The Party Crasher

www.penguin.co.uk

The Party
Crasher

sophie kinsella

BANTAM PRESS

TRANSWORLD PUBLISHERS
Penguin Random House,
One Embassy Gardens, 8 Viaduct Gardens,
London SW11 7BW
www.penguin.co.uk

Transworld is part of the Penguin Random House group of companies
whose addresses can be found at global.penguinrandomhouse.com

Penguin
Random House
UK

First published in Great Britain in 2021 by Bantam Press
an imprint of Transworld Publishers

A CIP catalogue record for this book
is available from the British Library.

ISBNs 9781787632455 (hb)
9781787630307 (tpb)

Typeset in 11.5/15.5pt Palatino by Jouve (UK), Milton Keynes
Printed and bound in Great Britain by Clays Ltd, Elcograf S.p.A.

The authorized representative in the EEA is Penguin Random House Ireland,
Morrison Chambers, 32 Nassau Street, Dublin D02 YH68.

Penguin Random House is committed to a sustainable
future for our business, our readers and our planet. This book
is made from Forest Stewardship Council® certified paper.

In memory of Sharon Propson

ONE

I know I can do this, I *know* I can. Whatever anyone else says. It's just a matter of perseverance.

'Effie, I already told you, that angel won't stay,' says my big sister Bean, coming up to watch me with a glass of mulled wine in her hand. 'Not in a million years.'

'It will.' Firmly I continue wrapping twine round our beloved silver ornament, ignoring the pine needles pricking my hand.

'It won't. Just give up! It's too heavy!'

'I'm not giving up!' I retort. 'We *always* have the silver angel on the top of the Christmas tree.'

'But this tree is about half the size of the ones we normally have,' points out Bean. 'Haven't you noticed? It's really spindly.'

I briefly survey the tree, standing in its usual alcove in the hall. Of course I've noticed it's small. We usually have a huge, impressive, bushy tree, whereas this one is pretty puny. But that's not my concern right now.

1

'This *will* work.' I tie my final knot with a flourish, then let go – whereupon the whole branch collapses, the angel swings upside down and her skirt falls over her head, exposing her knickers. Drat.

'Well, that looks super-festive,' says Bean, snorting with laughter. 'Shall we write "Happy Christmas" on her pants?'

'*Fine*.' I untie the angel and step back. 'I'll brace the branch with a wooden stick or something.'

'Just put something else on top of the tree!' Bean sounds half amused, half exasperated. 'Effie, why are you always so stubborn?'

'I'm not stubborn, I'm *persistent*.'

'You tell 'em, Effie!' chimes in Dad, passing by with a bundle of fairy lights in his arms. 'Fight the good fight! Never say die!'

His eyes are twinkling and his cheeks are rosy, and I smile back fondly. Dad gets it. He's one of the most tenacious people I know. He was brought up in a tiny flat in Layton-on-Sea by a single mother, and he went to a really rough school. But he persevered, got to college and then joined an investment firm. Now he is where he is: retired, comfortable, happy, all good. You don't achieve that by giving up at the first hurdle.

OK, so his tenacity can sometimes segue into irrational obstinacy. Like that time he wouldn't give up on a charity 10K run, even though he was limping and it turned out he'd torn a calf muscle. But as he said afterwards, he'd raised the money, he'd got the job done, and he'd survive. Dad was always exclaiming 'You'll survive!' during our childhood, which was sometimes cheering and sometimes bracing and sometimes totally unwelcome. (Sometimes you don't want to hear that you'll survive. You want to peer at your bleeding knee and wail and have someone say kindly, 'There, there, aren't you brave?')

Dad had obviously been at the mulled wine before I even arrived today – but then, why not? It's Christmastime *and* it's his birthday *and* it's decorating day. It's always been our tradition, to decorate the tree on Dad's birthday. Even now we're all grown-up, we come back to Greenoaks, our family home in Sussex, every year.

As Dad disappears into the kitchen, I edge closer to Bean and lower my voice. 'Why did Mimi get such a small tree this year?'

'Don't know,' says Bean after a pause. 'Just being practical, maybe? I mean, we're all adults now.'

'Maybe,' I say, dissatisfied by this answer. Our stepmother, Mimi, is artistic and creative and full of quirky whims. She's always loved Christmas decorating, the bigger the better. Why would she suddenly decide to be practical? Next year, I'll go tree shopping with her, I decide. I'll remind her subtly that we always have a massive tree at Greenoaks and there's no reason to stop that tradition, even if Bean *is* thirty-three and Gus is thirty-one and I'm twenty-six.

'At last!' Bean interrupts my thoughts, peering at her phone.

'What?'

'Gus. He's just sent over the video. Talk about cutting it fine.'

About a month ago, Dad said he didn't want presents this year. As if we were going to take any notice of that. But to be fair, he does have a lot of jumpers and cufflinks and things, so we decided to be creative. Bean and Gus have put together a video montage, which Gus has been finalizing, and I've done my own surprise project, which I can't wait to show Dad.

'I expect Gus has been pretty busy with *Romilly*,' I say, winking at Bean, who grins back.

Our brother Gus has recently landed this amazing girlfriend called Romilly. And we're not *surprised*, we're definitely not *surprised*, but . . . well. The thing is, he's Gus. Absent-minded. Vague. He's handsome in his own way, very endearing, and very good at his job in software. But he's not exactly what you'd call 'alpha'. Whereas she's some kind of amazing power-house with perfect hair and chic sleeveless dresses. (I've looked her up online.)

'I want to have a quick look at the video,' says Bean. 'Let's go upstairs.' As she leads the way up the stairs, she adds, 'Have you wrapped up your present for Dad?'

'No, not yet.'

'Only I brought some extra wrapping paper, just in case you needed it, and ribbon. I've ordered the hamper for Aunt Ginny, by the way,' she adds. 'I'll tell you what you owe me.'

'Bean, you're brilliant,' I say fondly. Which she is. She's always thinking ahead. She's always getting stuff done.

'Oh, and something else.' Bean delves into her bag as we reach the landing. 'They had a three-for-two offer.'

She hands me a Vitamin D spray, and I bite my lip, trying not to laugh. Bean is turning into this crazed health-and-safety officer. Last year she kept getting me cod-liver-oil capsules and before that it was green tea powder.

'Bean, you don't need to buy me vitamins! I mean, thanks,' I add belatedly.

We head into her room and I look around it affectionately. It's been the same since I can remember, with the hand-painted furniture she's had since she was five – twin white wooden beds, a chest, wardrobe and dressing table, all decorated with Peter Rabbit. Throughout our childhood she kept intending to upgrade to something cooler, but she could never quite bear to say goodbye to it, so it's still here. I associate it so strongly with her, I can't even see Peter Rabbit without thinking 'Bean'.

'Did you think of inviting Dominic along today?' asks Bean as she opens up her iPad, and I feel a glow at the sound of his name.

'No, it's a bit early for "meet the family". We've only had a few dates.'

'But good dates?'

'Yes, good dates.' I smile happily.

'Excellent. OK, here we go . . .' She sets up her iPad on the dressing table and we both watch a whizzy title sequence reading *The one and only . . . Tony Talbot!* A still photo appears next, of Dad in his local Layton-on-Sea paper when he was eleven and won a maths prize. Next comes a graduation photo, followed by a wedding photo with our birth mother, Alison.

I gaze at her pretty, wide-eyed face, feeling the weird sense of disconnect I always do when I see pictures of her, wishing I could feel more of a bond. I was only eight months old when she died, and three when Dad married Mimi. It's Mimi I remember singing to me when I was ill, baking cakes in the kitchen, being there, always. Mimi's my mum. It's different for Bean and Gus – they have dim memories of Alison. Whereas I have nothing except family resemblance – which, to be fair, I have big-time. We all take after her, with our wide faces, strong cheekbones and eyes set well apart. I look permanently startled and Bean's big blue eyes always seem questioning. Meanwhile Gus generally looks absent, as though he's not paying attention (which is because he never is).

A series of old home videos begins on the screen and I lean forward to watch. There's Dad holding a baby Bean . . . a family picnic . . . Dad building a sandcastle for a toddler Gus . . . Then a video I've seen before: Dad walking up to the door of Greenoaks and theatrically opening it, the day it became ours. He's often said it was one of the biggest moments of his life, buying a house like this. 'A boy from Layton-on-Sea made good,' as he puts it.

Because Greenoaks isn't just any old house. It's *amazing*. It has character. It has a turret! It has a stained-glass window. Visitors often call it 'eccentric' or 'quirky' or just exclaim, 'Wow!'

And OK, yes, there might be those very few, mean, misguided people who call it 'ugly'. But they are *blind* and *wrong*. The first time I ever overheard Greenoaks described as 'a monstrosity', by a strange woman in the village shop, I was shocked to my core. My eleven-year-old heart burned with indignation. I'd never come across an architectural snob before; I didn't know they existed. And I passionately loved everything about my home; everything that this unknown, mean grown-up was mocking. From the so-called 'ugly brickwork' – it is *not* ugly – to the mound. The mound is a slightly random, steep hill that we have in the garden, to one side of the house. The woman laughed at that, too, and I wanted to yell, 'Well, it's brilliant for bonfires, so there!'

Instead, I stalked out of the shop, throwing a resentful glance at Mrs McAdam, who ran it. To her credit, she looked a bit shocked and called out, 'Effie, love, did you want to buy anything?' But I didn't turn back, and I still don't know who that mocking stranger was.

Ever since then, I've watched people's reactions to Greenoaks with a close eye. I've seen them step back and gulp as they survey it and scrabble for positive things to say. I'm not saying it's a test of their character – but it's a test of their character. Anyone who can't find a single nice comment to make about Greenoaks is a mean snob and dead to me.

'Effie, look, it's you!' exclaims Bean, as a new video appears on the screen, and I peer at the toddler me, staggering around the lawn, holding an eight-year-old Bean's hand. 'Never mind, Effie,' she says cheerfully, as I tumble down. 'Try again!' Mimi always says Bean taught me to walk. And ride a bike. And plait my hair.

We've scooted straight past the dark year of Alison's death, I register silently. This video is just of the happy times. Well, why not? Dad doesn't need to be reminded of that. He found happiness with Mimi and he's been content ever since.

The buzzer rings, and Bean ignores it, but I look up, alert. I'm expecting a parcel with Mimi's Christmas present in it. I arranged for it to arrive today especially, and I don't want Mimi opening it by mistake.

'Bean,' I say, pressing Pause on the iPad screen. 'Will you come to the gate with me? I think that's Mimi's sewing cabinet arriving, and I want to bring it in secretly. But it's quite big.'

'Sure,' says Bean, closing the video down. 'So, what do you think?'

'Amazing,' I say emphatically. 'Dad's going to *love* it.'

As we hurry down the stairs, Mimi is winding greenery through the bannisters. She looks up and smiles at us, but her face seems a bit strained. Perhaps she needs a holiday.

'I'll get the gate,' I say hurriedly. 'It's probably a package.'

'Thanks, Effie love,' says Mimi in her soft, comforting Irish brogue. She's wearing an Indian block print dress and her hair is caught back in a hand-painted wooden clasp. As I watch, she ties a deft knot with red velvet ribbon and, needless to say, nothing collapses. Typical.

As Bean and I crunch over the gravel drive to the big iron gates, the afternoon air is already taking on a wintery, dusky gloom. A white van is parked outside and a guy with a shaved head is holding a cardboard box.

'That can't be it,' I say. 'Too small.'

'Delivery for the Old Rectory,' says the guy as we open the pedestrian gate. 'They're not in. Mind taking it?'

'Sure,' says Bean, reaching for it, and she's about to scribble on his device when I grab her hand, stopping her.

'Wait! Don't just sign. I signed for a package for my neighbour and it was this glass vase which was broken, and they couldn't get a refund because I'd signed and they blamed me.' I stop breathlessly. 'We need to check it first.'

'It's fine,' says the guy impatiently and I feel my hackles rise.

'You don't know that.' I rip the lid open and draw out the invoice. '*Yoga sculpture*,' I read. '*Assembly included*.' I look up, feeling vindicated. 'You see? It's not fine! You're supposed to assemble it.'

'I'm not assembling nothing,' says the guy, giving a revolting sniff.

'You have to,' I point out. 'It says so on the paper. *Assembly included*.'

'Yeah, right.'

'Assemble it!' I insist. 'We're not signing for it till you do.'

The guy glowers at me silently for a moment, rubbing his shaved head, then says, 'You're a stubborn pain in the arse. Has anyone ever told you that?'

'Yes,' I reply, folding my arms. 'Everyone.'

'It's true.' Bean nods, grinning. 'You'd better assemble it. What's a *yoga* statue, anyway?' she adds to me, and I shrug.

'I'll get my tools,' says the guy, now glowering at both of us. 'But this is bollocks.'

'It's called being a good citizen,' I retort.

After a minute he returns with his tools and we watch curiously as, with impatient huffs, he starts screwing together metal parts into . . . What *is* that, exactly? It's some kind of

8

representation of a person ... no, two people, male and female, and they seem to slot together ... *what* are they doing?

Hang on.

Oh my God. My stomach rolls over and I glance at Bean, who seems transfixed. Does *yoga sculpture* actually mean *X-rated sex sculpture*?

Okaaay. Yes, it does.

And quite frankly, I'm shocked! Andrew and Jane Martin wear matching padded waistcoats. They exhibit dahlias at the summer fete. How can they have ordered *this*?

'Is his hand meant to go on her tit or her bum?' the guy queries, looking up. 'There's no instructions.'

'I'm ... not sure,' I manage.

'*Oh* my God.' Bean comes to life as the guy pulls the final, most graphic male body part out of the box. 'No! No way. Could you please stop a moment?' she adds shrilly to the guy. Then she turns to me and says in an agitated undertone, 'We *can't* take this round to the Martins. I'll never be able to look them in the eye again!'

'Me neither!'

'We didn't see this. OK, Effie? We did *not* see this.'

'Agreed,' I say fervently. 'Um, excuse me?' I turn back to the guy. 'Slight change of plan. Do you think you could take it all apart again and put it back in the box?'

'You *are* bleeding joking,' says the guy incredulously.

'I'm sorry,' I say, in humble tones. 'We didn't know what it was.'

'Thank you for your trouble,' adds Bean hastily. 'And happy Christmas!' She reaches in her jeans pocket and finds a crumpled tenner, which mollifies the delivery guy slightly.

'Bloody shambles,' he says, briskly unscrewing the parts again. 'Make your bloody minds up.' He regards the naked female figure with disapproval. 'Anyway, you ask me, she'll give herself knee trouble, messing about like that. She wants a couple of pillows, cushion the joints.'

I glance at Bean and away again.

'Good idea,' I manage.

'Can't be too careful,' adds Bean, with a tremor in her voice.

He stuffs the last metal body part back into the box and Bean scribbles on his electronic screen, and as he gets back into his van we glance at each other again.

'Knee trouble,' says Bean, her voice almost exploding.

'The Martins!' I rejoin in slight hysteria. 'Oh God, Bean, how will we *ever* talk to them again?'

The van finally drives away, and we both dissolve into gales of laughter.

'I'll tape it up again,' says Bean. 'They'll never know we opened it.'

She's just reaching down to pick up the box when something catches my eye: a figure about ten metres away, walking towards us along the village road. It's a figure I'd know anywhere, from the dark hair to the pale, strong chin, to the long-legged stride. Joe Murran. And just the sight of him causes my hysteria to melt away. Instantly. As if it never happened.

'What?' says Bean, catching my expression, and she turns. 'Oh. *Oh.*'

As he nears us, there's a clenching in my heart. A python's grip. I can't breathe. Can I breathe? Oh, stop it, Effie. Don't be ridiculous. Of course I can *breathe*. Come on. I can see my ex-boyfriend without actually perishing on the spot.

'Are you OK?' murmurs Bean.

'Of course!' I say quickly.

'Right.' She sounds unconvinced. 'Well, tell you what, I'll take this box in and you two can . . . catch up.'

As she disappears towards the front door, I take a step backwards so that I'm standing on the gravel of the drive. On home territory. I feel like I need the ballast of home, of Greenoaks, of family love.

'Oh, hi,' Joe says as he approaches, his eyes unreadable. 'How are you?'

'Fine.' I shrug nonchalantly. 'How are you?'

'Fine.'

Joe's eyes shoot to my neck and I instinctively put a hand to my beaded necklace – then curse myself. I shouldn't have reacted. I should have blanked him. *What? Sorry? Did I once wear something around my neck with some kind of significance between us? Forgive me, I don't quite remember the details.*

'Nice necklace,' he says.

'Yes, Bean gave it to me,' I say carelessly. 'So it's quite special. You know. Meaningful. I love it, actually. I never take it off.'

I could probably have stopped at 'Bean gave it to me'. But I made my point. I can tell that from the look on Joe's face.

'Work going well?' he says, with stilted politeness.

'Yes, thanks.' I match his politeness. 'I've moved department. I'm mostly organizing trade events now.'

'Great.'

'And you? Still aiming towards heart surgery?'

I speak with deliberate vagueness, as though I'm not quite sure what stage of his medical career he's at. As though I didn't once sit with him, helping him study till two in the morning.

'That's the plan.' He nods. 'Getting there.'

'Great.'

We lapse into silence, Joe's brow knitted in one of his customary intent frowns.

'What about ...' he begins at last. 'Are you ... with anyone?'

His words are like salt on sore skin. What's it to him? Why should he be interested? *You don't get to ask about my love life, Joe Murran*, I want to retort hotly. But that would be giving myself away. Also, I have something to boast about.

'Yes, I *am* with someone, actually,' I say, putting on my most dreamy expression. 'He's really great. So great. Good-looking, successful, kind, *reliable* . . .' I add pointedly.

'Not Humph?' says Joe warily, and I feel a flicker of annoyance. Why does he have to bring up Humph? I went out with Humphrey Pelham-Taylor for three weeks as an act of revenge on Joe and yes, it was petty and yes, I regret it. But does he really think that Humph and I would ever have been a thing?

'No, not Humph,' I say with elaborate patience. 'His name's Dominic. He's an engineer. We met online and it's going brilliantly. We're so well matched. You know when it just *works*?'

'Great,' says Joe, after a long pause. 'That's . . . I'm glad.'

He doesn't look glad. In fact, he looks kind of tormented. But that's not my problem, I tell myself firmly. And he probably isn't tormented at all. I thought I knew Joe Murran once, but I clearly didn't.

'Are *you* with anyone?' I ask politely.

'No,' says Joe at once. 'I'm . . . No.'

We lapse into another silence, during which Joe hunches his shoulders and thrusts his hands into his coat pockets.

This conversation really isn't working. I take a few deep breaths of the crisp winter air and feel sadness overcome me. On that awful night, two and a half years ago now, I didn't just lose the love of my life. I lost the friend I'd had since we were both five years old. Joe grew up here; his mum is still headmistress of the village school. We were playmates. Then teenage boyfriend and girlfriend. Together through university. Young adults, planning to make a life together.

But now we're . . . what? Barely able to look each other in the eye.

'Well,' says Joe at last. 'Happy Christmas.'

'Same. Happy Christmas.'

I watch as he walks away, then turn and trudge back across the drive to the house, to find Bean hovering outside the front door.

'Are you OK, Effie?' she asks anxiously. 'Whenever you see Joe, you get all . . . prickly.'

'I'm fine,' I say. 'Let's go in.'

I've never told Bean about that night. Some things are just too raw to share. In fact, I try not to think about it, full stop.

I need to focus on the here and now, I tell myself. All the good things. Decorating the tree. Christmas around the corner. All the family gathered together at Greenoaks.

Feeling lighter already, I follow Bean inside, shutting the door firmly against the weather. I look forward to this day every single year, and I'm not letting anything spoil it. Least of all Joe Murran.

An hour later, my spirits are even higher, which might have something to do with the two glasses of mulled wine I've downed. We've finished the Christmas tree and are assembled in the kitchen, watching the video that Bean and Gus made for Dad, on the propped-up iPad. I'm curled up in the ancient wicker chair in the corner in a contented haze, watching myself, aged four, in a smocked flowery dress made by

Mimi. It's a summer's day on the screen and I'm sitting on a rug on the lawn, unstacking my Russian dolls and showing each one carefully to Dad.

I turn to Dad now to see if he's enjoying it and he smiles back from his chair, toasting me with his glass of mulled wine. That's a typical charming Dad gesture. My best friend Temi thinks Dad should have been an actor, and I know what she means. He has looks and poise and people are naturally drawn to him.

'Ephelant, you were *adorable* when you were little,' says Bean fondly. My whole family calls me 'Ephelant' when they're not calling me Effie – it was my baby-word for 'elephant'. No one ever calls me by my proper name, Euphemia (thank *God*) but then, no one calls Bean 'Beatrice', either, or Gus 'Augustus'.

'Yeah, shame you turned out like you did,' adds Gus, and I absently reply, 'Ha, ha,' without moving my eyes from the screen. I'm captivated by the sight of my pristine Russian dolls, new out of the box. I've still got them – five hand-painted wooden matryoshka dolls that stack inside each other, with lustrous painted eyes, rosy cheeks and serene smiles. They're knocked about now, and stained with felt tip, but they're the most precious souvenir I have of my childhood.

Where other children had a teddy, I had my dolls. I would take them apart, arrange them in a row, make them have 'conversations' and talk to them. Sometimes they represented our family: two big parents and three smaller children, with me the tiniest doll of all. Sometimes they were different versions of me. Or else I gave them the names of friends from school and acted out the quarrels of the day. But more often, they were just a form of worry beads. I would stack and unstack them, barely seeing them, letting the familiar ritual comfort me. In fact, I still do. They live by my bed to this day and I still sometimes reach for them when I'm stressed out.

'Look at your *dress*,' Bean is saying now, gazing at the screen. 'I want one!'

'You could make one,' says Mimi. 'I still have the pattern. There was an adult version, too.'

'Really?' Bean's face lights up. 'I'm *definitely* making that.'

Yet again, I marvel at how Bean has taken on Mimi's creative mantle. They both sew and knit and bake. They can turn a space into a magical domain, with a velvet cushion here and a plate of oatmeal cookies there. Bean works at home in marketing, and even her office is beautiful, all hanging plants and art posters.

I buy cushions and oatmeal cookies. I've even tried a hanging plant. But it never looks the same. I don't have that flair. However, I have other skills. At least, I think I do. (Is being a stubborn pain in the arse a skill? Because that's what I'm best at, apparently.)

Our kitchen is the prime example of Mimi's creativity, I think, my eyes drifting fondly over it. It's not just a kitchen, it's an institution. A work of art. Every cupboard is a panel of intricate forest, drawn in Sharpie, built up over the years. It all started with a tiny mouse that Mimi drew to cheer me up when I'd cut my knee, aged about three. She sketched the mouse in the corner of a cupboard, winked at me and said, 'Don't tell Daddy.' I gazed at it, enchanted, unable to believe that she had drawn something so amazing, and *on the furniture*.

A few weeks later, Gus was upset over something and she drew him a comical frog. Then, over the years, she added drawing after drawing, creating elaborate forest scenes. Trees to mark birthdays; animals at Christmas. She let us add our own little contributions, too. We would draw them holding

15

our breath, feeling momentous. A butterfly . . . a worm . . . a cloud.

The panels are pretty filled up with drawings now, but Mimi still squeezes in new touches, now and again. Our kitchen is famous in the village and it's the first thing our friends want to see when they come over.

'*No one* else has a kitchen like this!' I remember Temi gasping when she first saw it, aged eleven, and I immediately replied, bursting with pride, 'No one else has a Mimi.'

On the iPad screen now is a montage of Dad at various parties we've had over the years and I feel waves of nostalgia as I watch Dad dressed up as Father Christmas when I was eight . . . Dad and Mimi in black tie, dancing at Bean's eighteenth . . . So many happy family celebrations.

Happy Birthday, Tony Talbot! appears on the screen as a final frame, and we all applaud exuberantly.

'Really! Children!' Dad seems overcome as he smiles around the kitchen. He has a sentimental streak, and I can see his eyes are damp. 'I don't know what to say. That's an incredible present. Bean, Gus, Effie . . . Thank you.'

'It's not from me,' I say hastily. 'That was Bean and Gus. I made you . . . this.'

Feeling suddenly shy, I present him with my gift, wrapped in Bean's paper. I hold my breath as he unwraps the large, flat book and reads out the title.

'*A Boy from Layton-on-Sea*.' He looks at me questioningly, then starts leafing through the pages. 'Oh . . . my goodness.'

It's a kind of scrapbook I've put together of Layton-on-Sea in the era of my dad's childhood, sourcing old photos, postcards, maps and newspaper cuttings. It became totally engrossing as I was making it – in fact, I could probably do a thesis on Layton-on-Sea now.

'The arcade!' Dad's exclaiming, as he flips over the pages. 'The Rose and Crown! St Christopher's School . . . that takes me back . . .'

At last he looks up, his face suffused with emotion. 'Effie, my love, this is wonderful. I'm so touched.'

'It's not artistic or anything,' I say, suddenly aware that I just stuck all the clippings in and Bean would probably have done something super-creative with them. But Mimi puts a hand on my arm.

'Don't do yourself down, Effie, darling. It *is* artistic. This is a work of art. Of history. Of love.'

Her eyes are glistening, too, I notice with surprise. I'm used to Dad's sentimentality, but Mimi's not really a weeper. Today, though, there's definitely a softening around her edges. I watch as she picks up her mulled wine with a trembling hand and glances at Dad, who shoots a meaningful look back.

OK, this is weird. Something's up. I'm only just noticing the signs. But what?

Then, all at once, it hits me. They're planning something. *Now* it all makes sense. Dad and Mimi have always been the kind of parents who have private chats and then make fully fledged announcements, rather than floating suggestions first. They've got a plan and they're going to tell us and they're both kind of emotional about it. Ooh, what is it? They're not going to adopt a child, are they? I think, wildly. No. Surely not. But then, what? I watch as Dad closes the book and glances yet again at Mimi, then addresses us.

'So. All of you. We've actually . . .' He clears his throat. 'We've got a bit of news.'

I knew it!

I take a sip of mulled wine and wait expectantly, while Gus puts down his phone and looks up. There's a long, weird beat of silence and I glance uncertainly at Mimi. Her clasped hands are so tense her knuckles are showing white, and for the first time I feel a slight sense of unease. What's up?

A nano-second later, the most obvious, terrifying answer comes to me.

'Are you OK?' I blurt out in panic, already seeing waiting rooms and drips and kindly doctors with bad news on their faces.

'Yes!' says Dad at once. 'Darling, *please* don't worry, we're both fine. We're both in great health. It's not . . . that.'

Confused, I peer at my siblings, who are both motionless, Bean looking anxious, Gus frowning down at his knees.

'However.' Dad exhales hard. 'We need to tell you that . . . we've come to a decision.'

TWO

Eighteen months later

I've had an out-of-body experience precisely three times in my life.

The first was when my parents told us they were divorcing, boom, out of the blue, for no good reason, as far as I can make out.

The second was when Dad announced he had a new girlfriend called Krista, who was an exercise-wear sales executive he'd met in a bar.

The third is happening right now.

'Did you hear me?' Bean's anxious voice is in my ear. 'Effie? They've sold Greenoaks.'

'Yes,' I say, my voice weirdly croaky. 'I heard you.'

I feel as though I'm floating high up, looking down on myself. There I am, leaning against the front wall of 4 Great

Grosvenor Place, Mayfair, in my waitress uniform, my head twisted away from the bright sunlight, my eyes closed.

Sold. *Sold*. Greenoaks. Gone to strangers.

It's been on the market for a year. I'd almost come to believe it would always be on the market. Safely tucked away on Rightmove. Not *gone*.

'Effie? Ephelant? Are you OK?'

Bean's voice penetrates my thoughts and I snap back to reality. I'm in my own body again. Standing on the pavement, where I really shouldn't be. Salsa Verde Catering does not encourage the waiting staff to take phone breaks. Or loo breaks. Or any kind of breaks.

'Yes. Of course! Of course I'm OK.' I straighten my back and breathe out sharply. 'I mean, God. It's a house. It's no big deal.'

'Well, it kind of is. We grew up there. It would be understandable to feel upset.'

Upset? Who said I'm upset?

'Bean, I don't have time for this,' I say briskly. 'I'm on a job. The house is sold. Whatever. They can do what they like. I'm sure Krista's already picked out her luxury villa in Portugal. I expect it's got a built-in jewellery cabinet for all her bracelet charms. Sorry, what does she call them, again? Her *trinkies*.'

I can feel Bean's wince through the ether. She and I have different views on many topics, from balconette bras to custard – but most of all on the topic of Krista. The thing with Bean is, she's so *nice*. She should have been a diplomat. She looks for the good in Krista. Whereas I just look at Krista.

My mind automatically conjures up a vision of Dad's girlfriend: blonde hair, white teeth, fake tan, annoying dachshund. The first time I met her, I was astounded. She was so young.

So . . . different. I was already gobsmacked that Dad had a girl-friend in the first place. And then we met her.

I tried to like her. Or at least, to be polite. I really, really did. But it's impossible. So I kind of . . . went the other way.

'Did you see them on Instagram today?' I can't help twisting the knife, and Bean sighs.

'I've told you before, I don't look.'

'Oh, you should!' I say. 'It's a really fab photo of Dad and Krista in a bubble bath together, holding champagne glasses, hashtag *sexinyoursixties*. Isn't that nice? Because I *was* wondering if Dad was having sex, obviously, and now I know. So that's good. To have that confirmed. Although isn't Krista in her forties? Shouldn't she be represented? Oh, and he's definitely been at the fake tan again.'

'I don't look,' Bean repeats in her quiet, resolute way. 'But I have spoken to Krista. Apparently, there's going to be a party.'

'A *party*?'

'A house-cooling. A chance to say goodbye, I guess. It's going to be a big deal. Black tie, caterers, all that.'

'Black tie?' I echo in disbelief. 'Whose idea was that – Krista's? I thought she was spending all the cash on a villa, not some pretentious party. When is it, anyway?'

'Well, that's the thing,' says Bean. 'Apparently it's been under offer for a while, only Dad didn't tell anyone in case it fell through. So they're really far along. They're completing a week on Wednesday and the party's on Saturday.'

'A week on *Wednesday*?' I feel suddenly hollow. 'But that's . . . That's . . .'

Soon. Too soon.

I close my eyes again, letting the news ricochet through me in bounces and jabs of pain. My mind can't help hurtling back yet again to that day our world changed for ever. Sitting in the kitchen, drinking mulled wine, feeling all happy and warm, with no idea of the bombshell about to hit us.

Of course, in hindsight I can see there were signs. Mimi's tense hands. Dad's damp eyes. Those wary looks they kept shooting each other. Even the downsized Christmas tree feels significant, now.

But you don't see a small Christmas tree and automatically think, *Wait a minute . . . small tree . . . I bet my parents are divorcing!* I had no idea. People say all the time, 'You must have had *some* idea.' But I truly didn't.

Even now, I sometimes wake up and have a few blank, blissful moments before suddenly, *whoomph*, I remember it all. Mimi and Dad are divorced. Dad's dating Krista. Mimi lives in a flat in Hammersmith. Life as we knew it is over.

Then, of course, all the other catastrophic elements of my life pile into my head. Not only have my parents broken up, our whole family has pretty much broken up. I'm engaged in an ongoing feud with Krista. I never speak to Dad. I was made redundant four months ago. I'm just not on *top* of my life any more. It's like I'm in a fog. Sometimes I almost feel like someone died, only we didn't get any flowers.

And I haven't had a proper boyfriend since Dominic, who turned out to be totally two-faced. (In fact, if we're counting a 'face' for each girl he was secretly shagging, he was five-faced, and I can't *believe* I wrote out all his Christmas cards for him because he said my writing was nice. I'm a gullible sap.)

'I know it's all happening really fast,' Bean is saying apologetically, as though this is her fault. 'I don't know what's happening about the furniture, I guess it'll go into storage till they find a place. I'm claiming my stuff, anyway. Dad and Krista are going to rent somewhere meanwhile. Anyway,

Krista says she's emailing invitations out later today, so . . . I wanted to warn you.'

Everything's been happening so fast, I think, my chest tight. Divorce. Girlfriend. Sell the house. And now, throw a party. I mean, a *party*? I try to imagine going to a party at Greenoaks that isn't hosted by Mimi, but it just feels wrong.

'I don't think I'll go,' I say, before I can stop myself.

'You're not going to *go*?' Bean sounds dismayed.

'I'm not in a party mood.' I try to sound casual. 'And I think I'm busy that night. So. Have a good time. Send everyone my love.'

'Effie!'

'What?' I say, determinedly playing ignorant.

'I really think you should go. It's the last ever party at Greenoaks. We'll all be there. It's our chance to say goodbye to our house . . . to be a family . . .'

'It's not our house any more,' I say flatly. 'Krista's ruined it with her "tasteful" paint. And we aren't a family any more.'

'Yes, we are!' protests Bean, sounding shocked. 'Of course we're a family! You mustn't say that!'

'OK, fine, whatever.' I stare morosely at the ground. Bean can say what she likes, but it's true. Our family is shattered. Splintered into shards of glass. And no one will ever be able to put us back together.

'When did you last talk to Dad?'

'Can't remember,' I lie. 'He's busy, I'm busy . . .'

'But you have spoken to him properly?' Bean sounds anxious. 'You have patched things up since . . . ?'

Since the night I yelled at Krista and stormed out of the house, is what she means. Only she's too tactful to say so.

'Of course,' I lie again, because I'm not having Bean get all stressed about me and Dad.

23

'Well, I can't get through to him,' she says. 'Krista always answers.'

'Huh.' I put as little interest into my voice as possible, because the only way for me to cope with the whole Dad situation is not to engage with it. Especially with Bean, who has a way of stirring up my heart just when I thought I'd calmed it.

'Effie, come to the party,' Bean tries again, in a cajoling voice. 'Don't think about Krista. Think about *us*.'

My sister is so reasonable. She sees other people's points of view. She says things like *On the other hand* and *You do have a valid argument* and *I hear where you're coming from*. I should try to be reasonable, like her, I think, in a gust of self-reproach. Or at least, I should try to *sound* reasonable.

I close my eyes, take a deep breath and say, 'I hear where you're coming from, Bean. You do have a valid argument. I'll think about it.'

'Good.' Bean sounds relieved. 'Because otherwise Greenoaks will be gone for ever and it'll be too late.'

Greenoaks will be gone for ever.

OK, I can't deal with that thought right now. I need to finish this phone call.

'Bean, I have to go,' I say. 'Because I'm *working*. In my very important job as a *temporary waitress*. I'll talk to you later. Bye.'

As I sidle back into the huge marble kitchen, it's buzzing with catering staff. A florist is unloading flowers, there are big buckets of ice everywhere and I can see the guy they call the 'house manager' discussing the table settings intently with Damian, who owns Salsa Verde.

Putting on a big fancy lunch like this is like putting on a performance and I feel more upbeat as I watch the chefs at work. I just need to work and keep busy. Yes. That's the answer.

It was a big shock when I lost my job in events. (It *wasn't* because I was crap. At least, even if it was, I wasn't the only one, because they culled a whole department.) But I'm doing my best to stay positive. I apply for at least one new position every day and the waitressing is keeping me going financially. And you never know when opportunity might strike. Maybe Salsa Verde will be my salvation, I think, glancing around. Maybe this will be my route back into events. Who knows what might happen?

My thoughts come to a halt as I notice that the florist, a pleasant-looking grey-haired woman, seems beleaguered. She catches me watching her, and immediately says, 'Would you do me a favour? Pop this in the hall?' She jerks her head at a huge arrangement of white roses on a metal stand. 'I *need* to save my peonies, but this one's cluttering up the place.'

'Sure,' I say, and grab hold of the stand.

'Oh, you shouldn't have!' says Elliot, one of the chefs, as I lug it past him, and I grin back. He's tall and tanned, with blue eyes and an athletic frame. We chatted a little bit earlier, while I surreptitiously checked out his biceps.

'I know you like white roses,' I reply, with a flirty smile.

Would it be too much to pluck a single bloom out of the arrangement and give it to him?

Yes. Too much. Also: theft.

'Hey, are you OK?' he says more quietly. 'I saw you outside. You seemed kind of stressed.'

His face is so open, so genuinely concerned-looking, that I can't help confiding in him. Just a little.

'Oh, I'm fine, thanks. I just heard they're selling my family home. My parents split up eighteen months ago,' I explain, since he looks blank. 'I mean, I'm *over* it. Obviously. But still.'

'I get it.' He nods sympathetically. 'It's a shame.'

'Yes.' I nod back, grateful for his understanding. 'Exactly! It *is* a shame. It's like, *why*? Because it was totally out of the blue. Our family was *happy*. You know? People were like, "Wow! Look at the Talbots! They're so amazingly happy! What's their secret?" Until suddenly my parents are like, "Oh, guess what, kids, we're splitting up." It turns out *that* was their secret. And I still don't . . . you know. Understand,' I finish, more quietly.

'Wow. That's . . .' Elliot seems flummoxed. 'Although, lucky they waited till you were grown-up, right?'

This is what people always say. And there's no point disagreeing. There's no point saying, *But don't you understand? Now I look back at my childhood and wonder if the whole thing was fake.*

'You're right!' Somehow I muster a cheerful tone. 'Silver linings. So, are your parents still together?'

'They are, as it happens.'

'That's nice.' I smile encouragingly. 'That's really nice. Heartwarming. I mean, it may not last,' I add, because it's only fair to warn him.

'Right.' Elliot hesitates. 'I mean, they seem solid . . .'

'They *seem* solid.' I point at him triumphantly, because he's nailed it. 'Exactly! They *seem* solid. Until suddenly, boom! They're living separately and your dad has a new girlfriend called Krista. Anyway, if it happens, I'm here for you.' I squeeze his arm in advance sympathy.

'Thanks,' says Elliot, in a slightly weird voice. 'Appreciate it.'

'No problem.' I smile at him again, as warmly as I can. 'Better move these flowers.'

As I manhandle the floral arrangement up the stairs to the entrance hall, I feel a little glow inside. He's nice! And I *think* he might be interested. Maybe I'll ask him out for a drink. Just casually. But also making my intentions plain. What's that phrase they use in personal ads, again? *For fun and more.*

Oh, hi Elliot, just wondering, would you like to go to the pub, for fun and more?

No. Aargh. Definitely not.

Anyway, as I return to the kitchen, I can tell this isn't the right moment. It's busier than ever and the stress levels seem to have gone up a notch in my absence. Damian's having a row with the house manager and Elliot is trying to interject comments while piping cream on to a chocolate dessert. I admire his courage. Damian is pretty scary, even when he's in a good mood, let alone when he gets in a rage. (I've heard a story of a chef hiding in a fridge rather than having to face Damian, although that *can't* be true.)

'Hey, you!' barks another chef, who is standing over a huge saucepan of pea soup. 'Stir this a moment.' He passes me his wooden spoon and heads over to join in the argument.

I stare nervously down at the pale green liquid. Soup is above my pay grade. I hope I don't do it wrong. Although, can you ruin soup? No. Of course you can't.

As I stir it round and round, my phone bleeps and I pull it awkwardly out of my pocket, still stirring with the other hand. It's a text – and as I see the name *Mimi*, I can already hear her comforting Irish brogue. I open her text and read her message:

Darling, I just heard about the house. It had to happen. I hope you're OK. You have a tender heart, Ephelant, and I'm thinking of you. Found this photo today in a clear-out, remember this day?

See you soon my love
Mimi xxx

I click on the attached photo and am instantly overwhelmed by a cascade of memories. It's my sixth birthday party – the day Mimi turned the whole house into a circus. She tented our huge vaulted sitting room and blew up a million balloons and even learned how to juggle.

In the photo I'm wearing my ballet tutu, standing on the old rocking horse. My hair is in dishevelled bunches and I look like the happiest six-year-old in the world. Meanwhile, Dad and Mimi are on either side of me, holding my hands, smiling at each other. Two loving parents.

Swallowing hard, I zoom in, studying my parents' young, animated faces, moving from one to the other as if I'm a detective looking for clues. Mimi's face is glowing as she beams at Dad. His smile is equally affectionate. And as I stare, my stomach feels like it's in a vice. What went wrong? They *were* happy, they *were* . . .

'Oy!' A voice interrupts my thoughts. A loud, irate voice. My head jerks up, and as I see Damian bearing down on me, my heart spasms.

No. Nooo. Not good. I drop my phone with a clatter on the counter and quickly stir the soup with brisk intent. I'm hoping his 'Oy!' might have been directed at someone else – but suddenly he's two feet away, glowering straight at me.

'You. Whatever your name is. What's up with your face? You got a fever?'

Confused, I lift my hand to my face. It's wet. Why is it wet?

'Wait.' He comes closer, looking appalled. 'Are you *crying*?'

'No!' I hastily rub my face and plaster on an upbeat smile. 'God, no! Of course not!'

'Good,' says Damian with ominous politeness. 'Because if you were . . .'

'I'm not!' I say over-brightly, just as a big fat drop lands on the green surface of the soup. My stomach clenches in horror. Where did that come from?

'You *are* crying!' he explodes. 'You're getting fucking tears in the fucking soup!'

'I'm not!' I say desperately, as another tear falls with a splash. 'I'm fi-ine!' My voice breaks into a sob and, to my horror, another larger drop falls down into the soup.

Oh God, I don't think that one came from my eye.

Trembling, I raise my head to meet Damian's gaze, and his expression makes me quiver. From the silence around us, I can tell that everyone in the kitchen is watching.

'Out!' he erupts. 'Out! Get your things.'

'Out?' I falter.

'Tears in the fucking soup.' He shakes his head, repulsed. 'Go.'

I swallow several times, wondering if there's any way to redeem the situation, then deciding there isn't.

'Get back to work!' Damian suddenly bellows at the rest of the kitchen, and frenetic activity once more breaks out.

I take off my apron, feeling a bit unreal, and head towards the door as everyone else avoids my eye.

'Bye,' I mutter. 'Bye, everyone.'

As I pass Elliot, I want to pause, but I'm a bit too shaken to pull off an insouciant invitation right now.

'Bye,' I say, addressing the floor.

'Hang on a minute, Effie,' he says in his deep voice. 'Wait there.'

I feel a flame of hope as he washes his hands, dries them, and comes towards me. Maybe he's going to ask me out, and we'll fall in love, and this will be our cute story of how we met . . .

'Yes?' I say as he gets near.

'Just wanted to ask you something before you go,' he says, more quietly. 'Are you seeing someone?'

Oh my God! It's happening!

'No,' I say, trying to sound nonchalant. 'No, I'm not seeing anyone.'

'Well, maybe you should.' His eyes run over me pityingly. 'Because if you ask me, you *really* haven't got over your parents' divorce.'

THREE

As I arrive home, I still feel stung. I *have* got over my parents' divorce. Of course I have. You can be 'over' something and still discuss it, surely?

And I wasn't crying. Now I think back, I'm sure of it. My eyes were running because of the *soup*. The *soup*.

I push open the door to our flat and slouch in gloomily to find Temi sitting on the floor, her laptop open, her braids sprinkled over her shoulders.

'Hi,' she says, looking up. 'How come you're home?'

'Finished early,' I say, not wanting to get into the whole thing. (Actually, it's not as bad as I thought. The agency were quite calm when I told them about Damian chucking me out of his kitchen. They said he's always doing that and they wouldn't send me to work with him again for about a week. Then they booked me for ten corporate lunches.)

'Oh, OK.' Temi takes me at my word. 'So, I'm on Rightmove. It says "Sold". Looks amazing,' she adds.

I texted Temi earlier on with the news about Greenoaks. She's a bit of a property obsessive, so I knew she'd be interested. Plus she spent a lot of the school holidays at our house, so she's pretty invested.

'*Visitors to this Victorian Gothic home on the edge of the pretty West Sussex village of Nutworth will be bowled over by the grand and imposing entrance,*' she reads out. 'Yes! True! I remember the first time I stayed with you, I was like, "Oh my days, this is where Effie lives?"'

'*Arched stone-mullioned windows allow light to flood into the house.* And draughts,' she adds. 'It should say, "The windows also allow windy, freeze-your-ass-off draughts to flood in. As well as *actual* floods. Which are a regular benefit of this fine property."'

I can't help laughing – I know she's trying to cheer me up – and she winks at me. Temi and I bonded at school through dancing – we were both in the modern jazz group. I was a day girl, but she was a boarder, because her parents both worked insanely hard in banking. They moved from Nigeria when she was two, to France for a few years, then to London, which is where they've stayed. Now Temi's in banking, too. When people say, 'Isn't it really tough?' she smiles back and says, 'Yes, that's what I like.'

'How was work?' I say, hoping to change the subject, but she carries on reading.

'*The house sits within whimsical gardens and grounds, which complement the unconventional architecture.*'

'"Whimsical" means "weird",' I say, narrowing my eyes. 'And "unconventional" means "ugly".'

'No, it doesn't! Effie, I love Greenoaks to bits, you know I do, but you have to admit it's different. Special,' she adds tactfully. '*A spacious hall leads to a large panelled reception room with mullioned window seat,*' she reads out now, and for a moment we're both silent, because we *lived* in that window seat when we were schoolgirls. We pulled the ancient, thick curtains round us to make a kind of fusty cave, where we read magazines and tried on make-up. When we were older, we swigged vodka miniatures and talked about boys. When Temi's granny died, we spent an afternoon there, just in each other's arms, not saying anything, in our own space.

I perch next to Temi on the floor and watch as she scrolls through all the photos with a jokey running commentary. But as she reaches the pictures of the plain gleaming kitchen with its plain gleaming cupboards, her finger stops scrolling and we're both silent. Even Temi can't find anything funny to say. What Krista did was wanton, gratuitous destruction. She took Mimi's forest – something beautiful and unique – and she obliterated it.

And people wonder why I have a feud with her.

A timer goes off in the kitchen and Temi gets to her feet.

'I need to stir my stew,' she says. 'Cup of tea? You look like you need it.'

'Yes, please,' I say thankfully. 'It's been a bit of a day.'

It's not just the news of Greenoaks being sold, or even being thrown out of the kitchen . . . it's everything. It's all churned up in my mind.

What no one will believe is, I tried to give Krista a chance. I really did. That day we first met her at Greenoaks, I went along determined to be positive.

OK, yes, I found it weird, watching a strange, glamorous woman tottering around Mimi's kitchen in tight jeans and high heels. Running a manicured hand down Dad's back. Calling him 'Tone' and nestling up to him on the sofa like a teenager and roaring at some private joke clearly involving sex. But I wasn't 'against her from the start', which is what everyone seems to think.

Bean said afterwards we should have met first at some neutral venue, and I expect she's right. It was always going to be hard, seeing another woman in Mimi's place. In most families the mum stays in the family home, but as Mimi kept saying, it was Dad's house long before she was on the scene. So Mimi insisted on moving out, and after what seemed about five minutes, Krista moved in.

And that was never going to be easy. But, hand on heart, I was prepared to tolerate and even like Krista. It wasn't until the third time I met her that the alarm bells really started ringing. And that was the day when things first went badly wrong for Dad and me.

Our relationship had already disintegrated a bit. For quite a while, after the announcement about their divorce, I couldn't really talk to Dad or Mimi, because all I wanted to do was wail, '*Why?*' or 'How *can* you?' or 'You've made a terrible mistake!' and Bean said this wouldn't be helpful. (Nor would she join in my short-lived plan to get Dad and Mimi back together again by re-creating their first date and tricking them into going on it.)

So it was hard. And we were all a bit unnerved by the way Dad had changed. He'd clearly tried to shape up for Krista by buying new clothes (bad jeans) and putting on fake tan (he denied it, but it was obvious) and buying cases of champagne the whole time. He and Krista didn't ever seem to drink anything but champagne, which had always been a special-occasion thing before.

They kept going for luxury mini-breaks and posting photos of themselves in bathrobes on Dad's new Instagram account. And talking about buying a villa in Portugal, where Dad had never even been before. It was all Krista's idea. He even bought her a diamond pendant for their 'four-month-iversary', and she talked about it constantly, showing off and playing with it. *Mind my sparkler! Look at the light on my sparkler!*

It was as if a whole new, different Dad had emerged. But at least I was still talking to him. I still felt like he was on my side. Until that day.

I'd gone to Greenoaks for lunch – just me. It was when Dad was on the phone that I wandered into the sitting room and found Krista taking a photo of the bureau. Then she murmured 'bureau, six drawers, gold handles' quietly into her phone, as if she was dictating. I was so startled, I couldn't even move for a moment, then I tiptoed away.

I tried to give her the benefit of the doubt. All through lunch, I tried to think of an innocent explanation for what she was doing. But I just couldn't. So I asked Dad if I could see him in the office about a 'family thing', and then spilled it all out.

The conversation didn't just go badly. It went terribly. I can't remember exactly what he said, but I can remember his angry, defensive voice, telling me I shouldn't snoop around, that I had to accept he was with Krista now, and I should be happy for him, not invent problems, and I must promise not to mention this to Gus or Bean, as it would turn them against Krista.

I remember staring back at him, my face tingling. I was so shocked that he'd taken Krista's side against me, I could barely stutter a reply before leaving as quickly as I could.

I never did tell Gus or Bean about that day. I kept my promise to Dad. But I hadn't promised not to start a feud with Krista, had I?

So I did that instead.

My first strike was at Krista's birthday. Dad had summoned us all to this gruesome lunch to 'celebrate' Krista's big day. She was turning 'forty-one years young', as she told us about a thousand times.

35

Did we want to 'celebrate' Krista's birthday? No. Are we her proper family? No. Was it just a chance for her to get out all the expensive china and hire caterers and pop champagne bottles and show off? Yes.

But Bean said we should make an effort, and I should stop saying 'celebrate' with snarky quote marks, and maybe if we truly tried to be happy for Krista, we would start to bond with her.

I sometimes give up on Bean.

So I trooped along, and gave Krista a gift-wrapped framed photo as her present. It was a gold-tinted picture of her. In a gold frame. And it had two comedy speech bubbles. One read, 'Look at my sparkler!!!' and the other read, 'Ker-ching!!!'

OK, 'Ker-ching!!!' might have been going a bit far. But I just couldn't resist it.

I was all ready to defend it vigorously as an innocent, playful gift – but I didn't even need to. Krista stared at it for a few seconds, her face rigid, then said, 'Super!' and shoved the photo straight in her bag before anyone else could see it.

And then she threw her drink over me. The official version was that she accidentally dropped her drink over me. But she knows and I know: it was no accident. She chucked her Kir Royale over my new cream dress, then instantly played the innocent by grabbing her dachshund, Bambi, and stroking his head, saying, 'What did Mummy *do*, Bambi? Silly Mummy dropped her dwinkie on poor Effie!'

So that was the day she and I tacitly declared war. And for a while we were in quite active battle. Our weapons were mostly passive-aggressive emails, back-handed compliments on Instagram and insults dressed up as affection.

It was almost fun, goading her and waiting to see how she would retaliate. It was a kind of game. I still went to family gatherings, bristling silently, watching Krista with a wary eye, but there was never anything I could actually *object* to. Until one evening, two months ago. We all three arrived for supper at Greenoaks together – Gus drove us down – and I was actually in quite a good mood. Until Dad said on the doorstep, avoiding looking us in the eye, 'Oh, by the way, Krista's repainted the kitchen. Don't worry, I took some photos of it first, as souvenirs.'

Just like that. I still can't believe it. That he let Krista do it in the first place. That he told us so casually. That he didn't understand how devastated we would all be.

Gus just gasped as he walked in and saw the white-painted cupboards. Bean's face kind of crumpled. As for me, I felt shell-shocked. I remember standing there, feeling as though my whole childhood had been wiped out.

The worst thing was, Krista was *proud* of her desecration. She kept telling us the paint was called 'Wimborne White' and saying it looked so much fresher now. I was so dismayed by that point I could barely speak, but when I heard the word 'fresher', I couldn't help snapping, 'You know, I'm sure the *Mona Lisa* would look fresher if you plastered that with Farrow and Ball, too. You should offer your services to the Louvre!'

Which didn't go down brilliantly.

Gus and Bean seemed to get over it after a few minutes. They pulled themselves together. They had a glass of wine and made chit-chat. But I couldn't. I was too wounded. Too fraught. I started trying to explain how upset I felt, and I gradually got more and more worked up . . . until suddenly I was yelling at Krista, 'You know what? There's not enough room in this house for us and you, Krista, so we're off. OK? We're *off*. For *good*.'

Then it all got really embarrassing, because I'd assumed Bean and Gus would stalk out with me, but they didn't. They stayed put on the sofa. I strode into the hall, flushed, breathing hard, ready to high-five my siblings – who would naturally be by my side in solidarity – then realized I was on my own. I was so flummoxed, I put my head back into the sitting room and said, 'Aren't you coming?'

Bean said, '*Effie . . .*' in agonized tones without moving, while Gus just looked absent.

So I had to do a second exit, trying to hold my head high, and I swear I heard Krista giggle.

I was *so* livid. I nearly refused to forgive them both. Bean said afterwards she'd been really torn, but she'd had this awful instinct that if we all walked out, the family would be broken for ever, and she was trying to be the bridge.

I snapped, 'Yes, you *are* the bridge, because you let Krista walk all over you!' (Whereupon she looked hurt and I wished I hadn't.)

So then I tackled Gus. He said he hadn't realized he was supposed to walk out, and next time I should send him a WhatsApp.

My family are *useless.*

And since that evening, I've barely communicated with Dad. Nor have I been down to Greenoaks. I haven't launched any more strikes at Krista, and nor has she at me – but that doesn't reassure me. It's like a phoney war. I'm continually wary, wondering what bomb will drop next.

Now, as Temi sinks back down beside me and hands me a mug of tea, she surveys the blank, repainted kitchen again. She loved Mimi's creation too, and one Easter she even added her own little drawing of a chick.

'Bitch,' she says succinctly.

'Yup. Oh, guess what, she's holding a house-cooling party,' I add glumly. 'A big show-off event so everyone can say goodbye to Greenoaks and she can swan around and be queen bee.'

'What are you going to wear?'

'I'm not going,' I say flatly. 'It's *Krista*'s party.'

'So what?' retorts Temi. 'Ignore her! Say goodbye to the house, see your friends and family, have some drinks . . . If it were me, I would dress up in the most *awesome* outfit and I would *show* that woman.' Temi's eyes go distant and I can tell she's already planning what she would order from Net-a-Porter.

At that moment, my phone buzzes and I open WhatsApp to see a message from Bean:

Just got my invitation. By email, from Krista. Have you got yours yet?

I log on to my emails and scroll down – but there's nothing new from Krista, so I send back a reply:

Nope.

A moment later, she messages again:

It'll be on its way. I'll forward mine. It sounds fun! I really think you should come.

'It's Bean,' I explain to Temi, who's been watching me. 'She thinks I should go.'

'She's right,' says Temi firmly. 'You should drink all the drink, eat all the food, have yourself the best party ever.'

At that moment, Bean's email arrives on my phone and

with grudging interest I open the attachment. It's a posh e-invitation, with a virtual envelope and a card with grand swirly writing.

'So pretentious,' I say at once. 'It looks like a Royal wedding.'

'*Ms Krista Coleman and Mr Antony Talbot cordially invite you to a house-cooling party at Greenoaks. Champagne and Cocktail Reception, 6.30–9pm,*' Temi reads over my shoulder. 'Champagne *and* cocktails. You see? It'll be amazing!'

'There's another card,' I say, clicking on the second. '*Family Dinner, 9pm till late.*'

'Two parties!' exclaims Temi. 'Even better!'

' "Family Dinner" sounds dire.' I make a face. 'Do I have to stay for that?'

'The family dinner is for the A-list!' Temi contradicts me. 'It's the VIP event. She'll serve at least five courses.'

Temi's right. It'll be the most massive swanky show-off-fest of a dinner and now I secretly want to see it.

'She'll serve lobster,' I say, gazing at the grand swirly writing. 'No, roasted swan.'

'A roasted swan, *inside* a deep-fried ostrich.'

'With a sparkler round its neck.'

By now, both of us are giggling, and as my phone lights up with a call from Bean, I'm still smiling.

'Hi.'

'So, did you see it?' she says, in her typical eager-yet-anxious manner. 'Are you going to go?'

'Dunno,' I say. 'Maybe. It sounds pretty big. The drinks bit, anyway.'

'Oh yes, Krista's gone super-grand. She's inviting stacks of people. People from the village, friends of hers, friends of Dad's . . .' Bean pauses, then adds cautiously, 'She's asked the Murrans. But I don't know if they're all coming.'

She means *I don't know if Joe's coming*. I close my eyes briefly. Great. Joe Murran. Just to add to everything.

'Well, I'll think about it.'

'Oh, come!' Bean's enthusiasm pours down the phone line. 'It won't be the same without you, Effie. Anyway, you want to see the house, don't you? And pick out whatever things you want to have? The packers are coming on Monday, and they're going to deliver all my stuff to me, so you could do the same. I'm going to have all my old books. And my old bedroom furniture.'

'Your Peter Rabbit furniture?' I laugh in surprise. 'Where will you put it?' Bean's cottage bedroom is already furnished, with a proper, grown-up, super-king bed.

'I've cleared out the spare room,' says Bean triumphantly. 'My guests can have Peter Rabbit, and anyone who laughs at it needn't come to stay.'

'No one will laugh at it!' I say fondly. 'And I'm definitely coming to stay in your Peter Rabbit room.'

There's a pause, then I add reluctantly, 'So . . . what are you wearing?' and Bean whoops.

'You *are* coming!'

'Maybe,' I allow.

Perhaps I'm not as stubborn as I think. Perhaps I do want to raise a glass to Greenoaks. Perhaps I'll make it up with Dad.

Put it another way, if I don't go, will I *ever* make it up with Dad?

I click on my emails to see if there's anything from Krista yet – but nothing.

'You know, I haven't actually got an invitation to this thing,' I point out, and Bean laughs again.

'You know what Krista's like. She's so techno-illiterate, she's probably sending each one out individually. Oh, Ephelant, I'm so glad you're coming.'

'*Maybe.*'

'OK, *maybe*. Even so. Let me know when you get your invitation.'

As she rings off, I refresh my emails again. Still nothing from Krista. You'd think she would have sent out all the family invitations together. But perhaps she's delayed mine. In fact, what am I saying? Of *course* she's delayed mine. She's trying to make a point. Well, whatever. Let her make her point. I don't care.

Except I do care, it turns out, because an hour later I've refreshed my emails about a hundred times. Where's this sodding invitation? She really knows how to wind me up. Does she not think that Bean and I talk? Does she not realize I see her little game?

'Just be patient,' advises Temi, who's sitting on the sofa, her hair in a shower cap, emitting a strong smell of coconut hair-mask. 'And do your hair while you're waiting.' She gestures at her head. 'I've got another sachet of this stuff. It's great.'

But I'm too wound up to apply a hair-mask; I can't wait a moment longer. I pull my laptop towards me and open a new email.

'What are you doing?' demands Temi, her eyes narrowing.

'Calling Krista's bluff,' I reply shortly. 'She can't play games with me for ever.'

I type out a message, my fingers quick and determined.

Hi Krista.

Your latest Instagram post is so much fun!!! How's your sparkler? Hope it's well. Just wondering if you were around Saturday evening? I was thinking I might pick up some stuff, but if you're not going to be in, I'll come another time.

Effie.

I press Send and wait for her reply. Krista's always got her phone on her, in a jewelled belt thing, so I know she'll see the email soon. Sure enough, within minutes, a reply arrives.

Hi, Effie!

Long time! We had started to think you didn't exist, in fact your dad and I talk about 'the two kids' now. Joke!!!!

We will be in on Saturday night, but we're having a little gathering. You're very welcome to come! Since you told me you never wanted to set foot in the house again or see my face, I didn't think you would appreciate an invitation, but of course if you want to, we'd be super-thrilled to see you. Black Tie, drinks from 6.30pm.

Krista

I read the email twice through, my shock rising as I take it in.

She wasn't just delaying my invitation – I wasn't going to be invited at all. To my own family home. To my own family party, to which the entire rest of the world has been invited. I wasn't on the list.

This is Krista's bomb, after all these weeks. She must have been waiting and *waiting* to drop it and I can just see her triumphant, pink-lip-glossed smile.

My face is burning hot. My brain feels all jangly. It never even *occurred* to me they wouldn't invite me; that they would actually cut me out of this last chance to say goodbye to our family home.

'So, did you get the email?' says Temi, and I look up, trying to appear cheerful.

'NFI,' I manage, and watch as her face drops in utter shock.

'Not invited? You're kidding!' She grabs the laptop out of my hand and scans it intently. 'Wait. You *are* invited.'

'That's not really invited, though, is it? I wasn't on the list. Krista's "allowing" me to come to the party. It's different. In fact, this entire email is pretty much an *anti*-invitation.'

'This is unreal,' Temi breathes. 'It's your house!'

'Not any more.'

'Wait, but . . . your dad.' Her eyes widen. 'Is he OK with this? He can't be!'

'Not sure,' I say, trying to force my lips into a smile. 'Guess he must be. You know we don't really talk any more. So. This must be . . . what he wants, too.'

I lapse into silence. I feel as if a door has clanged shut somewhere. I didn't even know it was open, but now it's definitely shut.

'This is outrageous!' Temi erupts. 'How long did you live in that house? And how long has Krista been on the scene? And as for your dad . . .' She breaks off in disbelief and for a few moments we're both silent.

'Well, anyway,' I say at last, my voice trembling. 'Give me that.' With stiff hands, I take my laptop back, and press Reply.

'What are you doing?' asks Temi.

'I'm going to decline Krista's charming anti-invitation.'

'No.' She shakes her head. 'Don't yet. Sleep on it.'

I've never understood the 'sleep on it' thing. What, have a miserable, sleepless night, brooding on your problem, simply in order to do the thing you were going to do the night before – only now you've delayed by twelve hours. How is that a good idea?

'Nothing to think about,' I say, and start typing, fast.

Dear Krista

What a wonderful, inviting email!!!

I was lucky enough to catch a glimpse of the invitation
you sent Bean, which I see was a bit different. How clever
of you to do different invitations for everyone.
Super-personalized!

Unfortunately, I must decline your welcoming offer. I've
remembered I will have another engagement that night.
I'm just not sure what it is yet.

You must be so looking forward to showing off our
house to the whole village!!! I do hope all goes well, and
thanks again for including me on the email that you sent.

All best regards

Effie

I press Send before I can have second thoughts, or indeed
any thoughts – my head feels weirdly empty – then get up.

'Where are you going?' demands Temi. 'Effie, are you OK?'

'I'm fine,' I say. 'I'm going to Mimi's.'

FOUR

Our family is broken, and that's just a fact.

As I stride along the street to Mimi's flat, my thoughts are fast and furious and wretched. Bean can say whatever UN peacekeepery things she likes, but *look* at us. We used to be the closest-ever family, meeting up for lunches, picnics, cinema outings . . . But now we never get together. I haven't seen Dad for weeks. Gus has gone AWOL. Even Bean is on the quiet side. And now, this.

Miserably, my mind travels back to how my rift with Dad began. Because it wasn't my fault, it really *wasn't*. The day after I stormed out of Greenoaks, I phoned him up. I didn't get through, but I left him a message. I suggested maybe we could have lunch or something.

Then I waited. A day went by. Two days. Three days. I kept planning all the things I would say when we talked it over. I even wrote myself a kind of script. I would apologize for over-reacting. And for yelling at Krista. But then I would explain that we three didn't see a nice 'fresh' kitchen, we saw our childhood wiped out. I would explain that I feel constantly uneasy round Krista. I would explain that this has all been harder than he maybe realizes . . .

But we never did talk it over. On the fourth day, Dad sent me an email, and my heart thumped frantically as I opened it – but it was the most soul-crushing missive I've ever received. He said that my post was still arriving at Greenoaks and perhaps I should get it redirected.

Post? *Post?*

Nothing about that night. Nothing about Krista. Nothing about anything that mattered.

My hurt rocketed to a whole new level. For a while, I considered not answering at all. But then I decided to send a short, dignified reply back: *Sorry my post has been troubling you, I do apologize, I will get it redirected forthwith.* And that's been the tone of our exchanges ever since. Short. Functional. Formal. The next correspondence we had was when Dad informed me that some distant relative I'd never heard of had died. I expressed my condolences as though I was addressing the Royal Family. Then, a week later, he said he was sending me some old school reports he'd found in the clear-out, and I replied that he needn't trouble himself. And that's it. Our only communication. In two months.

It's as if Dad's whole personality has changed, along with his outfits and his fake tan. He doesn't care about the things he used to care about. And I miss my old Dad so much, it makes me ache. I miss asking his advice when things go wrong in the flat. WhatsApping him jokes about the news. Texting him photos of wine lists in restaurants, asking, 'What should we order?' and waiting for him to joke, 'The second-cheapest one, of course,' before sending some proper advice.

I never understood headlines or TV shows about estranged families. I would wonder, 'How can that even *happen*?' But now I'm in one myself. And I feel a kind of dizzy horror whenever I let myself think about it.

I can't bring myself to tell Bean how bad things are. It's just too awful. Plus, she's so soft-hearted she'd get all stressed and probably decide it was somehow her fault. In fact, there's only one person I can think of who could possibly help. It was Mimi who patiently solved all our tearful arguments when we were growing up, unpicked the rights and wrongs, sorted out our burning injustices. If anyone could listen, counsel and gently negotiate, it would be her.

But, of course, she's the one person I can't possibly ask.

I find Mimi in the garden, pruning her single rose bush, looking tanned after her recent trip to France. Mimi's taken to travelling a lot, recently: she does city breaks and art trips and went on a wine-tasting tour of South Africa that took a whole month.

'Darling! Didn't hear you!' Her face lights up as she sees me, and she comes forward to hug me. I'm fully intending to make small talk before launching into the main subject – but then I discover that I can't.

'So, there's this party,' I say.

'Yes, I've heard about the party,' replies Mimi in neutral tones, resuming her pruning.

'Just so you know, I'm not going,' I say, a touch defiantly.

Maybe Mimi and I will spend Saturday night together, I'm suddenly thinking. Maybe I'll take her out for supper. Yes. We'll hold our own little party.

'You're not going?' She seems genuinely surprised, and I try to think how to explain without getting into it all.

'Don't feel like it. Anyway, never mind about that,' I add quickly. 'How have *you* been?' Finally, I've got to the small talk I should have started with. 'You look really well. And the garden looks nice!'

'Thank you, my love. We'll get there. I'm thinking of putting in a plum tree.'

'Plum crumble!'

'Exactly.'

We always used to make plum crumble together, Mimi and I. It was our thing. We'd pick the plums, dodging the wasps, and then cut them up and disagree about how much nutmeg to grate and then Gus would wander in and his eyes would light up and he'd say, 'Does this mean we're having custard?'

Mimi deadheads a few more roses, then, as though following the same train of thought, says, 'Have you spoken to Gus recently? He seems very preoccupied at the moment.'

'Not for ages,' I say, relieved to talk about someone else. 'He's a bit rubbish at replying to messages. But when we did last speak, he seemed quite stressed out.'

'Hmm,' says Mimi non-committally. Then she adds lightly, as though changing the subject, 'Is Romilly coming to the party?'

Ha. This is her secret code. Mimi wouldn't bitch about Romilly, because that's not her style. But it's clear she thinks exactly the same way as both Bean and I do: Gus is stressed out because of his nightmare girlfriend.

We can all see why Gus fell for Romilly. She's very attractive and dynamic and has the most adorable little girls, Molly and Gracie. At first sight, she seems like the whole package. Except, then you *unwrap* the package ... and find a control freak who is obsessed by her daughters' schooling and happy to use Gus shamelessly as a car service/chef/maths tutor. (Opinions my own.)

I think Gus has realized it by now. He knows Romilly isn't right for him, he knows he's unhappy, he just hasn't got round to doing anything about it. I feel like 'Leave Romilly' is probably on a to-do list somewhere on his desk, but he's put a cup of coffee down on it.

'I haven't heard,' I say. 'But I'm sure she'll be there.'

'Mmm-hmm. And Bean?' adds Mimi softly. 'Is there . . . anyone?'

Immediately my heart creases up. Because Gus's love life may be what you'd call sub-optimal, but Bean's . . .

Thinking about it still gives me actual pain, even a year on. It is the saddest, simplest story. Hal – who we all loved – asked Bean to marry him. He did this proper proposal in the park and we were all so thrilled . . . Bean was so happy . . . But then three days later, he changed his mind and ended it. Not just the engagement, the whole relationship. Over.

They'd been about to choose a ring. Bean was actually on her way to the jeweller's to meet him. Oh God. It was awful. *Awful*. I had the happiest sister in the world, and then I had the most heartbroken. Lovely, kind, sensitive, generous Bean. It's just not right. That stuff *should not happen to her*.

And yes, I know it wasn't Hal's fault. He was totally frank with Bean about how he'd got carried away and then realized he just wasn't ready, and he was desperately sorry and screwed up about it. I guess he had to do what he had to do, but . . .

God, love is crap. It's *crap*.

'Don't think so,' I say, gazing at a dead leaf. 'She hasn't mentioned it.'

'Mmm-hmm,' says Mimi again, in that tactful way she has. 'And you, darling? Is there anyone . . . interesting?'

'Nope,' I say, more bluntly than I intended. 'No one.'

'I hear the Murrans are going to the party,' says Mimi lightly, snipping a rose.

'Yup,' I say, even more curtly. 'I heard that too.'

'Joe's turned into quite a celebrity, hasn't he?' She sounds entertained by the fact. 'Although his mother says he can't stand it. We had coffee the other day. He's left Twitter, she said. Apparently he was besieged, after he was on the TV. Besieged! The clip's still on the Internet, you know.'

'I'm sure it is,' I say after a pause.

'Have you watched it?'

'No,' I say, staring at the sky. 'Can't say I have.'

Which is a lie, but I'm not going to say, *Of course I have, every single female in Britain has watched it and half of them have proposed marriage to him while the other half have Fedexed him their knickers.*

Mimi has clearly received the message that I do not wish to talk about Joe. She shuts her secateurs, puts a hand on my arm and smiles.

'Come on. Let's have some tea.'

As I enter the kitchen, I stop dead and gaze at the cupboard in front of me. There's a little illustration in the corner of the door, done in Sharpie. A tree and a bird. Simple and gorgeous.

'You've been drawing!' I exclaim.

'Yes.' Mimi smiles. 'Just a little. You like it?'

I can't answer for a moment.

'Yes,' I manage at last. 'I love it.'

'It's a new start,' says Mimi, her eyes crinkling. 'Darling, would you like supper?'

'Yes, please.' I draw breath. 'And listen, Mimi, d'you want

to go out on Saturday night? Just you and me? Go out to a restaurant or something?'

'What about the party?' says Mimi, flipping on the kettle, and I feel a spike of frustration. Wasn't she listening?

'I'm not *going*. I'd rather be with you!'

Mimi exhales softly, then turns to face me.

'Effie, my love, I'm busy on Saturday night. I have . . .' She hesitates. 'I have a date.'

My insides slither around for a few hideous seconds. A date? My mum? A *date*?

'Right,' I say, in a strangled voice. 'That's . . . You know. Great!'

My mind is suddenly full of unwanted images. Mimi clinking champagne glasses in a restaurant with a smarmy silver-fox type wearing a cravat, saying he'd like 'fun and more'.

Argh. No. Stop. I cannot compute any of this.

'And I think you should go to the party,' Mimi continues implacably. She puts a gentle hand on my arm. 'Darling, is there more to this than you're saying?'

For a moment I'm silent, trying to think how to answer.

'It's just been hard,' I say finally. 'You know. With Krista. And Dad. And everything.'

At the word *Krista*, Mimi twitches just the tiniest bit. She never talks about Krista, but when she first saw a photo of her, I did notice her face kind of cave in slightly.

'Of course it's been hard,' she says at last. 'But you love Greenoaks. This is your chance to say goodbye. And there must be things you want to collect from the house—'

'Nothing,' I contradict her, almost in triumph. 'I cleared out my bedroom, remember?'

I should probably have cleared out my room years ago.

But Bean and I – and Gus, for that matter – never properly 'moved out'. We were always going back for the weekend before the divorce, so it made sense to keep some stuff at Greenoaks. Bean actually moved back in for a while, when she was redecorating her own place, and she's still got so many belongings there, it looks as if she still lives there.

But not me. Not any more. A month ago, in a kind of defiant gesture, I hired a company to go and pack up everything in my bedroom that wasn't furniture, stow it in boxes and put it in a lock-up.

'Furniture?' Mimi persists. 'Books?'

'No. There's nothing there I want. Anyway, it'll all go into storage. It's not exactly urgent.'

The kettle comes to the boil, but neither of us moves.

'I still think you should go to this party,' says Mimi gravely. 'I feel it strongly, Effie.'

'Well, I've already declined,' I say, in a light, almost flippant voice. 'So, too late. I can't.'

We don't talk about the party again. Mimi cooks me supper and we watch TV, and as we hug goodbye, I'm actually quite cheerful.

At home, I wallow in a hot bath for a while, then get ready for bed. And it's only when I'm giving my phone a last check that Bean's WhatsApps start arriving.

Mimi says you've DECLINED??

Ephelant, you do realize this is our last chance to see Greenoaks???

Don't ignore me. I know you're there.

OK, fine, you don't want to talk. Well, here's what I think. I think you should email Krista and say you're coming to the party after all. You don't have to talk to her. You can ignore her all night. Stick with me and Gus.

I'll do it, if you like. I don't mind.

Shall I try to speak to Dad?

Talk to me!!!

I don't reply to any of her messages. Instead, I turn my phone off, get into bed and burrow under the duvet, my eyes squeezed shut. I don't care what Bean says. Or Mimi. My resolve is growing stronger with every minute.

I don't need to attend some pretentious, pointless party, or see Greenoaks for the last time. There is absolutely nothing there that I want or desire or have any interest in at all. *Nothing*.

I'm already drifting off to sleep, reiterating my points dozily in my mind. What would there even be for me to take from Greenoaks? Exactly. There's nothing! My mind runs idly through the rooms on the ground floor, as though checking them off. Hall ... sitting room ... dining room ... study ... then up to the first floor ... along the landing ...

And then I sit bolt upright, my heart pounding hard, my hand clapped to my mouth.

Oh God. Oh my God. My Russian dolls.

FIVE

I need my Russian dolls. It's not a question of 'want', I *need* them. If I close my eyes, I can see them vividly, smell their faint woody, homey smell. One with a crack on her head where Gus threw her at me mid-fight. One with a blue felt-tip mark, right across her floral apron. One with a water stain from when I tried to use her head as a cup. All loved; all cherished. The thought of never touching them again, never feeling them in my hands, never seeing their familiar faces, makes my stomach curdle with panic.

But right now they're at Greenoaks, hidden up a chimney in the box room, which is where I stuffed them six months ago.

The irony being that I did that to keep them safe. *Safe*. We'd had a burglary here at the flat. Thankfully the dolls weren't touched – we only lost a bit of cash – but it freaked me out. I decided my precious dolls would be better off safely cocooned in Greenoaks than in our Hackney place.

But I didn't want to leave them lying around for Krista to get her mitts on. She was already in her clearing-out and 'freshening-up' phase. She might easily have 'freshened up' my dolls into the bin. So I put them right away, in a hiding place that only I knew about.

At the back of my mind, I planned to retrieve them sometime. I was relaxed about it. I thought I had for ever. I didn't foresee that I would stop visiting Greenoaks. Or that the house would be sold in such a rush. Or that I would be 'anti-invited' to the final family event there.

I guess everything in the house will go into storage – but the packers will never look up a chimney. The dolls will be left behind. The new people will redecorate, because that's what people do. I can already see a burly contractor putting his hand up the chimney and pulling them out: *What we got here then? Some old set of dolls. Chuck 'em on the skip, Bert.*

The thought makes me cold with dread. I haven't slept properly since that night I sat bolt upright in bed, which was five days ago. I have to get them.

Which is why I *am* going to the party tonight. But not as a guest. I've got it all planned. I'll get in while everyone's distracted by the festivities, creep to the box room, grab my dolls and leave. In, out, gone. I'll be ten minutes, tops, and the only crucial things are: 1. No one must see me, and 2. Krista must *definitely* not see me.

'Are my trainers squeaky?' I ask, pumping them up and down on our dingy green kitchen lino as though I'm in a cardio class. 'Can you hear anything?'

Temi looks up from scrolling on her phone and peers blankly down at my feet.

'Your *trainers*?'

'I need to be silent. I can't be caught out by a squeaky trainer. It's quite essential,' I add, as she doesn't seem to be responding. 'You know, you could help.'

'OK, Effie, slow down.' Temi lifts her hand. 'You're wired. Let me get this straight. You're going to crash your own dad's party. A party that you have, in fact, been invited to.'

'I was *anti*-invited,' I retort. 'As you well know.'

I stretch out a hamstring, because I have a vague sense I'm going to need all my physical powers to pull this off. I won't exactly be ziplining in, but . . . you know. I might have to get in through a window.

I'm wearing all black. Not chic party black, but *Mission Impossible* black, as befits my quest. Black leggings, top, trainers and black leather fingerless gloves. Black beanie, even though it's June. I feel slightly hyper, slightly nervous and slightly like, if I pull this off I could be the next James Bond.

Temi looks at me and bites her lip.

'Effie, you know, you could just go to the party.'

'But then I'd have to "go to the party",' I retort, making a face. 'I'd have to ask Krista for an invitation . . . and *smile* at her . . . It would be *hideous*.'

'Couldn't you ask Bean to get the dolls?'

'I suppose. But I don't want to ask her for a favour.' I look away, because the subject of Bean is a bit sensitive.

Bean still thinks I should go to the party. In fact, we've kind of argued about it. (It's hard to argue with Bean, as she keeps backtracking and apologizing even as she's landing killer points – but we got close.) If I *once* let slip to her that I'm going to be in the vicinity of Greenoaks tonight, she'll try to convince me to join the party again. She'll make me feel guilty. And I don't want to feel guilty. I want to get my dolls and go.

'You should take a dress, at least,' says Temi, surveying me. 'You might change your mind and want to join in the fun. What if you get there and the food and drink look really great and you think, "Damn, why didn't I just go to the party?"'

'I won't.'

'What if you see someone you want to talk to?'

'Won't happen.'

'What if you get caught?'

'Stop it!' I protest. 'You're being so negative! I'll never get caught. I know Greenoaks inside out. I know all the secret routes, all the attics, all the trap doors, all the hiding places . . .'

I can see myself now: sidling into the box room, a mysterious silhouetted figure. Grabbing the dolls in one seamless move. Clambering down a drainpipe and doing a forward roll on the lawn before I dash through the darkness to safety.

'You want a partner in crime?' says Temi, and I shake my head.

'Thanks, but I'll be better going solo.'

'Well, if you need me, I'm available. I'll triangulate your position. Sort out a chopper for your escape.'

'I'll let you know.' I grin at her.

'What if you see Joe?' Temi's words catch me off-guard, and I hesitate. Because this has crossed my mind, too. Of course it has. Endlessly.

'I won't,' I say. 'So it's fine.'

'Hmm,' says Temi sceptically. 'When did you last see him?'

'Couple of Christmases ago. He was walking past our gate. We chatted. No big deal.'

I head out of the kitchen before Temi can question me any further, sink down on the sofa in the sitting room and pretend to be checking my phone. But now I'm thinking of Joe. And that night, four years ago, when I returned from the States and everything imploded.

We'd always had insecurities about being high-school sweethearts. We both kept wondering, *Is* everyone right? *Are* we too young? So when an exchange programme to San

Francisco came along at my work, it seemed the perfect opportunity for a trial break. We would spend six months apart and hardly even text each other. We would be free to date other people, explore life without each other. And then when I came back . . .

We never actually said it out loud, but we both knew it. We would commit.

The night before I left for the States, we went out for dinner at a posh restaurant that we really couldn't afford, and Joe produced a tiny gift-wrapped parcel which made my nerves flutter, because his finances were pretty stretched.

'I know you say you're not a "big diamonds" kind of girl,' he began and I felt a jab of alarm, thinking, *Oh God, has he taken out a mortgage to pay for some stupid rock?*

'I'm really not,' I replied hastily. '*Really* not. And you know, there are always refunds.' I nodded at the parcel. 'If you wanted to take that back, I wouldn't mind. We could pretend this didn't happen.'

Joe burst out laughing – and of course, I should have known he was cleverer than that.

'So I went a different way,' he continued, his eyes crinkling. 'And I'm very proud to say I have bought you . . .' He handed it over with a flourish. 'The Smallest Diamond in the World. Trademark.'

I started laughing myself – partly in relief – and began to unwrap it.

'It'd *better* be the smallest one in the world,' I said, as I pulled the paper off a jewellery box. 'Don't be palming me off with "quite little".'

'It's actually invisible to the naked eye,' Joe replied, deadpan. 'Luckily I took a microscope along with me when I bought it. You'll just have to take my word for it that it exists.'

Joe could always make me laugh. And cry. Because as I opened the box and saw a little silver candle charm, with a tiny diamond for a flame, my eyes went misty.

'That's me,' he said. 'Burning steadily for you all the time you're away.'

As I looked up, his eyes were sheeny too, but he was smiling resolutely, because we'd already vowed we weren't going to be anything but upbeat tonight.

'You have to have *fun*,' I said. 'With . . . you know. Other girls.'

'You too.'

'What, have fun with girls?'

'If you like.' His eyes glinted. 'In fact, great idea. Send me the photos.'

'Seriously, Joe,' I said. 'This is our chance to . . .' I broke off. 'To *know*.'

'I already know,' he said quietly. 'But yes. I get it. And I promise to have fun.'

I enjoyed San Francisco, I really did. I didn't mope around or pine. I worked hard, I got a tan, I cut my hair differently, and I went out on dates with American men. They were nice. Polite. Funny. But they weren't Joe. They couldn't compete. And with every *meh* date, I felt more sure.

Joe and I were deliberately keeping our messages to a minimum, but sometimes, late at night, I would send him a photo of my candle charm, which was now hanging round my neck on a silver chain. And sometimes my phone would ping with a photo of a candle, burning on his desk. And I knew.

It was my idea to reunite in the tree house at Greenoaks on Midsummer's Night, where we'd hung out so many times, over the years. I'd landed the day before, but I'd told Joe not to meet me at the airport. Airports are stressy, functional places and it's never like the movies. Everyone watches you greeting each other and you're always struggling with some extra carrier bag full of crap and then you have to get on the Tube. I was very much *not* up for that. So instead, we would have our grand reunion in the tree house at Greenoaks, under the midsummer sky. I didn't tell any of the family, just took the train to Nutworth, crept round the house and into the field. It was going to be our precious secret encounter.

It took me a long time to realize he wasn't coming. A stupidly, mortifyingly long time. I'd arrived early, jittery but exhilarated, wearing new underwear and a new dress and the tiny diamond candle. I had wine ready, tea lights, a rug, music, even a cake. At first, when he didn't arrive, I wasn't concerned. I swigged the wine and let my anticipation happily build.

After half an hour, I sent him a photo of my candle charm, but there was no reply. So I sent another, and got no reply to that, either, which is when I started to worry. Abandoning all restraint, I sent him a series of cheery texts, wondering if he'd forgotten the date? The arrangement? Everything we'd talked about? Then, slightly more desperately: was he OK???

Then I started to panic. I'd been sitting there for nearly an hour. Joe's not the naturally late type. I started to catastrophize. He was dead. Knocked down on his way to our reunion, holding a bunch of flowers. Or kidnapped. Or at the very least, trapped under heavy furniture.

Which is my only defence for what I did next, which was to go round to his mother's house. Oh *God*. The memory still makes me cringe. Tottering up Isobel Murran's path, almost hyperventilating with worry, tears brimming in my eyes, jamming my finger desperately on the bell.

I don't know what I'd hoped for. Some happy, heart-warming scene in which it turned out Joe had been delayed by rescuing a kitten stuck up a tree.

Instead, Isobel opened the door in her towelling dressing gown. She'd been in the bath. The *shame*.

'Effie!' she exclaimed. 'You're back!'

But I was too frazzled even to return her smile.

I gabbled out my fears, and her surprise turned to alarm. She instantly fetched her phone, sent a text, and a few seconds later watched the reply come in.

It was her expression that confirmed to me the dark, unthinkable suspicion that had been lurking the whole way along. She looked embarrassed. Troubled. Pained. And worst of all, pitying.

'Effie . . . he's fine,' she said softly, her whole face creased up, as though she could hardly bear to deliver the news that her son was not in fact dead or trapped under heavy furniture.

'Right,' I said, feeling nauseous. 'Right. Sorry. I . . . I understand.'

The full enormity hadn't hit me yet, but I had to get away. My legs were already stumbling backwards . . . but then I paused a moment.

'Please don't tell anyone,' I begged, my voice husky. 'Don't tell my family. Mimi. Bean. They don't know I'm here. Don't tell, Isobel. Please.'

By now tears were streaming down my face, and Isobel looked nearly as distraught as me. She muttered, 'He needs to talk to you. I don't know what . . . I can't *understand* what . . . Effie, come in. Let me give you a cup of tea. A drink.'

But I just shook my head mutely and backed away. I had to find somewhere dark and private, to digest the nightmare that seemed to be happening.

The worst thing was that I still had hope; I couldn't help myself. It was the phone call half an hour later that finished me off. Joe rang. He apologized. He said he was sorry, about a hundred times. He told me he'd treated me badly, about a hundred times. He told me there was no excuse, about a hundred times.

What he didn't tell me was *why*. Every time I asked why, he just said he was sorry. I couldn't get past his blank, impenetrable wall of apology. But apology didn't help me.

My distress turned to fury and I demanded a meeting – *It's the least you owe me* – and so we had a dismal coffee the following day. But it was like talking to a witness in a court case. I didn't even know where my warm, witty, loving Joe had gone.

In hollow tones, he said he hadn't met anyone new, but he didn't think he could commit. He'd panicked. He hadn't meant to hurt me, although he realized that he *had* hurt me. If he said 'I can't even explain it myself, Effie' once, he said it about six thousand times, his gaze fixed on the far wall.

You can take a guy to a coffee shop, but you can't make him bare his soul. In the end we were going round and round in circles and I gave up, weary and defeated.

'Well, it's lucky you only gave me the smallest diamond in the world,' I said as a savage parting shot. 'I didn't mind too much when I chucked it in the bin.'

It was a childish thing to say and I saw Joe flinch, but I didn't care. In fact, it felt *good*.

Which is why, the following Christmas, when I was fairly sure I might bump into Joe, I did another childish thing that I knew would make him flinch. I hooked up with Humph Pelham-Taylor, our local aristo.

Humph lives five miles away from Nutworth and he's

properly posh. Family tree, checked shirts, old nanny still living with them, that kind of thing. He'd pursued me endlessly at school – I hadn't been interested, obviously – but now here was my chance to get revenge on Joe.

I mean, it kind of worked. When I turned up to that year's carol service, arm-in-arm with Humph, wearing a spectacular fake-fur hat, Joe did look pretty flabbergasted. And when I loudly exclaimed, 'Humph, darling, you're *hilarious*,' I saw Joe do a double-take in disbelief. (To be fair, I saw quite a few people do a double-take in disbelief. Including Bean.)

But that's all I achieved. One flabbergasted expression and one double-take, then radio silence. Joe left before the mulled-wine reception. We didn't even exchange words.

And for that I had to put up with Humph's braying voice and terrible kissing and alarming views on life. ('I mean, women's brains *are* smaller, Effie, that's a scientific *fact*.') Until I kindly parted ways with him on Boxing Day. We'd been together three weeks, but that was already too much.

We never slept together, a fact I often reiterate to myself. I found a list online – *10 excuses not to have sex* – and went down them methodically, from 'I've got a headache' to 'Your dog's watching me.' But we were an item, which was enough.

Of course, I regret it now. It was an immature thing to do. But then, I regret a lot of things, like believing that Joe and I would have grandchildren together one day.

The noise of throat-clearing breaks my thoughts and I look up to see Temi watching me.

'So, Joe's no big deal?' she says. 'Effie, you should have seen your face just now. You didn't even notice me come in. And *don't* pretend you weren't thinking about him.'

Temi doesn't know the whole story of what happened with Joe, but she knows he's still under my skin. (It *really* doesn't help that he's on the *Daily Mail* website nearly every day.)

'He split up from his girlfriend, didn't he?' she adds, as though reading my mind. 'It was in the *Mail*. What was her name again?'

'Not sure,' I say vaguely, as though her every detail isn't etched on my brain. *Lucy-Ann. TV research assistant. Very pretty, with flowing brown hair. They were photographed in Hyde Park, arm-in-arm.*

'I'm going to ask again,' says Temi patiently. 'What if you see him? You need a game plan.'

'I don't,' I contradict her. 'Because I *won't* see him. I'll be in the house for ten minutes, if that, and I won't go *near* the guests. I'm going to creep in through the back field, up through the shrubbery . . .'

'Someone'll spot you,' objects Temi, and I shake my head.

'The shrubs go pretty much up to the kitchen door. Remember how we used to play hide and seek? So I'll get in there, dodge up the stairs—'

'Won't there be people in the kitchen? Caterers or whatever?'

'Not all the time. I'll hide in a shrub and wait till I have my moment.'

'Hmm,' Temi says sceptically – then her face changes. 'Hey, what's happening to the tree house?'

'Nothing.' I shrug. 'The new people will have it.'

'Damn.' Temi shakes her head sorrowfully. 'I mean, fair enough, but, damn. We used to *live* in that place.'

Despite everything that happened there, I can still appreciate it's a good tree house. It has two storeys, with a rope ladder and even a trapeze. On summer nights we would go out and lie on the wooden boards with blankets, looking up at the stars. Dreaming, listening to music, planning our lives.

And then having our hearts broken. Or maybe that was only me.

'Whatever,' I say brusquely. 'It's only a tree house.'

'Effie . . .' Temi's eyes meet mine, suddenly serious. 'Listen. Are you *sure* about this?' She sweeps a hand over my black outfit.

'Of course.' I jut out my chin. 'Why wouldn't I be?'

'This is your last farewell to Greenoaks.' She looks wistful. 'Even *I* loved that house, and I didn't even live there. You should be saying goodbye properly, not slinking around in the shadows.'

'Goodbye to what?' I can't help having an edge to my voice. 'The house isn't the same . . . our family isn't the same . . .'

'Even so,' she says, refusing to give up. 'You need to take a moment while you're there. Be with it. Feel it.' She clasps her heart. 'Or you might look back and regret that you just rushed through, you know?'

Her eyes are on mine – my oldest, wisest friend, gazing at me in concern – and I flinch inwardly, because she's reaching a secret, tucked-away part of me. My innermost Russian doll, the tiniest baby one. Which still, after all this time, feels raw and hurt.

I know that what she's saying makes sense. But here's the truth: I don't want to 'feel it'. I'm tired of 'feeling it'. I need my outer, protective layers to click shut, quickly. Doll after doll. Shell after shell. Click, click, shut, shut. Safe inside.

'Whatever.' I pull down my beanie, until it's nearly over my eyes. 'It's just a house. I think I'll be fine.'

SIX

OK, I'm not fine. Not fine at all. This is *not* going as I envisioned.

How I envisioned it: I would approach the house under cover of the shrubbery, silent as a jaguar, stealthy as a fox. I would shimmy silently through the kitchen and be upstairs in three minutes. I would be out again in five. It would all be seamless and easy.

Instead: I am stuck behind a rose bush in the front garden, breathing in the scent of mud and leaves, watching the front door as well-dressed guests approach the bouncer to have their names checked off a list. The *bouncer*. Krista hired a *bouncer*. How pretentious is that? I never imagined that. Nothing is as I imagined it. And I don't have a new game plan.

I'm refusing to panic; not quite yet. But I do feel a little wired. And I'm still pulsating with rage at whoever cut back the shrubbery and *ruined my whole plan*.

It was all going so well. I'd arrived in Nutworth without anyone seeing me. I'd arrived by train, sneaked through the back roads of the village, and surreptitiously made my way down a little lane used by tractors. And OK, yes, I was planning to trespass, but only on farmland owned by our neighbour, John Stanton. He's an old man with a kind soul and I felt instinctively he wouldn't mind. Sometimes you just know these things about your fellow human beings.

I climbed over a fence, ripping my leggings slightly on the barbed wire, but never mind. I hurried along the side of John's field, dodging cowpats, until I was at the boundary with our land and the turret of Greenoaks was in view. I clambered over the next fence into our field and automatically glanced up at the tree house.

At that point, I felt a sudden pang. A yearning to climb up into the tree house again. To lie down on the smooth wooden boards, gaze up at the sky through the open windows and just . . . remember.

But I chose to ignore it. If you listened to every pang, you wouldn't get anywhere in life.

So instead I crept along the hedge line, ignoring the gaze of curious sheep, towards the yew hedge that marks the beginning of the garden. By this time, I was pumped. I was energized. I was ready to scamper through the shrubs, light-footed and swift, just like when I was nine years old.

And then, as I emerged from the yew hedge, I got the shock of my life. All the shrubs had been cut down. Cut down! The back of Greenoaks was exposed, with a dismal brand-new patio area laid down, complete with shiny black firepit. It looked naked and uncomfortable and just . . . *wrong*.

I felt such a visceral pang of dismay that tears came to my eyes. Because how much time did I spend playing in those shrubs as a child? How much affection did I have for their woody, peaty, leafy embrace? They always felt like benevolent, ancient members of the family, ready to shield you at a moment's notice. And now they'd been brutally chopped down . . . by who? Dad? Krista?

And more urgently: where was I supposed to hide now? I couldn't conceal myself on the new, bare patio.

Then things got worse. As I was peering out from behind a beech tree, a couple of people came out of the kitchen. They looked like catering staff. One dumped a couple of empty bottles in a plastic tub; the other lit up a cigarette and leaned against the wall. And I realized the awful truth: the caterers were using the patio as a service area. They would be constantly in and out. They would spot me in a heartbeat.

I was stuck. Stuffed.

For a few minutes I just stood there, thinking hard. From where I was standing, I could see a glimpse of white canvas on the west side of the house. I realized there must be some sort of marquee or awning off the dining room. That's where the party was going on. That was where I should avoid.

So I sidled up the garden on the other side of the house, stopping dead every time a member of the catering staff appeared outside, trying to blend into the foliage, barely daring to breathe, half thinking, *Could I climb in through an unobtrusive window?* But I already knew it was hopeless. The east side of Greenoaks has hardly any windows. It's the dead side, all mossy stone and storerooms which no one uses.

I carried on creeping slowly, silently, stealthily round, until I emerged on the front drive. And then my nerves really did start twanging, because there were guests. Actual guests. People I knew, crunching over the gravel, holding small gifts or bunches of flowers. I could see a distant guy in a hi-vis jacket directing cars to turn into a field to park. It was all more formal than I'd imagined. More organized.

No one noticed me slinking breathlessly from the horn-beam hedge to the ornamental bench to a crouching position in the rose border, about five metres from the house. And this is where I still am. Hiding behind a rose bush, trying to formulate a plan.

I can hear the distant hum of conversation and the bass thrumming of music playing over a sound system. The odd trill of laughter, too. Everyone's clearly having a *wonderful* time at Krista's *wonderful* party.

Meanwhile, my legs have started to ache, and I cautiously change position, wincing as I catch my arm on a thorn. Two women in sparkly dresses are walking up the circular drive to the door. I don't recognize them; maybe they're friends of Krista's. They give their names to the bouncer and he squints at his list. Then he mutters something into his headset – his *headset* – and finally lets them in.

I mean, who does Krista think she is? Victoria Beckham?

I stare resentfully at the bouncer with his clipboard and broad shoulders and steady gaze. If it weren't for him, I could easily dart in, between guests.

Could I distract him?

In an action movie I would have a hand grenade about my person that I would roll unnoticed along the ground. It would explode and the bouncer would rush forward, drawing his weapon, and by the time he looked round again, I'd be safely inside. That's what I need: a hand grenade. Only without explosions. Maybe I should appeal to a higher being.

Dear God, please send me some form of hand grenade . . .

And just then, into my field of vision appears pretty much the opposite of a hand grenade. The softest, gentlest, least explosive person in the world: Bean.

She's not in party gear – she's wearing jeans, a T-shirt and

Ugg boots and is lugging along something which is made of stone and clearly heavy, as she's panting with the effort. As she dumps it down and mops her brow, I recognize it as the bird bath from the walled garden. She takes her phone out of her pocket, taps at it, and a moment later, my own phone buzzes with a WhatsApp notification. Shit! She's WhatsApping me!

I jump in alarm and peer through the tangle of rose branches at Bean, to see if she heard the tell-tale buzz. But the hubbub from the party is obviously loud enough to mask it. Now I just have to decide whether to reply.

What's she bothering me for, anyway? Doesn't she have a posh party to go to?

But she might have some gossip or important news. I can't ignore her. Feeling slightly surreal, I click on her message and read it.

Hi Effie, I'm at Greenoaks. Just to let you know, I'm going to take the bird bath. I really wish you were here. Do you want me to take anything from the garden for you? Any pots or anything? Like, the terracotta one with herbs in? You might want it one day? Xxx

Part of me thinks I should stay silent right now. But on the other hand, I don't want Bean getting worried that I haven't claimed some manky old terracotta pot and will regret it for ever. So I type briskly back:

No thanks, I'm good on the pot front. Have fun. Xxx

'Good evening!' comes a jolly, booming voice, and through the rose bush I see the Martins from the Old Rectory, coming up the drive towards the house. As they greet Bean, she jumps and blushes furiously, and I smirk, safe in my hiding place. We haven't been able to look the Martins in the eye since the yoga statue incident.

We went for drinks at the Old Rectory last year, and Bean and I were surreptitiously looking *everywhere* for it, but no sign. Not even in Jane's bedroom, where we brushed our hair. So we agreed it must be in their secret sex room and got a bit hysterical, and then Jane came up, in her nice floral dress, and said, 'What's the joke?' pleasantly, and we nearly *died*.

'Hi!' says Bean now, in a slight fluster, and she gestures at her jeans and Uggs. 'Don't look at me, I'm not party-ready yet.'

'You always look lovely,' says Jane kindly, giving her a kiss. 'Is Effie coming?'

'Don't . . . think so,' says Bean, after a pause. 'She couldn't make it. But the rest of us will be here.'

'Big night for you all,' says Andrew, looking around the grounds. 'You've been here a long time. Hard to say goodbye to a house like this.'

'Yes,' says Bean, her cheeks becoming pinker. 'Quite hard. But . . . you know, good, too. Good in lots of ways.'

There's a short pause and I can tell no one knows quite what to say. The Martins are very tactful people, the type who would never take sides or bitch or say, '*What* has your dad's girlfriend done to that beautiful kitchen?' like Irene in the pub did.

'Well, see you in there!' says Jane. 'Goodness, a doorman!' she adds, twinkling at the bouncer. 'How very grand!'

The Martins give their names to the bouncer and are admitted to the house and I continue watching Bean. I'm expecting her to hurry in to the party, but she doesn't seem in any rush. Her face creases up as though with an anxious thought – then

she pushes her hair back off her brow and starts typing again.
A moment later, my phone buzzes.

> Are you all right?? You're not sitting on your own in the
> flat, brooding, are you? Mimi told me you wanted to have
> supper with her but she couldn't make it. I know she was
> hoping you would change your mind about tonight. Hope
> you're OK xxxxx

As I read her words, I'm simultaneously touched and offended. So, is this what everyone thinks? That I'm some tragic, brooding loner? I am not sitting alone in my flat. I am sitting alone *behind a rose bush*. I almost want to inform Bean of that fact. But then I have a better idea. Briskly I type a new message:

> Actually I've got a date. So don't worry.

I send it, then add a casual follow-up:

> You could tell people at the party. Like Krista. Or Joe, if
> you see him. You could tell him I'm on a date.

From behind the bush, I can see Bean's face. She looks so genuinely delighted by my news, I feel a fresh pang of affection for her. She types something hurriedly and a moment later it arrives:

> A date! That's fantastic! You never said. Details?

Details. Right, come on, Effie, details. As I start typing, I forgive myself for fibbing, because all I'm trying to do is set

73

my sister's mind at rest. She will enjoy the evening far better if she thinks I'm on some shit-hot date.

> Yes, it's amazing! I only met him today, at an event I was waitressing at. He asked me about the lemon sorbet and we took it from there. He's an Olympic athlete.

Even as I'm pressing Send, I'm wondering if 'Olympic athlete' is going a bit too far, and sure enough, Bean's reaction proves it.

> WHAT?? Which kind?

Yikes. I don't know anything about the Olympics. Jumping? Throwing? Better dodge that one.

> He doesn't do it any more. He's a businessman. And philanthropist.

I'm about to add something about his yacht when Bean exclaims, 'Joe!' and I drop my phone, then scrabble to pick it up.

Oh God. He's here.

I mean, I knew he might be. Obviously. But I never expected—

OK, Effie, breathe. *Breathe*. It's fine. He can't see me. He'll never look in this direction. And in a way, it's interesting to view him like this, neutrally, from a distance, now that he's a celebrity.

As he comes into view, I can't help scanning him greedily through the rose branches. Hair a bit longer than the last time I saw him. Eyes a bit more tired-looking? Smile just as intriguing.

There's always been something about Joe's smile. It's not just an expression of happiness. It hints at wryness and wisdom, a rueful amusement with life.

Although he's looking more wry and less amused, tonight. His dark hair is swept back and his face is thinner than last time I saw him, which makes his cheekbones stand out. He's in a very elegant dinner jacket, I'll give him that.

Now he's kissing Bean on the cheek and my own cheek tingles in a weird kind of sympathy.

'Hi, Bean,' he says in his deep, familiar voice, and without wanting to, I have a sudden memory of lying with him on the grass, aged about seventeen, dappled sunshine on our faces, feeling as though we had for ever.

More memories start cascading in, and I don't know which is worse – remembering what went wrong or what went right. That night we edged together for the first time at the sixth-form disco. The blissful intoxication of that first, dreamy summer. The way it all seemed meant to be.

It's only now I've tried making it work with other guys that I realize how natural Joe and I were together. Sex came easily. I never winced or said 'Ow! Sorry ...' or invented sexy noises to fill a vacuum. I never fibbed or faked. Why would I fib to Joe?

We learned everything together. How to be students. How to survive a hangover. The names of bones. That was for Joe's exams, but it mattered to me too, so I was his revision buddy. One time, I decorated his room with all the Latin words on Post-its, and for months, 'Tibia' was stuck on the wall above his bed.

Then we were out in the real world, with new challenges. Work. Colleagues. Finding a London flat in about Zone 1,000. Building a bed out of a box. For a while I cajoled Joe into rowing on the Thames every weekend. We were both pretty rubbish, but it was fun.

We didn't have to explain ourselves. We knew we were on the same side. Yes, we got stressed out and yes, we argued, but in the same way that we used to argue in English lessons at school. Respectfully. Never bitterly or meanly.

And somehow, however well we got to know each other, there was always a magic. A mystery. We could lie in bed looking silently at each other, not needing to speak. Joe's eyes were never boring. He was never boring.

What I've learned since being out in the dating field is: a lot of men are really boring. Or else, they're not boring, they're super-fun and exciting, but they have four other secret girlfriends they never mentioned . . .

I heave a familiar sigh and screw up my eyes, willing my brain to clear.

'So, end of an era,' Joe's saying to Bean, in the grave, empathetic tones that the whole nation has come to love. 'How do you feel about it?'

'Oh, fine!' says Bean brightly. 'I mean, it's all for the best. So.'

'Right.' Joe nods several times, looking wistful. 'I always loved this place,' he adds. 'I mean, how much time did I spend here as a kid? Remember those bonfire parties up on the mound?'

Both he and Bean automatically turn their eyes towards the grassy mound, looming up on the east side of the house.

'Yes, they were fun,' says Bean after a pause.

'And the tree house.' He shakes his head reminiscently. 'I think one summer we spent every single day in the tree house. Slept out there, everything. It was like a second home.'

I'm breathing hard with indignation as I listen. The tree

house? How can he refer to the tree house so casually? Does he not have any feelings?

Maybe that's it. Yes. I made the mistake of falling in love with a man without any feelings. *Now* it all makes sense.

'We were very lucky, growing up here.' Bean's smile is fixed and even from this distance I can see her eyes are starting to shimmer.

Joe seems to realize it too, because he adds, 'But, all for the best.'

'Exactly. All for the best!' Bean says, even more brightly. 'You have to move on.'

'Of course,' says Joe, a sudden kindness to his voice. Then he adds, almost casually, 'Is Effie here?'

'No, she couldn't come.' Bean pauses, then adds in a rush, 'She's got a date, actually. An Olympic athlete. She passed him lemon sorbet and they took it from there.'

'An Olympic athlete?' Joe looks surprised. 'Wow.'

Yes, I think silently behind my rose bush. So. Take that, Joe.

'He's a philanthropist now,' Bean adds breathlessly. 'Businessman and philanthropist.'

I want to *hug* her.

'He sounds quite the catch,' says Joe and there's a sudden edge to his voice. Or did I imagine that?

'Anyway, I should go in.' Bean shoots a worried glance at her watch. 'I'm late. You're coming to the family dinner, aren't you?'

'Apparently so.' Joe raises his eyebrows. 'Although I'm not sure how I qualify.'

'Oh well, you're practically family,' says Bean vaguely, her cheeks a little pink. 'So I expect Krista thought . . .' She trails off awkwardly.

What she's not going to say is, *Krista invited you because you're famous now*. But that's the honest truth. Krista's shameless. She'll want to boast about how she's best friends with him. And Joe's wry smile tells me that he fully understands this.

'Very kind of Krista,' he says politely. 'Thoughtful.'

'Yes. Well.' Bean passes a flustered hand through her hair. 'I really must go. See you later! . . . I'm on the list,' she adds to the bouncer as she hurries to the front door. 'Bean Talbot.'

'What's that?' The bouncer points a fleshy finger at the bird bath, still sitting on the drive. 'Is it a present for the family?'

'No,' says Bean patiently. 'I *am* the family. It's a bird bath.'

The bouncer looks as though he's never heard the term 'bird bath' before and doesn't believe in it for a moment. He scrutinizes it suspiciously, then looks up to scrutinize Joe, too – at which point his brow suddenly clears.

'Wait. You're that doctor. Off the telly.'

'Yes,' allows Joe, after a pause. 'I am.'

'My girlfriend's obsessed with you!' The bouncer is suddenly full of friendly animation. 'Obsessed! She changed her free pass from Harry Styles to you. And she wouldn't do that lightly, because she loves Harry Styles. I was like, "Babe, you sure?" and she was like, "That doctor is *hot*."'

He looks at Joe as though expecting an appropriate reaction and I bite my lip hard, because otherwise I'm going to splutter with laughter.

'Right,' says Joe. 'Well. Thanks. That's . . . an honour. Although you should be aware, I have a policy of not taking up free passes with women whose boyfriends could flatten me with one blow.'

'I'm telling her now.' The bouncer has stopped listening and is texting. 'Listen, I'm not supposed to do this, but can I get a selfie?'

He grabs Joe and beams at his phone screen, while Joe

gazes pleasantly ahead – not exactly ignoring him, but not doing a cheesy grin either. Then Joe's phone rings and he says in evident relief, 'So sorry, I'd better answer this.'

As he moves off to take his call, Bean disappears inside the house, and for a few moments there's quiet. Cautiously I shift position again, because a muscle in my leg has started to spasm. This is getting ridiculous. What am I going to *do*? How do I get into the house? I still need a hand grenade. Or a different plan altogether, except I don't have one.

Guests are still arriving in dribs and drabs. An entire family in black tie approaches and is admitted. I have no idea who they are, they must be more friends of Krista's. Kenneth from the golf club arrives, wearing a tartan bow tie, mistakes the bouncer for a guest and starts groping politely for his name – 'Now, I'm *sure* we've met before . . . ' – before the bouncer puts him right and sends him inside.

Then Joe wanders past, still on the phone, and I stiffen.

'Hi, Mum?' he's saying. 'Did I miss a call just now? Yes, I'm here. Oh, I see. Well, no worries, I haven't gone in yet, I'll wait for you.' He listens a moment, then says, 'No, don't be silly. We'll go in together. See you in ten minutes.'

He moves to one side of the house and starts reading something on his phone. It's gallant of him to wait for his mum, I admit to myself grudgingly. But then they've always been close. Joe's father died when he was small, and his sister Rachel is eleven years older than him. So after Rachel went to university, it was just his mum and him at home. Joe was teased a bit at junior school, his mum being the headmistress, but he tolerated it calmly, almost as though it were irrelevant. He stayed focused on what he wanted from life. He could see the bigger picture long before the rest of us could.

She must be super-proud of him now, I think, a little

bitterly. Everyone in the country loves her precious, talented doctor son. From bouncers to the Prime Minister. Everyone in the whole country loves Joe. Except me.

Maybe you have to have a streak of cruelty to be a good surgeon. Maybe that's why he was able to treat me so badly and just walk off. I don't know. For all that I loved him, I never got to the core of Joe. I never reached his innermost Russian doll. He always kept a part of himself locked well away.

When he got into King's College London to read medicine, for example, it took *everyone* by surprise. I don't know what I'd thought he was aiming for in life. I knew he had good, strong, sensitive hands – but I saw them as pianist's hands, not surgeon's hands. He played jazz piano in the school band and used to joke about making his living in bars. I took him at his word.

I didn't even know he was applying for medicine. He'd kept it completely quiet. He'd talked vaguely about physics at Birmingham, or maybe taking a year out to study piano, or maybe teaching, like his mum ... But it was all a smoke-screen, hiding the truth, hiding his fierce ambition.

After he announced that he'd won his place, he admitted it to me: he hadn't wanted to reveal what his goal was, in case he failed. He'd secretly volunteered at a local hospital, worked into the small hours, done what he needed to do to apply for medicine, without sharing a word with anyone except his mother. Not even with me. There's something tungsten protecting the core of him.

I'm not surprised he's doing well. His brain is like a machine. And he has a streak of arrogance. I can see him in an operating theatre, talking firmly, never wasting words, everyone else obeying his orders.

And now, on top of it all, he's famous. It happened about three months ago. Joe had been shadowed in a fly-on-the-wall documentary about his hospital. It was quite a serious documentary, which might have had a small, niche audience, but it was somehow featured on breakfast TV, which is where he became a viral hit.

It was a bit of a comedy interview, to begin with. Joe was being interviewed by a rather inane presenter called Sarah Wheatley, who couldn't pronounce 'cardiovascular' and kept attempting different versions. Every time she got it wrong, she giggled, and although Joe stayed polite, it was obvious he was unimpressed.

He looked spectacular. That's just stating a fact. He was in blue scrubs, his dark eyes at their most intent, his hands moving expressively to make his points. You could see that Sarah Wheatley was falling for him even as she interviewed him. And then the famous quote came. 'Think of it like this,' he said, staring gravely at the screen. 'We need to love our hearts.'

Well, Twitter went wild. *I'll love your heart!!!! You can have my heart, Doctor Joe!! That guy can look after my heart any day he likes!!!*

Memes of him went around. The quote popped up everywhere on Instagram. It was used by the Prime Minister in a speech. Joe was christened *The Doctor of Hearts* by the tabloids, who ran a series of splashy pieces about his love life. Apparently he was offered his own TV show.

But if Mimi is correct, he left Twitter, instead. Which doesn't surprise me. Joe's uncompromising. I guess you have to be, if you want to be a surgeon. He wouldn't be interested in some short-lived fame. He's always played a longer game. His own game.

He's typing something now, his brow creased with concentration. I watch him through the thorny branches, imagining him in an operating theatre. Surveying another human's life before him on the operating table. Deciding where he must deploy his scalpel to save them. He wouldn't do it lightly. I'm not sure he does anything lightly.

He pauses to stretch out his fingers and I'm suddenly trans-fixed by his hands. Hands which used to roam over me, caress me, make love to me. I know how much emotional intelligence is in those hands. I know how he balances thoughtful, cerebral caution with audacious risk-taking, all without a flicker.

He hurt me so much I can hardly bear to look at him. But if I ever needed someone to use a scalpel to save my life, he's the one I'd turn to. Like a shot.

A breeze brushes across my face and I shiver, not with cold, but with muscle fatigue. Or maybe with bitter thoughts. I'm getting a bit desperate here, still crouching on the peaty ground with no plan. I need help. I asked the gods for a hand grenade and they sent me Bean, which was clearly their idea of a joke. But now . . .

My eyes rest again on Joe, who is oblivious, ten yards away, still typing on his phone.

Is he my hand grenade?

The idea of asking Joe for help makes me wince. It's humili-ating. It's opening old wounds. It's my worst option. But it's my only option.

Slowly I draw my phone out of my pocket. I scroll down to Joe's number. And I send him a text. It's very short and to the point. In fact, it just reads:

Hi.

SEVEN

He jolts as he sees my text. He actually jolts. Which is . . .

Nothing, I tell myself quickly, chiding myself for even noticing. Joe's reaction to my text is irrelevant. I simply need to know if he's going to help me. Although – I must be honest – I'm feeling quite a *frisson*, secretly watching him like this. I feel as if I'm spying.

Well, let's face it. I am spying.

He's still staring at his phone screen, his brow furrowed as though he's processing a load of complex, not necessarily positive thoughts. As I watch, he rubs his face. He winces. He looks as if he wants to say something. Now he's shaking himself down, almost as though getting rid of a bad dream.

As I watch him, I start to bristle slightly. Am I the bad dream he's trying to escape? Was I so awful? Who does he think *he* is? Saint Joe? Before I can stop myself, I type a new text:

For someone who looks after hearts, you can be careless.
You know you broke mine, don't you?

83

I watch the shock on his face as the words arrive on his screen, and feel a surge of satisfaction. There. Just saying it like it is.

I was hoping he would come straight back with a reply, but he seems stricken. He's staring at his phone, motionless. I've clearly bludgeoned him into silence, which might have been a tactical error.

I'm not going to backtrack, because it's true. He *did* break my heart. And from his expression, he knows it. But it's strange: watching him now, I realize I don't feel quite as raw as I once did. I don't feel quite as broken. I feel like I can have a conversation, at least. And maybe I can turn that conversation to my advantage. I briskly type a new message:

Anyway. I'm not here for recriminations. I'm here to help you.

Joe looks startled, which is what I intended, so I press on quickly with a follow-up.

I expect you've been wondering all these years how you can ever make it up to me. I expect you lie awake at night, desperately racking your brains. I expect you're longing for me to suggest a way that you can make amends. Aren't you??

As he reads the message, Joe's face lightens a little. His mouth twitches in amusement; he seems to come alive.

Just seeing his reaction reminds me of how we used to make each other laugh, which gives me a little stabbing pain in my chest. Oh God, I wish I didn't have to engage with Joe

84

to achieve my goal. It's not good for my health. But I don't have any choice.

I watch breathlessly as he types a reply, and a moment later it arrives on my phone.

You read my mind.

Is he being serious? Or sarcastic? I don't really care. I tap out my answer:

Great. I always was a mind-reader. By the way, your shoelaces are undone.

They're not, but I couldn't resist making him start. He looks down at his shoes, frowns, then swivels on the spot, looking cautiously all around the drive. Then he peers up at the windows of the house, while I bite my lip, trying not to giggle. At last he sends a message:

Where are you?

At once I reply:

Never mind. You've agreed to help me, right?
    Well, I suggest that we form a pact. We will drop everything and help each other out if we ever text each other the single word 'rosebush'.

Joe stares at his phone, then types a new message, an expression of concern coming over his face.

Effie, do you need help?

Thank you! At last, the response I needed! I briskly type two words and send them.

Yes. Rosebush.

Immediately he replies:

I get it. We have a pact. I agree.

Oh. Duh. I should have expressed myself more clearly.

No. ROSEBUSH. Look at the rosebush.

I watch, breathing hard, as Joe swivels. He glances cautiously at the bouncer, still standing at the front door, then surveys the row of rose bushes lining the drive. His gaze moves over them, peering, questioning, half-suspicious, as though this is a wind-up . . .

Then, as he sees me, his eyes explode with shock. Disbelief. And some expression I can't read. For a while we're both motionless, gazing at each other in silence. This is the longest eye contact we've made for years. It feels as if we're connecting almost like we used to – even if it is through a tangle of rose bush, half-obscured by leaves. I feel an irrational craving to gaze at his familiar face from this place of safety all night.

But I can't. And I'm being stupid, because this isn't old Joe, whom I loved and understood. This is new Joe, who is cruel and inexplicable. They just look the same. So I tear my eyes away and type:

Come over.

He doesn't move a muscle at first, just stands there, looking annoyingly handsome with the evening sunlight behind him. But at last he responds. *Not* by coming over, which is typical, but by typing another text:

I understand you're on a date. I wouldn't want to interrupt. Where is your beau, by the way?

For a few moments I just stare back fixedly, my cheeks blooming with colour. Damn it, *damn it*. I almost can't bear to reply, but I have to. So at last, reluctantly, I type:

'Date' may have been an exaggeration.

To be fair, he doesn't laugh, although his mouth twitches. I'm half tempted to tell him not to bother after all – but that won't get me my Russian dolls. *Come on, Effie*, I tell myself firmly. *Who cares what he thinks, anyway?*

One of Mimi's stock phrases suddenly floats into my head – maybe because I associate her with the scent of roses. Whenever something mortifying happened to us at school, she would sympathize, up to a point, but then would say the same firm words: *No one ever died from embarrassment.* Exactly. So. Proceed.

With as much dignity as I can muster, I type another message:

Come over. Pretend you're looking at the rosebush.

As I wait for his response, I feel a sudden tension, because if he doesn't agree, I don't know what I'll do. But as he looks up, his mouth is twitching again and I know he'll play along.

He pauses for a couple of seconds, then addresses the bouncer conversationally.

'Nice roses.'

'Huh,' says the bouncer, staring blankly at my bush. 'I wouldn't know.'

'Oh, they're exceptional.' As he speaks, Joe strolls across the gravel towards my hiding place. 'Let me examine the pruning. Yes, well pruned . . .'

He comes to a halt, right in front of the bush. From my position, I'm looking directly at his black-trousered knees. I tilt my head back and see his face peering down at me.

'What are you doing?' he enquires in a polite undertone. 'Wonderful specimen,' he adds, more loudly, for the bouncer's benefit.

'I need to get into the party,' I mutter in quick, quiet tones. 'I need you to help me.'

'Through the door is traditional,' replies Joe, raising his eyebrows.

'Yes. Well. No one knows I'm here, not even Bean.' I scuff the leaves underfoot. 'I haven't spoken to Dad for weeks. I wasn't originally on the guest list. It's a mess.'

There's silence for a few moments, except for the distant thumping music and a sudden gale of laughter from the party. As I look up at last, Joe's expression is grave.

'I'm sorry,' he says, taking hold of one of the branches to examine a rose bloom. 'I knew the divorce was difficult. But I had no idea—'

'It's fine. Whatever.' I cut him off brusquely. 'But I need to get inside, just for ten minutes. I'm on a mission. But the bastard doorman's in the way.'

'What's your mission?'

'None of your business,' I snap back before I can help my-self, and his face closes up a little.

'Fair enough.'

'So, will you help me?'

I know I sound short – but I'm trying to hide how unnerved I am by his closeness. My hands feel damp; my eyes are a little hot. Maybe I'm not quite as raw as I once was, but I'm not quite healed, either.

Joe looks strained, too, although I have no idea why. He was the one at fault, not me. He glances warily at the bouncer – who is now staring vacantly up at the deep-blue summer sky – then turns back.

'Effie, it's your family's official farewell,' he murmurs gruffly. 'You should be in there as a guest. How about you come in as my plus one?'

'No,' I say, too quickly, and he flinches.

'I didn't mean—'

'I know. I know you didn't.' I rub my nose with an awk-ward gesture. 'But anyway, I'm not here for the party. I'm here for my own thing.'

Joe nods. 'OK. What do you want me to do?'

'Create a distraction. Get that guy away from the door somehow. Set off a hand grenade.'

'A hand grenade.' His eyes flash with sudden humour.

'Please don't tell me you haven't got a hand grenade about your person,' I deadpan. 'Or I'll be very disappointed.'

Joe pats his pockets. 'Of course I do. Should be here somewhere.'

'Good. Well, maybe you could deploy it. And . . . thanks, Joe.' I meet his gaze again, realizing that this may be the last time I ever see him. I'll dash in and out of the house – then

I'll leave the neighbourhood for ever. He'll lead his life, full of plaudits and achievement . . . and I'll lead mine. Whatever that turns into. 'Congratulations on all your success, by the way.'

'Oh, that.' Joe seems to dismiss it all – career, prestige, fame – with a single hand gesture, which is *so* him.

'Who would have thought?' I try to laugh lightly, although I'm not sure I pull it off.

'Indeed,' says Joe after a pause. 'Who would have thought?'

There's another long, strange silence. We're gazing at each other through a barrier of thorny branches, not moving a muscle. It's as though neither of us wants this moment to end.

'You all right, mate?' The bouncer's voice makes me start. He suddenly seems to have noticed that Joe has been standing in front of the same rose bush for a solid five minutes.

'Absolutely fine!' Joe calls back to him, then adds to me in an undertone, 'OK. I'm on.'

'Thanks so much,' I whisper in heartfelt tones – and I mean it. He didn't have to help.

'Chocks away,' he replies, in his 'World War Two pilot' voice. 'We'll all be home for Christmas.' He winks at me, then swings away towards the bouncer.

'How would your girlfriend feel about a little video message? You'll have to film it, though.'

'Mate!' The bouncer's eyes widen. 'You kidding?'

'Let's do it here.' Joe beckons the bouncer away from the door, across the drive. 'Better light, you see. No, even further. Yes, this is a good place. OK, face me with your phone, keep it steady . . . What's your girlfriend's name?'

I have to admit, Joe's a genius. Not only is the bouncer now several metres away from the door, he's totally engrossed in filming Joe. As quietly as I can, I emerge from behind the rose bush. The coast is clear. I carefully tiptoe over the gravel, then skitter the last few feet, dive breathlessly through the front door and into the oak-panelled hall, where I immediately dart into the Christmas-tree alcove.

I'm in. I'm in! Now, I just need to get up the stairs—

Shit.

I freeze as I see Jane Martin at the end of the hall, chatting to a woman in a green dress and gesturing at the bannisters. What are they doing in the *hall*? I thought the guests would all be nicely contained in the party area, not roaming, free-range, around the house.

And now they're moving this way. Oh God, I'm done for. Any moment, they'll spot me. I can already imagine Jane's cheerful greeting: 'Oh Effie, you *are* here!'

I only have one option. The coat-cupboard door is open, a foot away from me. It's a big, built-in cupboard, full of old coats and junk. Without pausing, I dive in, pull the door closed, curl myself into a ball behind an ancient overcoat and shut my eyes, as if I'm still a child, playing hide and seek.

After a few motionless moments, I open my eyes again. I think I'm safe. Soundlessly I release my right foot, which was pinned uncomfortably underneath me. I'm starting to relax, because this terrain is so familiar. How many times have I hidden in this cupboard? The very smell of it is whisking me back to my childhood: the pungent scent of rained-on wellingtons, Barbours, old wood and the faint, chemical aroma of glue. The glue dates from that model-making craze Gus once had, and as I feel around in the dark, my hand touches the old pot he used to use. I can't believe it's still here – I guess Krista hasn't got as far as clearing out this cupboard. The glue must be twenty years old, at least, dried up and desiccated. A piece of useless rubbish to anyone else – but to me an instant reminder of my brother, aged twelve, sitting at the table, earnestly joining pieces of wood together to make a fighter jet, while Mimi told him he'd have to clear it all away in a minute for supper. He would protest, 'But Mimi, this is a *crucial* bit,' every single time, not even looking up. And she would laugh, 'Oh, a *crucial* bit. I *see.*'

Funny how memories come back, sometimes in dribs and drabs, sometimes in enormous sweeps.

I glance at my watch and wince in disbelief. It's already 7.30 p.m. I thought I would be long gone by now, not stuck in the coat cupboard, with pins and needles in my foot. Cautiously I stick my head out, then hastily pull it back again as I hear the tell-tale creak of floorboards at the other end of the hall. My one advantage, after all those years of hide and seek, is that I know this house. I can tell when someone's approaching. And they are, right now.

I huddle back into the shadows of the cupboard, hoping that whoever it is will walk straight past – but the footsteps stop. It sounds like a woman in heels. Now she's swivelling. What's she doing? Who is it? There's an old spyhole in the door of the cupboard, where two planks don't quite meet, and I can't resist leaning forward stealthily to spy out and see who it is . . .

Nooo! Gross!

It's Krista, adjusting her Spanx in the hall mirror. I can't see her face, but I can see the charm bracelet around her wrist and her manicured nails tugging the stretchy waistband back into place. She's obviously alone and has lifted up her dress to give her underwear a good tug – and from where I'm crouching, I've got a prime view. *Great.* Some people dive into coat cupboards and get Narnia, I get my stepmother's crotch.

And yes, I know she's not really my stepmother – but she behaves like it. As if she owns the place. Including all the furniture, all our friends, and Dad.

I silently watch her, aghast, but fascinated. Her fake tan is streaky on her stomach, but I guess she thought no one would see. Except Dad, in the hot tub . . .

No. Noooo. Do not visualize *#sexinyoursixties*. Or *#viagra-works!* which Dad posted on Instagram last month, with a picture of him and Krista in matching white fluffy dressing gowns. (I nearly *died*.)

Just then her phone buzzes and I hold very still as she answers it in her nasal voice.

'Hi, Lace. I'm in the hall.' She listens, then adds in lower tones, 'Yeah, I'm announcing it at the dinner. Should cause their feathers to fly. OK, see you in a sec.'

She puts her phone away and I blink through the spyhole. Announcing what? Whose feathers?

As she steps back from the mirror, her face comes into view and I swallow at the sight. She looks stupendous, in a Krista way, all bronzer and sparkly eyeshadow. She always wears fake lashes, but tonight she's really gone to town. They're like two huge, black, fringed wings over her eyes.

'I am a beautiful woman,' she informs her reflection, and my heart sinks. *Don't* tell me I've got to sit through Krista's self-affirmations. She lifts her chin and surveys herself with satisfaction. 'I am a beautiful, strong, sexy woman. I deserve the finest things in life.'

Whatever. I roll my eyes. She certainly didn't buy the finest fake tan.

'I deserve to be loved,' Krista tells herself, with even more conviction. 'I deserve the world to shower me with goodness. I have the hair of a twenty-year-old.' She runs her fingers complacently through her highlighted blonde hair. 'I have the body of a twenty-year-old.'

'No you don't,' I say before I can stop myself, then clap my hand over my mouth.

Shit. *Shit.*

Krista stiffens and looks all around her. With lightning instinct, I shuffle silently backwards. There's a panel missing at the back of this cupboard and you can pretty much disappear into a dingy recess, if you want to. I quickly squish myself through the gap, smelling the musty atmosphere of the hidden space, pulling my feet up, trying to be motionless and invisible.

It's just in time, because Krista wrenches open the cupboard door.

'Who's there?' she demands, and I hold my breath desperately. I *can't* be caught. Not now. Not by Krista.

I can see her through a lattice of broken timber. She peers around and swishes some coats back and forth, her eyes narrow and suspicious. But ha ha, Krista, I win, because I *know* this house. I've squished myself into this space a million times. And I'm wearing black. And thankfully, no one's ever replaced the bust light bulb.

'I'm going mad,' she mutters to herself at last, and closes the cupboard door. 'Oh, hi, Romilly,' she adds more loudly, over the sound of new footsteps approaching. 'Enjoying the party?'

'Very much,' says Romilly, in her usual chilly tones.

Romilly's here, now? I thought all parties were supposed to end up in the kitchen, not the hall.

'And Gus!' Krista exclaims. 'I've barely spoken to you, love.'

Gus! I instinctively squirm forward. I haven't seen him for *ages.*

'Hi Krista,' says Gus dutifully. 'Lovely dress.'

'Well, thank you, Gus! Sets off my sparkler nicely, I thought.'

'Absolutely. And how's Bambi?' he adds politely. 'I didn't ask, earlier.'

I know Gus is only enquiring after Krista's dog because Dad once sounded off at us all on the subject. He said we could *try* to be welcoming to Krista and why couldn't we ask after Bambi, once in a while?

'Bambi's very well, thank you, Gus,' says Krista. 'Bit frightened of all the guests, though.'

'Don't blame him,' says Gus. 'I am, too.'

I can't resist pressing my face up against the spyhole to get a squint of Gus. But instead, I get an eyeful of Romilly. Great.

She looks good, I admit. Romilly always looks good, in that athletic, clean-cut way she has. She's wearing a very plain black cocktail dress which shows off her impressive tanned, muscled arms. Her make-up is minimal. She has a straight blonde bob to the chin, with discreet highlights. She has a firmer jaw than Gus does and, I should think, a harder punch.

She's smiling socially at Krista – but there's still a tightness round her eyes and her mouth, which is very her. Over time, I've picked up a few of Romilly's little ways. When she's angry, she looks tense, but when she's pleased, she somehow looks even *tenser*. Her laugh doesn't relax you, it puts you on edge. In fact, is it a laugh at all? Is it just an aggressive noise which sounds a bit like a laugh?

I don't understand how Gus can live with her. He's so mild and easy-going, and she's such a ball of stress. Somehow they've gone from dating to living together in Romilly's house, where Gus does all the cooking, as far as I can make out, and is always too busy to meet up with me because he's driving Molly and Gracie to ballet or something.

When they were first dating he used to tell us endlessly about how great Romilly was, how strong she was, how focused on her job in human resources, how tough it was for her, being a single mother. But since then, the torrent of praise has dried up a tad. These days, if I ask after her, he usually looks evasive and disengages from the conversation. Bean's theory is that he's disengaged from the whole relationship, and she's probably right. But the trouble is, how's he ever going to leave Romilly if he won't engage with her? It's like one of those child-proof bottles, where you have to press the lid *in* first, to release it. Gus is just clicking, round and round, because he can't bring himself to do anything more forceful.

I can hear Krista leaving, her heels clip-clopping on the wooden floor. By twisting round a little, I manage to get a view of Gus through the spyhole, and my heart crunches, because my brother is just like he ever was. He's sitting on the bottom stair, a place where he always used to perch whenever he wanted to think. He's leaning against the bannisters, running his hand idly up and down one of the spindles, and has obviously tuned out of proceedings.

I can only see a slice of his face through my spyhole, but I can tell he has the distant, abstract expression that got him in trouble at school a million times. His teachers said he wasn't paying attention, but he was. It's just that he was paying attention to a more interesting thought than whatever they were droning on about. He's probably thinking about some piece of computer code right now.

He turns and I see his face fully – and feel a jolt of dismay. He doesn't just look distant, he looks wiped out. There's a heaviness to his expression and he seems older, somehow. When did I last see him? Only a month ago. He can't have aged like that in a month.

'Gus?' Romilly snaps. 'Gus, are you even *listening*?'

I wasn't listening either, I realize. I was too busy watching Gus.

'Sorry.' Gus's face jerks guiltily. 'I thought you were talking to Krista.'

'Krista's *gone*,' says Romilly, rolling her eyes scathingly, as though Gus is a moron, and I gaze at her through the cupboard door in mute fury. I always suspected she was meaner in private than in public, and here's the proof.

This is why Gus has aged. It's Romilly. She's bad for his health. He *has* to get rid of her.

'I was telling you the good news!' she adds crossly, and I clap my hand over my mouth, trying to stifle my snort. This is Romilly relaying *good* news? What would she look like if it was bad?

'Oh, yes?' says Gus.

'We're on the list!' says Romilly, with a kind of suppressed triumph. 'She'll fit us in tomorrow morning! Annette Goddard,' she adds, as Gus looks blank. 'Remember? The go-to children's violin teacher that Maya's mum tried to keep secret from me? Well, we're in! I'll have to leave first thing in the morning,' she adds, and looks at her glass. 'I probably won't drink any more.'

'That's a shame,' says Gus, his face falling. 'There's a family brunch tomorrow. I thought we'd have a nice lazy morning.'

Romilly surveys him as though with incomprehension.

'It's *Annette Goddard*,' she says. 'If Molly and Gracie learn violin from Annette Goddard, they'll be in there! They'll be noticed! Luckily, I brought their violins with me, just in case,' she adds, breathing out sharply. 'Because I would *not* trust Doug to remember them.'

Doug is Romilly's ex-husband, and I haven't heard her say one good thing about him, ever.

'The girls are only four and six,' says Gus mildly. 'Do they need to be noticed?'

Romilly has started quivering. She does that when people challenge her; I've noticed it before. Her nostrils flare and she begins to tremble, as though her whole body is reacting to the unthinkable notion that someone could – oh my God – *disagree* with her.

'Of course the girls need to be noticed!' she retorts. 'Do you *know* how competitive it is out there? Do you want me to read you the stats?'

I can see a tiny shudder pass across Gus's face, though I'm not sure Romilly notices. 'No, I don't want you to read me the stats.'

'Do you know how hard this is for me?' There's a sudden crack in Romilly's voice and she lifts a hand to her beautiful brow.

'Look.' Gus puts a hand on her arm. 'I'm sorry. I just . . . reacted badly. Well done.'

Wait a minute. Romilly is bailing out on the family event, but Gus is apologizing? How does *that* work?

'I do my best for the girls,' says Romilly in martyred tones, pulling away from Gus and stalking over to redo her lipstick in the mirror. 'You know? I just do my best.'

She's only about two feet away from my spyhole now, side-on to me, and as she bends down to adjust the strap on her shoe, I suddenly notice that she has the most amazing breasts. I blink at them in surprise, wondering how I've never registered this before. Maybe it's just that I've never glimpsed them from this angle? Or is that dress particularly revealing? Either way, I'm getting more access than usual – and they're spectacular.

Pah. Trust Romilly to have spectacular breasts. This might explain why Gus hasn't ditched her yet. But he needs to look beyond breasts. *Beyond* breasts. I might try to convey this to him, somehow.

'Hi Romilly!' I hear Bean's voice, then glimpse her approaching. She's still in her jeans and Uggs. Of course she is.

'Bean!' Romilly looks her up and down. 'Aren't you coming to the party?'

'Yes!' says Bean breathlessly. 'I just got chatting to some old friends in the garden. So, in a way, I *have* been at the party, just not in the right clothes.'

'Of course.' Romilly smiles sweetly at Bean. 'Well, I'm going to find a non-alcoholic drink. See you later.'

As she strides off, her heels like gunfire on the wooden floor, Gus breathes out as if someone's removed a vice from his head.

'Hi,' he says to Bean. 'How's it going?'

'Oh.' She shrugs. 'It is what it is.' She sinks down beside him on the bottom stair, slumping slightly.

'The cocktails are good, at any rate,' he says, lifting his glass to her. 'My game plan is basically to get slaughtered.'

'Good one.' Bean nods.

'Shame Effie's not here,' adds Gus, his face falling. 'I know she doesn't get on with Krista, but . . .' He spreads his arms around the hall. 'This is the last hurrah. It should be all of us.'

I can't help feeling a little swell of love for Gus. I wish I could just very quickly give him a hug.

'I know,' says Bean sadly. 'I tried to persuade her to come, but she's gone on a date. He's an Olympic athlete, apparently,' she adds, more positively. 'Slash philanthropist. He sounds really impressive! Isn't that great?'

'Oh, really?' Gus looks up with interest. 'Who?'

'She didn't say.'

'A rower, I bet. Or a cyclist.' Gus is googling on his phone. 'Him?' He turns the phone round to show her a photo.

'Oh, I hope so!' says Bean with enthusiasm. 'He looks lovely!'

I feel a twinge of guilt, which I quell. It's only a white lie. And all's fair in love and war-with-Krista.

'I need to get changed.' Bean's voice breaks my thoughts. 'I'm just going to see if there are any bits and bobs from the kitchen that Effie might want. She always liked the jelly moulds, didn't she?'

'Jelly moulds?' Gus looks vague. 'Dunno.'

Oh my God, the jelly moulds! I'd forgotten all about them – but now, in a rush, I passionately want them to be saved. Especially the pineapple one. We used to make yellow jelly in it. I loved it so much. It reminds me of happy Sunday afternoons in the kitchen, and it's exactly the kind of battered old item that Krista would chuck out.

I gaze at Bean anxiously through the spyhole. Should I quickly text her? But I can't. I'm supposed to be on my date. Although maybe I could drop that in?

Having fab date with Olympic athlete in luxury London restaurant!! He's everything I hoped for!! We're toasting each other in champagne!! Also, I just had a random thought: let's keep the jelly moulds.

No. Too suspicious.

'I think Effie liked the pineapple one,' says Bean, getting up, and I subside with relief. 'OK, I'm going to get changed. See you in there.'

'I'll go along in a moment.'

As Bean walks off, Gus leans against the bannister again, texting. Then he suddenly says, 'Shit,' in a low voice and I stiffen. That didn't sound good.

For a few moments we're both utterly silent. I can't quite believe Gus is oblivious of me. Can't he feel my presence? I'm right here! But I could be a ghost, for all he's aware of me.

Gus seems transfixed by the screen of his phone and I'm transfixed by him – or at least, the slice of him that's visible. At last, he dials a number, then in low tense tones, says, 'Hi. I just saw your text. Are you serious?'

There's silence for a few moments, during which I hardly dare breathe. I feel half consumed by curiosity and half guilty for eavesdropping on a private phone call. But he is my brother, after all. And I won't tell anyone.

(Except Bean. I'll tell Bean.)

'Don't think so,' says Gus in an even lower voice. 'No, of course I haven't told anyone. If it gets into the press, it's definitely not . . . Well, what . . .' He exhales suddenly and I glimpse him rubbing his face. 'I mean, if charges *are* pressed . . .'

I can't help a sharp intake of breath. Charges? What charges?

For a long time, Gus is quiet, listening to the other end.

'OK, thanks,' he says at last. 'Listen, Josh, I have to go. And anyway, I can't speak for . . . Yes. We'll talk tomorrow . . . Yup. Not great. But let's hope it's not the worst-case scenario.'

He rings off and breathes out heavily, while I stare at him anxiously. What worst-case scenario? Who's Josh? Is Gus in some kind of trouble?

Abruptly Gus gets to his feet, checks his phone one last time, then shoves it in his pocket and strides away down the hall. And as I watch him leave, I feel suddenly bereft. Crouching here in the dark, my plan seems like madness. What am I doing, hiding like a thief? This is a *terrible* way to attend a party. I'm shut out of crucial conversations, I'm worried about my brother, my thighs are aching and I'm not even getting any of the good cocktails.

Should I, even now, admit defeat, come out of this cupboard, find something to wear and join in? Should I bury the hatchet with Krista?

With Dad?

The very thought makes my stomach flip over with painful nerves. I'm not prepared. I'm on the back foot. I don't know what I would say, how I would begin . . . I rub my face, feeling a sudden surge of frustration. Why am I even thinking this? This wasn't how tonight was meant to go. I wasn't supposed to see my family. I wasn't supposed to overhear troubling conversations.

And then I freeze as I hear a deep, familiar voice, booming through the cupboard door.

Oh God. Oh *God*.

All at once, I'm petrified. Striding along the hall towards the cupboard, with his unmistakable tread, laughing in that distinctive way he has, is Dad.

As he comes into view, I feel as though someone's gripped me tightly by the throat. I hadn't expected to see him tonight. I thought he'd be far away, surrounded by guests. But there he is, a few feet away, unaware of my watching eyes.

'This is the painting I was telling you about,' he says to some elderly man I don't recognize. 'Bought it three months ago. If you ask me, this painting sold the house for us!' He laughs uproariously and takes a slug of his drink.

I'm barely listening to what Dad's saying; I'm too fixated by studying him. He's wearing a double-breasted dinner jacket, his grey hair is glossy under the lights and he's laughing. He looks like the epitome of a successful man in his later years.

'Oh yes,' he's saying now, in response to some question. 'Yes, it's the right move for us. I've never been happier. Never been happier!' he repeats, as though for emphasis. 'Now, Clive, you need a drink!' he adds, and the two of them move away, while I watch them go, my eyes glassy.

Never been happier.

I slump back on the cupboard floor, my trembling thigh muscles finally giving way. To my horror, tears are edging over my lashes and I blink them away.

Our family has disintegrated, we're losing our childhood home, Dad hasn't talked properly to his younger daughter for weeks . . . but he's *never been happier.*

Fine. Well, I guess we'll have to disagree on our definition of 'happy'. Because I couldn't be happy if I was estranged from a family member, but I guess you can, Dad, because you have the consolation of Krista and her pert bum. Which is down to Spanx, did you even realize that, Dad? Not muscle tone, *Spanx.*

I'm talking to my dad in my head, I realize. I'm actually losing it. I need to get out of here, pronto. Any idea of joining the party has vanished. I'm going to get my precious dolls and go. For ever.

Cautiously I push the door open. The hall is empty. The staircase is empty. I can't hear any movement overhead.

OK, and . . .

Go.

With lightning-quick movements, I dart out of the cupboard, across the floorboards and up the stairs, two at a time, levering myself up with the bannisters. I'm in my comfort zone now. I know how to dodge the worst creaks. No one's heard me; no one's spotted me. I *knew* it would be easy.

As I near my bedroom, I feel an urge to go into it, even though I don't have any stuff in there any more. I want to see the wallpaper, touch the curtains, look at the view . . . Just be in my room for a few last moments. But as I reach the open door, I blink in shock. The wallpaper's gone. The curtains have gone. I'm staring into a plain, white-painted box, with varnished floorboards that never used to be there.

My heart falls, just for a second, then I tighten my chin and resolutely close the door. Who cares? My life in this house is over, anyway. No point brooding. Crack on.

I tiptoe along the landing, swiftly but cautiously. Nearly there. I'll be out again in less than three minutes. I turn the corner to the box room, already mentally grabbing my Russian dolls – then stop dead.

What?

In disbelief, I stare at the blockage in my way. It's a pile of tea chests. Who put them there? Why there? Experimentally I reach for one – then pause. It's going to make a noise if I shift it.

Do I dare? The party's pretty noisy anyway . . . I can hear thumping music coming through the floorboards. Anyway, what choice do I have? I need to get rid of this barricade. I wrap my arms round one of the top chests, lift it up and realize it's empty. OK. I can do this. I just need to move, say, four chests, just enough to clear a path to the door . . .

Then I hear an unmistakable creak, and my heart sinks. I don't *believe* this. Someone's coming upstairs with swift steps. This house is impossible. Feeling a spasm of fright, I replace the tea chest crookedly, hurry back along the corridor and, purely on instinct, dive into the welcoming sanctuary of Bean's room.

A split second later, I realize my error. It's Bean herself

coming up the stairs, I can tell now from her steps, and she'll be coming in here to get ready. I'm a *moron*.

Feeling a bit demented, I look about for somewhere to hide. The curtains are too short. The wardrobe is too full, and she'll be opening it to get dressed, anyway. Come on, Effie, *think* . . . In a flurry of panic, I leap into one of Bean's twin wooden Peter Rabbit beds, hurriedly heap up as many cushions as I can, then carefully pull the duvet over me. I once won a game of hide and seek in *exactly* this spot, disguised with a pile of teddies. That trick can work again. I just need to keep still.

As Bean enters the room, I close my eyes tight. My own shallow breathing in my cocoon sounds like the roaring of a furnace. Through the mound of cushions, I can hear the muffled sounds of Bean moving around her bedroom. A faint chinking as she puts something down on her glass-topped dressing table. The click of a cupboard door being opened. Now she's humming. It's worked! She hasn't noticed me!

As I lie there, motionless and tense, I'm willing Bean with every cell to speed up, to get ready, to leave the room and let me get on with my mission . . .

Then suddenly, with no warning, blows are being rained on me. I'm being hit by something through the duvet. Something hard.

'You motherfucker!' Bean is suddenly bellowing. 'You dirty motherfucker! Get out! I've already called the police! Get out!'

EIGHT

I'm so startled, it takes me a moment to react.

'Stop!' I yell, trying to protect myself, but Bean doesn't seem to hear. She keeps on thwacking me with . . . what is that?

'I'll tear off your balls!' she's yelling wildly. 'I'll tear off your balls and feed them to your gerbil! Get out, you motherfucker!'

'Bean!' I roar, finally managing to throw the duvet aside. 'Stop! It's me! It's Effie!'

Bean halts mid thwack, breathing hard, and I see that she's been hitting me with a pink painted coat hanger decorated with daisies. That is *so* Bean.

'*Effie?*' Her voice rockets through the room in astonishment.

'Ssh! You *hurt* me!' I exclaim reproachfully.

'I thought you were an intruder!' she exclaims, equally reproachfully. 'Effie, what the hell? What are you *doing* here? You're supposed to be on a date!'

For a few moments there's silence between us, except for the distant thud and hubbub of the party, overlaid with a distant yapping, which must be Bambi. He's always getting shut in rooms and yapping to be let out.

'*Effie?*' prompts Bean.

I can hardly bear to admit the truth, but there's no way out of it.

'I made up the date,' I confess at last.

'You made it up?' Bean looks utterly crestfallen. 'But what about the Olympic athlete?'

'Invented him.'

Bean sinks heavily on to the bed as though I've ruined her evening, not to say her entire life.

'I've told *everyone* about him,' she says. '*Everyone.*'

'I know. I heard you.'

'You heard me?'

'Talking to Joe. I was in the rose bush.'

Bean's eyes nearly pop out of her head. 'Oh my God, Effie, you're insane!'

'*I'm* insane?' I retort in disbelief. 'You just told me you were going to tear off my balls and feed them to my gerbil! Where the hell did *that* come from?'

'Oh, that.' Bean looks pleased with herself. 'That's from the anger workshop I did. It was really good. I sent you the link, remember?'

Bean is always sending me helpful links to workshops, so I don't remember, but I nod.

'Did they tell you to express your anger with a coat hanger?'

'I was flustered!' says Bean defensively. 'I just grabbed the first thing. Sorry if I hurt you,' she adds as an afterthought.

' 's OK. Sorry if you thought I was an axe-murderer hiding in your bed.'

Bean lifts her hands as though to say, 'Any time.' Then she surveys me again.

'You're wearing a hat.' She eyes my black beanie, per-plexed. 'You do know it's summer?'

'It's part of my outfit.'

Actually, the beanie is making me swelter. I take it off and put it on Bean's bedpost, while she gazes at me.

'But Effie, what are you *doing* here?' she repeats. 'Are you coming to the party?' She gestures in the direction of the noise.

'No,' I say vehemently. 'I'm here to get my Russian dolls. Then I'm going.'

'Your Russian dolls?' Bean frowns.

'I hid them up the box-room chimney, ages ago. No one knows they're there. They would be lost if I didn't rescue them.'

'*Ohhh.*' Bean emits a long, drawn-out sound. And this is the good thing about sisters: I don't have to explain to her how I need my Russian dolls. She knows.

She also knows without asking why I put them up the box-room chimney. There's a handy ledge, about six inches up, which is where we always stuffed contraband sweets. A secret cavity that even all-knowing Mimi never seemed to cotton on to. (The sweets got a bit sooty, but you just had to give them a rinse.)

'But, wait, Effie . . .' I can see Bean's brain cranking into action. 'Why have you come tonight, when everyone's here? It's the worst night! It's madness!'

'It's not!' I say defensively, because doesn't she think I've worked all this out? 'It's the best night! Everyone's distracted with the party. It was the one time I could creep in and *not* be noticed. At least, that was the theory.' I roll my eyes. 'Hasn't quite worked out like that.'

'You could have asked me to get them for you.' Bean

suddenly looks a little hurt. 'Or at least, told me you were coming and not invented a date with an Olympic athlete.'

'I know,' I say, after a slight pause. 'Sorry. But I thought you'd tell me I should go to the party.'

'You *should* go to the party,' returns Bean at once and I heave an exasperated sigh.

'You see? And by the way, you're not exactly hurrying to get there, are you?'

'I'm on my way,' says Bean, guiltily glancing at her watch. 'Look, Effie, it's not that bad. Why don't you change your mind?' She adopts a cajoling tone. 'There are heaps of nice people downstairs. You can borrow a dress of mine . . .'

She goes over to her wardrobe and swings the door open. Immediately I clock a familiar printed fabric and draw in breath.

'Is that my Rixo dress?' I demand, pointing at it accusingly.

'Oh!' Bean jumps. 'Er . . . is it?' she muses in suspiciously vague tones. 'Yes, I suppose it is.'

'I *knew* you had it! I've been asking you about that dress for ages and you said you couldn't find it!'

'Right,' says Bean evasively. 'Well, I did find it. There it is.'

I narrow my eyes at her and she looks away shiftily.

'Were you going to wear it tonight?' I ask, in the tones of a Stasi inquisitor.

'No,' says Bean after a pause.

'Yes, you were.'

'Well, maybe.'

'But it's mine!'

'Well, you left it here,' says Bean, as though that proves anything.

'*By mistake!*' I yell, then suddenly realize I'm about to give myself away to the whole party. 'By mistake,' I repeat more

109

quietly. 'You said you'd find it for me, but you never did, and now I know why.' I fold my arms as though to indicate the gravity of this situation. 'I know exactly why. I can see your whole plan.'

'I was only *thinking* of wearing it,' says Bean, rolling her eyes. 'But if you're going to be so possessive . . .'

'Yes,' I say. 'I *am* possessive. Wear something else.'

'Fine.' Bean rattles her hangers along noisily. 'Whatever. I mean, honestly. It's only a dress.'

I treat that remark with the disdain it deserves. There's no such thing as 'only a dress'. I watch as Bean gets out her black sleeveless dress (nice, but inferior), steps into it, and starts applying speedy make-up, peering into her dressing-table mirror without bothering to sit down.

'Shall I tong your hair?' I offer, out of habit.

'No, thanks. Can't be bothered. I'll put it up in a clip.' She looks at herself and grimaces, as her phone bleeps with a new WhatsApp. She reads it and rolls her eyes. 'Krista, asking where I am. *Just coming!*' she says, typing the message, then puts her phone in her evening bag. 'Humph is here, by the way. I ran into him in the garden.'

'*Humph?*' I gape at her.

'I know.' Bean starts to giggle. 'Krista's beside herself with glee. She keeps introducing him as "the Honourable Humph".'

'Oh my God.' I clap a hand over my face. 'Is he wearing his tweed cap? Has he brought six Labradors with him?'

'No, no!' Bean wheels round, her face alight with laughter. 'Haven't you seen Humph recently? He's totally changed. He's wearing a black shirt under his dinner jacket. No tie. And he's got a beard. And he does transcendental meditation.'

'Transcendental meditation?' I blink at her. Someone less

likely to do transcendental meditation than Humph, I can't imagine. Unless it was transcendental meditation on a horse, while drinking sloe gin.

'And he's telling everyone he's a feminist.'

'*What?*'

'I know. He said it without even blinking. Apparently he dated some nutritionist in London who changed his life.'

'Is she here?' I ask, agog.

'No, they split up, but he still does the meditation. He's coming to the family dinner, too.'

'*Humph* is?' I exclaim in outrage. 'He's not family!'

'Oh, I know, but Krista got her mitts on him a couple of months ago. She's such a social climber. You should have heard her. "Have you met the Honourable Humph, Bean? Isn't he a charmer?" I was like, "Krista, we all know Humph, and he's a prat."'

'But how on earth can she justify inviting him to a family dinner?' I stare at Bean.

'She's calling him a "close friend".' Bean rolls her eyes. 'You can't believe how brazen she is. Humph has started some woo-woo health clinic, and of course Krista goes to it, so now they're besties.'

'Urgh.' I make a face, then suddenly remember the conversation I overheard downstairs. 'Bean, listen. Krista's announcing something at dinner that's going to cause feathers to fly, apparently. Don't know what. I overheard her telling someone called Lace.'

'That's her sister, Lacey,' says Bean slowly. 'Oh God, Effie. You don't think Krista and Dad ... they're not planning to ... ?'

My eyes widen as I take in Bean's meaning. I have a sudden appalling image of Krista sashaying down the aisle in a white body-con dress, smirking through a veil, while Bean and I follow dismally behind, sprinkling rose petals.

'It *can't* be that,' I say in horror. 'Can it?'

'Guess I'll find out later,' says Bean, sounding resigned. 'I'll text you. Oh, and Krista's asked Joe to the family dinner, too. Because he's famous – sorry, I mean, a very dear, close friend.' She gives a sudden snort. 'At least that's true in Joe's case . . .' Then she swivels round, as though suddenly worried she's hurt me. 'At least . . . he *was* a friend.'

'He still is,' I say staunchly. 'Joe is a close friend. Nothing that happened between us changes that.'

'Hmm.' Bean looks as though she wants to say more – then thinks better of it. 'Well, you're missing out,' she adds, swivelling back to put away her mascara. 'It's obviously going to be the dinner party of the century. What are you going to do now? You can sit here, if you like. I'll bring you a drink.'

'No, I need to get on.' I leap to my feet, inwardly berating myself for sitting here, chatting away with Bean. 'Will you help me before you go? Can you shift those tea chests? I don't dare to myself.'

'Sure,' says Bean, putting her phone in her evening bag and slinging the chain over her shoulder. 'But then I'd better go down. Are you going to leave as soon as you've got the dolls?'

'Straight away,' I say firmly.

'Well then, I'll say goodbye now.' Bean comes over and gives me a hug. 'I'll miss you tonight, Ephelant.'

'Me too.' I wrap my arms around her and hold her tightly. 'Have fun. Or whatever.'

'Definitely "whatever",' she says wryly. 'Shall I tell Gus you were here?'

'Better not,' I say, after a moment's thought. 'He might let it slip. As far as everyone is concerned, I'm still on my hot date.'

'Fine. By the way, don't use my bathroom,' she adds. 'In case you were planning to. The loo's broken.'

'I'm not going to stay long enough to need the loo,' I say, rolling my eyes. 'Didn't you hear me? I'm out of here.'

As we draw apart, we smile at each other – then Bean strides out. A few moments later I hear a loud scuffling and bumping from the landing – then Bean's head reappears round the doorframe. 'It's clear. You can get in now. Good luck. And let's meet up next week, OK?'

'Definitely. Oh!' I add, suddenly remembering. 'I *do* want the pineapple jelly mould.'

'What?' Bean goggles at me.

'I heard you. I was in the coat cupboard.'

Bean stares at me incredulously, then shakes her head, blows me a kiss and vanishes.

As soon as she's gone, I remember that I never told her about Gus's phone call. Damn.

Well, I'll have to do that later. It's time to make my move. At the door, I pause to look both ways – then, like a mouse, make my way along the landing, tiptoeing on the floorboards. I creep between the tea chests, hardly breathing . . . and I'm in!

The box room has the same sparse furniture as it always did: a single bed, a yellow Formica bedside table dating from about the 1950s, a broken exercise bicycle and a few old pictures stacked against the wall. The fireplace is never used but still operational, and that's where I head without pausing. I crouch down and reach up the rough, bricky shaft of the chimney, feeling for the familiar ledge and the smooth surface of my dolls. My beloved, cracked, felt-tip-stained dolls.

My dear, cherished friends. After this, I'm never letting them out of my sight, I promise myself as my hand moves upwards. This has been *way* too stressful.

When my fingers don't touch anything that feels like a set of Russian dolls, I sweep my hand around the chimney a few times, groping, shutting my eyes so I can concentrate. They must be there. They have to be there. I mean, they were there.

They were *there*.

Feeling slightly light-headed, I retrieve my hand – now black with soot – and take a few breaths. I'm not even *allowing* my brain to process the possibility that . . .

Stop. Come on. I know they're there. I'll reach in again properly, and this time I'll find them. I just went in at the wrong angle or something. This time, I lie flat and shove my arm up so far I scrape it against the brick. I extend my fingers as much as I can, probing, swivelling, pushing, scratching the brickwork, desperate to find *something*, some hint . . .

Nothing.

Panic is ballooning inside me. I pull my hand out of the chimney and rub my face, realizing too late that I must be covering it with soot. Where *are* they?

Feverishly I start to look around the room. I flip on the dim, overhead pendant light and peer under the bed, even as I'm thinking, *How would they have got under the bed?* I glance between the stacked-up pictures. I open the old built-in cupboard, but the white painted shelves are empty, just as they always are. I reach up the chimney one more time, feeling like an absolute fool, because I *know* they're not there . . .

As I finally bring my manic search to a halt, I'm breathing hard. I can't contain my distress, I have to share it. On instinct,

I haul out my phone from my pocket and type a desperate WhatsApp to Bean:

I can't find them!!!!!!!!! 🙁🙁🙁🙁🙁🙁🙁🙁🙁

It only takes a moment for her to reply, and when she does, her measured response feels like salve on my soul.

Don't worry, Ephelant. I'm sure they're somewhere in the house. They wouldn't just disappear.

A moment later, she adds another message:

You go home, if you like. I'll look for them tomorrow and keep them safe for you. In fact, now I think about it, I'm pretty sure I've seen them around somewhere.

Oh my God. Where? I'll go and get them! My fingers fly over the keys:

Where????

It seems about a month before she replies:

Don't know, it's just ringing a bell. I think they're on a shelf or in a cupboard or something? You probably moved them yourself and forgot! So don't panic! PS This party doesn't end, there's a DJ setting up in the sitting room!!!!

She's so calm and matter-of-fact, I'm forced to consider this theory. Did I leave them somewhere else?

I've been quite stressed out. Maybe I've had some brain

lapse. Maybe I transferred them somewhere else and forgot. I close my eyes, thinking hard. My room? No. I never trusted Krista not to go and poke around my room. I would never have left them there. Anyway, it's been stripped now.

The window seat? That's where we always kept a lot of our secret treasures when we were growing up. It would make sense. I might have done it and then somehow blanked it . . .

Oh God, I want to rush down and check inside the window seat. Only I can't, because a bloody DJ is setting up in the same room. This evening is *unreal*.

A gale of laughter from outside draws my attention and I walk out of the box room, along the landing and into my empty bedroom, following the sound. From my window, I have a direct view down into the garden . . . and there they all are. Guests have spilled out of the marquee on to the lawn, and I survey them, in their dinner jackets and posh dresses. There's Bean . . . Gus . . . Dad . . . Krista . . . Joe . . . My heart pings as I see that Joe is talking to an attractive woman in a floral strappy dress, and firmly I tell my heart off for even noticing.

My phone buzzes, loud in the empty room, and I jump. It's Temi, checking in on WhatsApp.

Found the dolls yet? You've been for ever! You said you'd be ten minutes!!

Her message brings me back to the task in hand, and I type a reply:

They're gone!!!

Already, Temi is typing a message in return, and moments later it appears:

Shit!!! What are you going to do???

I perch on the ledge to reply:

Think maybe they're in the window seat. But can't get to it ATM. Need to sit it out in secret.

In seconds, her response pops up:

Sit it out in secret? Effie, just give in and go to the party!!

As I read Temi's words, my chin tightens obstinately. I'm not going to the party. Not in a million years. But I'll admit, I feel a bit left out, watching everyone from up here. And I'll also admit I'm quite curious about the dinner party of the century. I wouldn't mind *seeing* it, at least.

I gaze down at the party again, feeling like a ghost at the window. Dad is standing on the top step down to the lawn, waving his glass around as though he's a conductor, just like he always used to when we had family birthdays. Gus is talking to some man I don't recognize. Bean is . . . where's Bean?

I peer through the glass, wondering if she's in the marquee – when suddenly I spot her, alone, behind a yew hedge, in a secluded place where no one else can see her. I don't blame her for escaping.

As I watch, her shoulders suddenly heave and I grin with appreciation. I bet she's laughing because Krista said something unspeakably awful and she had to dash off for a silent moment of mirth.

But then she turns and my grin fades in shock – because it's not mirth. She's crying. Why is Bean *crying*? In dismay, I watch as she clasps her face, shaking, as though unable to control herself. Then at last she pats her eyes with a tissue, redoes her lipgloss, puts on a bright smile and goes to join the throng again. No one even seemed to notice her absence except me.

In consternation, I try to think of all the innocuous reasons why Bean might go off to cry secretly at a party. Is it leaving Greenoaks? It would be just like Bean to hide her real feelings and put on a brave face. Or . . . is it something else? Something *worse*? Oh God. What's up with my big sister? And for that matter, what's up with Gus? And what's Krista planning to announce at dinner? I'm *desperate* to know.

I rest my head against the cool window and watch my breath mist up the pane, feeling a rising sense of frustration. I was supposed to be in and out of here like a streak of lightning, focused only on getting my dolls. Not overhearing troubling conversations. Not worrying about my sister. Not wishing I was down there with them. Not wondering what's going to happen at dinner.

I should leave, I tell myself firmly. Just go, right now. Get Bean to find the dolls. Creep out and sprint down the drive, catch a train back to London, shake the whole place off my feet. I've already overrun my schedule, it's time to *go*.

But somehow . . . I can't. Something's keeping me here. Some force I can't seem to fight. This family may be broken. It may be shattered. But it's *my* broken, shattered family. And I want to be here, I finally admit to myself. To be at the party, even if I'm invisible. This *is* the last hurrah, even if no one's cheering. I can't just walk away.

What do I do, though? Give in and tell everyone I'm here? The very thought makes me cringe in horror. I'd have to ask Krista if she could possibly lay an extra place for dinner. I'd have to make some grovelling apology.

No. No way. I *won't*.

But then, what?

I sit up straight, still watching the colourful figures of the party guests, laughing and talking, with no idea they're being observed. And now I'm getting the beginnings of a plan. An audacious idea is crystallizing in my head. I mean, it's mad. I admit it's mad. But then, this whole evening is a bit mad – so what's new?

NINE

All plans need a goal, and I know exactly what mine is. There's a console table in the dining room, a massive great thing, which always has a tapestry cloth on it, reaching down to the floor. You can sit under that cloth, absolutely concealed, while still getting a view round the edge of it. If you're careful. And that's what I'm going to do.

I want to hear Krista's announcement. I want to keep an eye on Bean. I want to try to find out what's up with Gus. And I want to be at the party. To see everyone, even if they can't see me. Then, as soon as the sitting room becomes empty, I'll look in the window seat for my Russian dolls.

So, I have a plan and my only issue is the tiny matter of getting into the dining room. I've made it down to the hall without being seen, and I'm silently tiptoeing into the sitting room, looking just like a burglar, when I hear Krista's voice saying, 'This way,' and the click of her heels approaching.

Shit! She's coming. I'll never make it to the console table in time. In panic, I turn instinctively towards the nearest, safest hiding place: behind the old blue sofa. This trusty piece of furniture has concealed me many times over the years; I'll just wait there till the coast is clear. Good plan. I dive behind it a split second before Krista walks in and breathe out heavily in relief – then nearly scream in shock.

I'm not alone. There's a boy crouching behind the sofa alongside me. He looks about six years old, is dressed in a smart collared shirt, and seems unfazed at my arrival.

'Hello,' he whispers politely. 'Are you playing, too?'

For a moment I can't find a reply. Who is he? He must belong to a guest.

'No . . . no, I'm not,' I mouth, then put a finger over my lips, and the boy nods sagely.

He beckons to me to lean down and whispers into my ear, 'The fountain's homey, if you want to play.'

I give him an agonized smile, hoping this indicates, *No thank you and could you please be quiet?* But it doesn't work, because he adds, in the same breathy whisper, 'Chloe's seeking. She's my sister. She's got a scab on her knee. Who are you?'

I don't reply, but cautiously peep through a gap in the back cushions of the sofa. Krista has been followed by a pot-bellied guy who looks like he's the DJ, and he quite clearly can't keep his eyes off her.

I don't blame him. She's spectacular. I didn't get a good look at her earlier, only her Spanx, but now I have the leisure to eye her party outfit up and down. Her cleavage is showcased in a low-cut purple body-con dress, adorned with her sparkler, and her feet are in diamanté sandals with heels so high I can't believe they're even feasible. In fact, her whole look is gravity-defying, including her lashes and amazing blonde ringlets. (Hair extensions. *Surely.*)

'Nice place you've got here,' says the DJ. 'Historic, like. Done much to it?'

'Oh, this and that,' says Krista carelessly. 'You've got to put your stamp on a place.'

'Lucky you.' The DJ is still looking around. 'Shame you're selling.'

'Well, life goes on.' She shrugs. 'Can't live in a musty old house for ever.'

Musty old house? I feel a stab of hurt on behalf of Greenoaks. It is *not* musty. Well, OK, it is musty in places. But that's not its fault.

'Where are you off to, then?' says the DJ.

'Portugal's the plan,' she informs him. 'Get a bit of sun . . . new life . . . Forget all this.'

'Life of leisure, eh?' He laughs.

'Leisure?' retorts Krista. 'Not likely! I want to open a restaurant. Mexican-themed. *If* I can persuade my other half,' she adds meaningfully.

A Mexican restaurant? I haven't heard this plan. My head suddenly fills with a surreal image of Dad serving fajitas, wearing a poncho.

No. Just, *no*.

'Who are you?' the boy repeats breathily in my ear, making me jump. This is *all* I need. If I don't reply, he'll keep pestering. But what do I say? I can't say, 'I'm Effie.' Nor do I want him telling his family about the stranger dressed in black, hiding behind the sofa.

'I'm a ghost,' I whisper back, before I've fully thought this through.

'Oh!' The boy's eyes open wide and immediately he reaches out a hand to prod me. 'But I can touch you.'

'I'm the kind of ghost you can touch,' I whisper, trying to

sound convincing. 'Only people with extra-special brains can see that kind of ghost. I bet you have an extra-special brain.'

'Yes,' says the boy, after a moment's thought. 'I do.'

'Well, then.' I nod.

'Doesn't he want to open a restaurant, then, your other half?' the DJ is enquiring.

'You know men.' Krista twinkles at him. 'But I'll get my way.'

'I bet!' The DJ laughs, then adds, 'Couldn't grab a glass of water off you, could I?'

'Of course!' responds Krista with another charming smile. 'Come this way . . .'

Thank God! They're leaving!

'You should go,' I whisper to the boy. 'Chloe's bound to find you here. There's a much better hiding place in the garden. Behind the statue of the lady in the walled garden, there's a little dip in the hedge. Hide there and you'll easily get to the fountain.'

One good turn deserves another, I always think. And after all, he didn't give me away. He's earned a little hiding tip.

'OK!' The boy's face lights up and he scrambles to his feet. 'I knew you were a ghost,' he adds carelessly, 'I just didn't say.' Then he scampers out of the room.

At once I rise up on to my tiptoes. As I creep back out into the room, I glance longingly over at the window seat, which is covered with the DJ's heavy-looking boxes and cables. Could I quickly heave off the boxes and have a look?

No. Too risky. So instead I scurry silently into the adjoining dining room, stopping only for a moment to survey the table setting, which is jaw-dropping. There's a purple damask cloth, covered in glittery table confetti, on which are five silver candelabras, holding purple candles. There are three huge vases stuffed with white flowers. Each place setting has its own tea light in a silvered glass, plus individual salt and pepper pots and a little sculpture of . . . I peer more closely.

Is that Marie Antoinette? And is that bit of cotton wool supposed to be a *sheep*?

OK, that's bizarre. But I don't have time to linger. I crouch down, crawl under the tapestry cloth that covers the console table and collapse in relief. Made it!

But only a few seconds later, my triumph ebbs away as I have a terrible new realization: I'm starving. I didn't plan on being here all evening, there's no prospect of getting any food and I'm about to watch my family guzzling a whole roasted swan with quail garnish, or whatever. Why didn't I eat something in Bean's room? I'm an *idiot*.

I poke my head out, in case there's a spare Mars bar or something lying on the floor, and my eyes scan the room a bit hopelessly – then halt. There's a basket of bread rolls on the sideboard. Delicious-looking, white and fluffy, half covered with a napkin.

Now I've seen them, I'm fixated. All my stomach juices have come to life. I've never craved anything as much as I crave one of those bread rolls, right now. And if I *don't* have one, I point out to myself logically, I might faint from hunger. My unconscious body will flop out from under the console table like a corpse and my plan will be ruined.

This last thought decides me. I emerge from under the console table, tiptoe to the sideboard, deftly grab two bread rolls – then stiffen as I hear high heels swiftly approaching. And a distinctive laugh. It's Krista coming back again. *Shit.*

I don't have time to get back to the console table. As Krista appears, I descend to the floor behind a dining chair in one seamless curtsey. I clutch the back of it for balance, hold my breath and pray.

She strides up to the table, holding a stack of printed menu cards. She's only a few feet away. She's *right there*. I'm utterly exposed. As I'm crouching, my knees start to tremble. What if one of my bones cracks? What if my phone buzzes?

There's a huge old mirror on the opposite wall, and with a lurch, I realize I must be visible in that, too. But thankfully, Krista's not checking her reflection, for once. She's too engrossed in her task. As she moves along the table, distributing menu cards and humming to herself, I surreptitiously crawl along the other side, back towards the console table. She finishes arranging her menu cards, then pauses, and I freeze.

I watch her tensely through the wooden lattice of a chair back, trying to work out which way she's going to move next. But to my surprise, she looks furtively around the room, as though checking she's alone. Then, to my horror, she peels up her tight body-con dress. She grabs hold of the waistband of her Spanx and breathes out with a groan.

Please. Not Krista's Spanx *again*. What did I do to deserve this? I don't dare look away, in case she makes a sudden move towards me, so I'm compelled to watch the ghastly spectacle. Her face is intent, as though she's coming to some momentous decision – then she starts hauling off her Spanx completely. Argh. No! This isn't happening. This is—

I breathe out as I realize she's wearing a nude thong underneath. Could be worse. Could be a *lot* worse.

As she releases her streaky fake-tanned stomach from its elastic confines, she groans again in what sounds like massive relief. From the effort it took her to get them off, it's clear that her Spanx are about two sizes too small. No wonder they hurt. She's holding them, panting from her efforts, still with her dress hoiked right up, when footsteps suddenly sound and the DJ's voice says, 'Krista?'

At once, Krista stiffens in panic. Laughter swells up inside me and I desperately cram a fist into my mouth. I'm biting my knuckles, trying to keep silent, as Krista tugs her dress back down, looks around feverishly, then chucks her Spanx into a big blue pot on the sideboard, just as the DJ comes into view.

'Oh, hi!' she greets him, her voice only slightly more shrill than usual. I can't help admiring her cool. (Also – quick moment of female solidarity – she looks fine. That dress is solidly constructed. She didn't need Spanx in the first place.)

'Quick question about the playlist?' he says. 'I've scribbled down some thoughts in the kitchen, if you didn't mind having a look . . .'

Krista's eyes swivel briefly to the blue pot on the sideboard and away again.

'Of course.' She smiles brightly and follows him out.

The moment she's gone, I scamper along on all fours till I reach the console table. Once I'm safely hidden behind the tapestry cloth again, I exhale, my heart thudding. This is *stressful*. But at least I have food now. I sink my teeth into one of the bread rolls and start chewing vigorously.

'. . . obviously he's busy, but even so—'

'I know. Does *anyone* talk to Dad any more?'

I lift my head, alert. That sounds like Gus and Bean coming into the sitting room. I move towards the edge of the tapestry cloth, wondering if I dare peep out.

'It's impossible,' Bean is sighing. 'I can't seem to get to him for a proper conversation.'

'Same,' agrees Gus. 'Every time I try his mobile it gets picked up by Krista. She's like his henchman. She says he'll ring back, but of course he never does.'

'Me too!' exclaims Bean. 'Exactly!'

'What about Effie?'

'She says she can't remember when she last spoke to him. Says she's been busy.' Bean sighs again. 'But I don't think that's the whole story. I think things are still tense between them.'

Their footsteps pause and I imagine Gus perching on the arm of a sofa, like he always does.

'That situation's so fucked up,' he says gloomily. 'It really is a shame Effie isn't here. Everyone was asking after her.'

'Er . . . yes,' says Bean, sounding strangled. 'It's . . . a shame she didn't come. I haven't seen her at all. Not for ages.'

Is that the best she can do? She's a *terrible* liar. If Gus weren't so absent-minded, he'd pick up on it at once.

'Have you seen Effie's Russian dolls, by the way?' Bean adds. 'She was looking for them.'

'No,' says Gus. 'Sorry.'

'I reckon they might be in the window seat,' says Bean thoughtfully. 'I'll wait till the DJ's gone, then have a look.'

Now they're coming into the dining room, towards me. I angle my head so that I can peer round the side of the cloth, and see their approaching feet.

'Wow,' says Gus, coming to a halt in front of the dining table.

'I know,' says Bean. 'Krista's new hobby is tablescaping. Apparently the theme is "Versailles".'

'Why Versailles?' says Gus, sounding baffled.

'No idea. Help me light the candles, will you? Krista asked me to.'

I hear the sound of two matches being struck and gradually, infinitesimally, the lighting of the room becomes more mellow.

127

'This place card says "Lacey",' comments Gus. 'Who's she?'

'You know,' says Bean. 'Krista's sister. Red hair? You must have met her earlier.'

'Oh, her,' says Gus without enthusiasm. 'Hey, look, there's a menu. *Lobster ravioli with sorrel, fillet of beef . . .*'

Feeling more courageous, I peek out properly, and catch a glimpse of Gus reading out the menu card as Bean finishes lighting the candles. 'This looks great!' he exclaims. 'What time's dinner?'

I *knew* there would be lobster. My stomach is rumbling at the mention of food, and I clutch a hand over it. I'll try to get hold of some of the leftovers before I go.

'Soon, I guess,' Bean replies. 'Most of the cocktail-party guests have gone. I've said all my goodbyes. I've had enough of goodbyes,' she adds, sounding doleful.

'Me too. Oh, someone just asked me if the house is haunted,' says Gus, sounding puzzled. 'One of her children saw a ghost in here, apparently.'

'A *ghost*?'

'That's what she said.'

'Weird.'

They fall silent and I try my best to see what's going on, but it's impossible. I should have brought a periscope. Along with a hand grenade. I'll know next time.

'How are you, anyway?' Bean breaks the quiet. 'Apart from all this? You look tired.'

'Oh . . . you know.' Gus sounds evasive. 'Just the usual ups and downs.'

'Anything in particular?'

I wait breathlessly. Is he going to share the contents of his stressed-out phone call? Is this where I'll learn everything in some heartfelt outpouring?

'Nope,' he says at last. 'Nothing . . . no.'

There is! I want to cry out indignantly. *There's whatever you were talking about on the phone with Josh!*

'How about you?' Gus adds, and Bean looks away, studying her nails.

'Oh . . . er . . . pretty good,' she says, and I feel my face screw up in shock. *Pretty good?* When she was just crying in the garden?

I had no idea my brother and sister were so secretive and duplicitous. I'm shocked and I will tell them so at some point, when I'm not hiding from them under the console table.

'How are things with Romilly?' asks Bean politely.

'Oh . . . you know,' says Gus distantly. 'It's, um . . . Anyone on *your* horizon?' He changes the subject quickly as though fearful of further questioning.

'I . . .' Bean seems unable to answer. 'It hasn't been . . . It's . . .'

My heart swells with sympathy. Oh God, poor Bean. She hasn't been able to talk about her love life since the whole sorry business with Hal.

'I'm sure.' Gus backtracks. 'Really tough. Sorry. Didn't mean to . . .'

They're on the move again, and I crane my neck anxiously for a glimpse, trying to see if Bean looks upset. Then, as I finally catch sight of her, a burst of indignation sweeps all my sympathy aside. She's wearing my Rixo dress! The nerve! She must have gone and changed into it as soon as she thought I'd left!

Footsteps have been approaching, and they come to a halt.

'Champagne!' says Gus to someone I can't see. 'Great, thanks!'

Champagne, now. Pah. And all I have is a crummy old bread roll. I eye my siblings slightly resentfully as they clink glasses, notching up my grievances. Especially against Bean, who is not only enjoying the fruits of Krista's party, but doing so in *my* Rixo dress.

'I need a cigarette,' says Gus fervently, as the footsteps retreat.

'Gus!' exclaims Bean. 'You don't smoke!'

'Only at family reunions. I'm going in the garden. Coming?'

'Well, I'm not staying here on my own!'

As they move away, I subside. I hadn't realized that I'd been sitting in such a state of tension. I'm all squished up. In fact, can I even feel my toes?

My thoughts are broken as I hear a man's footsteps entering, swift and decisive.

Familiar footsteps?

No, I'm imagining things.

Except ... I'm not. It's Joe, striding into the room, his phone to his ear. Even though it's risky, I can't resist pulling the tapestry cloth aside slightly to have a proper look at him. His hair is gleaming in the candlelight and he's frowning slightly, his face taut with concentration.

He shouldn't be so attractive *and* be a doctor *and* be so oblivious of his looks, I think, watching him morosely. That shouldn't be allowed.

'Yup,' he's saying. 'No, you'd laugh.'

Who would laugh? I wonder jealously before I can stop myself. That beautiful girl he was pictured with in the *Daily Mail*? The one who was 'flaunting' her legs in a perfectly normal skirt?

Joe's been checking out the name cards on the table, but now he pauses.

'Yes, well, she is.' He hesitates. 'I saw her. Hiding in a rose bush, would you believe? No. No idea.'

I stare at him, unable to move. My head is prickling all over. *Hiding in a rose bush.* That's me. He's discussing me.

'Well, how do you *think* I reacted?' He sounds terse and instinctively I crane forward, because I want to know the answer myself. 'How do I *feel* about her? I . . . I think I feel . . .' He breaks off for an unbearable pause and rubs his brow. 'Essentially the same way.'

Breathlessly, I wait for him to elaborate. But he just listens a few moments more, then says, 'I'd better go. Yup, see you . . . Thanks. Appreciate it.' He puts his phone away and I peer at him for further clues, my heart hammering, despite myself.

The same way as what? As *what*? I'm so consumed by trying to read his face that as he walks away I lean further forward than I mean to, and suddenly, to my horror, I lose my balance. As I topple out inelegantly from under the tapestry cloth, I cry out, then clap my hand over my mouth and gaze desperately up at Joe, who looks flabbergasted.

'What the—'

'Shh!' I whisper. 'Ssssh! Forget you saw me. I'm not here.'

Cursing myself, I crawl hastily back under the tapestry cloth and readjust it. When I'm safely concealed again, I peek out – and Joe's still standing right there, staring in my direction, his mouth open. Honestly. He'll give me away.

'Go away!' I mouth, and motion for him to leave.

He swivels away and takes a few steps, but a moment later, my phone buzzes with a WhatsApp.

WTF???

Without missing a beat, I send a reply.

Pay no attention to that girl behind the curtain.

I know he'll get the *Wizard of Oz* reference, because once, when we were kids, we played a game with forfeits. His was to watch *The Wizard of Oz* twice through with me. Which he duly did, and we took to quoting it at each other for a while. Sure enough, he sends a new WhatsApp.

Why is the great and powerful Effie hiding under a table?

At once, I type my response.

I told you, I'm on a mission.

Then, biting my lip, I add a follow-up, trying to make it sound heartfelt.

Seriously, please don't tell anyone. Please.

I send it, then risk a tiny peek around the side of the tapestry. Joe is facing away from me, but as though he can sense me, he swivels back. As he sees me peeping out, his mouth twitches, but his face stays grave. He puts a finger to his lips and slowly nods. For a few moments, neither of us moves. His dark, steady gaze is impossible to read. I don't know what he's thinking. Except that he was thinking about me.

And that he still has feelings about me.

Of some sort.

Essentially the same way. My stomach churns as I consider all the different ways he could feel about me. He must know I overheard him just now. Will I ever find out what he meant?

More footsteps sound from the hall, breaking the spell, and I blink, coming to my senses. I've let him get under my skin. Which is a *mistake*. Why am I even interested in Joe

Murran's opinion? So what if he was talking about me on the phone? Who cares what he feels about me?

I need to get this message across to him. And luckily my face is pretty expressive. We're still gazing at each other, and slowly I transform my demeanour into that of steely antagonism. I can see him frown in slight puzzlement at my change of expression, and I mentally high-five myself. *That*'ll show him.

I'm feeling cross with myself for wondering about Joe's view of me. He's not worthy of my curiosity. And that is what I will say to him, if I get the chance—

'Joe!' We both start as Krista greets him, and I duck hastily back behind the tapestry. *Come on, Effie, get a grip.* I need to stop fixating about Joe, focus on my mission and find a comfortable sitting position. The night is still young, and I've still got a whole bloody dinner party to get through.

TEN

OK, my biggest problem is the dog. Which I did not foresee.

It was Lacey, Krista's sister, who brought Bambi into the dining room, holding him under her arm like a clutch bag. In fact, he looks even more like a clutch bag than usual tonight, because of his sparkly party collar, which I must admit is quite cute.

'Bambi's going to sit with me, aren't you, Bambi my love?' she said as she sashayed in – but of course, the minute she took her place, Bambi scrabbled off her lap on to the floor. He did several circuits of the dining room, then came to sniff around the console table in an incriminating way, while I furiously muttered, 'Bugger off, Bambi!' I've been so busy trying to get rid of him I haven't been able to concentrate on proceedings at all. But thankfully someone must have dropped a piece of lobster ravioli or something, because he's scooted off to the other side of the room.

Right. Finally, I can observe my family at close quarters. Or at least, see enough to get the gist of what's going on. If I tilt my head this way and that, and keep peeking through a useful moth hole I've discovered in the tapestry, I can see everyone's face to some degree, even if it's only in the mirror. (Except Romilly's. But I don't want to see Romilly's face, so that's fine.)

In between cursing Bambi, I've been trying to monitor the conversation at the table like an MI5 operative, but so far I've learned nothing. Everyone's just been talking aimlessly about how great the cocktails were. Apart from Romilly, who's been banging on about her daughters' violin lessons with this uber-teacher. As if anyone's interested.

My eyes slide along to Krista's sister, Lacey. This is the first time I've ever seen her and she's quite something, all flicky auburn hair and tight turquoise dress and bare, tanned shoulders. I swear she put on an extra wiggle when Joe politely held out her chair for her, and now she seems entranced by him. As I watch, he refills her water glass and she murmurs, 'Thanks, Doctor Joe,' in a husky, sultry voice, then brings the glass to her lips without taking her eyes off his.

' "Joe" is fine,' says Joe politely, whereupon Lacey bats her eyelashes at him.

'Oh, I couldn't possibly! You'll always be "Doctor Joe" to me. You do know I'm already in love with you?' She laughs, tossing her hair back again.

She's even sexier than Krista, with mesmerizing green eyes. Also, she's younger than Krista, maybe mid-thirties. Although still older than Joe, I note to myself. (Not in a bitchy way. Just in an accurate way.)

'I'm a very honest person,' she adds to Joe. 'I *have* to say things the way I see them. It's Lacey's way.' She twinkles at him. 'And if you don't like it, then don't sign up for the programme, excuse my French.'

'Right,' replies Joe, sounding a bit baffled. 'Are you in exercise-wear too?' he asks politely.

'No, but I've modelled for Krista's company,' says Lacey. 'I'm a contortionist in my spare time. She gets me walking on my hands, that kind of thing.'

'You're a *contortionist*?'

'You should see her,' puts in Krista proudly. 'Lacey can get her thighs right behind her ears, can't you, Lace?'

'Oh yeah, easy.' Lacey nods complacently and I swear all the men shuffle slightly in their chairs.

'Now, attention,' says Dad, tapping a fork on the rim of his wine glass. 'Before we proceed, I just want to say how marvellous it is to have all of us here tonight – including you, Lacey.' He smiles kindly at her. 'And Joe, of course, and Humph, although I don't know where he's got to . . .'

'Thank you, Tony,' says Lacey charmingly, raising her wine glass to him. 'And thank you for welcoming me, everyone.'

'It's not quite all of us, though, is it?' Bean's voice bursts out of her in a tremor. 'What about Effie?'

There's a long, charged silence around the table. In the mirror, I can see that Gus has winced and put his hand to his brow. Romilly has turned to look at Bean in astonishment. Joe has frozen, his hand clenched rigidly around his glass, his dark gaze unreadable. Krista is smiling glacially as though no one has uttered a word. I can see Lacey's eyes swivelling around the motionless scene in gleeful fascination.

I swallow several times, feeling hot all over, suddenly claustrophobic in my hidden space.

'Effie . . .' says Dad at last, his voice light but strained. 'Effie made her choice about tonight. And we must . . . respect that.' He takes a deep breath and seems about to continue, but then another voice comes booming forth, breaking the tension.

136

'Greetings, all! Sorry I'm so late!'

It's Humph, striding through the sitting room. *Great*. My entire being recoils. All I need to make this evening even more super-fun is another ex-boyfriend appearing on the scene. Especially one with eyebrows like caterpillars and a laugh like—

Wait. I blink as Humph swings into my restricted view. Is that *Humph*? I can scarcely believe it. I know Bean said he'd changed, but he's practically unrecognizable. His eyebrows are groomed. His hair is almost cool. He's thinner, bearded and wearing a black dinner jacket which is kind of . . . sleek.

The idea that 'Humph' and 'sleek' might go together is unbelievable.

'We didn't meet earlier,' I can hear him saying to Lacey as he extends a hand. 'Humphrey.'

'You're the Honourable Humph!' exclaims Lacey in delight. 'Does everyone around this table have a fancy title, or is it just these two gorgeous men? I'm a sucker for a good-looking man,' she adds to Bean. 'You know? A really *handsome* man. It's Lacey's way.' She beams and throws back her hair.

'I prefer hideously ugly men,' says Bean, deadpan, but Lacey completely misses the irony.

'Do you?' she says with a bright vagueness, her attention already back on Humph. 'And what do you do?' She gives a sudden, excited gasp. 'Don't tell me, Squire of the Manor.'

'I'm a medical practitioner,' says Humph pleasantly, and I frown, puzzled. A medical practitioner? Surely Humph went to agricultural college?

'Snap!' says Lacey, looking from Joe to Humph. '*Two* doctors in the house.'

'Not really,' says Joe, taking a gulp of wine.

'I practise alternative medicine,' explains Humph. He takes a small brown bottle out of his pocket and drops a colourless liquid into his water glass.

'What's that?' queries Lacey eagerly.

'It's a digestive compound,' says Humph. 'Everyone should take it.'

'In your unqualified opinion,' puts in Joe, and Humph gives a long, pitying sigh.

'I'm fully qualified in Dr Herman Spinken's techniques of internal alignment,' he says smoothly to Lacey. 'There's a website I can point you to. We have some impressive testimonies.'

'Impressive prices, too,' says Joe. 'Or wait, do I mean extortionate?'

Humph glares briefly at him before turning back to Lacey. 'Unfortunately, the Establishment doesn't yet understand Dr Spinken's theories. Joe and I have already had to agree to disagree on that one. But if you *are* interested, Lacey, I have a regular clinic near by. Do come along for a half-price starter session.' He's already produced a business card, which he hands to Lacey.

'*Humphrey Pelham-Taylor, Associate Practitioner, The Spinken Institute,*' Lacey reads off the card. 'Sounds very grand!'

'How long was your course, Humph?' says Joe evenly. 'A month?'

Humph doesn't even flicker.

'More attack from mainstream medicine,' he says sadly. 'The length of the course is irrelevant. It's not about learning facts, it's about awakening our minds to what we already know instinctively.'

'Oh, really?' says Joe. 'So, are you instinctively qualified in pharmacology, Humph?'

Humph gives Joe a baleful look, then turns back to Lacey.

'When we were babies, we understood instinctively how to align our spines, our inner organs, and our *rhu*.'

'What's our *rhu*?' says Lacey, looking fascinated.

'*Rhu* is a Spinken concept,' says Humph, and Joe snorts into his wine. 'It's the energy of our internal organs. It produces a transcending, healing power. Healthcare begins and ends with the *rhu*.'

He taps his chest and Krista chimes in, 'Humph's a marvel, Lace. That herbal drink I swig? Got it from Humph. Perks me right up, that does!' She twinkles at Humph, who beams back, pleased.

'Well, I'll definitely look into it.' Lacey puts the card in her bag. 'Lucky me, meeting a Spinken expert *and* the Doctor of Hearts!'

'Yes, you're quite the A-lister now, aren't you?' says Humph snidely to Joe. 'I'm amazed you've got time for any patients, in between all those interviews and red carpets.'

I see a ripple of annoyance pass over Joe's face, but he doesn't rise to the bait.

'We've been trying to keep up with your girlfriends in the media, Doctor Joe,' Krista joins in teasingly. 'But there are just too many. You're such a Casanova!'

'Not really,' says Joe. 'Most of my apparent paramours are simply women I happened to be adjacent to in the street for thirty seconds, on my way to work.'

'You can't fool us!' says Krista with a knowing smile. 'Yes, please clear the plates,' she adds to a hovering waiter.

Conversation lulls as the waiters remove the starter plates, then come in with plates of beef. There's some kind of fragrant sauce served with it, and I don't know what spice is in it – Cloves? Nutmeg? – but the smell instantly takes me back to Christmas. Christmas in this house. As the guests start eating, murmuring to each other and exclaiming over the food, it could almost be us again, the Talbots, sitting round the table, wearing paper hats and laughing. Mimi still in her apron, because she always forgot to take it off when she sat down. It became a family joke. We called aprons 'Christmas dresses'. And there was the year we gave Mimi one as a surprise, all decorated with red tinsel. She loved it so much she wore it for years.

I suppose that joke's gone now, I think, with a kind of crunching sadness. Or at least, I don't know where it lives any more. Not with Mimi, she never talks about the past. Not here, either. All the jokes, the family fables, the silly slang and traditions that only we understood. Have they been divided up like the furniture? Or are they all in a box somewhere?

Then another childhood memory creeps into my mind. I hid here, under this very console table, one Christmas Day! I'd completely forgotten – but now it all comes flooding back. I was about seven and I'd had a fight with Bean over her cracker gift. (Should I now admit the truth? I *did* break her yoyo.) I slithered down from my chair in tears and hid here, half ashamed, half sulking. And after about ten minutes, Dad came to join me.

It was a magical little moment we had, father and daughter, hiding under the table from the rest of the family. He made me laugh with his opening gambit, 'Isn't Christmas *awful*? You're very clever to escape, Effie.' Then he sang a series of carols, getting all the words deliberately wrong. And then, when I was in fits of giggles, he asked if I wanted to bring in the Christmas pudding after he'd set it alight.

Which, thinking back, was surely a fire risk? Should seven-year-olds carry flaming plates? Well, whatever – I did it. I still remember making that careful procession in from the kitchen, mesmerized by the blue flames, by my huge importance. It made me feel on top of the world. Effie Talbot, fire goddess.

Dad's laugh interrupts my thoughts, and I breathe out shakily, snapping back to the present day. My heart is well and truly scrambled. How have things come to this? Back on that Christmas Day, I hid in here with my dad. Now I'm hiding from him. From everyone.

'Of course, Effie was one of Joe's girlfriends, once upon a time.' Krista's voice distracts me and I look up, blinking. 'She'll be in the *Daily Mail* next!'

'I don't think so,' says Joe tonelessly, and I feel myself prickle, although I'm not sure why. Does he mean I'm not attractive enough to be in the *Daily Mail*? I see him glance down towards my hiding place and immediately stiffen. He'd better not give me away.

'And, Humph, I understand you used to date Effie too?' Lacey chimes in provocatively. 'Popular girl! Such a shame she's not here. You two could fight a duel over her!'

'With all due respect, Lacey,' says Humph in reproving tones, 'I'm not sure that's a very *feminist* thing to suggest?'

'Are you a feminist now, Humph?' says Joe, in a strange voice. 'That's . . . new.'

'All Spinken practitioners are feminists,' says Humph, sounding offended.

'Well, I still think you'd fight a duel if Effie was here,' says Lacey, unabashed. 'Is it too late to get her here? Call her up, Krista!'

Oh my God. She's not going to call me right now, is she? I glance down in panic, just to make sure my phone's on silent. But in my next breath, I realize I don't have to worry. Krista would never do that in a million years.

'Wouldn't work,' says Krista briskly. 'I begged her to come tonight, didn't I, Tony? I sent her an email, saying, "You know what, Effie, my love? This is the last party at Greenoaks. You'll regret staying away. You're only cutting off your nose to spite your face."'

I'm almost breathless with shock. She did not say any such thing!

'But you know Effie,' concludes Krista. 'Goes her own sweet way. It's a shame, but there it is.'

'Is she the problem child of the family, then?' asks Lacey with interest.

'I wouldn't say she's the problem child, exactly, but ...' begins Dad with an easy laugh, and my heart constricts.

But ... ? *But ... ?*

How was he going to finish that sentence?

I'm suddenly desperate to see Dad properly. I poke my head round the side of the tapestry, but no one bats an eyelid. They're all waiting for Dad to carry on.

'Effie is stubborn,' he says at last. 'And when you're too stubborn, you can miss out on opportunities. You can find yourself ... trapped.'

I blink in utter disbelief. *Stubborn?* Dad can talk! Who hurt his leg because he wouldn't give up on that 10K? Exactly. And I'm *not* trapped, I think indignantly, shifting my ankle uncomfortably.

Well, OK. Maybe I'm a little bit trapped *right now*. But that's not the point.

'Poor old Effie!' says Lacey. 'There's stubborn and then there's perverse. Who doesn't come to a family party, for Pete's sake?'

She looks around the table with avid eyes.

'Effie *would* have come,' says Bean, glaring at Krista. 'If she'd been asked properly.'

'There was a mix-up with her invitation,' says Krista briskly, 'so she threw her toys out of the pram. The trouble with Effie is she's too emotional. It's all a roller coaster with her. Total drama queen.'

'*I'd* say the trouble with Effie is she's never quite grown up,' chimes in Romilly, and I glower at the back of her smug head. Who asked Romilly's opinion? 'She's still very much the baby of the family.'

I feel my cheeks start to blaze. What's *that* supposed to mean?

'Oh, I know those types.' Lacey nods sagely.

'She can't really *deal* with life,' Romilly continues. 'She lost her job, and ever since then she's been temping as a waitress. Can't seem to get it together. And as for her love life . . .'

Now my head is tingling. Is this how everyone talks about me when I'm not there?

'Stop it! You're all being unfair!' chimes in Bean, sounding distressed. 'Effie's had some really good temp work. It wasn't her fault she lost her job. She's just regrouping while she considers her next move. It's very sensible. And do you want to know where she is this very minute?' she adds triumphantly. 'She's out on a date with an Olympic athlete!'

My eyes are suddenly blurry as I listen to my sister defending me. I love Bean so much. She can have my Rixo dress. She can have it for ever.

'An Olympic athlete?' Krista bursts into derisive laughter. 'Has Effie told you she's on a date with an Olympic athlete? I mean, we all love Effie, but an Olympic *athlete*? I think someone's been telling porkies. Poor love. She could have just said she was washing her hair.'

For a moment no one speaks. Then Joe puts down his glass with a firm clunk.

'I believe the guy in question *is* an Olympic athlete,' he says pleasantly. 'A gold medallist, so I understand. Isn't that right, Bean?'

There's a slightly stunned silence around the table and I see Krista's eyes fly open in shock.

'A *gold medallist*?' says Romilly, sounding impressed in spite of herself.

'Yes!' says Bean, somehow keeping it together. 'Yes, he is. A gold medallist.'

'In the modern pentathlon, wasn't it?' Joe adds. 'Or rowing, I forget. But I do know he's now a successful businessman and philanthropist.' Joe looks expressionlessly at Krista. 'Quite a catch.'

'He must have made some serious money!' exclaims Humph, perking up. 'You know, the Spinken technique is ideal for professional athletes. Maybe Effie could introduce me.'

'If they have more than one date!' says Lacey snidely.

'I can't imagine he won't fall for her,' says Joe, in the same matter-of-fact voice. 'So. That'll be up to Effie.'

He darts the briefest of glances towards me, and I gaze back, unable to move, feeling unsettled. I know he's just winding up Krista; I know none of this is real. But . . . Oh God. I can't let him get under my skin. Not again.

'How do you know all this?' says Krista, smiling at Joe with a rather livid smile.

'Effie and I have been in touch recently,' says Joe nonchalantly. 'Didn't she mention it?'

'Do you know where this guy lives?' says Humph to

Bean. Clearly he's hoping to land a big celebrity sporting client.

'No,' says Bean. 'But I *do* know that right this minute, Effie is miles away, being wined and dined in some top luxury London restaurant. So, here's to Effie, wherever she is!'

She looks determinedly around the room, as though to convince everyone. Then she lifts her glass, high and confident – and as she sips, suddenly spots me peeping out from under the console table. Her face spasms with shock and she splutters violently, sending wine everywhere. Lacey gasps, and shrieks, 'Bean! Are you OK?'

'What's up?' demands Gus in alarm.

'Nothing! I just noticed the . . . flowers!' says Bean, a bit wildly.

As everyone looks in confusion at the flowers, Bean makes a desperate, incredulous face at me. I make an apologetic face back, then retreat under the tapestry.

'Shame Effie can't see them, isn't it?' says Joe conversationally to Bean. 'Effie loves flowers.' He nods almost imperceptibly at the console table and she stares at him, eyes widening.

'Yes,' she manages. 'Great shame.'

'Anyway, I'm glad she's having fun tonight,' continues Joe. 'Wonder what she's doing, right now?'

'Yes, I wonder too,' says Bean, sounding strangled. 'Who knows?'

'People-watching, I should think,' says Joe, with a straight face, and Bean gives another desperate splutter.

'Yes, I expect so.'

'I'm sure she's got a good view, wherever she is,' adds Joe.

'Yes, I'm sure she's got an excellent view,' manages Bean, her voice choked with laughter. 'Oh, pudding!' she adds in relief.

Great. I'm totally famished and now I have to watch them all eat *pudding*?

'Now, everyone,' says Krista, clapping her hands for attention, 'I thought we'd have a bit of a throwback tonight . . . so we've got an old-fashioned sweet trolley! Bring it in!' she raises her voice.

The next moment I hear trundling wheels, accompanied by gasps and cries of delight and even applause.

'Now, that *is* fun,' says Romilly, managing, as usual, to sound totally un-fun as she says it. 'That *is* witty. Yes. It's fun.'

'How do we choose?' says Bean yearningly. 'I want everything! Look at the pavlova!'

'Have everything!' says Lacey. 'Ooh, chocolate mousse. I love chocolate,' she adds confidingly to Humph. 'Love it. It's just Lacey's way.'

'You're a chocoholic,' says Humph, smiling, and Lacey gasps, as though she's never heard that term before and Humph is another Oscar Wilde.

'You got it!' She points at him triumphantly. 'I'm a chocoholic!'

'As long as you all leave some profiteroles for me,' says Dad jovially.

The trundling wheels are coming close to me, and they suddenly halt, right in front of the tapestry. I edge my face close to the gap and see the burnished metal trolley. I can smell pastry, chocolate, strawberries . . . This is torture.

'If I could just explain to everyone?' says a woman's voice above my head. 'Here we have a kiwi and pistachio pavlova . . . chocolate mousse . . . profiteroles . . . On this lower level, we have mini New York-style cheesecakes . . . pineapple carpaccio with lemongrass syrup . . . apricot parfait . . .

and fresh strawberries, served with cream. Madam? Some pavlova? And some parfait with that?'

I'm in a daze of hunger-lust, listening to all this. My stomach feels like it's turning in on itself, it's so empty. And the food's right there. Right in front of me. Could I . . . ?

No.

But if I was really careful?

'And a few strawberries?' the waitress is saying. 'Of course.'

Experimentally, I creep one hand out from under the tapestry and grope blindly towards the trolley. My mouth is watering as I reach the lip of the bottom shelf and start edging towards the nearest platter . . .

Noooo!

With no warning, the trolley trundles off again, and I snatch my hand back to safety. Ow. That scraped my skin.

Morosely I sit back in the darkness, preparing to listen to my family scoffing their way through profiteroles and pavlova while I quietly die of hunger. I hadn't realized how *greedy* my family was, I find myself thinking resentfully. Listen to them, all asking for about six different desserts and then saying, 'Oh, and some strawberries,' as though that'll make up for eating a pound of cream.

'This chocolate mousse!' Lacey moans. 'It's heaven.'

I'm just feeling in my pocket yet again to see whether there's even a stick of chewing gum I've missed, when a snuffling sound alerts me. It's Bambi, returning to investigate.

'Sod off, Bambi!' I hiss, but he doesn't take any notice. In fact, something's obviously attracted his interest, because he starts worrying at the tapestry. He's whining and scratching at it. Then he suddenly barks in his loud, yappy way.

'Stop!' I whisper desperately. 'Ssh!'

But his barking only gets louder, and I tense up in fright. Any moment now he's going to pull the tapestry aside like bloody Toto and it'll be the end.

'What's Bambi doing?' says Bean in a stagy voice. 'Here, Bambi! Come here!'

'I've never met Bambi before,' says Joe easily. I hear him push back his chair and head towards the console table. 'Let's see you properly. That's a lovely collar you're wearing. Come here, boy!'

Peeping round the side of the tapestry, I see him taking hold of the protesting Bambi with a firm grasp.

'Beautiful dog!' he exclaims loudly, then adds *sotto voce* to me, 'How's the mission going?'

'Terrible,' I whisper back. 'And I'm starving. If you could just pinch me about six cheesecakes and a chocolate mousse, that would be great.'

I catch a flash of Joe's face, looking amused.

'I'll see what I can do,' he murmurs, then stands up, still holding Bambi. 'You'd like to be let out?' he says, as though the dog is speaking to him. 'Good idea! Is that OK?' he adds casually to Krista. 'He seems a bit freaked out. I'll take him somewhere quiet.'

To my utmost relief, he strides all the way through the sitting room and dispatches Bambi into the hall, closing the door on him. I watch as Joe returns to the table. He takes a few mouthfuls of pavlova, not talking to anyone, his eyes distant. Then, as if with a sudden thought, he pulls out his phone and says to Krista, 'I do apologize, but I need to send an urgent text. It's a fairly important medical emergency.'

'A medical emergency!' breathes Lacey. 'Oh, Doctor Joe! What is it?'

'I'll leave the table . . .' Joe begins to stand up, but Krista bats him down again with an ingratiating smile.

'Don't be silly! We're all family here. Send your text, Joe.'

'Thanks.' Joe gives her a brief smile, then starts to type. A moment later, my phone lights up with a message from him.

You should try to stretch your legs. You'll get DVT in there.

Automatically, I try to extend one of my legs, but I can't, it's a ridiculous idea, so I type a reply.

No I won't. Anyway, if I do, Humph will cure me with the Spinken method.

I send it, then watch Joe reading it, his mouth twitching.

'Everything all right?' says Lacey, who is also watching him, agog.

'Patient's being a bit obstinate,' says Joe and flicks his eyes briefly my way – which Bean notices. She stares at his phone incredulously, then glances towards the console table. Then she gets out her own phone.

'So sorry!' she says to Krista in stilted tones. 'But Joe's reminded me, I need to send a text, too. It's a . . . um . . . a plumbing emergency.' She types quickly, and moments later, my phone lights up with her message.

What are you DOING????

Without pausing, I send a reply.

Hiding. Rixo dress looks nice, by the way.

I stifle a giggle as I see Bean's cheeks flame. She looks down at the dress guiltily, then towards me. Honestly, she's going to give me away! Quickly I type a follow-up.

Don't worry, you look lovely in it. X

Then, in sudden inspiration, I create a new group: *Bean and Joe*, and send them a joint WhatsApp.

Guess what?? Krista's Spanx are in the blue pot on the sideboard. She took them off. I saw her.

As Bean reads my message, she gives a sudden, violent gulp of suppressed laughter. A moment later, Joe makes a tiny snorting noise. He raises his head from his phone, looks at Krista, then at the blue pot, then straight at Bean, who makes another desperate snuffling sound.

'That's a beautiful blue pot over there,' he says, deadpan. 'Don't you think, Bean? I've never noticed it before, but it's a work of art.'

'Oh yes,' says Bean, in a wobbly voice which means she's on the verge of giggles. 'It's lovely.'

'Striking.' Joe nods. 'Shall we have a closer look at it? Krista, would you mind?'

For a moment, Krista stares back, her brows lowered, as though she can't tell if she's been caught out or not. Then, in suddenly strident tones, she exclaims, 'A toast!' She leaps to her feet, brandishing a wine glass. 'Here's to you, Tony, my handsome hero.'

'Hear, hear!' chips in Lacey.

'You know, Tone's had a *marvellous* year with his investments and all that,' says Krista proudly. '*Swimming* in profits.'

'Well,' says Dad, looking startled. 'I wouldn't—'

'Don't be modest! You've made a stack!' Krista cuts him off proudly and I see Bean wincing at Gus. Dad never usually talks about money. Nor does Mimi. It's just not what they do.

'Tony!' says Lacey, twinkling at him. 'You dark horse! Save some for me, won't you?'

'Get in line!' retorts Krista to Lacey. 'And now, since I'm standing up . . . we've got a very special announcement to make.' She simpers at Dad. 'Haven't we?'

I catch my breath. Oh my God. Here it comes. I glance at Bean, suddenly wishing she was down here with me and I could clutch her hand like I used to in scary films. She's looking questioningly at Gus, who raises his eyebrows back, clearly meaning *No idea*.

'Tony and I want to take things to the next level.' Krista beams at Dad. 'So we'll be holding a commitment ceremony in the autumn. In Portugal, probably. You'll all be invited.'

For a moment, I'm not sure how to react. A commitment ceremony. It could be worse. But it could be better.

'Congratulations!' exclaims Lacey. 'Aw, you two lovebirds!' She beams at Dad and he smiles back charmingly.

'Krista's idea,' he says, and I have an overwhelming urge to burst out, exclaiming, 'It was Krista's idea? No way! You're kidding!'

Bean and Gus haven't said anything yet, and Krista seems aware of the awkward atmosphere, because she springs into overdrive.

'And now, come on, time for some entertainment!' she exclaims. 'Someone needs to put some music on! Call this a party?'

'We could sing!' says Dad heartily. 'We're all here . . . How about "Auld Lang Syne"? Come on, everyone!' He crosses

151

his arms and extends them to Gus and Bean, who both look startled. *'Should auld acquaintance be forgot . . .'*

As he starts to sing, only Lacey joins in, followed by Humph, who promptly changes his mind and stops. Dad jigs his arms up and down a few times to the ragged, unconvincing tune, waiting for Gus and Bean to take his hands, but neither moves a muscle. In fact, Bean looks frozen in awkwardness.

'I don't really think . . .' she begins, whereupon Lacey stops singing, claps a hand over her mouth and gives an expressive look to Krista.

'Maybe . . . later?' says Gus, and Dad's tentative singing gradually dies away to nothing. He clears his throat, brings his arms back to where they were and takes a slug of his drink, while everyone stares silently at their dessert.

Oh God. This is hideous. It's mortifying. I can't look at Dad; in fact, I can barely look at anyone. I'm prickling with embarrassment, and I'm not even at the table.

'Anyway,' says Bean at last, in the most false, desperate voice I've ever heard. 'Congratulations on your . . . er . . . commitment, Dad and Krista. Sorry, I should have said straight away . . .'

'Yes, absolutely.' Gus coughs. 'It's . . . um. Great news.'

'Super!' says Humph. 'Lovely place, Portugal.'

'Let's dance!' Krista breaks in like a determined juggernaut. 'Come on, what are we all still sitting here for? This is a party! Let's get the music going!'

She gets up, strides into the sitting room and calls, 'Yoohoo! Where's that playlist? We want to part-ay!' Then she marches back to the table and starts tugging at chairs. 'Everyone! On the dance floor! Now! Finish your desserts later.'

I mean, you have to admire her tenacity. Within about two

minutes, she's chivvied everyone out of their seats, the DJ has taken up his position, coloured lights are flickering around the sitting room and 'Dancing Queen' is blasting through the house.

The dining room is empty. I'm alone. Do I dare . . . ?

Cautiously I start lifting up the tapestry, then hastily drop it again as I hear the gunfire of approaching heels. They're striding near. Is it Krista? Oh God. Oh shit. Has she discovered me?

I feel a spike of terror as the tapestry is suddenly lifted up, the light making me blink. It's all over. I'm revealed. I've failed. I shrink desperately back into the shadows, trying to make myself invisible . . . There's a soft *thwack*, and something fabric lands in my face, making me flinch. Then the tapestry falls down again. The heels retreat. I don't know what on earth's going on.

In utter bewilderment, I unpeel the fabric from my face. It's stretchy. It's—

Argh! Gross! It's Krista's Spanx!

She must have dumped them in here to hide them. Urgh. Urgh. They were on my *face*. With a shudder, I throw them down, as far away from me as I can. I need to get out of here. I've had enough of this hell-hole. My back aches and my legs feel squashed. But how do I dare creep out when Krista might come in at any moment with random shapewear to hide?

Then my phone lights up with a new message. From Joe. I look at his name warily for a moment – then click on it.

Dessert is served in the wine cellar. Bean and I will be your lookouts. You can make it if you go now. X

ELEVEN

The cellar is down a set of stone steps leading from a door just outside the kitchen. When I was little, I was terrified of it. Now, as I cautiously descend the steps on to the old brick floor, the place looks just as it ever did: musty and shadowed, with cobwebs thick in every corner. The wine racks are on the far wall, although they look pretty empty now. Dad must have been running down supplies before the move. Hanging on a cord from the ceiling is a single light bulb, glowing dimly. Beneath that a tea towel has been spread on an upturned tea chest, and on it is a platter bearing a selection of the most delicious-looking desserts I've ever seen. There's a mini cheesecake, a huge dollop of pavlova, a mound of chocolate mousse, five strawberries and a couple of slices of cheese, with crackers.

I can't help laughing out loud with delight. It's a feast! There's cutlery, a glass of water and even a napkin. This must be Bean's doing.

Without hesitation, I pull up an ancient metal stool and dig in. I'm almost swooning as I shovel chocolate mousse into my mouth – then I turn to the pavlova, which is just as good. Hats off to Krista: these caterers are awesome.

I've just taken a bite of strawberry when I hear the sound of the door opening above and leap to my feet in fright, still holding the half-eaten strawberry. Oh God. *Please* don't say I'm going to be caught here, scoffing the posh food . . .

'Don't worry,' comes Joe's voice. 'Only me.'

I hear his footsteps descending the stone steps and then there he is, impossibly elegant in his black tie, holding a bottle of champagne.

'Bean wanted to bring this to you, but she's been waylaid by Lacey,' he says. 'So I said I'd do the honours.'

'Oh,' I say awkwardly. 'Thanks. Also, thanks for not giving me away in there,' I add gruffly as he opens the champagne with deft hands. 'And backing up the Olympic athlete story.'

'Pleasure,' says Joe. He pours out two glasses and hands one to me. I watch the bubbles fizzing to the top, my stomach knotting up. As he lifts his dark eyes to mine, I draw breath, then stop. I want to know things I can't ask.

'What?' says Joe.

'Nothing.' I swallow. 'Just thinking about . . . you know. Moving on.'

'Yes. Of course.' He lifts his glass in a toast. 'To moving on.'

'To moving on,' I echo obediently, even though the phrase gives me a little pang in my heart. 'Don't let me keep you,' I add, after sipping.

'Oh, I'm in no hurry.' He nods at the chocolate mousse and perches on a nearby barrel. 'Eat some more.'

'I will,' I say as I sit back down, although I weirdly seem to have lost my appetite. I see Joe's eyes move briefly to my neckline and away again, and I can guess what's in his mind.

The candle charm. The Smallest Diamond in the World. It felt so precious when he gave it to me. A magical talisman that would protect us through all our months apart.

Well. So much for that.

Just then, music blasts through the air, and we both jump. They must have turned on some extra speakers above us, because the thud-thud-thud is coming right down into the cellar. I hear a distant whoop and imagine Krista or Lacey making shapes on the dance floor.

The beat of the music is infectious, even muffled by the ceiling. Joe takes a sip of his champagne, his eyes on me all the time, and I take a large gulp, trying to keep my cool. I had a lot of imaginings about tonight. But being alone with Joe Murran in the cellar, with chilled champagne and the seductive thud of music, was not a vision I ever had.

A shaft of light is illuminating his face, right on his cheekbone. Why does he have to be so *good-looking*?

'Last dance in this house,' he says at length, lifting his glass again.

'Yes. Except I'm not dancing. And neither are you.'

'No.'

There's silence between us and I realize that we're both moving almost imperceptibly to the thud-thud-thud. My body is shifting this way and that, by the tiniest fraction of a degree, and he's doing the same. We're almost-dancing, if that's a thing, and if it's not, we're making it a thing. We're deliberate. We're in sync. Our bodies always were in sync. We walked in time, we fitted each other perfectly in bed, we yawned simultaneously.

The music increases in volume and I feel my body responding. Joe's wordless gaze seems more intense, almost hypnotic. I suddenly remember dancing with him at that school event, as teenagers, before we were even an item. It was the first time I felt his hands on me like that. The first time we ever looked at each other in that way.

And now we're looking at each other in that way again. My spine is tingling. I'm in a kind of trance, lost in the connection between us. An outsider would probably see two people sitting in motionless silence. But if this isn't dancing, nothing is. All my cells are swaying in time with his. All my cells are yearning for his. The feel of his skin, his hands, his mouth . . . I feel intoxicated. I want him. Desperately. Even as I simultaneously know that a lot of things I might want in life are *not* a good choice.

People give up smoking by associating cigarettes with some horrible food, don't they? Therefore I can give up Joe by associating him with heartbreak. Which should be easy, because I already do.

Somehow I wrench my eyes away from his, break the spell and find a normal voice.

'Well, that was a weird evening.'

'Agreed.' Joe nods.

'A *commitment ceremony*.' I wrinkle my nose. 'What is that, even?'

Joe shrugs. 'I guess it's where you promise to, you know, be with each other. Stay with each other.'

He breaks off, and I feel a warmth travel through me, all the way to my cheeks. Because that's what we wanted, once upon a time.

'Anyway.' I try to move the conversation on. 'What they say is true. You don't hear anything good about yourself if you eavesdrop.' I make a wry, comical face and Joe laughs.

'What did you expect if you were a fly on the wall?'

'Well, obviously I was *hoping* they might all say, "Isn't Effie brilliant? Isn't she fabulous? Isn't she the best member of this family?" Joke,' I add quickly. 'I'm joking.'

'You are the best member of this family,' says Joe, straight-faced.

I know he's joking too, but I still feel a kind of longing inside me. I used to be his best. And he was my best.

Anyway. Whatever.

'I once made the mistake of looking at some online comments about me,' Joe adds, more lightly. 'I guess that's the equivalent of hiding under the table and eavesdropping. I don't recommend it.'

'Oh God!' I clap a hand to my mouth. 'But surely everyone loves you.'

'Not the guy who wanted me to stuff my arrogant cock . . .' He pauses. 'Don't remember exactly where. Nowhere edifying. At least your family didn't come out with anything like that.'

I can't help snorting with laughter. 'That puts it in perspective.'

I sip my champagne and look at Joe's face, and suddenly miss his wisdom. We used to talk everything through. He's not like Bean, he doesn't get anxious or over-protective. He just listens and gives his view. I'm still feeling raw after hearing myself discussed, and I want his take on it.

'Joe, do you think I'm still the baby of the family?' I say in an embarrassed rush, and he lifts his eyes in surprise.

'Maybe,' he says, after a few moments' thought. 'Although – quite hard not to be.'

'Bean does far too much for me,' I say, suddenly stricken. 'I just let her. She organizes everything and sorts out all the family arrangements and worries about me. She's like a mother hen. She even orders me vitamins.'

'Well, order her some vitamins, then.'

This is such a Joe response, I can't help laughing. Direct. Practical. To the point.

'You have a solution to everything, don't you?'

'Not always.' A strange flicker passes over Joe's face. 'Not always.'

There's a weird little silence. Joe's eyes meet mine directly and my throat tightens. Does he mean . . . ? What does he mean? But then he looks away and the moment's gone.

'My sister Rachel sometimes comes to meet me for lunch at the hospital,' he continues more lightly. 'And whenever she arrives, she says the same thing. "Little Joe! A doctor!" And then she pinches my cheek. So I get it. Once the youngest, always the youngest.'

'She doesn't pinch your cheek!' I laugh.

'She pinched my cheek once,' concedes Joe. 'As a joke, she said. I never let her forget it. My point is, you get cast in a role and it can be hard to escape. Baby of the family. Patriarch. Whatever.'

'Nation's heart throb,' I can't resist retorting, and he nods, his eyes raised ironically.

'Nation's heart-throb.'

I eye him silently, mapping his familiar, real-life face on to the face that sometimes pops up in the media. I still can't relate Joe – my Joe – with 'Doctor Joe, national treasure'.

'Some people are born into roles,' says Joe, as though reading my mind. 'Others have roles thrust upon them. You know, I wasn't even supposed to do that interview? I was a last-minute substitute.'

'It must be . . . fun, though?' I venture. 'The fame? All those people in love with you?'

'It was shocking at first,' he says. 'It felt ridiculous. Mad.

Then it was interesting for about twenty minutes.' He shrugs. 'But then it became a barrier to what I really want.'

It's my cue to ask what he really wants, but something's stopping me. Maybe pride. I used to know what Joe really wanted. Or at least, I thought I did. But that's all over, I remind myself furiously. *Over*.

'You split up with your girlfriend,' I say, almost brusquely, wanting suddenly to establish where we stand. 'I read about it in the papers. Sorry. That must have been hard.'

'Thanks.' He nods.

'Can I ask why? Or is that too personal?'

'I guess I just annoyed her,' says Joe, after some thought.

'You *annoyed* her?'

'I guess.' His voice is toneless and I stare at him, baffled.

'What annoyed her? Leaving the cap off the toothpaste? The way you slurp your tea? Because you don't seem like a very annoying person. I mean, you annoy *me*,' I add, 'but that's different. That's specific.'

Joe shoots me the kind of wry grin that used to make my heart twist around itself. That still does, truth be told.

'What annoyed her?' he says musingly, as though beginning a philosophical treatise. 'Well. I guess most of all, although she would never admit it, it was my levels of anxiety. My "inability to function like a proper human being" as she once charmingly put it. Maybe the toothpaste thing, too,' he adds after a beat. 'Who knows?'

I gaze at him in confusion. Joe? Anxiety? What's he on about?

'You don't know,' he adds, catching my expression. 'I wasn't well for a time. I guess it's ongoing,' he amends. 'But I manage it.'

I'm so stunned, I can't speak. If you'd asked me to describe

Joe Murran, I would have reeled off the words easily: *Selfish. Handsome. Talented. Cruel. Unfathomable.*

But *anxious?* That would never have figured.

'I'm sorry,' I say at last. 'I had no idea, Joe. No idea.'

'It's fine. One of those things.'

I'm trying to match up the mental image of Joe I've been holding on to all this time with the new version in front of me. *Anxiety.* I thought he was made of tungsten. What happened?

The party music is still thudding through the ceiling of our musty space. All the years that Joe and I have known each other seem to be passing through my head like a video. All those hours spent together, playing, talking, laughing, love-making . . . I should know him by now, surely. I should know the secret, vulnerable corners of his brain. Shouldn't I? But then, he did always keep part of himself hidden away, I remind myself. As though he couldn't trust it with anyone, not even me.

'Are you with someone?' asks Joe, as though wanting to push the conversation away from himself. 'You were with a guy called Dominic.'

'Oh, Dominic.' I wince as I remember myself telling Joe how utterly perfect Dominic was. 'No. He was . . . Anyway. No. There's no one.'

We both sip our drinks again, the music still thudding. Then Joe breaks the silence.

'You said you're here at Greenoaks on a mission, Effie.' His eyes crinkle. 'Can I be of assistance?'

'No,' I say, more shortly than I mean to. 'Thanks.'

Joe may have helped me out. And he may be a lot more vulnerable than I realized. But that doesn't mean we're reconciled, or that I'm ready to confide in him.

He looks slightly batted back by my rejection, but then draws breath again.

'Effie . . .'

He pauses, for longer than seems natural. In fact, so long that I stare at him.

'What?' I say at last. 'What?'

'There's – I need to say something . . .' He breaks off again and exhales sharply as though he's finding something a struggle.

'What?' I say warily.

There's another massive silence, and as Joe finally looks up, his whole face seems to have changed. He looks grim and determined, but daunted, too, like someone about to climb a mountain.

'You were right,' he says swiftly, as though he's speaking fast before he can have second thoughts. 'What you said in your text, earlier. I *have* been racking my brains about how I can make things up to you. All this time; ever since that night. I know I hurt you badly, I know I broke your heart, I think of it every day. And I've been . . .' He rubs his brow. 'Desperate.'

I feel a white-hot flash of nerves. Adrenaline is pumping round my veins. On the few times we've seen each other since the break-up, we've been cautious and formal. We've never 'gone there'.

But now we are. We're lifting up the scab on that part of our love affair that's never quite healed. I'm already steeled for hurt, but weirdly exhilarated, too, because I've imagined this moment about a zillion times.

'I was joking,' I say. 'In my text.'

'I know you were. But I'm not. I'm not joking.' He takes another deep breath. 'Effie, listen, I'm so—'

'Don't!' I cut him off almost savagely and see the shock

ripple over his face. 'Please,' I continue, my voice calmer but still trembling. 'Don't tell me you're sorry, Joe. You've said it a million times. I know you're sorry. I don't want to hear that. I want to hear *why*. Why? Did you go off me? Was there someone else?' I gaze at his face – so familiar but such an enigma – feeling suddenly desperate. *'Why?'*

For the longest time, neither of us speaks. I'm staring into Joe's dark eyes, like I used to endlessly in bed. Trying to fathom their depths. Willing them to relinquish whatever it is he's protecting. Is he going to let me into his innermost self? Finally?

'It was . . .' Joe begins hesitantly, his voice low. 'There's a lot you don't know.'

My heart starts to thump. My mind is already frantically scurrying around. What don't I know? What secret did he keep from me? Another woman? Another . . . man?

'So, tell me,' I manage, my voice barely above a whisper. 'Tell me, Joe.'

'Hi, you two!' Bean's cheery greeting makes me jump so violently I spill my champagne. I look up, dazed, to see her coming down the steps to the cellar.

Instantly, Joe's face closes up and he shifts slightly away from me. 'Bean,' he says. 'Hi. We were just . . .'

'Yes,' I say, inanely. I feel barely able to speak, as though wrenched from a dream.

'How are the puddings?' Bean continues, oblivious to the tension. 'Wasn't that dinner the worst? Effie, you nearly made me *die*. Oh, don't leave, Joe,' she adds, as Joe gets to his feet.

'I'd better leave you to it,' he says, sounding strained. 'Effie, we'll . . . catch up. Will you be around tomorrow?'

'Don't know.'

'Right. Well.' Joe rubs the back of his neck. 'I'll be here for the brunch.'

'Great.' My voice is barely working. 'Well. Maybe see you.'

'Goodnight, Joe,' says Bean cheerfully. 'Thanks for coming along. We all really appreciate it.'

As I watch him walking up the steps, I feel unreal. What was he going to say? What? Halfway up, he pauses and turns back to look straight at me.

'Good luck with your mission, Effie. It was nice to . . .'

He hesitates, and phrases sweep silently through my mind. *It was nice to not-dance. It was nice to feel your presence burning through my skin. It was nice to want you so badly it made me breathless, yet at the same time hate myself. It was nice to feel I was maybe – just maybe – on the brink of understanding you.*

'It was nice to remember,' Joe concludes at last.

'Yes.' I try to sound natural. 'It was.'

He lifts his hand in salute and disappears through the door, and I collapse inwardly. I can't cope with this. I need a new boyfriend. I need a new brain.

'I can't stay long,' says Bean, shoving some cheesecake into her mouth. 'I said I needed some water, but I'll have to go back or it'll look suspicious . . . Are you OK?' She peers at me. 'You look really pale.'

'Fine.' I come to and swig my champagne. 'Fine.'

'So why on earth are you still here? I thought you'd have left ages ago! I *told* you I'd look for your Russian dolls. I think they must be in the window seat.'

'I know.' I give her a feeble smile and take a bite of cheesecake to fortify myself. 'I guess I just couldn't stay away, after all.'

'Well, I'm glad you're here. Although, not the most comfortable place to spend dinner.' She gives a sudden snort of mirth.

'No. And not very comfortable hearing the whole table talking about me.' I grimace at the memory. 'Thanks for sticking up for me, back there.'

'Oh, Effie.' Bean winces. 'I wish you hadn't heard that conversation. Nobody meant anything by it.'

'They did,' I say wryly. 'But it's fine, I probably needed to hear it. Bean, thanks for all this.' I nod at the desserts, feeling a rush of remorse. 'You do too much for me. Far too much.'

'Don't be silly!' says Bean, sounding surprised. 'Anyway, this was Joe's idea.' She sweeps her hand round the plates. 'He's so thoughtful. And he said he'll try to find a specialist for my neighbour's knee. Remember I told you about George and his knee?'

'Er . . . yes,' I say, although I don't.

'Well, Joe said, "Leave it with me," and took my number. He didn't have to do that. You wouldn't think he was a massive celebrity now, would you? He's still really down-to-earth. I mean, he didn't have to come to this party at all, let alone make such an effort. And he talks about you a *lot*,' she adds, raising her eyebrows.

'What do you mean?' I reply, stiffening.

'Just what I say. He thinks about you. He cares about you.'

'He's just being polite.'

'Hmm,' says Bean sardonically. 'Well, you know my opinion—'

'Bean, I saw you crying.' I cut her off, suddenly desperate to change the subject. 'From the window, during the drinks party. You were hiding from everyone. And crying. What's wrong?'

A tremor of shock goes through Bean's face and her eyes slide away and I feel a clutch of fear. I've hit a nerve. What is it? But then, a moment later, her gaze is back on mine, frank and open.

'Oh, *that*,' she says, obviously doing her best to sound relaxed. 'That was just . . . a thing at work. Minor problem. It suddenly got me down. No big deal.'

'A thing at work?' I echo dubiously. 'What thing?'

'Nothing.' She brushes it off. 'I'll tell you another time. It's boring.'

She's almost convincing – but I'm suspicious. Bean never has 'things at work'. Unlike me, she's not a total drama queen and never seems to fall out with anyone, or complain, or get fired for crying into the soup.

But she's clearly not going to tell me what really is the matter. I'll have to bide my time.

'OK, well, there's something else,' I say, changing tack. 'Have you spoken to Gus much today?'

'Gus? Yes, a fair amount. We were together earlier.'

'Did he mention any trouble he's in?'

'*Trouble*?' Bean stares at me. 'What do you mean, trouble?'

Automatically I glance up at the steps, although I'm fairly sure there's no chance of Gus putting in an appearance here.

'When I was hiding in the hall,' I say quietly, 'I heard him on the phone, talking to someone called Josh. Do you know who that is?'

'Never heard of him.'

'Well, Gus sounded super-stressed and he was talking about facing . . .' I lower my voice to a hiss. 'Charges.'

'Charges?' Bean echoes, shocked. 'What kind of charges? Like, criminal charges?'

'I guess.' I shrug helplessly. 'What other kind of charges are there?'

'*Charges*?' Bean says again, in disbelieving tones.

'That's what he said. He talked about the "worst-case

scenario". And he was speaking in a really low voice, as though he didn't want anyone to hear.'

'You're quite the spy tonight, aren't you?' Bean still seems a bit shell-shocked. 'What else did you hear him say?'

'That was it. No, wait, he said something about getting into the press.'

'The *press*?' Bean looks appalled. 'What on earth's going on?'

'I don't know, but we need to talk to him. Urgently. Where is he now, dancing?'

'No, he and Romilly have already gone to bed. She just dragged him off. She was blathering on about needing an early start in the morning.'

'Don't tell me.' I roll my eyes. 'The famous violin teacher. I overheard her droning on about that, too. She can't talk about anything else. Apparently, if you go to this particular teacher, you end up at Oxford *and* Harvard *and* win a Nobel Prize. All at once.'

Bean laughs, half wincing. 'Oh God, she is awful. You know Gus is going to leave her? We did talk about that, earlier on in the garden. We had quite a heart-to-heart. He's had enough.'

'Finally!' I exclaim. 'But why didn't he leave her months ago? All the time he's wasted with her! All the time we've spent trying to be polite to her!'

'I think he's been worrying about hurting her,' says Bean, sighing. 'But the longer they're together, the worse it'll be . . .'

'He shouldn't worry. If Romilly loves him at all, it's because of what he can do for her, not who he is,' I say adamantly. 'She loves being able to boss him around.'

'What does he love about her, do you think?' queries Bean, and for a moment we're both stumped.

'Her body,' I say at last. 'Sorry. But it's true. And she's really into Pilates. She's probably really good in bed. Good core muscles, all that.'

'If he does love her, then maybe he's forgotten what love is supposed to be like,' says Bean, a bit sorrowfully. 'I think you can do that. You put up with this awful toxic version of it and then one day your eyes are opened and you think, "Oh right! I get it! *That*'s what love is supposed to be."'

'On your death bed, when it's too late,' I supply gloomily.

'No!' protests Bean, and I reach out to hug her fondly, because she is just *so* soft-hearted.

'So, what shall we do about Gus?' I return to the issue. 'We can't just leave it.'

'I think we should tackle him,' says Bean, with resolve. 'I'd better show my face again at the party – then we'll make a plan. You can sleep in my room. No one'll know you're there.'

'Thanks. Oh, and I do need the loo,' I add sheepishly.

'Well, don't use my one,' says Bean at once. 'It's—'

'Broken. I know. But I wondered, if I sneak up and use the cloakroom, will you keep guard?'

'Sure. But be quick!'

As we head up the stairs and tiptoe along the back corridor, the music is thundering even more loudly than before. I hurry into the cloakroom, take the opportunity to check my reflection and scowl morosely, because whereas everyone else is glammed up and looking their best, I am definitely not. My hair is dusty and my face is pale with streaks of soot. I could have done with putting on some blusher, I realize, as I view my washed-out skin. And lipstick. If I'd known I was going to see Joe . . .

No. Stop that train of thought right there. I would *not* have put blusher and lipstick on for Joe. So.

I emerge cautiously from the cloakroom and find Bean diligently keeping watch. At the other end of the hall, the door to the sitting room is open, spilling out music, disco lights and silver helium balloons – and I have a sudden craving to see the party.

'I want to have a quick look,' I mutter to Bean. 'Can you stand in the doorway? If anyone tries to come out, distract them.'

Bean rolls her eyes but dutifully goes and stands in the doorway, and I creep up behind her to have a peek. Not that anyone even notices us. The only people left dancing are Krista, Lacey and Dad – and as I watch, my jaw drops slightly. I've never seen them dancing before. Krista is all over Dad, her hands running over his torso. It's *embarrassing*.

'She's an octopus,' I mutter to Bean.

'She is a bit much,' Bean murmurs back resignedly.

I don't know if it's because of the champagne or because I'm all churned up after seeing Joe, but as I watch, my eyes start to blur. I remember Dad dancing with Mimi in this room, so many times. Not ostentatiously, but affectionately, shuffling around, smiling at each other.

Then there was the time we tried to put on a family Burns Night. We all wore kilts and attempted to dance reels and Dad read out Burns poetry in the worst Scottish accent ever, till we were all in stitches. For months, he just had to *look* at me and say, 'D'ye fancy some haggis tonight, Effie, lassie?' and I would collapse in laughter. And of course, we sang 'Auld Lang Syne'. Riotously and joyfully, pumping our arms up and down in unison.

We had all that. We had jokes and games and love and fun. And now we have Krista and her sister in body-con dresses, dancing with Dad like they're all in a music video.

'Remember the Burns Night?' I murmur to Bean, my voice a bit choked. 'Remember Mimi with that tartan ribbon in her hair? Remember Dad addressing the haggis?'

'Of course.' Bean nods – but her eyes aren't filling with tears. She's calmer than me. Bean's always calmer than me.

With a sigh, my eyes move to the window seat, still covered in cables, and I feel a sudden pull of longing. I feel as if I can *see* my Russian dolls inside it. They're calling to me. But there's nothing I can do about it right now.

I gesture at the stairs and Bean nods. Silently, we make it up to her bedroom, then Bean shuts the door and we collapse on her bed.

'Oh my God!' I exclaim. 'What was *that*? Strictly Come Dad-dance?'

'Ssh!' Bean retorts. 'Romilly and Gus are across the landing, remember?'

Oops. I'd forgotten that. I rub my face, trying to rid myself of the image of Krista and Dad, and focus on the task in hand.

'So, how are we going to talk to Gus? We need to get him away from Romilly.'

'I should get back to the party,' says Bean.

'Don't be silly.' I brush her objection aside. 'Dad's having a great time with Krista and Lacey. They're practically having a threesome on the dance floor. They won't notice if you're there or not. Let's text Gus.'

'I already have,' says Bean. 'He's not answering texts or WhatsApps.'

'Damn.' I think for a moment. 'Well, you'll have to get him out of his room. Say it's a family thing.'

I hover by the doorway, listening as Bean ventures over to Gus's door and knocks on it.

'Hi!' I hear her exclaiming as it opens. 'Romilly! Fab pyjamas! Um, can I have a quick word with Gus? Family thing.'

'He's in the bath,' I hear Romilly reply. 'Could this wait until tomorrow?'

'Well . . .'

'I need to get to bed, you see,' Romilly presses on, in that humourless, self-important way she has. 'Molly and Gracie have a very important violin lesson tomorrow, with a rather special teacher. She's extremely exclusive—'

'Yes, I heard about the violin teacher,' Bean cuts her off hastily. 'Amazing! But if you could tell Gus we need to speak to him urgently—'

'*We?*' queries Romilly crisply and I stiffen.

'I mean . . . me,' Bean amends. 'I need to speak to Gus. Just me. On a family matter. Urgently.'

'I'll tell him,' says Romilly, and a moment later the door closes. As Bean walks back towards me she makes silent gestures, and as our door closes safely, she emits a small squeak of frustration.

'She's such a cow!'

'I bet she doesn't say anything to Gus,' I predict. 'She'll say she forgot.'

'Why won't he look at his phone?' moans Bean, checking her screen. 'There's no way to get to him!'

'Yes, there is,' I say, feeling a little spike of triumph, because for the first time in my life, I feel like I have a superpower. 'I'll climb round to Gus's bathroom. I know the way from your attic to his.' I gesture to the trap door above our heads. 'Easy.'

Already I'm unhooking the trap door and letting down the old wooden ladder. We all used to clamber around the attics of Greenoaks when we were children, but no one got to know them as well as I did. There are eaves and trap doors every-where in the house, and on wet days, all I did was explore: crawling through the dusty lofts, balancing on beams, set-ting up secret camps wherever there was room. I know every hidden space; I can trace every route.

'But what will you do then?' protests Bean. 'You can't talk to him in the bath with Romilly in the next room. And if we try and talk in here, she'll only follow him.'

'I'll tell him to meet us in the Bar,' I suggest. 'No one'll ever find us there.'

The Bar is the biggest attic of all, with a tiny round win-dow that lets in a grey stream of light. It has an old chest of drawers in it, in which we used to stash illicit bottles, and it was always our secret meeting place.

'The Bar!' Bean's eyes light up. 'Of course! I haven't been up there for years. We should have a final drink there, any-way. For old times' sake.'

'You get the booze.' I say, already halfway up the loft lad-der. 'I'll get Gus. See you there.'

OK, the attics are smaller than I remember. Or I'm larger. Or older. Or something.

I remember nimbly scampering from beam to beam as a child, effortlessly shimmying past water tanks, dodging odd planks with ease. Not huffing as I crawl along and squeezing through tight gaps with an 'Oof!' sound and cursing as stray nails catch me. As I finally reach Gus's trap door, my back is aching and my lungs are protesting at all the dust.

Still. I've made it.

I sit on my heels, brush a cobweb off my face and survey the square trap door in front of me. All the trap doors in the attics open from both sides – it was a safety measure Mimi insisted on when she realized we were playing up here. Gus's bathroom is directly below me. I can get to him through that trap door in a nano-second. I've done it plenty of times before.

But now I'm having sudden qualms. It was all very well, crawling around and surprising each other when we were children – but we're adults now. What if Romilly's in there? What if they're naked together? What if they're having sex?

I lower my ear to the trap door – but I can't hear anything. I'll just open it a chink, I decide, and peep out. See what's going on.

I let the trap door down a few inches and peer through the gap, trying to make sense of the room below me. There's the bath, full of water, but Gus isn't in it. (Thank God. I don't particularly want to be a peeping Tom when my brother's washing himself, thanks very much.)

I crane my neck and see him sitting on the closed lid of the loo seat, fully dressed. And I'm about to call out a greeting to him, when his expression stops me. He looks wretched. No, worse than that, he looks desperate. Pale with shock.

My eyes fall to the object in his hand. It's a plastic stick. Hang on. Is that . . .

Oh God. *No*.

My heart starts thudding. She can't be. She *can't* be.

As he gets up and walks towards me, I get a full view of the stick. It's definitely a pregnancy test and it reads *Pregnant*. As I stare at the word, taking in its full reality, I feel suddenly leaden – so I can't even imagine how Gus feels. He was about to escape. He had his chance. You stupid, *stupid* brother, I've silently berate him.

'Gus!' Romilly's voice through the bathroom door makes us both jump. 'Have you finished?'

'Nearly!' calls Gus in a strained voice. He looks at the pregnancy test once more, then dumps it in the bin.

OK, this is really not ideal timing. But I have to move fast, before he lets Romilly into the bathroom. I allow him three seconds to gather his thoughts, then open the trap door wider, poke my head down and whisper, as loudly as I dare, 'Gus!'

Gus's head jerks up and as he sees me, his eyes widen.

'What the— *Effie*? What the *hell*?'

'Sssh!' I put a finger to my lips. 'We need to talk. It's important. Meet at the Bar, OK?'

'The Bar?' He stares at me. '*Now?*'

'Yes! Now!'

'Gus, I *really* need to do my face,' Romilly is saying sharply through the bathroom door. 'And we need to have sex. I have a lot of tension right now. I told you that, Gus. I need an orgasm at *least* every other day, and it has been seventy-two hours. I *really* wish you would listen to me on this.'

I'm biting my lip so hard, I'm going to chew it off. Gus meets my eyes, then hastily looks away again.

'Do whatever you have to do,' I say, rolling my eyes. 'But be quick and then come to the Bar. Bean's bringing the drinks. Be there.'

TWELVE

As I crawl through the entrance to the Bar, I'm instantly engulfed by nostalgia. How many hours have I spent in this place? It's almost head height, with a ratty old sofa on the floorboards, threadbare rugs, a chest of drawers with one drawer missing, and a bar made out of an old bookshelf. Propped up on the bar is a neon sign reading *Cocktails* that someone once gave Gus for a birthday present. I switch it on – and to my delight, it still glows. Now we just need some drinks. Where's Bean got to?

I pull out my phone to text her, but then hear a familiar voice, exclaiming, 'For God's sake!'

'Are you OK?' I hurry to the hole in the floorboards and peer down the loft ladder to see Bean standing in the spare room, grappling with a bottle and three glasses.

'How am I supposed to get drinks up there?' she says, looking ruffled. 'How did we *manage* it?'

'Dunno. We just did. Here, hand them to me. Be quick, someone'll see you!'

In a couple of minutes, Bean and the drinks are safely up in the attic, and she's looking around in wonderment.

'I haven't been here for years,' she says, poking at a moth-eaten cushion. 'It's pretty grotty, isn't it?'

'It's not grotty!' I say, feeling hurt on the Bar's behalf. 'It's characterful.'

'Well, I won't miss it.'

'Well, I will.'

'Effie, you miss *everything*,' says Bean with fond exasperation. 'Every brick, every cobweb, every tiny moment we ever had here.'

'They were good moments,' I say mutinously. 'Of course I miss them.'

As Bean's pouring out three glasses of white wine, Gus appears up the ladder, and looks around in apparent stupefaction.

'This place!'

'I know, right?' says Bean. 'I haven't been here for what, a decade? Come and have a drink. We need to talk.' Gus hoists himself up, shuts the trap door, takes a glass of wine and finds a seat on the sofa.

'Cheers.' He raises his glass, takes a sip, then turns to me. 'What are you doing here? I thought you weren't coming. Aren't you on a date with an Olympic athlete?'

'That was all made up,' I admit. 'I've been here all along. But I'm unofficial. *Don't* tell anyone. Only you and Bean know. And Joe.'

'Joe knows?'

'She was under the console table, listening to everything during dinner,' says Bean, and Gus splutters on his wine.

'*What?*'

'It was pretty entertaining,' I say.

176

'But *why*?' says Gus incredulously. 'Why not just come to the party?'

'I didn't want to come to the party,' I say patiently. 'I only came to get my Russian dolls. I was just going to pop in and out. But I ended up staying.'

'*That*'s why you were talking about the Russian dolls.' He looks at Bean. 'You could have warned me. Effs nearly gave me a heart attack when she popped out in the bathroom!'

'It was the only way to get to you!' I say defensively. 'You weren't checking your phone!'

'Well, lucky for you I wasn't in the bath. Or far, far worse.' He makes a terrible, comical face. 'So, have you found your dolls yet?'

'No. Have you seen them, Gus?' I can't help querying, even though I know Bean's already asked him. 'You remember what they look like?'

'Of course I do,' says Gus. 'Who doesn't know Effie's Russian dolls? But I haven't seen them. Not for years. They're not in the window seat, by the way. I had a look, before I went up. Got the DJ to move his stuff. It was empty.'

'Really?' I gaze at him in dismay. 'Are you sure?'

'Pretty sure. Sorry, Effs. But they'll be somewhere, I bet.'

'That's what I said,' chimes in Bean. 'I know I've seen them around the house.'

But where? I think in despair. *Where?*

'Thanks anyway, Gus,' I say, and he nods back. There's not a hint of suspicion in his face; I don't think he has any idea I saw him with that pregnancy test. It's etched on my mind, though, and I can see the strain beneath his relaxed veneer.

'Well, let's have a proper toast. To what?' Gus raises his drink aloft.

'To new beginnings,' suggests Bean, and I have a sudden,

awful fear that she's going to add something about Gus and Romilly splitting up and how marvellous that will be, so I quickly interject:

'To being honest with your siblings.'

'Right,' says Gus, looking confused. 'Who's not being honest?'

'Well, that depends on how you answer the following question.' I fix him with a narrowed gaze. 'What's going on, Gus? I heard you talking about "charges" downstairs, so if you're going to prison, you'd better let us know.'

'Prison?' Gus gives a shocked laugh. 'Don't be daft!'

'What are these charges, then?' says Bean anxiously. 'And why are you going to be in the press?'

'I'm not!' says Gus, looking scandalized. 'For God's sake! Don't you know you shouldn't eavesdrop, Effie?' He frowns at me. 'The charges are nothing to do with me. Not directly,' he adds.

'What, then?' I persist. 'Because you sounded pretty stressed out.'

Gus takes a deep gulp of wine, then breathes out.

'OK,' he says, looking from face to face. 'This goes no further. But Romilly has been accused of bullying by one of her staff and it looks like she might be taken to court. I was talking to a lawyer mate about it. But you don't know any of this, OK?'

Romilly? *Bullying?* Surely not! Not lovely, sweet Romilly. I glance at Bean and quickly away again.

'Oh . . . no!' says Bean, making an unconvincing stab at sounding sympathetic. 'Poor Romilly. That's . . . um . . .'

'Terrible,' I manage. 'I'm sure she didn't do it.'

'Yes,' says Gus. 'Well.'

There's a long, uncomfortable silence, during which all the

things we can't say seem to dance silently in the air between us all.

'Anyway,' says Gus at last, 'that's what that was about.' He raises a glass ironically. 'Happy days.' He swigs his drink, then adds, more seriously, 'Actually, I'm glad you dragged me up here. Seems only right we should have a last drink together.'

'Dad's happy, all right,' I say morosely. 'Have you seen him dancing with Krista?'

'It's quite a sight.' Gus raises his eyes.

'I kept remembering the Burns Night we did.' I turn to Gus, feeling a fresh pang. 'Dancing the reels, remember that? And the haggis? And the poetry?'

'That was fun.' Gus nods reminiscently. 'Dad's *accent*.' He gives a chuckle. 'Good whisky, though. Seems like another life, now.'

'Exactly.' I swallow. 'Another life. That we'll never have again.'

I wasn't really intending to talk about Dad, or the divorce, or any of it. But my hurt has been bubbling up all evening. And now that we're up here, in private, just the three of us, I can't stop it flooding out. 'I heard Dad downstairs earlier, saying he's never been happier.' I look miserably from Gus to Bean. 'He probably can't wait to get shot of this house. In fact, he was probably fed up the entire time he was pretending to enjoy being a family with us and Mimi. You know. All our lives.'

'Effie!' Bean protests. 'Don't say that. Just because Dad's happy now, it doesn't mean he wasn't happy before. And we're still a family. You need to stop talking like this.' She appeals to Gus. 'Tell her.'

'Remember how Humph's mum once called us a self-made family?' I say, ignoring Bean.

'That woman is a crashing snob,' says Gus, rolling his eyes.

'Well, anyway, she was wrong, because we're not self-made. We're self-shattered.'

'Shattered!' Gus raises his eyebrows. 'Well, you're as understated as ever, Effie.'

'Don't *you* feel shattered?'

'I feel shattered for lots of reasons,' says Gus, and takes another deep swig from his wine glass.

'We're a family who can't even manage to sing "Auld Lang Syne",' I say. 'I've never seen anything so painful. It was *awful*.'

'Oh God.' Bean winces. 'I feel bad about that. Poor Dad. But somehow it didn't feel right. You weren't part of it, Effie . . . I don't know . . .'

'It was weird,' pronounces Gus. 'It felt unnatural. Dad's lost his timing. He was faking it.'

'Exactly. That whole dinner was fake.' I look around bleakly. 'Face it, we're not us any more.'

'We just need to think positive!' says Bean, looking at me with troubled eyes. 'I know things are . . . difficult at the moment. But we can mend, we *will* mend.'

'Bean, stop being such a bloody *optimist* all the time!' I erupt in sudden, violent distress. 'Just admit the truth: it'll never be the same again. We'll never have Mimi and Dad dancing again . . . we'll never have Christmas here again.' There's an ache in my throat. 'We'll never have a bonfire on the mound. Or . . . I don't know. Play family charades. Everyone says, "At least you're grown-up," but I come back here and I don't feel grown-up. I feel like . . .'

Tears are suddenly rolling down my cheeks and I brush them away, and for a few moments no one speaks, or even moves.

'I know what you mean, Effs,' says Gus at last, and we

both look at him in surprise. 'I found it tough for a while. After they split. And you can't say anything. You're an adult. Get over it. You're like, *ashamed* of feeling crap.' He swigs his drink. 'You know what? I almost wish they'd done it when we were kids. At least then I wouldn't have Dad bragging to me about his sex drive and expecting me to high-five him.'

'Ew!' I make a face.

'Noo!' says Bean in horror.

'Yup,' Gus says with a wry grimace. 'I mean, great for him and all, but I really don't need to know.'

'It does make you look at marriage differently,' says Bean after a pause. 'And relationships. And all of it.' It's so rare for her to be anything but relentlessly positive that I glance at her, almost with a new respect.

'Agreed.' Gus nods. 'I sometimes think, Jeez, if Dad and Mimi can't make it work, what hope do I ever have of making it work?'

'Exactly!' I say, seizing on the fact that finally my siblings are agreeing with me. 'They were the perfect, happy couple and then, boom, out of the blue, they split up.'

'They *weren't* the perfect, happy couple,' retorts Bean, almost sharply. 'And it wasn't out of the blue. Ephelant, you have to stop seeing everything in such a rose-tinted way. Dad and Mimi were a complicated, mixed-up couple, like any other. They just didn't show it much. But I saw the reality when I was living here. Remember a few years ago, while my house was being done? I was here for six months, on my own with them, and it wasn't all sunshine. It was difficult.'

'What was difficult?' I stare at Bean, because she's never said this before.

'It was just . . .' She looks uncomfortable. 'The atmosphere.'

'Bean . . .' I swallow hard, because I'm venturing on to

new, toxic ground here. 'D'you think Dad was having an affair? Is *that* why they broke up?'

The official timeline of the split is that, first of all, Dad and Mimi agreed to separate. And then after that – very much *after that* – Dad met Krista in a bar. But I've always suspected that this timeline may not be quite accurate. And in my darkest moments, I sometimes wonder: was Dad two-timing Mimi all along? Not just with Krista, but with others?

'No,' says Bean after a pause. 'At least, not that I was aware of. But I think they put on a show whenever we came home, and the problems were there for longer than we realized.'

'I'll tell you something,' says Gus, looking up. 'And I only heard this tonight: Krista targeted Dad.'

'*What?*' I stare at him. 'What do you mean, "targeted"?'

'That sounds sinister!' says Bean, with a nervous laugh.

'I mean, she asked questions about him,' says Gus. '*And* she lied about how they met. The story is that their eyes met across the bar in the Holyhead Arms and Dad bought her a drink and she had no idea who he was, right? Well, bollocks. He'd been drinking in there a couple of times, and she'd spotted him, but she laid low. She asked the landlord all about him. Then she made her move.'

'Who told you that?' demands Bean.

'Mike Woodson.'

'He would know,' I say. Mike Woodson lives in Nutworth, next to the church. He took early retirement years ago, and his main hobby is patronizing all the pubs and hotel bars in the neighbourhood.

'He collared me at the cocktail reception and warned me about her. He reckons Dad's made a killing this year and he thinks Krista's got her eye on it. To quote Mike exactly:

"Make sure the new girlfriend doesn't nab all the cash and do a runner."'

'Really?' Bean stares at Gus.

'I *knew* it.' I look around, suddenly alert, feeling like a detective. 'I *knew* it. And did you know Krista wants to open a restaurant in Portugal? What if she's planning to fleece him? She's already got a socking great diamond out of him. What's that worth? Has anyone even checked if she's got a criminal record?'

'Effie!' exclaims Bean, half laughing. 'A *criminal record*?'

'Think about it! No wonder she's been trying to stop us all talking to him! It's all part of the plan! I think one of us needs to speak to Dad about it. Obviously not me,' I add.

'And say what?' Bean looks appalled. 'We'll cause huge damage if we start hurling unfounded accusations around. This family is in enough trouble already. We need to be healing, not finding new wounds!'

I roll my eyes, because I might have known Bean would react like that.

'Gus?' I turn to him.

'I'm not saying anything,' Gus says firmly. 'Bean's right, this is all hearsay. Opening a restaurant in Portugal isn't actually against the law, you know.'

'Also, Krista wants a commitment ceremony,' points out Bean. 'So why would she do a runner?'

Yet again I feel a surge of frustration at my siblings, who may be older but are *not* necessarily wiser.

'What if Krista spends all Dad's money and makes him wear a poncho and be a waiter in her restaurant?' I throw at them.

'A *poncho*?' Gus stares at me.

'And then she dumps him and he ends up destitute and miserable in Portugal? What will you say *then*?'

'I'll say, "Effie, you were right,"' says Bean patiently.

'I'll say, "Did *not* see that poncho coming,"' chimes in Gus.

'Ha ha,' I say. 'Hilarious.'

'But it's not going to happen,' Bean continues, reaching for the wine bottle and knocking over a crate. 'I honestly think Dad can look after himself—'

'Krista, love, I think you've got mice!' Lacey's distant voice comes from below us and all three of us freeze, exchanging looks of consternation.

'Did you see one?' Krista's equally distant voice replies.

'No, but I heard a right old scuffle just now. Maybe it's rats.'

'Rats!' Krista's voice is getting louder, and there's the clattering sound of approaching heels. 'That's all this bleeding place needs.'

'Well, not your problem any more, is it?'

All of a sudden, the heels stop dead, and I hear Krista saying, 'You know what, Lacey, you're right. I can't be arsed. The rats can eat their hearts out, for all I care.'

'This the chandelier you were talking about?' says Lacey. 'I'd say nearer four grand.'

'Really?'

'Oh yeah, for sure. Four, four and a half. And that mirror, two.'

'Two!' Krista sounds impressed.

Bean and Gus are exchanging wide-eyed glances, and I feel a sudden burning inside my chest. I always promised Dad I wouldn't reveal what happened that awful day. But I can't keep quiet any longer.

'I wouldn't give you five quid for it,' says Krista. 'Just goes to show.' There's a skittering sound on the floorboards below, followed by Bambi's distinctive yapping. 'Hello, baby boy,' she croons. 'Hello, my baybeee . . . Hey, Lace. Let's go and make ourselves vodka tonics.'

'Nice one,' says Lacey approvingly, and they move away. For a beat, none of us moves, then we all exhale.

'Oh my *God*,' breathes Bean. 'What was *that*?'

'I *told* you!' I say, agitation making my voice tremble. 'She's all about money! And you want to know something?' I lower my voice. 'I caught her taking photos of the furniture, ages ago. But when I told Dad, he got all defensive and took Krista's side. He said I mustn't tell you because it would prejudice you against her. So I didn't. But now . . .' I break off. 'You *see*?'

'I had no idea!' says Bean, looking appalled.

'Well. That's what happened.' I swallow hard, my face hot. It's been quite a stress keeping that secret all this time, I suddenly realize.

I can see Bean's brain ticking over and suddenly, with a confused frown, she bursts out, 'OK, I know what I was going to ask. Did Krista really send you an email saying, "Effie, my love, you must come to the party, you'll regret staying away"?'

'Of course not!' I roll my eyes. 'That was more of her bullshit.'

'I thought so! But Dad obviously believed her!' Bean stares at me in consternation. 'Effie, this is really messed up. He needs to know. I'm going to tell him.'

'Bean, don't.' I grab her arm. 'Don't. You do everything for me. You're always the go-between. You always take on the emotional load. And you've got enough on your plate with your . . .' I hesitate. 'Work problems. I'll sort things out myself.'

'I need to go,' says Gus reluctantly, putting his glass down. 'But this has been great. Really.'

'You can't *go*!' I exclaim. 'What are we going to do about Krista and the furniture and all that?'

'OK,' says Gus. 'If anyone sees Krista and Lacey manhandling a chandelier out of the front door, text the others, code word *glassware*. Repeat, *glassware*. Otherwise, regroup tomorrow?' He lifts a hand in farewell and pulls up the trap door.

'Wait, Gus,' says Bean, with sudden fervour. 'Before you leave.' She grabs one of his hands and one of mine, then pulls them together. 'We're not broken. We're *not*.'

For a few silent moments we look at each other over our clasped hands. My brother. My sister. These familiar, beloved faces. Grown-up now . . . but in my head, never grown-up. Always children, knocking around the attic, wondering how to make life work.

'Yup, well,' says Gus at last, breaking the spell. 'Goodnight, all. See you for another fun day of carnage tomorrow. Aren't family reunions the best?'

THIRTEEN

Getting ready for bed in Bean's room is like going back in time. We always used to be made to share when there were guests, and we used to squabble over everything. What time to turn the light out. Who was shuffling their duvet 'too loudly'. Who was being 'really annoying'. (Probably me, to be fair.)

But now we're all grown-up and polite and civilized. Bean even finds me a fresh toothbrush in an airline pouch, and a sample pack of moisturizer. I wander round the room in an old pair of her pyjamas, trailing my hand fondly over her Peter Rabbit furniture. The two wooden beds with their hand-painted rabbits on the bedheads. The wardrobe, decorated with trailing leaves. The dressing table with its dinky little drawer handles shaped like carrots.

'Where did this furniture even come from?' I say, opening the glass-fronted cabinet to examine Bean's collection of pottery nestling on leaf-decorated shelves. 'It's incredible.'

'There was a local furniture maker who built bespoke

pieces,' she says, brushing her hair. 'He's died now. Apparently it was Mum's idea to put carrots on the dressing-table drawers.'

'I never knew that,' I say after a pause. I'm feeling that slightly weird sensation of being out of the loop that I always do when people speak about Alison. (I can't think of her as Mum.)

'Do you want to read or anything?' Bean asks politely.

'No, I'm whacked. Let's just go to sleep.'

We both get into bed and Bean turns off the lamp, and I stare up into the darkness. I did *not* expect to be spending another night under this roof. It's surreal.

Without thinking, I reach out for my Russian dolls to soothe myself – then, with a sinking feeling, remember. And I don't even know where to look for them.

What if I can't—

No. Don't think that. I *will* find them. I just have to persevere.

To distract myself, I count off the members of the family, which is another thing I did as a child. I'd say goodnight to them in my mind, as if to reassure myself that everyone was OK. Dad . . . Gus . . . Bean . . . Then, as I reach Mimi, I can't help heaving a huge sigh.

'You OK?' says Bean through the darkness.

'Just thinking about . . . things.'

'Hmm.' Bean's quiet for a moment, then she says, gently, 'Ephelant, you keep saying the family's broken. But look at us. I'm here. You're here. Gus is here.'

'I know.' I stare up through the darkness. 'It's not the same, though, is it? We don't talk like we used to. Dad's all weird and false. And now we won't even have Greenoaks to gather at. We're all just going to . . . drift apart.'

'No, we're not,' says Bean stoutly. 'We'll still gather. We'll just do it somewhere else.'

'Krista doesn't want to gather with us. She wants to gather Dad off to Portugal.'

'Well, if he wants to go and he'll be happy there, then we need to respect that,' says Bean. 'Maybe it'll be a fun new chapter in all our lives. We can visit them. Go to the beach!'

'Maybe,' I say, although the idea of visiting the beach with Krista makes me want to hurl.

There's silence for a bit, then Bean takes a deep breath.

'Effie, I've been reading,' she says. 'You know it's a form of grief? We're called ACOD. Adult children of divorce. Apparently, it's really common, there are so many silver splitters. I even found . . . a group,' she adds hesitantly. 'We could go, maybe.'

A *group*, I think, in silent disdain. In a church hall with bad biscuits. Sounds super-fun.

'Maybe,' I say again, trying not to sound too discouraging.

'I think it hit you the hardest.' Bean's voice rises softly into the room again. 'Maybe because you're the youngest. Or maybe because you never knew Mum. Mimi *is* your mum.'

'I miss Mimi,' I say, my throat suddenly blocked as I utter her name. 'We're all here, but she isn't.'

'I know. It's strange.'

'It feels so empty without her.' I blink, my eyes hot as I remember Mimi in the garden, humming around the kitchen, sketching, laughing, always finding something life-enhancing. 'She was the heart of our family. She was the heart of everything. And I just wish—'

'Ephelant, don't,' Bean cuts me off, sounding suddenly troubled. 'Don't do that. Stop wishing.'

'*What*?' I raise myself on my elbow in slight shock.

189

'All you keep saying is you wish Dad and Mimi hadn't split up. But they did. And the house is going. We can't have what we had.'

'I know,' I say, feeling prickly. 'I *know* that.'

'But you talk as though it's still an option. As though we can go back in time and magically stop it happening.'

I open my mouth to contradict her, then stop myself. Because now she says it, maybe I do constantly flash back to that bombshell day in the kitchen, playing it out a different way.

'You just have to accept it,' says Bean, sounding sad. 'I know it's hard. When Hal dumped me, all I wanted was Hal. I wanted him so badly, I thought the universe must give him to me. It *must*.' Her voice trembles. 'But it didn't. I couldn't have him. I had to have something different. I had to be happy with something different. Otherwise, what am I going to do, just cry my whole life?' She sits up in bed, a ray of moonlight making her eyes glitter. 'What are *you* going to do, cry your whole life?'

I'm silent, feeling chastened. I hadn't thought of it like that. And yet again, I feel a swell of love for Bean, who is so stoical and was dealt such a crap hand.

'Bean, I heard you talking to Gus, earlier,' I say tentatively. 'How are . . . things? Like . . . love-life things?'

'Actually,' says Bean after a long pause, 'I've been seeing someone.'

'Oh my God, Bean!' I say in excitement. 'That's great! Why didn't you *tell* me?'

'I'm sorry. I've been meaning to tell you. But after what happened with Hal, I wanted to just see how it went, first.'

'Of course,' I say understandingly. 'And . . . how is it going?'

'It's all a bit up in the air.' Bean's voice is tense; she's turned her face away. 'Things are . . . complicated.'

I feel a clench of dismay. I don't want 'complicated' for Bean, I want 'happy and straightforward'.

'Is he . . .' I swallow nervously. 'Is he married?'

'No. He's not married. But . . .' Suddenly she gulps. 'Look, can we stop? I don't want to talk about it. I just . . .' Her voice wobbles perilously. 'I just . . .'

I feel a shaft of horror as I hear a sudden sob. She's crying. I've made her cry. *This* is what she was weeping about in the garden.

'Bean!' I say, leaping out of bed and wrapping an arm fiercely around her. 'Oh God, sorry, I didn't mean . . .'

'I'm fine.' She shudders with another huge sob, then wipes her face. 'I'm really fine. Go back to bed. It's a million o'clock and I've got this bloody brunch tomorrow.'

'But . . .'

'We'll talk about it another time. Maybe.'

'God, we're really cracking this relationship business, aren't we?' I say as I get back into bed, trying to cheer her up. 'We should start a self-help podcast.'

'Yup,' says Bean shakily. 'We're champions at love. Although at least you've got your philanthropist Olympic athlete.'

'Oh, didn't I tell you?' I deadpan. 'He chucked me.'

Bean starts to laugh, half choking. 'Oh, shame.'

'Yes, he said I wasn't very present in the relationship. He said he had more rapport with his javelin,' I add, and Bean splutters again. 'He said I didn't do it to his pole. Vault. He said it was a real hurdle.'

'I have to go to sleep,' says Bean. 'Seriously. Don't make me laugh any more.'

'Knock knock,' I say at once.

'Stop!'

'There was a young girl from Nantucket—'

'Effie!'

Still smiling, I look up into the darkness again. And as I listen to Bean's breathing grow calmer, I try to guess what 'complicated' might mean. Maybe he has an ex-wife. Maybe he lives abroad. Maybe he's in jail for a crime he didn't commit—

'Effie?' Bean's hesitant voice breaks my train of thought. 'There's something else I need to say, before I fall asleep. I . . . I don't think I've done you any favours. And I'm sorry.'

'What?' I say, taken aback. 'What are you talking about?'

'I've always tried to shield you from stuff,' she carries on. 'We all have. When you were little, we told you white lies. Father Christmas. The tooth fairy. The time Gus shoplifted.'

'Gus *shoplifted*?' I echo, aghast.

'It was for a bet,' says Bean, a little impatiently. 'He was suspended, big serious talk, he never did it again, blah blah. But we didn't tell you, because you wouldn't have understood. Anyway . . . ' She pauses. 'The point is, I guess I never got out of the habit of wanting to protect you.'

'You don't have to protect me any more,' I say at once. 'I'm an adult.'

'Exactly. But it's a hard habit to kick. And then, you and Mimi have this amazing bond. I've never wanted to spoil that.'

'What are you driving at?' I say uncertainly.

'There are . . . things I haven't told you,' she says, and the air in the room seems to grow thick.

'What things?' I falter.

'About Mimi. And Dad.'

'What about Mimi and Dad?' I say in a tiny voice.

'I love them both,' Bean says, after a pause. 'But when I was living here, it wasn't great. Mimi was quite intolerant. Quite judgy. Almost . . . mean.'

'*Mean?*' I echo, dumbfounded. '*Mean?* But Mimi's lovely to everybody! The whole world says that,' I remind Bean. 'They say, "Mimi's so lovely." '

'I know they do. But she wasn't where Dad was concerned.' Bean sighs. 'I couldn't believe it either, at first. She seemed to have the opposite of a blindspot. It was a glaring, kind of magnified spotlight on Dad, following him around the house, and nothing she saw pleased her. She picked him up on everything. The way he ate, the way he sat down, the way he drank his tea . . . Everything was wrong.'

'They always teased each other,' I say uncertainly.

'Maybe it started off as teasing, but it ended up . . .' Bean sighs. 'Snippy. It was like, Mimi didn't want Dad to occupy a Dad-shaped space in the world any more. She wanted him to be different. Or not there. And then Dad reacted by going all silent and sullen. He would ignore Mimi, which would drive her mad. It drove me mad, too. I would be thinking, "Just *answer* her, for God's sake!" '

'Silent?' I'm freshly dumbfounded. 'Sullen? *Dad?*'

'I know. You can't even imagine. And I used to hear them having a go at each other at the bottom of the garden, where they thought I couldn't hear. The pair of them were . . . let's just say, they weren't their best selves. Either of them.' Bean exhales. 'I didn't tell you because it was so grim. But now I think I should have done. Then you wouldn't have been so shocked when they split up.'

I'm quiet for a while, digesting Bean's story. Try as I might, I can't imagine it. Mimi is about warmth and comfort and nurture, not snippiness. And Dad is about charm and charisma. How could he be sullen?

'Dad's not perfect,' says Bean, as though reading my mind, 'and nor is Mimi, and they weren't in a constant state of bliss.

I'm sure they only behaved like that because they were . . . unhappy.'

The word *unhappy* lodges, heavy, in my heart.

'So, what, they were unhappy all the way along?' I retort. 'They never loved each other?' I'm feeling a miserable clench-ing inside, because isn't this what I've been saying? That our entire childhood was a fake?

'No!' says Bean at once. 'I don't believe that. I think it was only recently that things got difficult. But they didn't want to admit it.' She sighs. 'Maybe they should have been more open with us. Then you wouldn't keep putting them on such a pedestal.'

'I don't put them on a pedestal!' I protest, and Bean laughs.

'Oh, Effie, of course you do. It's endearing. But it makes it tougher for you. You see it as "We had heaven, and then, boom, it exploded into smithereens." Well, that's not right. It wasn't heaven. But nor is it smithereens,' she adds after a pause. 'It's just . . . difficult.'

'That's an understatement,' I say, staring into the darkness.

'I do get it, Ephelant,' says Bean gently. 'I do. I miss Mimi being here and so does Gus. It really hit me on Dad's last birthday. Krista had already decorated the tree, remember?'

'*Yes,*' I say with feeling – because how could I not? We all arrived for tree-decorating day, but the tree was already covered in brand-new ornaments which Krista had ordered, and we all had to admire them.

'Then she brought out that grand chocolate cake with the swirls, remember?' Bean continues. 'And I kept thinking, "But Mimi always makes him carrot cake." It's such a tiny thing, but I got really upset.'

'Did you?' I turn to her, feeling a swell of gratitude. 'You know, that makes me feel better. Realizing I'm not the only one.'

'You're not the only one,' says Bean. 'You're really not.'

'And by the way, that chocolate cake was *vile*.'

'*Awful*,' agrees Bean emphatically.

'Hideous.'

'Where did she even buy it? It was the worst quality chocolate. It was like plastic.'

'Yes, but you can't see the taste on Instagram, can you?'

'Of course!' Bean exclaims. '*That*'s why she got it. To show off on Instagram.'

'Bean, you're bitching about Krista!' I exclaim, in sudden, joyful realization.

It's so rare to hear Bean bitch, even about Krista, that I can't help smiling. We need to do more of this. Far more. (Except I won't call it 'bitching'. I'll call it 'sharing'. That can be our group. I'll even buy biscuits.)

'Oh God,' says Bean, sounding stricken. 'Effie, I'm *sorry* I've been so . . .'

'Diplomatic,' I supply.

'On the fence,' she corrects me. 'I was trying to give Krista the benefit of the doubt. Keep the family talking. I thought, *Well, Dad's chosen her, I need to respect that.* But now, after what you told me, I don't trust her an inch.'

'I've *never* trusted her,' I say darkly, just to make the point that I'm a better judge of character than she is.

Bean's breathing is growing heavier and I can tell she's drifting off, but I can't sleep yet. I'm too wired. I stare up into the darkness, my eyes wide open, trying to process this whole weird, unexpected evening. I came here for my Russian dolls. They were my only priority. That was all I wanted from this house. But I haven't found them and instead I'm tangled up in my family and all its problems.

My mind roams over all my family members. All keeping

secrets. From each other or from the world. Mimi and Dad . . . Krista and Dad . . . Gus and Romilly . . . Bean . . . Everyone's hiding something from someone.

And then, of course, there's Joe. I feel a painful twinge as memories from this evening stream into my brain: Joe's expression when he spotted me through the rose bush; Joe gazing at me in the cellar. He was about to explain himself, I'm sure of it. To tell me something. But what? *What?*

I heave another great sigh and turn on to my side, burrowing my head into the pillow, feeling a sudden wave of exhaustion. I can't think about it.

I need to focus on my goal again, I resolve sleepily. I'll search for my dolls first thing. They *must* be somewhere. In an attic? In the tree house, maybe? I just need to think . . .

Anyway. At least I got some cheesecake.

FOURTEEN

I wake up the next morning feeling a strange, unfamiliar sensation. I lie still for a moment, trying to work it out . . . then it hits me. I think it's lightness. I feel lighter. Softer. Easier.

It's nice. It's a relief.

Life has felt pretty wretched for a while, I admit to myself, staring up at Bean's ceiling. Maybe Bean's right: the divorce did hit me harder than the others. And maybe Dad's right, too: I have been trapped. Trapped in a grey, miserable place. But maybe, at last, things are starting to shift? Just a little bit?

I don't know how else to explain the way I feel. Nothing's changed tangibly since last night. All the problems I had then, I have now. But somehow they seem . . . different. More manageable. More in proportion.

Even when the vivid cascade of divorce memories hits me – as it always does in the morning, like a gruesome feature film, starting with that awful Christmastime announcement – it doesn't feel so visceral. I feel like I'm watching it with wry, almost detached sadness.

Nor do I have my usual, wrenching, *if only* feeling. Bean's right: I can't turn back time. I can't wish it all away.

The world is as it is. And I have to move on within it. Which will be good. It will be *good*. I take a deep breath, feeling my whole body galvanize itself. I just need to be myself: Effie Talbot. Or maybe a new, improved Effie Talbot. Not a child crying about her parents any more. Not the little one. But maybe the one who steps up to the plate. Who takes on responsibility.

My eyes slide over to Bean, still asleep in a hump under her duvet, and on impulse I get out my phone. I'm going to order her some vitamins. There. Already, I'm taking action.

I log on to a healthstore website and am immediately baffled by the choice. What vitamins do people need, anyway? What's 'chelated'? What's the difference between magnesium citrate and magnesium taurate?

I'll ask Bean.

No, wait, don't be stupid, I can't ask Bean.

I scroll a bit more, then decide on a supplement called Super Skin Radiance. You can't go wrong with Super Skin Radiance, can you? I pay for my purchase, feeling a glow of satisfaction, then look around Bean's room to see how else I can help her. Maybe I'll tidy up a bit. There's a little suitcase on the floor, which Bean must have brought for the weekend, and some clothes have spilled out of it. I'll sort those.

Silently I get out of bed and start folding up clothes. I'll put them into her wardrobe, I decide. But I'm just carefully tiptoeing over to it when my foot catches on the open case and I crash on to her bed.

'Ow!' She turns, still half-asleep.

'Sorry!' I whisper. 'Didn't mean to wake you. Go back to sleep.'

'What are you *doing*?' she says blearily.

'Helping you. Tidying.'

'Well, *don't*,' she says venomously and turns over, pulling her duvet around her.

OK, maybe I'll put the tidying on hold for now. I'll return to my original plan for this morning: finding my Russian dolls. I reach for my clothes, then recoil and decide to borrow some clean ones of Bean's. As I search in her wardrobe, making only the tiniest of rattling noises, she opens her eyes and gives me a resentful stare.

'What are you doing?'

'I'm going to look for my dolls,' I whisper, pulling on a pair of her jeans. 'Ssh. Go back to sleep.'

'What if you bump into Dad or Krista? Or Lacey? She's sleeping in the turret room, by the way.'

'Yes, I guessed she would be.' I nod. 'And I won't bump into anyone. I'm going round the attics. I might have hidden them up there and forgotten.'

'OK, well, good luck.' Bean turns over as I pull down the loft ladder. 'Don't get caught.'

Get caught? Not a chance. As I mount the ladder, I feel springy and determined. I roam around each attic in turn, peering into cases and into dark corners and under old, broken chairs. And all the time, my mind is on Joe. I just can't help thinking about him.

Last night was a revelation. I always knew Joe kept a part of himself tucked away, protected from outside scrutiny. But I never realized there was an anxious core to him. I'm still slightly stunned by this news.

How many versions of him are there? I find myself wondering. How many Russian dolls are locked away inside the Doctor of Hearts? What does he still have hidden? And *what* was he about to tell me last night?

By now, my arms and legs are starting to ache with all the crawling and climbing. My bouncy zeal is fading. I kick aside a pile of old medicine packets and climb over a cross-beam, wiping a cobweb off my head. By now, I'm fairly sure my dolls aren't in the attics, but I feel kind of superstitious. I'll still check each one, just in case. Only I need to go carefully now, because I'm coming into the attic above Dad's room.

Dad and Krista's room, I should say. Except I still haven't quite got my head round that concept. *Dad and Krista's room . . . Dad and Krista's future in Portugal, running a Mexican restaurant*. None of it feels real.

I head cautiously into the dusty space, then stop dead. The trap door down to their room is open, and I pause nervously. Are they in the room? I edge towards it. The area below seems empty and silent. I'll just have a quick scout about while the going's good—

'Ow!' Before I can think straight, I've tripped over a metal pipe, which seemed to loom up in my path out of nowhere. (Or maybe I wasn't concentrating.) As I hurtle helplessly towards the trap door, I feel both winded with shock and strangely calm. So, this is it. My life ends here. I'm going to fall through the gap and tumble down ten feet and break my neck and I'll *never* know what Joe was going to tell me—

'Thank *God!*' With a gasp, I manage to break my fall, grabbing on to the frame of the trap door just in time. I scrabble, trying to find firmer ground . . . but I'm stuck. My shoelace has snagged on something. I'm caught in a crouching position, perilously situated right above the open trap door, with only a wooden ladder to catch me if I fall. Gripping on for dear life, I joggle my foot, trying to free it, then stiffen as I hear voices.

Dad. Krista. *Shit*.

'Here we are,' Dad is saying as he ushers Krista into the room. They're both wearing silky dressing gowns and holding glasses of what looks like Buck's Fizz. Is that what they have for breakfast every day? Or are they just carrying on with their all-night party?

Either way, I need to get out of here. Urgently. But before I can move a muscle, Dad turns to Krista, his face flushed, and declaims, 'I am Julio, a rich Colombian drugs baron.' He waggles his eyebrows. 'Enchanted to meet you, pretty lady.'

I freeze in icy horror. Why is Dad calling himself Julio? And *what* is that terrible accent?

'Julio!' Krista simpers at him. 'How lovely to meet you! I am called Greta. Tell me how rich you are,' she adds breathily. 'I love a wealthy man.'

Oh my *God*. I'm trapped above my dad and his girlfriend embarking on some dodgy role play. It's like a bad dream. I *have* to escape. Silently, frantically, I tug my foot again – but I'm stuck.

'I have many thousands of money in the bank,' says Dad with a sexy swagger.

'Only thousands?' Krista bats her eyelashes at him.

'I have . . . six hundred billion pounds in the bank,' Dad hastily amends.

'Tony!' snaps Krista, coming out of character. 'That's too much! It's not believable! Even Jeff Bezos doesn't have six hundred billion pounds! It needs to be *believable*!'

Honestly, she's quite fussy, Krista. What's wrong with six hundred billion pounds?

'I have 2.4 billion pounds in the bank,' ventures Dad warily. 'And a yacht!'

'A yacht!' Krista's breathy voice returns. 'And such delicious champagne, Julio. They don't let us drink at the nunnery.'

The *nunnery*? Is she kidding?

Oh God, I mustn't laugh—

'Krista!' Lacey's nasal voice penetrates the room. 'Fashion emergency! Can you come here a sec, love?'

Both Dad and Krista start, and I send silent, fervent messages of gratitude to Lacey.

'Bloody hell!' says Krista, moving away from Dad, her voice normal again. 'It's Piccadilly Circus in here! Coming!' she calls back, then makes one last seductive shimmy towards Dad. 'Hold that thought, Tone. I mean, *Julio*.'

I'm fervently praying they'll both leave, but to my dismay, Dad lingers, directly below me. My legs and arms are juddering by now, but I manage to stay noiseless, breathing in tiny gulps of air.

As I gaze down, still desperately trying to free my foot, I notice the hair thinning on Dad's head. He doesn't look like Julio the drugs baron, or even Tony Talbot, the genial host. He looks tired. The book I made him, *A Boy from Layton-on-Sea*, is propped up on the mantelpiece, and I feel a wash of nostalgia as I see it. I remember Dad's face bursting with pleasure when he first saw it. I felt at that moment I really *knew* Dad. I'd really *got* him.

The atmosphere feels charged with memories as I struggle silently to get my foot free. It's just Dad and me. When was it last just Dad and me in a room together?

And although I'm really not a woo-woo person, I find myself thinking, Can't Dad sense I'm here? Can't he feel my presence, hovering above him like some sort of deranged angel?

It's me, Effie! I mentally cry out. *Your daughter! I'm here! Right above you!*

Almost as though he can hear me, Dad tilts his head, and I watch, transfixed. Slowly he gets out his phone from his dressing-gown pocket, hesitates, then summons his Contacts list. He taps on a name, and my heart jolts as I see it. *Effie*. Oh my God.

Suddenly my eyes are hot. I didn't actually expect . . .

Dad types *Dear Effie*, then stops. My heart is thudding feverishly as I watch, waiting for him to continue. What's he going to write? Something bland and impersonal? Or something real? About things that matter?

As I watch his hands hover over the screen, a desperate hope swells in me. Is he finally going to start the conversation I've been craving all this time? Are we finally going to *talk*?

By now my eyes are brimming, and I feel a sudden flash of panic as I realize I can't prevent my tears from falling down. Oh God. Dad will see the drips . . . he'll look up . . . Do *not* cry, Effie, I instruct myself strictly. Do *not*.

But it's too late. As though in slow motion, I feel a tear fall and watch it hit the carpet – just as Dad's phone jangles. The sound seems to jolt him out of the spell, back to life. He closes down the text without saving it. Then he accepts the call, his demeanour transformed. Tony Talbot is back in the room.

'Hello there! Well, thanks! Yes, we thought it was a terrific send-off for the old place . . .'

He strides out of the room, and I release the air I've been holding in my lungs. I yank my foot so hard my shoelace snaps, and I fall back, landing with a thud on the safety of the attic floor. I lie there for a while, feeling a bit numb.

After a while, I check my phone. But there's nothing from Dad. No texts, no emails, no WhatsApps.

I mean, whatever. Doesn't matter. I was stupid to think . . . What *did* I think, anyway? That he would write, *Effie darling, we all miss you and wish you were here*? He was probably writing about postal redirection again. That's where we are, now.

At last I get up, staggering slightly after my athletic feat. I feel wrung out. And I suddenly want to be with someone who *does* talk to me about things that matter. My sister, who's unhappy and maybe needs my help, even if she doesn't realize it. I'm going to find Bean.

'Let's go for a walk,' I say, as I clamber back down into Bean's room. 'It's still early. It can't be time for brunch yet.'

I'm not having a conversation here. This house is a leaky, creaky sieve. You can't share secrets without worrying that someone's overheard you.

'A walk?' Bean peers at me from under her duvet, looking dazed.

'I want to say goodbye to the garden,' I improvise. 'I need you as lookout. And it'll wake you up. Come on!'

It takes half an hour to cajole Bean out of bed and into some clothes, but at last we're outside. No one was around, so we managed to dodge downstairs and out of the front door without incident. We get to the bottom of the garden – Bean walking sedately on the lawn, me dashing from shrub to shrub – then step through the gate into the field below, where I breathe out. As we walk in step through the long grass, my spirits start edging upwards. It's a warm day; the sky is blue and hazy. Grasshoppers are already chirruping around us and wildflowers are shimmering between the grasses.

'Bean,' I say eventually. 'I know you think I can't help, but I can.'

'What do you mean?' Bean seems puzzled. 'Help with what?'

'You cried yesterday.' I touch her arm gently. 'Twice. And I know you said you didn't want to talk about it—'

'That's because I don't,' Bean cuts me off. 'I know you want to help, but you can't. So. Thanks, Effie, but let's leave it. Shall we sit down?'

Feeling deflated, I sit down in the long grass, breathing in the summery scents all around. Idly I watch a ladybird walk up a blade of grass, fall down, then start again on the other side. Maybe I should be inspired by that. Try a different tack.

'But Bean, you might feel *better* if you talk to someone,' I venture.

'I won't,' she says, looking at the sky.

'But you don't know until you try.'

'I do know.'

Honestly! And people say I'm the obstinate one.

'OK,' I say. 'Well, I'm here for you, any time you change your mind.' I hunch my arms round my legs, staring across the field, watching a flock of birds take off, all in perfect sync, like a functional family that *isn't* keeping a zillion secrets. 'Hey, you want to hear some more marvellous news? Only, I'm not supposed to know.'

'Go on, then.'

'Romilly's pregnant.'

'*What?*' Bean jolts so hard she almost levitates. 'Is she . . . How do you know? Did she tell you?'

'Are you serious?' I roll my eyes. 'You think Romilly and I have girly chats? No, I saw it through the trap door, last night. Gus found the test in the bin in their bathroom. He looked—'

I break off, because the expression on Gus's face will

always haunt me, but I can't convey it in words. It was too private, too painful. I shouldn't have seen it.

'Shocked,' I resume at last. 'He looked pretty shocked. I don't know if he's told Romilly he knows yet.' I look at Bean for a reaction, but she doesn't seem able to speak. 'I mean, they'll work it out,' I add reassuringly. 'Don't worry, Bean.'

'Did he . . .' She swallows, licking her dry lips. 'Was there . . . more than one test?'

'More than one test?' I say, confused. 'Don't think so. I could see the bin and it was empty. What, you think Romilly would take ten tests? You're probably right.' I give a sudden laugh. 'God, that would be *so* her—'

'It's me.' Bean's voice cuts me off.

For an instant the horizon seems to wobble and I grasp for the ground, because—

Bean?

Bean?

'I used their bathroom yesterday,' she's saying, her voice tiny, her gaze fixed ahead. 'My loo's . . . you know . . .'

'Broken,' I supply on auto-pilot.

'Exactly. I just chucked the stick in the bin afterwards. I was in such a state, I didn't think . . . I didn't *think* . . . I'm such a moron, I should have wrapped it up and put it in the kitchen bin . . .' She clasps her head in self-reproach and I come to life.

'Bean, stop! Where you threw the test isn't the . . . Bean . . . oh my *God*.' I throw my arms round her and squeeze hard. Bean! A baby! I don't know how . . . or who . . . but is that relevant? Does that matter?

Actually, it kind of matters.

'How?' I lift my head. 'I mean, who? Is this the guy you were telling me about?'

'Ye-es.' Bean's voice judders and once again she can't quite speak. 'He's . . . he's . . .' She fumbles in her pocket, pulls out her phone and finds a picture of a friendly-looking guy. Dark curls, warm brown eyes, waterproof jacket. Mutely she scrolls through photos of her beaming with him in cafés and by the river. On a walk. A couple.

'He looks . . . great?' I say tentatively, because I don't know how this story goes.

'He is. He's . . .' Bean swallows. 'But we've only been together for a few weeks, and now this has happened. I only found out yesterday. I was in total shock.'

'Is that why you were crying in the garden?' I venture and she nods silently. 'Oh, Bean.' I clutch her arm desperately. 'Whatever you want to do . . .'

'Oh, I'm having the baby,' she says with resolve. 'I'm having it. But . . .' She glances down at her phone.

'Does he know?' I ask warily.

'Yes. I was in such a panic, I couldn't wait a moment. So I called him . . .' Again she can't speak.

'What did he say?' I ask, ready to swipe this guy if he did the wrong thing.

'He's honest.' Bean wipes her nose. 'He takes his time. He's not like Hal. He's said he'll support me, whatever happens, but he wants to think about . . . That whatever we do, he'll do one hundred per cent. He already has a child,' she adds. 'So he's already . . . But he's not married,' she adds hastily. 'He's divorced. He's funny, and . . . he can cook,' she adds randomly. 'He's an architect. He draws!' She scrolls ahead to a sketch of a tree. 'He did this. And this one . . . and this one . . .'

'Amazing,' I say, looking not at the sketches but at the love blossoming in her eyes.

'But a baby is . . .' She seems unable to contemplate finishing that sentence. 'It's just . . . It wasn't meant to . . .'

She breaks off, and for a while we just sit there in silence, the breeze blowing through the long grass.

'Maybe it was,' I say softly.

A Bean baby. I can't imagine anything that would enhance the world more than a little Bean baby. Then something occurs to me.

'But you drank champagne! And wine . . .'

'I didn't *drink* it,' says Bean, rolling her eyes. 'It was subterfuge. I didn't want anyone saying, "Oh Bean, you're not drinking, why's that?"'

'Well, you fooled me,' I say, impressed. 'You're far more sneaky than you make out, you know.'

'I'm sorry I was so secretive, I just couldn't quite bear to say it out loud.' She shoots me a sweet smile. 'But I do feel better for telling you, Effie. I do. So, thanks.'

'Good.' I give her a quick, impulsive hug. 'And anything I can do, *anything* . . .'

Pregnancy vitamins, I'm already thinking. I am so on those.

'You're the only person in the world I've told,' says Bean. 'No one else knows, except . . .'

'Except Gus,' I say, suddenly remembering. 'Who thinks it's his.'

'Oh *God*.'

We meet eyes, aghast, and I can tell our minds are working exactly the same way.

'He *wouldn't* propose or anything stupid like that?' says Bean, looking slightly sick. 'I need to tell him. Pronto.'

'Let me do it,' I say at once.

'It's fine, I'll do it,' says Bean, already getting to her feet, but I plant both my hands strongly on her shoulders.

'Bean, stop. I'm doing this. I'm taking this on. You need to sit down and have a nice rest. *Don't* worry about Gus, worry about yourself, and . . .' I break off, glancing down at her abdomen, feeling a rush of love. Bean's tiny new baby Russian doll is nestling in there, and I suddenly, fiercely want to protect it. Both of them.

'Well . . . all right.' Bean subsides.

'Our family is changing shape.' I pause as the truth of this hits me. 'It's changing shape in all kinds of ways. But this is the most important.' I gesture at her stomach. 'So. Let me take over.'

'Thanks, Effie.' Bean gives me a grateful smile. 'I do feel a bit knackered this morning, actually. Maybe I'll walk back with you and have a nap.'

'What's his name, by the way?' I nod at her phone as we start to walk back across the field.

'Adam,' she says, her voice softening.

'Nice.' I smile.

Don't be a dickhead to my sister, Adam, I'm silently messaging him already. *Or I will break you.*

We head back to the house, approaching cautiously along the side of the drive. The caterers are already back, and a brunch table is being laid on the lawn, with a crisp white tablecloth and bunting strung from poles.

'No expense spared,' I mutter, rolling my eyes. 'What's being served at brunch, then, roast goose?'

'God only knows,' says Bean. 'Wait! Someone's coming.'

I hastily disappear behind a tree and Bean freezes, pretending to consult her phone, as a waiter comes out of the house, heading towards where the catering van is parked.

'Morning!' she says cheerily, and he nods back without

breaking his stride. When he's a safe distance away we resume our progress, tiptoeing across the gravel, and Bean suddenly starts giggling a bit hysterically.

'This weekend,' she says, *sotto voce*. 'It's mad. It's the maddest ever party, ever.'

'Agreed.'

'I can't believe you've stayed hidden this long,' she adds. 'You must want to leap out and say, "Surprise!"'

'Nope,' I say.

'Not even a tiny part of you?'

I try to imagine Krista's face if I popped up from under the brunch table, brandishing a pair of cheerleader's pom-poms, yelling, 'It's me!'

I mean, it would be quite funny. Until the recriminations and carnage began.

'Look – Gus!' adds Bean suddenly, pointing.

He's emerging from the house, looking dazed, holding a small violin case in each hand.

'Gus! Come here!' she calls, beckoning vigorously, but he shakes his head.

'I have to go,' he shouts back. 'Violin emergency. Romilly forgot them.' He lifts the little violins up as though to demonstrate.

'She forgot the violins?' Bean glances at me and I feel a spasm of laughter rising. 'After all that, she *forgot the violins*?'

'It's not funny.' Gus looks beleaguered. 'She's in a real state. I'm going to meet her at the lesson, in Clapham, then try to get back for the brunch. I need to go.'

'Tell him I'll meet him at the car,' I murmur to Bean. 'Tell him I've got some news for him. Then go and relax.' I give her shoulder a little squeeze. '*Relax*, Bean.'

As Bean approaches Gus, I creep along behind the hedge

at the side of the drive to the field that was operating as a car park last night. I dodge between the few remaining vehicles until I get to Gus's Vauxhall. It's unlocked, so I slide into the front passenger seat and sink down, till I'm barely visible.

As Gus opens the car door, he seems distracted, even for him.

'Hi,' he says. 'Bean says you've got something important to tell me?'

'Romilly's not pregnant,' I say, and watch his face go through about six different colours.

'How . . . ? *How* did you . . . ?' He swallows. 'Wait.' He checks his phone and winces. 'She's forgotten the music, too. I'll be back in a minute.'

I wait impatiently until he returns, gets in and plonks two dinky little music cases on the back seat.

'I don't get it, Effie,' he says, dazedly. 'How could you know about . . . ? How the hell could you even . . . ?'

'I saw you in the bathroom through the trap door,' I say swiftly, trying to cut through his confusion. 'You found a positive test. But it wasn't Romilly's. It was Bean's.'

'*What?*' Gus starts in shock. '*Bean?*'

'I know. So that's a whole other thing. But the point is, what you saw was misleading. It's *not* Romilly's baby. It's *not* your baby. And that means . . .' I can't finish the sentence, because what I want to say is, *You're free.*

For a moment, we're both silent. Then I realize that Gus's shoulders are shaking. His face is wet.

'Gus!' I say, aghast.

'I've been such a fool.' He brings two fists to his face. 'Such a bloody . . . I've been coasting along in a relationship I don't really want, because of . . . I don't know. Inertia. Procrastination. Denial.'

211

'Well, then, this is good!' I say encouragingly. 'Now you know how you feel! You can do something about it!'

'Yes. Thank *God*. I still can't believe it.' He still seems in shock. 'Effie, you don't know the night I've had . . .'

'I can imagine,' I say wryly.

'Wait, though. Wait.' He seems barely able to get the words out. 'Wait. What if that *wasn't* Bean's test? What if somehow Romilly is pregnant, too? What if they both are?'

I can feel his panic. He's had a glimmer of freedom. A moment of self-realization. What if the iron gate clangs shut after all?

'Find out?' I suggest. 'Call her?'

'OK.' Without hesitating, Gus speed-dials Romilly. 'Hi,' he says. 'Yes, in the car. Listen, I was wondering something. Are you pregnant?'

Beside him, I splutter incredulously. I thought he'd work up to it a tad more gradually. I can hear a stream of words on the other end, and suddenly Gus's face releases. He looks like a child let out to play.

'Right!' he says, glancing at me. 'So that's definite. You're not.'

Beside him, I let out a silent whoop, punching the air. I high-five Gus, who suddenly clutches me in a hug, the phone still clamped to his ear.

'Don't know,' he says. 'I just got a sudden strange idea about it . . . Anyway, good to know you're so sure.'

He breaks away from me, giving me the thumbs up, then silently he does a little victory dance with his arms. I join in, mirroring his ecstatic movements, both of us beaming in our exhilarated relief. All this time, Romilly has been talking, and now Gus chimes back into the conversation.

'I know we haven't, but I'm talking about it now. No, this

isn't my weird way of proposing.' He makes an appalled face at me, and I make an equally horrified one back. 'But yes . . . maybe we do need to talk. Yes, I did find the music cases,' he adds patiently. 'And yes, I am on my way.'

At last he puts the phone down and breathes out. He looks drained.

'That was the closest shave of my life,' he says at last. 'And I am a fucking . . . idiot.'

'Let's deliver the violins,' I say. 'And you can end it. I'll keep you company.'

And make sure you don't get talked round, I add silently.

'Yes. I need to end it.' Gus starts the car. 'I feel like I've woken up from a bad dream,' he adds, as we drive slowly over the grass. 'I'm like one of those frogs in the pots of water. They don't notice the temperature going up, because it's so gradual.' He turns on to the main village road, his brow furrowed. 'I couldn't tell you when things started going wrong, exactly. You wake up and you realize you've tipped over from happy to unhappy. But you blame yourself. You rationalize. You bury yourself in work and think things must surely get better. It's crazy.'

'Was Romilly happy?' I ask curiously. '*Is* she happy?'

'I can never tell,' says Gus honestly, and I can't help laughing, half in despair.

'Gus, don't you think you should be able to tell?'

'I guess.' He thinks for a moment. 'I can tell when she's pleased. But that's different from happy. She has this amazing energy, and for a while, that carried us both along. It was like a white heat. It was dazzling. Invigorating. But then . . .' He shakes his head. 'She's pretty hard work.'

'Did you love her?'

'*Love* her?' Gus sounds flummoxed, which is all the answer I need. He signals and turns on to the A road – then he frowns.

'Hey, the guy behind is flashing me. Is one of our doors not shut properly?'

'Don't think so.' I swivel in my seat and look around the car. 'Wouldn't it show up on the dashboard, anyway?'

'Weird.' Gus squints into his rear-view mirror. 'He's still doing it. He's trying to say something, too.'

'And those people are waving at us,' I say, as a car passes us. 'What's up? Are we leaking? Should we stop?'

'We'll be on the dual carriageway in a moment,' says Gus, sounding puzzled. 'I'll find a lay-by. This is all we need,' he adds with a sigh. 'We'll probably be shockingly late.'

'Gus, you're doing Romilly a massive favour,' I remind him. 'If we're a bit late, then too bad. Anyway, maybe it's nothing.'

But as we pull on to the dual carriageway, an entire car-load of people in the next lane starts gesticulating violently. I undo my seat belt, clamber into the back seat and lean out of the window. The whole family seems to be watching us, agog, from their estate car.

'What?' I shout, and the rear window of the estate car descends.

'On the roof!' comes a disembodied shout. 'Violins!'

For a moment I can't move. Violins? *Violins?*

'Gus,' I say in a trembling voice as I sit back down. 'Did you by any chance leave the violins on the roof of the car?'

'What?' He jolts. 'Shit. No! I . . . Shit! Did I?'

'You were pretty distracted,' I remind him.

'But I *can't* have . . . Fuck!' He shoots me a wide-eyed look. 'No!'

'That's why everyone's waving!'

'Oh God.' He's silent for a moment, then swivels his head briefly. 'OK, quick, Effie. You need to get them.'

'Do *what*?'

'Just climb out on to the roof and get them,' he says, almost impatiently. 'Simple.'

Simple?

'*You* climb out on to the roof and get them!' I retort, glaring at him. Then, almost against my will, I lean out of the car again. I pull myself up, using the window frame as leverage, and catch a glimpse of violin case – then a Mercedes zooms past, making me scream, and I duck back in again.

'There's not a chance in hell I'm climbing up there,' I say breathlessly. 'You'll have to stop the car.'

'I can't! If I stop the car, they'll fly off!'

A snort of laughter rises up through me, before I can stop it.

'It's not funny!' exclaims Gus hotly.

'I know.' I clap a hand over my mouth. 'Sorry. It's very bad. It's a terrible situation. What do we do?'

'OK. I need to stop gradually,' he says, staring ahead tensely. 'Decrease our momentum little by little. Yes. I should be able to work it out. If P is momentum and M is mass . . .'

'Gus, we're not in a bloody maths problem!' I erupt, although to be fair, this is exactly like a maths problem. I can even see it on the exam paper: *Gus and Effie are driving in a car with two violins balanced on top (see diagram).*

'I'm just trying to think it through!' he snaps back irascibly.

'Well, you've forgotten we're on a dual carriageway! We *can't* stop gradually.'

'Shit.' Gus screws up his face. 'Shit! This is . . . OK. Let's think. Maybe I can turn off at the next exit. Very gently. Before anything happens to them.'

'But how long are they going to balance on the roof for?' I

demand. A moment later, a bump answers my question and we both jump.

'Fuck! That was a violin!'

'Stop the car!'

As Gus frantically signals and pulls off the road on to the verge, there's another bump. I scramble out of the car and see something black on the road, already metres behind us. As I watch, the tyre of a passing lorry crushes it with ease, and I wince.

'One violin is toast!' I call.

'This can't be happening,' says Gus wildly, as he gets out. 'It cannot be happening. *How* did I leave them on the car?' At that moment, his phone buzzes and he winces as he glances down. 'It's Romilly. She says I can stay to hear the lesson, if I like.'

'It'll be tuneful,' I say, biting my lip.

'Oh *God*.' An almighty roar of laughter breaks through Gus, as though months of unbearable tension are being let out, and he clasps his head tightly in his hands. 'Oh *God*.'

As we're standing there, a car pulls up on the verge and an old lady gets out, followed by a teenage boy.

'We saw it all!' she says. 'So distressing!' She pats Gus's heaving shoulder as though to console him. 'But luckily my grandson was able to salvage some pieces.'

'There was a gap in the traffic,' says the boy. 'I picked up what I could.' He thrusts a bundle of pulverized bits of twirly wood and dangling strings at Gus, who stares wordlessly at them.

'Thank you,' he manages at last. 'Very helpful.'

'Perhaps it could be mended?' suggests the old lady earnestly. She plucks at one of the strings, which gives a dismal twang. 'They can do wonders these days.'

'Maybe.' Gus seems about to explode again. 'Well . . . we'll deal with it. Very helpful of you.'

As the woman and her grandson drive off, we sink down on the grassy verge. Gus dumps the assortment of shattered wood fragments and strings on the grass and stares up at the sky.

'Well, there we are,' he says. 'I guess it really is over, now.'

'Guess so.' I pat his shoulder, just like the old lady did. 'Now, go on. Make the call.'

FIFTEEN

Half an hour later, we pull back into the drive of Greenoaks. Gus parks the car and we both exhale.

'It could have been worse,' I say, after a moment. 'Imagine if we'd driven to Clapham. She might have *actually* torn your head off and fed it to the wolves, rather than just threatening to.'

'I need a drink. Or two.' As he turns towards me, Gus looks a bit giddy. 'Effs, don't ever let me do that again, OK? Ever.'

I don't know if he means *Drift into a terrible relationship* or *Drive off with two violins on the car roof* but I nod and say, 'Of course. Never again.'

'I feel like I've got out of prison,' he says fervently. 'I feel . . . light. Life's good again. The sun's shining!' he adds, as though only just noticing. 'Look! It's a beautiful day!' A smile sweeps across his face, and it's such an unfamiliar sight I give him an impulsive hug.

'Yes, it is,' I say. 'Beautiful.'

'I've been in such ridiculous denial,' he says slowly. 'I've spent the past six months focusing on everything but the emotional stuff. On the plus side, my work is going *splendidly,*' he adds, his eyes gleaming with his old sense of humour. 'So. Silver linings.'

As we get out of the car, I automatically look around to see if we're being watched, and Gus shakes his head incredulously.

'You're not still hiding from everyone, are you? Come to the brunch.'

'No, *thanks,*' I say. 'Anyway, I'm busy. I'm going to check the tree house for my Russian dolls.'

'OK.' He nods. 'But don't just disappear, will you, Ephelant? Touch base before you leave?'

'Sure.' I nod and squeeze his arm. 'Have fun at the brunch.'

I look around again, to check that we're not being observed, then cautiously make my way towards the boundary of the field. I'm dodging from car to car, trying to stay concealed, although there aren't many cars left parked on the grass. Behind me, I can hear Gus singing the *Mission Impossible* theme tune. Ha. Hilarious.

As I emerge through the hedge into the big field, I suddenly feel free, just like Gus did. Finally, I can stride. Stretch my arms, without fear of being seen.

It's a beautiful day, the sky a cloudless blue, and as I walk, my mind is full of memories of running over this grass, towards the tree house. As a small child, full of joyful anticipation, desperate to clamber up the rope ladder and swing on the trapeze. Then later, with Temi, giggling, holding rugs and illicit bottles of wine.

And then, of course, there's that dark, painful shadow which stretches over everything.

I spring up the ladder easily, my muscle memory coming back, then pause on the wooden platform, my gaze sweeping the horizon. I'm suddenly glad I came back to this familiar place one last time. Glad I'm here, looking at this view, breathing in the summer air. And I'm about to climb the steps to the upper level when I hear a creaking sound above me. I freeze uncertainly and look upwards. Is someone else here? If so, it has to be Bean, surely. No one else would come here.

'Hello?' I call tentatively. 'Bean?'

'Effie?' comes Joe's voice and I feel a lurch. *Joe?*

He clambers down the ladder, wearing a smart linen-shirt-and-trousers combo that screams 'brunch outfit'.

For a moment, neither of us speaks.

'Hi,' I say at last, trying to sound cool. 'I was just . . .'

'Of course.' Joe seems equally discombobulated. 'Sorry. I'll get out of your way.' He hesitates, then adds, 'Actually, I was writing you a letter. Trying to. But I haven't finished it. In fact, I've barely started.'

'A *letter*?' I swallow. 'What about?'

'About . . . everything,' says Joe slowly, as though choosing his words carefully. 'I have a lot to say. Now that I've decided to say it. But it's hard to know where to start.'

He sounds genuinely perplexed, and I feel a flash of impatience. I want to say, *Is it so hard? Start anywhere. Anywhere would do.*

But that might sound confrontational.

'I'm here now,' I say. 'So you don't need to put it in a letter. Why not start with where you were that night. With another woman?'

Joe's face jolts with what looks like genuine shock.

'Oh my God. Is that what you think?' He's silent for a few moments, his face heavy – then he looks up. 'OK, Effie, here's the truth. I was in Nutworth that whole evening.'

'*What?*' I stare at him.

'I was parked in a side street. When Mum phoned to see where I was, I was only minutes away. Holding the steering wheel of my car. I was . . .' He closes his eyes briefly. 'Frozen.'

'Frozen?' I echo blankly.

'I couldn't move. I couldn't tell Mum where I was. Let alone you.'

'But . . . why?' I stare at him, utterly bewildered – then I catch my breath. 'Wait. Is this related to what you told me last night? About being anxious?' As he nods, I feel a sudden wave of distress, because I'm suddenly – too late – working this all out. 'Joe, what went on while I was away? What haven't you told me? What is it I don't know?' I break off, breathing hard, suddenly desperate to put this story together. Every piece. Because it never made sense. It *never* made sense.

'Something happened at work while you were in the States,' Joe says, and I see a flicker of pain, deep in his eyes. 'It wasn't great. For a while, I thought I was going to lose my job. Be struck off. Maybe even prosecuted.'

'*Prosecuted?*' I echo, horrified. 'But . . . but what . . .'

'There was an incident at the hospital,' says Joe, in level tones, as though he's explained this story quite a few times. 'I came across a consultant . . .' He hesitates. 'Using.'

'Using what?' I say dumbly, before I realize. 'Oh. Right.'

'He was injecting himself with drugs,' Joe clarifies. 'Before operating. I was concerned, obviously, so I raised it with him. Privately.'

'What did he do?' I ask nervously, and Joe's face twists.

'To my face, he told me how glad and relieved he was that I'd called him out. He took me out for a drink. Said I was a responsible young man, clapped me on the back.' There's a long pause. 'Then, two weeks later, he stitched me up. He reported me for prescribing drugs wrongly to a patient. Falsified the paperwork before I had a chance to prove my case. Encouraged the patient's family to sue. Floated the word "negligence" around.' Joe's voice tightens. 'He tried to destroy me.'

I stare at him, unable to move. My whole body is in shock. Someone did that to *Joe*?

'I was powerless,' Joe continues, after a pause. 'And I fell into a spiral of panic. I wasn't thinking straight. I was already knackered from working and studying, and my brain went into a kind of emergency shutdown.'

'Why didn't you tell me?' I manage, my voice tangled.

'Because I couldn't tell anyone.' His dark eyes meet mine frankly. 'I couldn't, Effie. I couldn't tell a soul. It was too big. Too catastrophic.'

'Not even your mum?'

'Especially not Mum.' His face twists again. 'She'd helped me to get into medical school. I *couldn't* tell her I was going to lose it all. Sometimes I thought I'd have to leave the country. I actually googled places I could live. I thought maybe Costa Rica.'

'Costa *Rica*?' I give a weird half-laugh, although what I really want to do is cry, at the idea of Joe sitting alone, googling places to go and live in disgrace.

'I know. I was all over the place. I was . . . not thinking properly at all.' He shakes his head as though ridding himself of old thoughts, then looks up. 'And then, right in the middle of it all, you came back from San Francisco. You were happy. Your life was going well. I just couldn't bear to tell you what a mess mine was. *Hi, remember me, your doctor boyfriend? Well, funny story about that* . . . That's why I sat in Nutworth, clinging on to the steering wheel, in a kind of frozen panic.'

'But I would have helped!' I exclaim, breathing hard in agitation. 'I would have helped! I would have done anything—'

'Of course you would.' He looks at me with a kind of wry tenderness. 'I knew that then. I knew you'd throw everything you had into supporting me, and I couldn't stand it. What if I ended up in court? What if I ended up in the papers and you suffered some of my disgrace? I felt I didn't deserve you. I felt . . . tainted.'

'*Tainted?*' I echo in dismay and Joe winces.

'I was in a very bad place. For quite a long time.'

'But . . . wait,' I say stupidly, as it suddenly occurs to me. 'You're still in a job. You're Doctor Joe! What happened?'

'I was lucky,' says Joe wryly. 'The consultant was spotted injecting himself again, by a pair of nursing staff. Because there were two of them, he couldn't railroad them, and gradually it all came out. After a lot of meetings, I was cleared. But I was a wreck. I couldn't relax, couldn't sleep . . . Luckily a colleague spotted the signs and sent me off to get help. And now . . .' He gestures at himself. 'Good as new. Almost. Actually, I think the whole experience helped me when the TV thing kicked off,' he adds. 'I had perspective. Coping strategies.'

No wonder Joe was a wreck. I feel a total wreck, listening to all this, and it didn't even happen to me. I sink down on to the wooden floor, trying to digest it all, and after a moment, Joe follows suit.

I have a lot of questions I could ask, but there's only one I really want to.

'*Why* didn't you tell me before?' I say, trying not to sound as upset as I feel. 'It's been four years, Joe. *Why* didn't you tell me?'

'I know.' Joe squeezes his eyes shut briefly. 'I should have done. But I felt so shit. So utterly shit. I knew what I'd done to you was unforgivable. And the more I got my head back to normal, the worse I felt about the way I'd treated you. I didn't want you thinking I was asking for forgiveness. Or trying to get back into your life. I didn't want to sound as if I was . . . asking for sympathy.'

Asking for sympathy? After that ordeal? Only Joe Murran could be so hard on himself. It's the secret of his success, but it's the secret of his problems, too.

'I wouldn't have thought any of that.' I look at his face, wanting suddenly to give him a long, tight hug. 'You know I wouldn't.'

'The trouble is, the longer I left it, the harder it was.' He shrugs. 'If it makes you feel any better, I only told Mum the whole story about a month ago.'

'A *month* ago?' I stare at him. 'Your *mum*?'

'I know.' He nods, shamefaced. 'She was shocked. Really shocked. Quite distraught. Then, almost at once, she said, "Joe, you have to tell Effie." I actually came to this party hoping you'd be here. Hoping I might have a chance to . . . put things straight. Four years too late.'

My mind drifts back to that awful meeting, four years ago, in the café. Joe could barely meet my eye. He sounded like a robot. But instead of wondering if there was more to it, I took him at face value. I blamed him. But I should have known. I should have *known*.

'Joe, I feel terrible,' I say in a rush of remorse. 'I said some awful things to you.'

'I don't blame you,' says Joe quickly. 'You felt let down. It was understandable.'

As his eyes flick to my collarbone again, I remember my savage parting shot to him. *Well, it's lucky you only gave me the smallest diamond in the world. I didn't mind too much when I chucked it in the bin.*

Now I let myself remember the devastated look in his eyes as I said it. Why didn't I notice that? Why didn't I *realize*?

'I wish you'd told me, Joe.' I smile, but there are tears on my lashes. 'I understand why you didn't, but I really, *really* wish you had. It might have meant . . .' I swallow. 'We might not be . . .'

Our lives would be totally different now, I want to say, but it sounds a bit too drama queen. Even if it is, in my opinion, true.

'I know. But I wasn't right for a long time. And by the time I finally got my head together, you were in a relationship. You were happy. What was I going to do, disrupt that? Call up and say, "You know how I broke your heart? Well, guess what, I have an explanation now." It was too late. I couldn't expect you to forgive me.' Joe meets my eyes briefly, his face a little bleak. 'Maybe sometimes in life you just miss your chance.'

'I wasn't happy,' I say, my voice tiny. 'I wasn't.'

Joe is silent for a moment, as though digesting my words.

'You looked happy. You went out with that guy Dominic. And before that, you were with . . .' He hesitates, as though he can't believe he's saying the word. 'Humph.'

'*Don't* mention Humph.' I clap a mortified hand over my face. 'Please don't mention Humph. I'm *so* ashamed of that.'

'I'll admit it was a surprise. Even Mum, who was firmly on your side, wavered a bit when she saw you with Humph at the carol service.' He pauses. 'In that extraordinary fur hat. Calling him "darling".'

I peek out between my fingers to see him give a sudden snort of mirth.

'"Humph, *darling*,"' he says, imitating me. '"Humph, you're an absolute *scream*."'

'Don't!' I say, giggling in spite of myself.

'I didn't think it was funny then, obviously,' says Joe. 'But now . . . it is quite funny.'

I smile back at him, almost shyly. Can we still laugh? If we can, it feels like a small miracle.

'I'm sorry I behaved like that at the carol service.' I shake my head ruefully. 'It was all an act. I wanted to show you what you were missing.' I pause, then add awkwardly, 'Humph and I never . . .'

'Didn't you?' says Joe after another pause.

'No.'

Somehow, I need him to know this fact. But I can't tell if it makes any difference to anything. Joe's face is closed up, his eyes dark with thoughts I can't read. The atmosphere is getting too intense, and I swivel away.

'Funny we should wind up here,' I say, scuffing the wooden floor with my foot. 'The place where it ended.'

There's silence, and I watch the dust motes floating in a shaft of sunshine. Then Joe replies in a low voice, 'I don't think of it like that. I think of it as the place where it began.'

His words take me by surprise. For years, I've only thought of this tree house as the backdrop to devastation, humiliation, weeping. But now my mind is leapfrogging back to a previous time. A sundappled, endless afternoon. Two teenagers, finding their way with each other for the first time. If I close my eyes, I can still feel the scratchy rug. The rough, wooden floor. Joe's body on mine, more hard and assured and insistent than I'd ever known it. Sensations which seemed both new and timeless. Pain and bliss.

I'd forgotten. No, I hadn't forgotten, exactly. I'd chosen not to recall. But now ... Slowly I turn back to look at Joe, my head tingling. The air is coming alive; I can feel it. A prickling atmosphere is growing between us. And to match it, my body is coming alive. I'm filled with a strong, pulsating hunger.

Is it just a nostalgic yearning for what we had then?

No. It's not. It's a hunger for now. Right now. A longing to reclaim his body, this place, this man.

Restlessly I get to my feet, and Joe follows suit. I gaze past him, through the window, at the view which has been the same since before we were even born. Then, slowly, I turn back to face him.

'Maybe sometimes in life you get another chance,' I say, my voice barely a husk. 'Maybe you can go back. Right back to ... how it was in the beginning.'

Something shifts in Joe's face. His gaze is pinned on mine now, dark and urgent, as though with a question. The same question I'm silently asking too.

'I remember every moment of that day,' he says, his deep, gravelly voice mesmerizing me. 'Don't you? We were kissing, right here. And we both wanted it so badly, but we were kind of nervous, remember? Putting it off, almost. Then at last you said, "Is this the day?" And I said, "Is it?" Because I didn't want to ...' He breaks off, breathing hard. 'And you said, "Yes." And that's when we ...'

He takes a step forward, his eyes never leaving mine.

'First of all, you closed the shutters,' I manage, and Joe nods. 'Well remembered. I did.'

Unhurriedly, he goes to the window. He closes and latches the shutters firmly, then walks back as I wait, quivering.

'Is this the day?' he says softly, and I feel a white-hot surge of anticipation. Unlocked memories are flooding my brain, mingling with new imaginings.

'Is it?' I whisper, following the script.

'Is it?' He pushes the question back to me and I can see a genuine, last-minute uncertainty in his face. He wants to be sure; he wants to get it right.

For the past four years, all I could see in Joe's face was arrogance and cruelty. But now it's as though a curtain has been swept aside and I can see everything that's really in him. The compassionate, thoughtful, sensitive Joe I loved was there all the time.

'Yes.' My voice is constricted. 'Yes.'

For a heartbeat we're motionless, almost sizing each other up, prolonging the agony. Then suddenly his warm mouth is on mine and my hands are in his hair and the air is heavy with our frenzied, feverish breathing. *We should slow down*, I think in a daze. *I mean, no. The opposite. Don't slow down. Oh God . . .* Already he's pushing me up against the wooden wall of the tree house and the whole structure is rocking and my jeans are on the floor, and basically, we're not hanging about.

But then, we have got a few years to catch up on.

SIXTEEN

Afterwards, I can't quite speak. My senses feel fried. My skin feels raw. We both collapse on to the wooden floor, and Joe takes me in the crook of his arm. I nestle into his chest and we stare up at the ceiling, just like we did back then, all those years ago. The tiniest rays of sunlight are coming through the wood, here and there, making me blink.

'That was . . .' Joe seems equally shattered. He exhales in a sudden, disbelieving laugh. 'I guess there was quite a build-up to that.'

'Four years of build-up.'

'Four years is a long time to be storing sexual tension.'

'What's the cure, doctor?' I say innocently and he laughs again.

'Oh God. The cure is not to be a fuckwit.' He turns and buries his face in my neck. 'I should have told you everything. I should have *told* you.'

'I've missed you,' I say, which seems like a supreme understatement.

Joe sighs and stretches his arms upwards as though trying to catch a shaft of light. 'I've missed you too.'

'I could have been there for you.' I feel a sadness weighing me down. 'I can't *bear* that I wasn't. That you went through it all alone.'

'Well, same goes. I could have been there for you when your parents split up. It must have been . . .' Joe turns his head to study me. 'How are you about that?'

'Better than I was,' I say slowly. 'I'm starting to see the bigger picture. I could never *understand*, you know? Mimi and Dad seemed so perfect together. But last night, Bean told me some stuff about them which I never knew. And now I'm seeing it's not so black and white. I'm thinking . . . maybe they *didn't* have a perfect relationship. Maybe it *wasn't* out of the blue.'

'I'm sure it wasn't,' says Joe. 'These things never are.' He pauses, then adds, 'So. Why aren't you at the party?' His simple, direct question catches me off-guard, and I take a moment to answer.

'My dad and I aren't speaking. Things really disintegrated between us. You have no idea what Krista's like.'

'I got a flavour last night,' says Joe. 'But you and your dad – that's sad. You used to be so close.'

'I know.' I exhale a shuddery breath. 'It *is* sad. I guess . . . families are messy.'

'True.' Joe nods. 'Although at least you're not having fist fights.'

I can tell he's trying to cheer me up and I shoot him a grateful smile.

'I'm serious!' he retorts. 'I've seen relatives leave hospital rooms in tears because their beloved gran is ill. They'll be arm in arm, comforting each other, like the most united family you've ever met. Brings a tear to this jaded old medic's eye. Then half a minute later, you come across them brawling in the corridor. An overlooked category in medicine is "Patients whose injuries were caused by family strife in the waiting room". Think yourself lucky no one's been driven to A&E.'

'Yet,' I say, and he laughs.

'Yet.'

'Krista'll put my dad in A&E, if he's not careful,' I mutter, rolling my eyes. 'With an overdose of sex games.'

'Sex games?' He raises his eyebrows.

'I got stuck watching her and Dad role-playing this morning. That's what happens when you spy on your family. You see terrible things. Krista was being a nun.'

'A *nun*?' Joe erupts in laughter. 'Well, she's imaginative, I'll give her that.'

'Joe, Mike Woodson reckons she's planning to rip off Dad,' I say more seriously, suddenly wanting to hear his take on this. 'I'm not joking now. He warned Gus at the party.'

'On what grounds?' says Joe, looking taken aback.

'Apparently Krista deliberately targeted Dad. Asked all kinds of questions about him and then made her move. She's already got a diamond out of him, and now she wants them to open a restaurant together. In Portugal. I'm worried she's going to run through his money and then dump him.' I look at him anxiously. 'What do you think?'

'Huh.' Joe thinks about this for a moment. '*Could* your dad be ripped off? Isn't he too savvy for that?'

'I don't know.' I try to consider the matter honestly. 'I think maybe he could be, if he was flattered enough. He's quite vain.'

'Well, it's his life,' says Joe. 'Maybe someone could gently talk to him, though?'

'Maybe.' I feel my face close up. 'Maybe they could. But not me.'

'Hmm,' says Joe non-committally, then he glances at his watch. 'Are you hungry?'

'Starving,' I admit. 'I didn't have any breakfast.'

'Let's go and find you some, then.' He kisses me. 'You need to keep your strength up.'

'Is that a promise?' I wink at him and he laughs.

As Joe gets dressed in his trousers and linen shirt, I pull on Bean's T-shirt and jeans, then do a hasty sweep of the tree house, clambering up to the top level and peeking in every corner. But there are no Russian dolls. Just a few old sweet wrappers and a lot of memories.

'So, goodbye, tree house,' I say as we step down off it for the last time.

'I think we gave it a good send-off.' Joe nods.

'Not bad.' I smile back at him. 'And may I say how smart you're looking, Doctor Joe?'

'Well, thank you.' Joe puts on a pair of shades and instantly looks even more dashing. 'What are your plans now?' he adds, as we make our way through the long grass. 'Are you going to the brunch?'

'To the *brunch*?' I stare at him.

'Yes, to the brunch.' He shrugs, as though he's talking about the simplest thing in the world. 'Why not? Bit of food, bit of drink, say hello to your family . . .'

Has he heard nothing I've been saying, this whole time?

'Because I'm not *at* the party, remember? I'm not a guest, remember?'

'I know,' says Joe slowly, as though picking his words carefully. 'But I was just thinking. You're here. Everyone's here. This is your last chance to . . . I don't know. Be all together at Greenoaks. It's now or never.' He pauses, studying my face warily. 'I don't know what's gone on between you and your dad. I don't know the history and I'm sure it feels toxic . . .'

'My dad and I communicate in one-word emails, these days,' I say, gazing at the ground. 'About practical stuff only. It's grim.'

'It's unbelievable. You and your dad were always . . .' He shakes his head. 'But even so. You're part of this family, Effie. And I hate to see you hiding away like some sort of outsider. This is your house, too. *Your* house, too,' he repeats with emphasis. 'And you want to know what I think? I think you should be able to walk through that front door with your head held high. Proud and strong. Effie Talbot is in the house.'

'Effie Talbot is in the house,' I echo slowly, because I like the sound of that.

'Effie Talbot is in the house.' He pauses and gazes at me intently, as though trying to inspire me. 'You can still join in. You can still be part of this. And if you don't, maybe you'll always—'

'Ssh!' I cut him off in sudden alarm. 'Look! It's Lacey!'

Coming into the field is a figure with stunning red hair, in a pale-pink dress. She waves, and I stiffen, turning my face away.

'Walk the other way,' I say fervently. 'Quick!'

'And go where?'

'Don't know. But we need to escape. She mustn't see me.'

'She's already seen you,' points out Joe.

We both watch as Lacey pauses to take a photo of the landscape. She shouts something, and Joe waves cheerfully back.

'Don't wave to her!' I mutter.

'I can hardly ignore her.' Joe gives a sudden snort of laughter and I glare at him.

'You think this is funny?'

'Effie, you can't hide for ever,' says Joe patiently. 'Why not use this as an opportunity to come out from the shadows?'

'Not like *this*,' I say desperately. Then a sudden realization comes to me. 'Wait. Lacey doesn't know what I look like. OK, this can work. I'm not Effie, I'm someone else. Got it?' I turn to him with urgency. 'Got it?'

'Effie.' Joe blows out. 'This is ridiculous.'

'It's not! I can't have Lacey running off to Krista and telling her I'm here. It would just be . . .' I shudder. 'I *can't*. I'll be a friend of yours. OK? We're on a morning stroll. Having a chit-chat. Whatever. We'll say hello and you introduce me as . . . as Kate. Then I'll go.' I break off, breathing hard. 'Please, Joe? Please?'

Joe gazes at me incredulously for a moment, then sighs. 'Fine. You'd better put these on.' He hands me his shades. 'Otherwise your Talbot eyes will betray you.'

'*Don't* give me away,' I mutter as we draw nearer to Lacey.

'I won't!' says Joe – then raises his voice. 'Lacey! Lovely morning, isn't it?'

'Gorgeous! I'm taking a few shots for Instagram. And who's *this*?' she says, in the most insinuating voice possible, her eyes running swiftly over my drab jeans and T-shirt.

'Let me introduce Kate,' says Joe dutifully. 'A friend of mine. Kate, this is Lacey.'

'Hi,' I say, lifting my hand in greeting, trying to keep my face averted. 'I'd better go—'

'Nice to meet you, Kate!' Lacey holds out her hand to shake mine. Damn. I can't really avoid it. Gingerly I approach her, and shake her slim hand as quickly as possible.

'A *friend*, Doctor Joe?' Lacey raises her eyebrows suggestively. Honestly, she's got a one-track mind.

'Colleague, actually,' I say in brisk tones. 'I'm also a doctor. I was in the area, so I just popped along to give an update on a patient.'

Ha. Brilliant improvisation, though I say it myself.

'Very considerate of you, Kate,' says Lacey, in a tone I can't quite read. 'Very thoughtful, to pop round like that. And how's the patient?' She gives a sudden dramatic gasp. '*Don't* tell me they died.'

I feel a prickle on Joe's professional behalf. Of course his patient didn't *die*.

'No, the patient's much better, thank you,' I say pleasantly. 'Anyway, we're pretty much done, so I'll be off. Nice to meet you, Tracey.' I deliberately get her name wrong, which is another masterstroke, and I'm already turning away when Joe suddenly says,

'Oh, Kate, I didn't ask. What were the patient's levels like this morning?'

I swivel back, aghast, to see Joe regarding me with a bland, innocent expression. He thinks this is *funny*?

'They were satisfactory,' I reply after a pause. 'Broadly speaking. So that was good. Anyway, I'll be off . . .'

'Satisfactory?' He raises his eyebrows and I silently curse him.

'Satisfactory,' I repeat, nodding. 'Actually, I texted the levels to you,' I add, in sudden inspiration. 'They'll be on your phone. Have a look.'

'I must have missed your text.' He blinks back at me, deadpan. 'Remind me? Just a ballpark figure.'

I will *kill* him.

'Well.' I swallow. 'This morning, the patient's levels were

at . . .' I grasp for a number. 'They were at a solid thirty-five. Whereas during the night she was more of a twenty-one, twenty-two.'

'As low as that,' says Joe gravely.

'Yes. We were concerned, obviously. But then she rallied. So.'

'Yay!' exclaims Lacey, who has been following our conversation with bright, avid eyes. 'What does that mean to a layman?'

'Kate?' Joe inclines his head towards me. 'Care to explain?'

OK, he's really asked for it.

'It means the patient will live,' I say flatly, and Lacey clasps her hands together. 'Her life has been saved. Her grandchildren will walk with her in the park again. She'll feel the rays of sunshine on her face. And we couldn't ask more than that, because *that*'s why we're doctors. *That*'s why.' I look heroically into the distance. 'For that life. For that sunshine.'

I glance at Joe, who mimes applause, a smile on his face.

'Oh, I think you medical professionals are amazing!' says Lacey mistily. 'You should get medals!'

'I think Kate should get something, certainly,' says Joe sardonically. 'Walk you to the gate, Kate?'

'Lovely. Bye again,' I say to Lacey, and start striding away, through the long grass. 'Thanks a lot,' I murmur, as soon as I'm sure we're out of earshot. 'I really enjoy improvising medical details, how did you guess?'

'Oh, I had a hunch . . . Nice speech, by the way,' replies Joe, his mouth twitching with amusement. 'You should consider a career change.'

'Maybe I should.'

The twist of his mouth suddenly reminds me of the time I dressed up in a white coat, stethoscope and not much else, to surprise him for his birthday. It's been so painful to remember our past that I've almost blanked the fun times. But now the happier memories are returning, like nerves tingling back to life.

We walk silently till we reach the gate into the garden, where I automatically shrink into the laurel hedge, peering ahead for observers.

'So, what are you going to do?' says Joe.

I look past him for a few silent moments, at my beloved Greenoaks. At the distinctive turret. The stained-glass window. The 'ugly' brickwork that nobody loves but me. *It's now or never*, Joe said, and he was right. Greenoaks is going out of my life. For ever. And I'm not sure I've ever quite faced up to that. Not like I'm facing up to it now.

'I want to say goodbye to Greenoaks,' I hear myself saying. 'That's what I want to do. Go back in while everyone's at brunch and walk around and just . . . say goodbye.'

I'll look for my dolls as I go. But somehow my heart has shifted focus. My dolls might turn up in a box. Greenoaks will never turn up in a box. Temi was right: I need to take a moment. Be with it. Feel it.

'Good idea.' Joe's eyes crinkle sympathetically. 'You want some company? Can I help?'

'I don't need any company, thanks.' I squeeze his hand. 'But you could help by going to the brunch? Keep them all distracted outside. Buy me some time.'

'You got it.' He kisses me. 'You got it.'

SEVENTEEN

I'm going to say goodbye in my own way, on my own terms. As I circle the drive, breathing in the familiar scents of plants and wood and earth, I feel resolute. I'm going to walk through the front door, my head high, proud and strong, just like Joe said.

By now, I'm about twenty feet from the house and I square up to the front door, facing it head-on. I feel like a gymnast preparing to approach a tricky vault. Deep breath . . . rise up on the toes . . . go.

Lightly but briskly, I walk towards the front door of my childhood home for the last time. I must take this moment in. I must remember the details. The light glinting on the windows. The way the wind moves through the trees. The—

Hang on.

There's such an almighty gale of laughter from the brunch table that I can't help stopping dead. *Curse* my family. Why do they always have to get inside my head? What are they laughing about? How come they're having a good time?

As I listen to the sound of chattering voices and the occasional clinking of silverware against china, curiosity overcomes me. I want to see the brunch table, I realize. And the brunch outfits. And the brunch food. And who's sitting next to who. And basically . . . everything.

I'll just have the quickest of tiny peeks. And *then* I'll walk through the front door, proud and strong. Yes.

I edge round the house, then duck down low and crawl through the rose bushes until I can spy the table. It does look lovely, all white and silver, the bunting fluttering in the breeze, almost like an outdoor wedding. I always used to think I'd have my wedding reception here, I think, with a sudden swell of sadness. If I ever had one.

Anyway. Crack on.

I edge still closer, running my eyes over the guests. Krista is in a low-cut printed silk frock which displays her tanned boobs as though they're a museum exhibit on a plinth. Lacey's in her pale-pink dress. Bean is in a strappy floral print with a wide-brimmed straw hat to protect her face, and she's smiling but anxious-looking. Humph is in a cool black linen suit which I expect his nutritionist ex-girlfriend chose for him. Gus seems kind of exhilarated and I wonder how many drinks he's had. Joe's face is guarded behind his shades, and he's sipping what appears to be fizzy water. Dad is sitting at the end of the table, as well-dressed and debonair as ever, wearing one of his inscrutable smiles.

As I'm studying them, the sun comes out from behind a cloud. And I don't know if it's the bright light or what, but they suddenly look like a load of Russian dolls to me, lined up round the table. All hiding their inner layers. All protecting their secrets, whether it's behind glossy smiles or sunglasses or under straw hats. Or simply with lies.

'Lovely brunch,' Bean is saying politely to Krista. 'It's been a lovely party. So . . . um . . . relaxed.'

'Well, thank you, Bean,' says Krista, dimpling at her charmingly. 'I just wanted to give the house a good send-off. You know how fond I've always been of the dear old place.'

'Right,' says Bean, after a long pause, and takes a big glug from her water glass.

'You know, I'm not bothered about money,' Lacey is saying confidingly to Humph. 'I just can't seem to get *interested* in it. I have no idea what things cost. It's the last thing that matters!' She throws up her hands, and her bracelets glitter in the sunshine.

'That's a very refreshing attitude,' says Humph, smiling at her.

'Well, I don't know about that,' says Lacey modestly. 'It's just Lacey's way.' She turns to study Joe, sucking provocatively on a stripy paper straw. 'Doctor Joe's keeping very quiet. Did anyone else meet the lovely Kate this morning?'

Kate . . . ? Oh God, she means me!

'Kate?' Bean glances up, immediately alert. 'Who's that? Who's Kate?'

'A friend,' says Joe impassively.

'Oh, a bit more than a friend, I should say!' exclaims Lacey. 'She came all the way over here to talk about a patient. At the weekend! And you should have *seen* the way she was looking at him. Couldn't take her eyes off you, Doctor Joe, excuse my French.'

I stare at Lacey indignantly. That's rubbish! I was entirely professional in my demeanour. *Entirely* professional.

'You should have invited her to brunch!' says Krista. 'Any friend of yours is welcome here, you know that, Doctor Joe.'

'I did suggest that she might come to the brunch,' says Joe, after a pause. 'But she didn't want to impose.'

Bean looks all pink and ruffled. 'So are you and this Kate . . .'

'Colleagues.' Joe sips his water.

'Not just colleagues, if you ask *me*,' says Lacey.

'Really?' says Bean, crestfallen. Her disappointment for me is so touching, I half want to giggle and half want to set her straight. Do I dare text her and tell her Kate is me?

No. Not now. She'll only give me away.

'Oh, you should have *seen* them, Bean,' says Lacey. 'I had to turn my eyes away!'

'Isn't that quite unprofessional, Joe, flirting with a colleague?' says Bean, looking twitchy. 'Quite unethical?'

'It was simply a meeting about a patient,' says Joe blandly.

'Come on, Doctor Joe.' Lacey laughs, throwing Joe a flirty look. 'Admit there was a sizzle between you and this Kate.'

Joe looks at her for a few moments, as though deciding how to answer. Then he nods. 'I would agree she's attractive.'

'Knew it!' crows Lacey.

'Indeed, beautiful,' adds Joe. 'In fact, now I think about it, I'd say she's the most beautiful woman I know.' He meets Lacey's eyes impassively. 'Bar none.'

Instantly, my face flames. I know he only wants to wind up Lacey. But still.

'Wow!' says Humph with a laugh. 'I'd like to meet her!'

'The most beautiful woman you know!' exclaims Lacey, bridling.

'We've simply *got* to meet her now,' chimes in Krista. 'Lace, you never said she was a stunner!'

'I obviously didn't look at her carefully enough.' Lacey tosses back her luxuriant, blow-dried hair, and although her glossy smile is still carefully pasted on, I can tell she's offended. 'Beauty really *is* in the eye of the beholder, isn't it?' She trills with laughter. 'Because I would have said your Kate was a bit of a nondescript mouse. But each to his own!' She flashes a savage smile at Joe. 'I don't really notice looks, actually. Couldn't be less interested! It's Lacey's way. For me, it's the *inside* of someone that counts. You know?' She turns to Humph, as though for validation. 'The heart. The soul. The person.'

'I guess I'm just quite shallow,' says Joe with a shrug, and I bite my lip, trying not to explode with laughter.

My legs are already aching from crouching in the bushes and I shift position slightly. I need to stop gawping. I need to go and say goodbye to the house like a strong, proud woman. But I'm gripped. I can't tear myself away from watching the cabaret that is my family at brunch.

'Yes, unfortunately Romilly and I have broken up,' Gus is telling Joe now. 'We came to our natural end. Which is obviously very sad.'

'Very sad,' agrees Joe cautiously.

'Very . . . very . . . *very* sad.' Gus gives Joe a brief, beatific smile, then claps his hand over his mouth in self-reproof. 'Sorry. Didn't mean to smile. That was inappropriate. Because it's very sad.' He gives a sudden snort of mirth, then tries to straighten his face. 'Very . . . very sad.'

Oh my God, Gus is drunk. Not that I blame him.

'I'm sorry to hear that,' says Joe, his mouth twitching. 'It does sound extremely . . . sad.'

'It is.' Gus swigs his wine. 'It's a great sorrow to me that I will never hear her saying, "Gus, you fucking moron," ever again.'

'That is a loss,' says Joe gravely.

'Indeed. I don't know how I'll bear it.' Gus reaches for the bottle of wine and nods at Joe's glass. 'Care to drown my sorrows?'

'Of course, it's no secret why Effie isn't here this weekend.'

The sound of my name makes me look over sharply to the other end of the table. Humph is in full flow to an admiring Lacey, who is leaning so close to him her red hair is tumbling over his shoulder.

'Why's that, then?' asks Lacey, then breathes in. 'Wait! I can guess the answer. She's avoiding you!'

'She was always in love with me, poor thing,' says Humph, and I feel a flash of indignation. Is *this* what he says when I'm not around?

'Of course she was.' Lacey nods wisely.

'After I let her down, she was pretty devastated. Begged me to reconsider, bombarded me with letters . . .' Humph pauses, his eyes distant, as though with memories. 'I felt for her, as a compassionate human being. But do you want to know something I really believe, Lacey?'

'What's that?' responds Lacey, agog, and Humph gives her a wise, noble smile, as though he's the Dalai Lama.

'You can't force love. Simple as that. You can't force love.'

'That is *so* profound.' Lacey blinks at him in admiration.

'No, it's not!' chips in Bean scornfully. 'And Humph, you're totally inventing this. Effie wasn't in love with you!'

'With respect, Bean . . .' Humph gives her a pitying look. 'I don't think Effie shares everything with you.'

'Yes, she does.' Bean glowers at him. 'And I know she wasn't in love with you.'

'If that's what you want to believe . . .'

He makes a little face at Lacey, who bites her lip in amusement and says, 'Oh dear. Poor Effie. Awkward,' she adds, wrinkling her nose.

'Don't you dare say "poor Effie"!' retorts Bean furiously. 'You don't know anything about it! The idea that she's avoiding *Humph*, of all people! It's ridiculous!'

To be fair, I decide silently, I would probably try to avoid Humph, in any given situation. But not because I'm hopelessly in love with him.

'Well, why else isn't she here, then?' shoots back Lacey, her eyes dancing maliciously. 'Who doesn't come to their own family party?'

'She had a date,' says Bean at once. 'She had a date with an athlete!'

'She could have brought him!' Lacey trumps her. 'If you ask me, it's weird. Everyone's here but Effie! Don't tell me there isn't some socking great reason. And we all know what it is. Or rather, *who* it is.' She points at Humph, as though she's just proved her case in court, and he lifts his glass appreciatively.

'What are you talking about?' says Dad, looking up suddenly, and everyone jumps. With a lurch of surprise I realize that this is the first time I've heard him speak. He's been completely detached from the rest of the party, sitting at the end of the table, staring at his phone. But now for the first time he's looking up and joining in; he's even taking off his sunglasses.

He's shifted position slightly and I can't quite see his face from where I am. So I creep along a bit, staying behind the bushes, until I can get a proper view of him.

'What are you talking about?' he says again, filling his wine glass.

'Effie,' says Bean, shooting daggers at Humph.

'Oh, Effie.' Dad's face crinkles slightly and he takes a deep sip of wine. His hand is just a tad shaky as he replaces the glass and I suddenly realize that he's been drinking, too. 'Dear little Effie,' he says reminiscently. 'I can still see her, running across that lawn in her pink fairy wings. Remember those?'

'Those fairy wings!' Bean's face softens. 'God, yes. She refused to take them off for what, a *year*?'

'Remember when you put them in the washing machine by mistake, Bean?' Gus suddenly chimes in. 'And we had to order a new pair and we spent a day pretending we couldn't remember where they were?'

'Oh God!' Bean collapses into laughter. 'She wouldn't stop asking! "Fairy wings? Where fairy wings gone?"'

'And we were like, "Oh, Effie, don't worry, I'm *sure* they'll turn up."'

My cheeks are beetroot as I listen to them. I shouldn't be eavesdropping on my family. It's wrong. It's deceitful. I need to leave. Now.

But somehow I can't.

Everyone has politely tilted their heads to listen to the family reminiscences, and as Dad draws breath to speak again, there's a kind of expectant hush.

'Remember Effie's circus birthday party? Her face!'

'That was amazing.' Bean nods. 'Best one ever.'

'Such happy times.' Dad takes another deep swig of wine. 'Happy, happy times. Happiest time of my life, maybe.'

What?

What did Dad just say? I'm transfixed as I stare at his oblivious face. *Happiest time of his life?*

I can feel my crumpled, beaten heart slowly starting to puff out again.

'Bean, you were right.' Dad suddenly turns to her. 'Effie should be here. I'm sure she had her reasons for refusing to come, and I know she's very stubborn, but . . .' He breaks off, his face bleak. 'I do wish she'd changed her mind. It should be all of us here today.'

'She's a woman scorned, Tony,' says Lacey knowingly. 'Nothing more determined than a woman scorned.'

'For the last time, it's nothing to do with Humph!' erupts Bean in exasperation. 'It's because she wasn't bloody invited!'

'Of course she was invited,' says Dad, looking perplexed. 'Don't be ridiculous, Bean.'

'Now, as I said before, there *was* a small misunderstanding,' chimes in Krista smoothly. 'I sent her invitation out late, I told you that, Tony. A simple mistake, but she took umbrage. But then, she hadn't set foot in this house for weeks before that, so . . . no surprise there!' She gives a short laugh. 'Anyone need topping up?'

'It wasn't just late!' says Bean, her face pink. 'It was a passive-aggressive anti-invitation. It made her feel unwanted. Dad, didn't you *see* the so-called invitation Effie got?'

'I . . .' Dad glances uncertainly at Krista. 'Well, Krista kindly took care of those arrangements . . .'

'You didn't see it!' Bean sounds incredulous. 'You didn't check. You have no idea what's been going on in your own family! We can't get through to you, Dad! We can't talk to you! No wonder Effie didn't come! I nearly didn't come myself! And Krista?' She swivels round. 'You're a big fat liar, because you *didn't* email Effie whatever bullshit you said last night. You *didn't* beg her to come. That's bollocks!'

There's a kind of general gasp, and Lacey puts a hand over her mouth, as though she's watching a bull fight.

'Maybe I typed an email and never sent it,' replies Krista crisply. 'My mistake. But really! All this fuss over nothing! I sent Effie a perfectly nice, personal invitation. If she'd wanted

to be here, she'd be here. She chose to stay away. *Her choice.'*
Krista lifts her chin pugnaciously.

'You say she felt *unwanted*?' Dad stares at Bean as though this makes no sense to him.

'Yes!'

There's silence. Dad seems absolutely staggered, and I gaze at him through the leaves in disbelief. How does he *expect* me to feel? What does he *think* has been going on all this time? Doesn't he *realize* how hurt I've been?

I'm mouthing my thoughts aloud, my heart beating faster and faster with righteous indignation. And suddenly, as I see myself, I flush with humiliation. What's *happened* to me? What am I *doing*? Hiding behind a bush, talking to myself, clutching on to all my grievances. When I should be . . . what?

Tackling them, says a small voice in my head. *Dealing with them*. I'm as bad as Gus was with Romilly, I realize with a sudden flare of shame. Avoiding the issue, instead of taking action. Gus hid behind his work; I'm hiding behind a bush. But it's the same. You can't fix something if you're hiding from it.

Maybe I don't understand where Dad's coming from. And maybe he doesn't understand where I'm coming from. But we'll never work it out until we start a conversation. Even if it's awkward. Even if it's painful. Even if I have to make the first move.

But . . . what can I do? How can I even begin? Should I just stand up behind this bush?

The idea petrifies me. Maybe I'll just wait a moment longer. Plus, I'm desperate to hear more of this conversation.

'Bean, why didn't you mention this before?' Dad is saying now. 'Why didn't you tell me?'

'I tried!' she explodes. 'The minute Effie told me about the invitation, I called you. I left messages . . . I tried everything! But I couldn't get through! I've tried calling you so many times this week, but Krista's always answered and fobbed me off.'

'He was busy!' Krista lashes back defensively. 'Tony, you told me you were too busy to talk to the children! I was following instructions.'

'I couldn't even talk to you properly at the party. Nor could Gus.' Bean shakes her head disbelievingly. 'It's as if you've been avoiding us. And then Effie said, "Don't bring it up." But it needed to be brought up.' Bean comes to a halt, then takes a deep breath and speaks more calmly. 'Effie wasn't being stubborn, Dad. She was hurt.'

Immediately, my brain tries to play fair with this comment. If I'm absolutely honest, I *was* being quite stubborn. But I was also hurt. And I think that finally, *finally*, Dad is getting this. I can see it in his face. I can see him processing it. His eyes are distant and he keeps wincing as though with realization. Is he only just now putting it all together? What planet has he been on?

At last, he blinks into focus again, his face a little craggy.

'Is anyone in touch with Effie?' he says. 'Does anyone know where she is, right now?'

Without quite meaning to, I get half to my feet, then duck back down again in panic.

'Right *now*?' Bean looks wrong-footed. 'You mean . . . actually this minute?'

'Yes,' says Dad. 'Does anyone know?'

A weird frisson passes round the table. Bean looks wildly at Joe, then at Gus, who also glances at Joe, who clears his throat and nods towards the house under the guise of shifting his chair.

Honestly. What a pantomime. Do they think they're being subtle?

'I'm not *exactly* sure,' says Bean in a stilted voice. 'Gus? Do you know where Effie is?'

'I . . . umm . . .' Gus rubs his face. 'Difficult to say. She could be anywhere. In theory.'

'Exactly.' Bean nods. 'That's what makes it hard. To . . . know. Where she is.' She reaches for her glass and takes a large gulp.

'You know, I nearly sent her a text this morning, but . . . I have no idea why I didn't, in the end.' Dad draws a deep breath, looking agonized. '*When* do we all stop making mistakes?'

Everyone at the table seems a bit dumbstruck by this rhetorical question, apart from Lacey, who says brightly, 'I'm sure you don't make any mistakes, Tony! A top businessman like you!'

Dad gives her a blank glance, then reaches for his phone. A moment later, there's a buzzing in my pocket. Fumbling, I pull out my phone. And even though I know who it is, my throat still thickens as I see the word. *Dad*. There on my screen. *Dad*. At last.

Already my thumb is automatically moving to accept the call – but then I stop, flustered. No. Don't be stupid. I can't answer him here, under the rose bush, where everyone will hear. But I can't not answer, either. What do I do?

I crouch, frozen, watching my phone buzzing away, my head in turmoil – until suddenly I know exactly what I'm going to do. Breathing hard, my leg muscles burning, I edge backwards, away from the brunch, towards the house.

'She's not answering,' I can hear Dad saying as I straighten up and start tiptoeing swiftly towards the back door.

I'm not answering yet. But I'll be in touch very, very soon. And not by phone. In person.

*

As I rattle the hangers along Bean's wardrobe rail, I feel apprehensive, almost jittery. I want to build bridges with Dad. I really want to. There are still things in our history that don't make sense to me; there are still things that seem to put reconciliation out of reach. But then, I thought Joe was out of reach. Maybe nothing's impossible.

As long as I'm in a good dress. This is key. Krista and Lacey are still downstairs with their fake lashes and immaculate outfits, and I'm *not* having them looking at me pityingly.

It only took me a few seconds to sneak in through the back door and up the stairs, and now I'm moving as quickly as possible. I want to turn around and get back down to the brunch as soon as I can. Sooner.

At last, I find the frock I was searching for – the flattering blue print one with the sash – and drag it on, then hastily apply a bit of make-up. My hair is a disaster, but it can go in one of Bean's sparkly party hair clips.

I give myself a final lashing of bronzer for Dutch courage, survey myself in the mirror, then turn and almost skip out of the room. As I fly down the stairs, at the half-turn I can see the brunch table out of the French doors that lead to a little mezzanine-level balcony. And even though I'm in a hurry, I can't help pausing to survey the scene. It couldn't look more idyllic: a family gathered in a sunny garden around a beautiful table. The bunting is fluttering in the breeze. The glasses and dishes are glinting in the sunshine. Everyone looks well-dressed and handsome, with Dad sitting at the head of the table like some noble patriarch.

At the idea of surprising them all, my heart starts thumping with nerves. How will I do it? I'll go straight up to Dad. And I'll say . . . what?

Dad, it's me.

No, that's stupid. He knows it's me.

Dad, it's been too long.

But that sounds like I'm blaming him already. Oh God, maybe I should just wing it . . .

A sudden burst of clapping makes me jump and I see that Humph has adopted some kind of yoga-type position on the grass. He's wearing leather flip-flops with his linen suit, I notice, and he looks pretty uncomfortable, with his legs crunched above his face.

Oh, I *have* to find out what's going on. And before I know what I'm doing, I'm pushing open the doors to the mezzanine balcony, formulating a new plan. I'll just stand here until someone looks up and notices me, then casually say, 'Oh hi, everyone!' and watch their jaws drop.

Humph's voice is floating upwards on the summer air, from between his thighs.

'My internal organs are aligning as you watch,' he's calling out breathlessly. 'I can feel the flow of my *rhu*, actually *feel* it. Coursing through my body, healing any imperfections it finds along the way.'

'Did he say, "I can feel the flow of my poo"?' Dad says to Joe, looking baffled, and Joe chokes on his drink.

'*Rhu*,' he says, obviously trying to control his laughter. 'He said *rhu*. It's a Spinken concept, apparently.'

'Amazing!' says Lacey, applauding. 'You should do contortioning, Humph. You'd be a natural.'

'Lace, show them your splits,' calls out Krista, as Humph uncurls himself. 'You've got to see Lacey's splits!'

But Lacey wrinkles her nose. 'Not in this dress, love.'

No one has noticed me yet, so I step forward, right to the front of the balcony, and lean over the old wooden balustrade, my dress lifting in the breeze, listening as the conversation moves on. They've *got* to see me now, surely? And I'm just wondering whether to call out, when Bean's sharp, distressed voice draws my attention.

'What?' she's saying to Krista. '*What* did you just say?'

She looks devastated and my stomach flips over in alarm. What's happened?

'Bean?' says Dad, but she ignores him.

'They've sold my furniture,' she says, turning to Gus, her voice a half-sob. 'Just sold it without telling me. My Peter Rabbit furniture. It's going to the buyers, along with the house.'

I feel a streak of utter shock. They've done what? *What?*

'You can't do that!' says Gus to Dad, who seems flummoxed. 'You sold Bean's *furniture?*'

Dad swallows, looking totally out of his depth, then says, 'Krista?'

'The buyers wished to purchase some items from the house which took their fancy,' says Krista defensively. 'I worked it all out with the agents. You never told me the furniture was special.'

'Why on earth was it up to *Krista?*' Bean explodes.

'I was simply helping your dad out,' snaps Krista. 'He's had a lot on his plate recently. You children should realize that, instead of bothering him about some manky old furniture.'

'Mimi would have known.' Bean looks at Dad with tormented, impassioned eyes. 'Mimi would never have let that happen. I wanted that furniture in my cottage. In my spare bedroom. I wanted it for—' She stops abruptly and looks away, flushing.

For her baby, I suddenly realize, with a shaft of anguish. Maybe she wanted the furniture for herself originally. But now she wants it for her baby. And as I gaze at her anxiously, she seems strained beyond the limits of her endurance.

'You know what?' she says, suddenly pushing back her chair. 'Effie was right. She was right all the time, and I wouldn't listen. This family is over. We're broken.'

'Now, Bean,' says Dad, looking dismayed. 'We'll sort this out, I promise.'

But Bean doesn't even seem to hear him.

'I've done everything,' she says, her voice shaking. 'I've tried to bond, I've tried to forgive, I've read books, I've listened to podcasts. I've come to this fucking party and put my hair in a fucking updo and it's hurting my head and I am *over* this. I'm *over* it.' With erratic movements, she wrenches off her hat, then starts pulling grips out of her hair, still talking jerkily. 'Effie was right! This family is broken. Shattered. A bomb went off and we can never be put back together. Never. We're like a broken plate. Like this broken plate right here.' She grabs the nearest plate, a white filigree china one.

I'm so thrown by her outburst, I have to cling on to the balustrade. This can't be happening. Bean was the optimistic one. Bean was the conciliatory one. If *Bean*'s giving up . . .

'That plate isn't broken,' says Krista, staring at Bean as though she's mad.

'Oh, isn't it?' says Bean shrilly. 'My mistake.' As everyone watches, dumbstruck, she throws it down on to the terrace flagstones, where it smashes. There's a general gasp, and Lacey screams. 'Oops,' says Bean to Krista. 'Hope you weren't planning to sell that, too. Maybe you can put it down as wear and tear. Oops,' she adds, grabbing another plate and smashing it on the flagstones, too. 'More wear and tear. Such a shame when people spoil things you love, isn't it, Krista?'

She picks up a third plate and Krista stands up, her nostrils flared.

'Don't you break that plate,' she says ominously, her chest rising and falling in her silk dress. 'Don't you break it.'

'Why shouldn't I?' Bean gives a weird laugh. 'You've spoiled enough! You painted over Mimi's kitchen, you ruined our house, you threw your drink over Effie . . . and now you're complaining about *plates*?'

Krista's eyes run over her coldly. 'That's your dad's plate.'

'Is it?' says Bean hysterically. 'Well, you should know! You were eyeing him up before you even met him, Krista, weren't you? Asking questions about him, pricing up the house. Is this plate worth something, then? Maybe he's going to leave it to me in his will! Are you, Dad?' She turns and hurls it at the sundial on the lawn and a piece of jagged china ricochets off, straight at Humph.

'Ow!' he yells. 'You've cut my foot!'

Bean halts, drawn up short, and for a breathless beat, no one moves a muscle.

'Well, I'm sorry,' she says, breathing hard. 'I truly am. But you know what, Humph? Your foot is just another piece of collateral damage. Like my furniture. And Mimi's kitchen. And everything we loved.' Tears start running down her pink cheeks. 'It's all broken. Effie was right.' She sinks down into her chair and gives an almighty sob. 'It's all broken.'

I can't bear it. I can't bear it. I can't bear to see my lovely, patient, hopeful, well-meaning sister sobbing.

'Bean!' I come out of my transfixed spell and lean desperately over the balustrade, tears pricking my own eyes. 'Bean, please don't cry! We'll be OK!'

'*Effie*?' Bean raises an incredulous, tear-stained face.

'We'll be OK!' I lean even further over, wishing I could reach her hands. 'I swear it! We'll find a way. We'll—'

I break off mid-sentence as I hear a crack – and then, for the second time today, it comes to me that I'm about to die, as the wooden balustrade suddenly gives way under my weight, splintering into bits.

I can't even cry out. I'm crashing down through the air before I can stop myself, breathless, numb with shock, unable to think—

Crump.

'Ow!'

'*Shit.*'

Somehow Joe's arms are around me before I land, breaking my fall, so that we hit the ground as a tumbling pair. We roll a couple of times, then come to a halt. For a few seconds I look into his face, breathing like a piston engine, unable to compute what just happened. Then slowly, gradually, he releases me.

He looks white. And I feel a bit white.

'Thanks.' I swallow. 'Thanks for . . . Thanks.'

My head is spinning. I'm going to be sick. Am I going to be sick? No, maybe not. I take a deep breath and give a weird, shaky laugh as I survey my limbs.

'Not even a bruise,' I say. 'Not even a scratch. You're good.'

'Can you move everything?' Joe demands.

'Um . . .' Experimentally I jiggle my arms and legs. 'Yes, I can. How about you?'

'Yes.' Joe flashes me a grin. 'Thank you. Now, get up *slowly*. And tell me if anything hurts.'

I obey him, standing up and cautiously shaking out my limbs. 'I'm fine. My ankle's a bit twisted. But I'm fine.'

'Good.' He breathes out. 'Good. Might want to get that railing fixed.'

All this time, there's been a deathly silence over the rest of the group, as they've watched us, but now Lacey points at me in sudden recognition.

'Kate!'

'Effie,' Gus corrects her. 'That's Effie.'

'*Effie?*' Lacey's eyes narrow in disbelief. 'That's Effie? I *knew* you weren't really a doctor! I knew that was all a load of bollocks!'

'*Kate?*' Bean goggles at me, and I can see everything falling into place in her brain. 'Oh, thank God! *You're* Kate! That's one weight off my mind, anyway. So you . . .' Her eyes dart between Joe and me. 'You two . . . ?'

'You can stop lecturing me about inappropriate workplace relationships now, Bean,' says Joe, taking my hand and kissing my fingertips. 'How do you feel?' he adds to me.

'Bit shaky,' I admit. 'But . . . you know. OK. Bean, are *you* OK?' I add anxiously.

'Not really,' says Bean. 'But I'll survive.'

'Have some water.' Joe pours me a glass and watches me as I drink it down. 'And take it easy.'

'Look at the lovebirds,' says Lacey, her voice acid. 'So, you came to the party after all, Effie. Couldn't stay away? Your ears must have been burning!'

'Oh, believe me, they were.' I shoot a scathing little glance at Humph, who looks hastily away.

'Yes, nice of you to drop in, Effie.' Gus cracks up at his own joke. 'Get it? Drop in.'

Krista hasn't said anything yet, and as I turn to face her, I can feel the old animosity crackling between us. But I don't mind. I'm going to be the bigger person. Calmly, crunching over the ravaged crockery, I walk up to her with my most dignified expression.

'Thank you for your kind invitation, Krista,' I say formally. 'On reflection, I find I am able to accept.'

'Well, you're very welcome, Effie, I'm sure,' says Krista, her mouth tightening. 'You always were.'

'Thank you,' I say for good measure. 'Most considerate of you.'

'My absolute pleasure,' says Krista, folding her arms.

And now there's just Dad. Finally, Dad. I haven't even looked at him yet. I haven't got to that. But now . . .

As I turn to face him, I feel a lurch, because he's so pale.

'I thought you were going to die,' he says. 'I thought . . . Oh God . . .' He makes an inarticulate sound like a rusty music box, then breathes out sharply. 'But you're OK. You're OK. That's all that matters.'

'Dad . . .' I swallow hard.

'Oh, Effie.' As his eyes meet mine, they're the eyes I remember from my childhood. The warm, twinkling eyes of my dad.

'Dad . . .' I try again. But I don't know how to continue. Where do I start? 'Dad—'

'Ahem. Excuse me.' A man's throat-clearing noise makes us both jump.

In a daze, I swivel my head to see a balding man in a suit standing on the terrace, holding a briefcase, looking at us awkwardly. 'I'm sorry to interrupt this . . . um . . . family moment.' He takes a few steps forward, carefully avoiding all the bits of shattered crockery. 'My name is Edwin Fullerton. I'm from Blakes Estate Agents. I'm here on behalf of the Van Beurens.'

'The *who*?' Gus wrinkles his brow.

'The Van Beurens. The buyers of this property.' He gestures at the house, and we all glance at each other uneasily.

So the buyers are called the Van Beurens. I've never heard

their name before, I realize, and to my ear, it sounds instantly sinister. No wonder they went around the house, stealing all our stuff.

'What do they want?' says Dad.

'They wished me to clarify how much space there was for their delivery vans in the drive. If you didn't mind me measuring up?' He clears his throat again. 'Although, please do mention if this isn't a good time.'

I can see him carefully trying not to notice the shattered plates, or Humph's bleeding foot, or Bean's tearful face, and in the end he aims his gaze at the sky as though he's suddenly interested in the clouds.

'Of course. Please go ahead. We were just having . . .' Dad pauses, as though he's not sure how to describe the spectacle in front of him. 'Brunch.'

'Indeed.' Edwin nods tactfully. 'There were also a few further small matters I wanted to check, if I could beg a moment of your time, Mr Talbot? Although, as I say, this might be an awkward . . . um . . .' He shuffles his feet. 'I did leave a message on your mobile phone.'

'You and the rest of us,' says Bean pleasantly. 'Our father has been spectacularly unavailable this week. So. No surprise there.'

I glance at her, a bit discomfited. She doesn't sound like Bean. She sounds cynical. Her face is tight and jaded. She looks as if her expectations of life have sunk so low she's not going to bother having any, any more.

Edwin's eyes dart nervously between Bean and Dad.

'It's really no problem,' he says.

'Maybe not for an estate agent,' agrees Bean. 'For his children, it's a bit of an issue. What with stepmothers selling off cherished possessions, that kind of thing. But there we are.

That's our family, for better or for worse. Tell me,' she adds, in friendly tones, 'were the Van Beurens intending to buy these plates?' She picks up an undamaged one and brandishes it at him. 'Because some of them might be just a *teensy* bit cracked. Sorry about that.' She gestures at the carpet of broken china. 'Wear and tear.'

Edwin Fullerton looks speechlessly at the shattered bits of plates, then up at Bean again, as though not sure whether she's joking.

'I would have to consult the contract,' he says at last.

'Well, do let us know,' says Bean. 'Because we'd hate to let down the Van Beurens. That would be our worst nightmare.' She blinks at him. '*Literally*, our worst nightmare.'

'Right.' Edwin Fullerton seems unable to find an answer. 'Well. Indeed.'

'Let me . . .' Dad seems to gather himself. 'Let me show you into my office.'

'Worst nightmare!' calls out Bean, as the two men walk away. 'We just want the Van Beurens to be happy!'

I exchange glances with Joe, and I can tell he's also startled by Bean's whole new personality. What's *happened* to her?

'I'd better pop along too,' says Krista to Lacey. 'See what they're talking about. Have some more wine, or whatever you want, love. You too, Humph.'

She strides off without even looking at the rest of us, and I immediately draw breath, but Humph gets in first.

'I'm actually bleeding rather badly?' he says fretfully. 'I need to go to A&E, but I haven't got my car here. My dad dropped me. Can anyone take me?'

'To A&E?' Joe gives a bark of incredulous laughter. 'What, to a hospital, with, what do you call it, "mainstream medicine"?'

'Why don't you just align your whatsits?' suggests Gus,

pouring himself another glass of wine. 'Internal thingummies. Your *rhu* will sort you out, Humph. Trust your *rhu*.'

'Funny,' says Humph tightly. 'But you really don't understand what you're talking about, so I suggest you don't try.'

'I thought the *rhu* was supposed to heal everything with its transcendent power?' says Joe. 'Healthcare begins and ends with the *rhu*, isn't that right?'

'There. Are. Exceptions,' says Humph, spitting out each word.

'Oh, *exceptions*.' Joe grins at Humph, then seems to relent. 'Well, as someone who took a different route to medical qualification, I would say that you should definitely go to A&E and have that seen to. It looks a bit nasty. Technical term.'

'I've called a cab,' says Lacey, standing up in a businesslike way. 'I'll take you, Humph. I'll mop your fevered brow. Not just mock your beliefs, like *some* people.' She shakes her hair back and addresses Joe squarely. 'People believe in penicillin, don't they? So why shouldn't they believe in the *rhu*?'

Joe stares back at her, dumbfounded. 'Because . . .' He rubs his face. 'OK, I don't even know how to answer that.'

'Exactly!' says Lacey triumphantly, as though she's scored a direct hit. 'Humph, my love, you come with me. I'll stay with you, make sure you're all right. And then maybe you can show me your studio.' She bats her eyelashes seductively. 'I'd love to learn more about your work.'

I bet she would. And his stately home. And his title. Although she'd better not be holding out for his massive great fortune, even I know that much.

She extends an arm for him to lean on, and the pair of them move off together, Humph hopping along beside her determined stride.

'Oh,' he suddenly says, remembering his old-school manners and turning back. 'Please thank your father and Krista for a delightful party and tell them I'm sorry I couldn't say goodbye in person. I'll write, obviously.'

'Of course. And good luck!' I say, suddenly feeling a bit sorry for him. I wouldn't like to be relying on either the *rhu* or Lacey for my happiness.

We watch them making their way round to the drive – then, as they disappear from view, we all subside and look at each other.

'I knew someone would get taken to A&E,' says Joe. 'Don't want to say I called it, but I called it.'

'It's not brunch unless there's a trip to A&E,' I say, feeling a bit hysterical. 'Everyone knows that. Oh God . . .' As I look around at the broken china littering the terrace and lawn, I start to laugh a slightly painful laugh. 'Look at this place! That estate agent seemed absolutely freaked out.'

'He's phoning the Van Beurens right now,' says Gus. 'He's saying, "Quick! Move in before they wreck the place! They're all crazy!"'

'Oh God, you're right. His *face*!' I give another gurgle of laughter. 'Joe, are you sure you want to be associated with me? Because I have to warn you, I have a pretty sketchy family.'

'Oh, I'm used to you lot.' Joe flashes me a quick grin, then glances at Bean and back at me, a question on his face.

I turn to survey Bean and feel a little wrench inside. She's sitting with her bare feet pulled up on to her seat, her arms hunched round her knees, staring into the distance, not listening to any of us.

'Are you OK, Bean?' I ask anxiously. 'You seem quite . . . stressed.'

'I'm not stressed,' she contradicts me at once.

'Bean.' I bite my lip. 'Be honest.'

'Really, I'm not.' She turns to face me. 'I'm not anything.

261

Couldn't care less. I'm over it. Don't care about the house . . . don't care about the family . . . don't care about anything. It's quite freeing, actually!' She gives a strange little laugh, which doesn't sound anything like her.

I make a worried face at Joe, who frowns.

'Bean, listen,' I try again. 'I'll talk to Dad about the furniture—'

'Don't bother.'

'But—'

'Whatever!' Bean cuts me off determinedly. 'I mean, really, whatever. I feel like I'm an elastic band and I've been pulled too hard, too many times, and you know what? I'm out of bounce. I give up. I'm going to the pub to eat crisps.' She pushes her chair back, slips on her sandals and picks up her handbag. 'All the crisps.'

'The pub!' exclaims Gus. He drains his wine glass, then stands up, teetering so much he has to grab on to his chair. 'The pub. Tremendous idea. We should have gone to the pub in the first place. Why didn't we?' He gestures emphatically, as though he's giving a lecture to thousands. 'It's always a mistake not to go to the pub. Yet we never learn. We *never learn*.'

'Come on, then,' says Bean. 'Let's go. My round.'

'Will you go with them and make sure they're OK?' I murmur quickly to Joe. 'Bean's in a really strange mood and Gus is totally pissed.'

'Of course,' he murmurs back. 'But what about you? Aren't you coming?'

'In a bit. I just have a bit of . . . unfinished business.'

'OK.' He nods and squeezes my arm briefly. 'Got it.'

'Effie . . .' Bean comes over to me and gives me a sudden, unexpected hug. 'I just need to say sorry. You were right. You were right about everything. You could see it all clearly and

I was the deluded one.' She shakes her head. 'We're not a family any more. It's shattered. It's broken. Over.'

'Bean, don't say that.' I stare at her, dismayed.

'You said it yourself!' she retorts, with yet another weird laugh. 'And it's true!'

She gives me another hug, then walks off, scooping up Gus's arm as she does, and I watch them go, feeling all jumbled up. I know I said it. I know I believed it. But somehow, when Bean says it, it feels wrong. I want to grab her and protest, *We're not broken! It's not too late! We can still be fixed!*

But can we?

Slowly my eyes turn towards the house, standing silent in the afternoon sunshine. There's only one way to find out.

EIGHTEEN

As I line myself up in front of Greenoaks again, like a gymnast ready for her second go, I'm determined. This time I'm not going to be distracted by anything.

Lightly but briskly, I walk towards the familiar front door of my childhood home for the last time. I must take this moment in. I must remember the details. The intricate (*not* ugly) brickwork. The distinctive chimneys. The stained glass. The way the . . .

Wait, what?

Humph?

I do not bloody believe this. Humph has appeared through the door and is now on the doorstep, holding on to the doorframe as though he'll keel over otherwise. Of all the people to pop up. I thought he would be at hospital by now. Or being seduced by Lacey. Or both.

'Hi,' he says plaintively as I approach. 'Lacey's just getting her things. Then we'll be off to hospital.'

'Right. Well, I hope they look after you. Bean didn't mean to hurt you,' I add, with a twinge of guilt. 'It was an accident.'

'Oh, I know,' says Humph. 'Bean wouldn't hurt a fly. She seemed a little bit . . .' He wrinkles his brow. 'Hassled?'

'Yes,' I say. 'Just . . . you know. Everything.'

'I don't blame her.' Humph nods with what seems like genuine sympathy.

'Do you know if that estate-agent guy is still with my dad?'

'No, he came out a few minutes ago,' says Humph, jerking his finger vaguely towards the left of the house. 'Don't know where he went.'

'OK, thanks.' I smile politely, and am about to head past him into the house when he says,

'Wait. Can I ask you something? Effie, how long were you standing on that balcony before you fell?'

I look at him curiously, not sure why he's asking. Then I see the sheepish expression on his face and instantly get it.

'Are you wondering if I heard you saying I've always been passionately in love with you and bombarded you with love letters?' I give him a pointed look.

Humph's cheeks turn crimson, and he suddenly looks a lot more like the gawky guy I dated than a smooth Spinken practitioner.

'I know you weren't ever in love with me,' he mumbles, his head downcast. 'Sorry.'

'That's OK,' I say.

'I'm a bit hassled myself,' he says miserably. 'I think my parents might be splitting up.' He raises his eyes to mine. 'It's all a bit hellish, over at our place.'

'Really?' I wince. 'There's a lot of it about.'

'I guess.' All his pompous veneer has dropped away. In his

eyes I can see a worried, fearful expression I recognize, and I feel a wash of sympathy for him. Even affection.

'You know what?' I hear myself saying. 'It'll be OK. *You*'ll be OK. If you ever want to talk, give me a call. As friends.'

'Thanks,' says Humph. 'Really.'

'You'll have ups and downs, but hang in there, because you'll get through. You'll find a way.'

I'm saying words I don't recognize. Words I've never thought before.

Am I finding a way? At last?

'That's good to hear.' Humph seems to be hanging on my every utterance. 'It's inspiring. You always seem so together, Effie.'

I explode with laughter before I can stop myself.

'Together? Me? *Together?* Weren't you listening at dinner to the Effie Car Crash Show?'

'But you weren't at dinner!' exclaims Humph, looking startled. 'How do you know that?'

'I was under the console table,' I explain. 'I heard everything.'

'Oh.' Humph rubs his nose and I can see him adjusting his thoughts. 'I see. Well, for what it's worth, I thought you were maligned. I've always found you a very together sort of person. That's why I admired you.'

'Humph, you didn't *admire* me,' I say, rolling my eyes.

'I did,' he insists. 'I always did.' A strange sort of flicker passes over his face before he adds, 'So, you're with Joe again now?'

'Yes.' I can't help smiling happily. 'I'm with Joe.'

'Huh.' He nods several times. 'I mean . . . yes. Makes sense. Absolutely.'

'And you're . . . with Lacey?' I venture.

'Oh, I can't afford Lacey,' he says frankly. 'She'll find out soon enough, but I'm hoping she'll get me to the hospital first.'

I'd forgotten that Humph can be quite funny and self-deprecating. I painted him in a really negative way in my mind, over the years – but that picture wasn't quite true. Maybe I did it so I wouldn't feel bad about the way I treated him.

'Sorry,' I say impulsively.

'For what?'

'Humph, I was dreadful to you. Back then.'

'Sorry, too,' he says, shrugging. 'I realize now I was a really bad kisser. I've improved.'

I can't help laughing again and he grins back, and I decide I will definitely get him out for a drink sometime.

'Well, see you,' I say, and touch him a little awkwardly on the arm.

'See you.' He glances up at the house. 'Good times.'

I nod. 'Good times.'

There's a moment of silence – then I lift my chin firmly and walk into Greenoaks. Effie Talbot is in the house.

As I walk through the quiet hall, I feel hollow with nerves. I don't know what I'm going to say to Dad. My thoughts are like Formula One cars, screeching round and round my brain.

Then Dad's office door opens. He sees me and both of us freeze.

'Effie,' he says at last, looking as wary as I feel.

'Dad,' I reply, my voice strangled. 'I thought . . . maybe we should talk?'

'Come in.' He nods at his office as though I'm here for a job interview and, feeling a bit unreal, I head in. It's still the room I remember: his old desk, his computer screens, his chessboard set up by the fireplace. Dad and I used to play chess, I recall with a twinge. After Bean and Gus had left for uni and it was just me living at home. I'd come in here after I'd done my homework. Dad would be drinking a G&T. We'd play a few moves, then leave the board for next time.

I look up to see that Dad is gazing at me ruefully.

'I thought you weren't coming to the party,' he says. 'But I'm so glad you changed your mind, Effie. Even if your entrance was on the dramatic side. *Please* don't ever sky-dive into a party again, darling, or I'll be the one going to A&E, with a heart attack.'

He sounds as though he's trying to make me laugh, and I try to smile, but it doesn't quite work. There's too much hurt swilling around the room. Or am I the only one who can feel it?

'Dad . . .' I pause, as possible openers fill my head. *I've been so upset . . . I've felt so shut out . . . Why did you ignore my messages?* But instead of any of them, I hear myself saying, 'Dad, we're worried about you.'

'Worried?' Dad stares at me, as though confused. '*Worried?*'

'We all are. Me, Gus, Bean . . .' I take a step forward, suddenly desperate to express my fears. 'Dad, how well do you know Krista? What's her background? Because she's got an agenda, she really has. She was secretly pricing up the furniture with Lacey. We heard her. And did you know she targeted you before you met? Mike Woodson told Gus.'

'Mike Woodson?' Dad seems staggered. 'Mike Woodson's been *discussing* me?'

'Everyone's worried!' My words tumble out in a fervent rush. 'People are just looking out for you!'

'Well, they needn't, thanks very much,' begins Dad tightly, but I'm not having him brushing me off again.

'*Please* listen,' I say urgently. '*Please*. Krista was asking people about you at the Holyhead Arms, but then she pretended she just met you by chance. She lied, Dad! She's after your money! She's already got a great big diamond. You never bought Mimi a great big diamond. And she wants to invest all your money in a restaurant in Portugal and we just feel . . . we're so worried . . .' I break off as I hear the approaching gunfire of Krista's heels.

Oh God. My heart starts to hammer. Did she hear me? What exactly did she hear? In a way, if she heard me, I'm glad. This has to come out, one way or another.

Krista sweeps into the room, accompanied by Bambi – and from her icy glare, it's obvious: she heard.

'You just can't leave it, can you?' she says, in tones of contempt. 'I know you think I'm a gold-digger. What a bloody joke! There's no gold in this house.' She strides up and looks me right in the eyes, her stony gaze unblinking. 'I'm not a gold-digger. I own a business. I pay my way. This isn't a bloody diamond – what do you think I am, a fool?' She jiggles her sparkler at me so aggressively I flinch. 'It's Diamonique. If I want to spend money on something pricey, I'll buy shares in a Nasdaq fund. *Won't* I, Bambi?' she adds, and Bambi answers with a yap.

Diamonique?

I look dumbly at the pendant, still sparkling away against her tanned skin.

'*Isn't* it a diamond? I'm sure you and Dad said—'

'Maybe we said it was a diamond,' Krista cuts me off impatiently. 'What's the difference? We used to laugh about it. I told your dad, "Your kids think I'm a gold-digger," and it was funny. But you just couldn't let it go, could you? Every time he wants to have a bit of fun, you kids are right there, stomping on him. You especially, Miss Effie.' She jabs a finger at me. 'Jeez! Drives me mad. Oh, and while you're still mouthing off, you might like to know my sister Lacey's doing you all a *favour*. Her ex is an antiques dealer. So she knows a bit and she's got contacts. Your dad's strapped for cash. *That*'s what you should be worrying about, not my poor little sparkler.'

'Strapped for cash?' I echo, nonplussed.

'Krista!' Dad interjects, looking pained.

'It's time they knew!' says Krista, wheeling round to Dad. 'Tell her, Tone!'

'Effie . . .' Dad rubs his brow, looking beleaguered. 'I do think you've got the wrong end of the stick.'

'What do you mean, strapped for cash?' I stare at him.

'That's overstating it,' Dad says, his hands gripping his desk tightly. 'But . . . I have had financial concerns. And they did distract me for a while.'

'Why didn't you *say*?' I gaze at him, stricken.

'I didn't want to worry you, darling,' says Dad, and Krista makes a loud exclamation of impatience.

'Give me strength! You're always talking about "worrying the children". They're grown-ups! Let them worry! They *should* worry! And if I hear one more word about that *bloody* kitchen . . .'

She sounds like she wants to explode, and I swivel back to her, my blood up. I can't *believe* she's got the nerve to mention the kitchen.

'Mimi's kitchen was a work of art.' My voice trembles with anger. 'It was magical. It wasn't just us who loved it – everyone in the village loved it, too. And if you can't appreciate that—'

'It was a liability!' Krista cuts me off scornfully. 'Every estate agent said the same thing. Great house. Well – weird, ugly house.' She shrugs. 'But saleable, just about. As long as you do something about that eyesore of a kitchen. Clean it up. Paint it. Get rid of the squirrels and rats and shit.'

I stare at her, blinking in shock, unable to speak. Squirrels and rats and shit?

'There weren't any drawings of *rats*,' I say, finally finding my voice. 'There weren't any *rats*.'

'They all looked like rats to me,' retorts Krista, unmoved. 'So I say, "Fine. I'll do it myself." I'm quite nifty with a roller. But your dad starts wailing on about Mimi and all the precious memories and how the kids will kill him. So I said, "Blame me. Tell them it was my idea. I don't care what your kids think of me." Then you come round, the kitchen looks a million dollars, and guess what? The house has already had a load more viewings. But do I get any thanks? No, of course I don't. I knew you'd flip out,' she adds, her eyes flicking over me. 'I said, "Effie's the one, she'll throw the hissy fit." And sure enough. Like clockwork.'

My face is burning. It never occurred to me . . . I never realized.

'Why didn't you *say*, Dad?' I turn to him in sudden agitation. 'You should have *said*. You could have explained about the estate agents, talked us through it. We would have understood . . .'

'Don't you think your dad's got enough on his plate?' Krista glares at me. 'He's been stressed as fandango, excuse my French. You think he's got time to ring you lot up and talk you through *cupboards*? I said to him, "Don't discuss it with them, Tone. We'll just do it. Job done, end of."'

'Stressed about what?' I say blankly, and Krista erupts.

'What do you think? I already told you! *Money*. Like I say, there's no gold in this house.'

'But I don't understand,' I say, feeling as though I'm going a bit mad. 'You said it had been a great year for Dad's invest-ments at dinner last night! You said he was swimming in profits!' Abruptly I realize I've given myself away. 'I was hid-ing under the console table,' I add awkwardly. 'In fact . . . I've kind of been at the party the whole time.'

'*What?*' Dad gapes at me, then gives a sudden snort, which I think might be laughter. 'Oh, Effie.'

'You were under the console table?' says Krista sharply.

'Before dinner, too,' I add. 'When you were . . . dressing the table.'

And undressing yourself, I message her silently. From the snap in Krista's eyes, I can tell she's understood.

'Might have figured you'd sneak yourself in,' she says coldly. 'I should sue that bouncer. He was supposed to keep crashers out.'

'Well, he couldn't keep *me* out. And I heard you at dinner, saying how great Dad's year had been. How he'd made a stack. Didn't she, Dad?' I appeal to him.

'Krista tries to boost my ego,' says Dad, wincing. 'She means well, but . . .'

'Whose business is it?' says Krista defiantly. 'Put your best face on, that's what I say. Spread a little party dust. Why not let everyone think your dad's on great form. Better than tell-ing the truth, ruining everyone's evening.'

'So . . . what's the truth?' I say, looking from face to face.

'Things have been tricky, ever since the divorce,' says Dad slowly. 'And Krista . . . Krista has tried to help.'

'Much thanks I get.' Krista folds her arms. 'Much bloody thanks I get.'

My head is spinning in confusion. I keep looking from Krista – vibrant, colourful, prickling with indignation – to Dad, who looks a bit grey and worn out in comparison.

Have I misjudged Krista? Have we all misjudged Krista? But no. *No.* My mind rebels. She didn't invite me to the party, remember? She threw her drink over me, remember?

'Effie,' Dad says, his voice grave. 'Did you really refuse to come to the party simply because you didn't approve of my choice of partner?'

'No!' I say, stung. 'No, of course not! OK, so Krista and I don't get on. But I wouldn't not come to a party because of that. It was the invitation. The anti-invitation.'

Dad sighs. 'Darling, Krista explained she made a mistake. Everyone can make a mistake—'

'It *wasn't* a mistake,' I say, feeling fresh hurt. 'It was deliberate. And . . . I assumed it was from you, too,' I add in a smaller voice. 'I assumed you didn't want me to come.'

'*What?*' Dad sounds scandalized. 'How could you think that?'

I stare back, almost exploding with frustration.

'Come *on*, Dad. You've been blanking me for weeks. The day after the kitchen row, I left you that voicemail, but you didn't even reply. Then you send me some awful email about post redirection. I was like . . . OK. I get it. Dad doesn't want to talk. Fine. We won't talk.'

'But I asked you out to lunch!' Dad retorts, his brow creased in consternation. 'I asked you to lunch, Effie. You didn't reply.'

'What?' I gape at him.

'I suggested lunch. When I sent you the hamper. And I never got a voicemail from you.'

I stare at him, aghast. Does he think I'm *lying*?

'I left that voicemail the very next day,' I say, breathing fast. 'The very next day. And what do you mean, hamper? I never got any hamper.'

'It was from Fortnum's.' Dad looks confused. 'A little peace offering. Effie, you *must* have got it.'

'Dad, I think I would know if I'd had a hamper from Fortnum's,' I say shakily. 'I think I might have noticed.'

'But we sent it! At least, Krista sent it,' he amends. 'I was very preoccupied, and she insisted on ordering it, to save me time.' He turns to Krista, and when he sees her brazen, defensive expression, his look changes from disbelief to horror. 'Krista?' he says with ominous quietness.

'I forgot, OK?' says Krista. 'I had a lot on! Anyway, a hamper from Fortnum's, Tone? What nonsense! You couldn't afford a hamper from Fortnum's!'

She forgot? Or she just didn't bother?

'What about my voicemail?' I say in sudden, sharp suspicion and Krista shrugs.

'Your dad gets a lot of voicemails.'

'Do you deal with them?' I meet her gaze directly and she juts out her chin.

'I protect him from them. I'm like his PA. My job is to filter out the crap.'

I'm almost speechless. Crap?

'You don't pass anything on, do you?' I say in sudden realization. 'What, do you *delete* messages? Are you deliberately cutting Dad off? It's Bean and Gus, too,' I add, turning to Dad. 'No one can get through to you, Dad. Everyone tries, everyone wants to talk to you, but it's impossible.'

'Krista?' Dad turns to face her, a vein pulsing in his forehead. 'Krista, what have you been doing?'

'You told me to use my judgement,' says Krista, who seems completely unabashed. 'Well, my judgement is, you do too much for those kids. Jeez! They're not kids, they're *adults*. Ask me, they need to grow up, the lot of them.'

I glance over at Dad and feel a twinge of nerves, because he's pale and trembling.

'Maybe they do,' he says, as though finding it hard to control his voice. 'But that's for me to decide. My relationship with my children is for *me* to decide.' He gazes at Krista for a few silent moments, then adds, almost to himself, 'I knew we had different priorities, but . . .' Again he breaks off, then draws breath. 'Effie, could you give me a moment alone with Krista, please?'

My heart gives an almighty leap. Oh my God . . .

'Um, of course,' I mumble.

My heart juddering, I back away, out of the room. I close the door and take a few steps into the hall – then pause. I can hear their voices, coming from the office. Raised, angry voices.

I just stand there, still a bit stunned, following the distant ebb and flow of heated conversation, wondering desperately what's being said. Whether I should tactfully leave. But somehow I can't. I feel rooted to the floor. What's going *on*?

Then suddenly the door is flung open and Krista strides out, her eyes sparking, breathing furiously.

Shit. I should have escaped while I could. I feel a swoop of fright as she comes right up to me, her jaw set. She tosses her blonde hair back and surveys me contemptuously.

'Well, you win, Miss Effie. Me and your dad – we're over.'

'It isn't about winning,' I say feebly.

'Whatever.'

She flicks her eyes over me again, then reaches in her bag for a packet of cigarettes.

'Gold-digger. Bloody nerve. Yeah, I targeted your dad. But you want to know why? I felt *sorry* for the guy. He looked like a wreck. Didn't want to land myself with some psycho, so I asked around. But, of course, it was just the usual story.

Wife wakes up one morning, wants a divorce, cleans him out. Guy hits the bar, Krista picks up the pieces. Don't know why I do it, I must have a saviour complex.'

'Mimi didn't clean Dad out!' I stare at her uncertainly.

Krista shrugs, putting a cigarette in her mouth. 'Let's say, she did nicely for herself.'

'She's got a flat in Hammersmith!' I exclaim. 'It's hardly the Ritz.'

Krista surveys me for a moment, then starts laughing in genuine mirth.

'Oh, you have no idea, do you?' She gets out a gold lighter and flicks it, trying to get a flame. 'Mimi got a lot more out of your dad than a flat in Hammersmith. You want to see her bank account. I mean, good for her. But not so good for your dad. I've heard a lot about your precious Mimi,' she adds, as her cigarette finally catches light. 'People talk about her. I know she's warm and lovely. With the cutesy drawings. Linen dresses. Baskets. All that.' She takes a long, deep drag, then adds with cool appraisal, 'But if you ask me, you can be warm and lovely, and hard as nails when you want to be.'

Mimi? Hard as nails?

I can't even compute that idea. But then maybe I haven't seen the full picture, I reluctantly allow. Just like I couldn't imagine her being snippy with Dad. I've never seen Mimi doing business. And I guess a divorce settlement is a kind of business.

'Bambi! Come on! We're going!' Krista is already turning on her heel to leave – and I have a sudden realization. She knows stuff about Dad that nobody else knows, and this is my only chance to hear it.

'Krista, what *really* happened?' I ask quickly. 'With Dad's finances?'

Krista turns back, and for a moment I'm not sure if she'll even answer. But then she shrugs.

'He started making riskier investments, didn't he? Ended up staring at that wretched computer screen all day long.' She puffs out smoke. 'My dad was a bookie. I know the fear in people's eyes. That's why I stepped in, started fielding his calls, trying to help him out a bit. You can think what you like of me.' Krista meets my eyes through the cloud of cigarette smoke. 'But I was Team Tony. Well, there we are. All over now. Nice enough guy, Tone. I like him. But his *baggage*. God help me!' She runs her eyes over me again disparagingly and I gulp. I've never thought of myself as baggage before. '*There* you are, Bambi, love,' she adds, as he patters up to her. 'Let's go.'

'Wait!' I say. 'One more thing. Do you admit you threw your Kir Royale over my dress on purpose?'

'Maybe I did,' she says unrepentantly. 'So shoot me. You called me a gold-digger!'

'And you didn't invite me to the party.' I feel a familiar jab of hurt. 'Our last family party at Greenoaks. You deliberately cut me out and didn't tell the truth to Dad.'

Krista inhales and narrows her eyes.

'Maybe I should have sent you an invite.' She shrugs, as though in a brief moment of self-reflection. 'But you *really* got under my skin. You pissed me off. Can't say more than that, really. I felt arsey with you.'

'OK,' I say, suddenly wanting to laugh. 'Well, thanks for your honesty.'

'Maybe because I can see you've got guts,' she adds thoughtfully. 'More than your sister. Bless her. But you two are quite different. You're worth picking a fight with.'

'Oh,' I say, not sure if this is a compliment or not. 'Um . . . thanks?'

'Welcome,' says Krista.

I stare at her immaculate, heavily made-up face, slightly mesmerized. I'm having the weirdest feeling – that I wish I'd got to know Krista. This is the woman I've been having a feud with. Who wrecked my relationship with my dad without even thinking. She's caused so much harm in our family, she nearly broke us up for good. But I can also see now that she gave Dad a good time and livened up his life and gave him practical help. She might be totally immoral, but she's strong and feisty and there's more to her than I realized.

'You're more of a Russian doll than any of us,' I say, before I can stop myself – and Krista instantly bristles.

'A Russian doll?' she retorts indignantly. 'You're calling me a Russian doll? I'm not bloody Russian and I'm not some plastic dolly bird. This is all me!' She gestures over her impressive body. 'Apart from my boobs. But it's only polite to have your boobs done. It's only manners.' With an offended huff, she stubs out her cigarette on a nearby ornamental plate. 'C'mon, Bambs. We're off.'

'Will you be . . . OK?' I hear myself saying.

'Will I be OK?' Krista gives a derisive laugh and swivels to face me. 'I've built up a business and I've turned off my mum's life-support machine and I've punched a shark in the face. I think I can cope with this.'

She flicks her hair back and strides up the stairs, and I watch her go, feeling slightly winded. Then I hear Dad's voice calling, 'Effie? Effie, darling, are you still there?' and I hurry forward.

'Yes,' I call. 'I'm still here. Still here.'

As I enter the office, Dad's sitting in one of the chairs by the fireplace, the chessboard in front of him, and just for a moment, it's as though we've gone back in time.

278

'I've poured us both a drink,' he says, nodding at two glasses of whisky next to the chessboard.

'Thanks,' I say, sitting down opposite him. Dad lifts his glass to me and I smile back hesitantly, and we both sip.

'Oh, Effie.' He breathes out as he puts his glass down. 'I'm so sorry.'

'Well, I'm sorry too. It's been . . .' I search for words. 'I guess we've had some miscommunication.'

'That's diplomatic,' says Dad wryly. 'I still can't quite believe Krista—' He breaks off and closes his eyes.

'Dad,' I say. 'Let's not.'

I really don't think it'll help Dad and me to start discussing Krista. (Plus, I'll do it with Bean, later.)

Dad opens his eyes and surveys me incredulously.

'Were you really at the party, all the time?'

'All the time.' I nod. 'Hiding here and there.'

'But *why*? Not just to avoid Krista?'

'No!' I can't help laughing. 'I was looking for my Russian dolls. You haven't seen them, have you?'

'Your Russian dolls?' Dad frowns thoughtfully. 'Now, I *have* seen them . . . But I'm blessed if I know where.'

'That's what Bean said.' I sigh. 'I guess the packers will turn them up.'

'They won't be lost,' says Dad reassuringly. Then he gives a sudden laugh.

'I can't believe you were hiding under the console table. Remember the Christmas you hid there, when you were a little girl?'

'I was remembering that, too.' I nod. 'You came and hid with me. And then you let me carry in the Christmas pudding.'

'We've had some happy times here,' says Dad and a shadow passes over his face as he reaches for his glass. Now that I'm properly close up to him, I can see that he looks more lined than the last time I saw him. Older. Worrieder. Not at all like someone who's *never been happier*.

He's such a performer, Dad. He can fool his guests and even his own family. But life's difficult, I realize. More difficult than he's been letting on.

And I feel a sudden wash of shame. Have I ever asked Dad how he's doing? Have I ever looked at him as a person? Or only as my dad, who was supposed to be super-human and not get divorced and not sell the house and basically never falter in any way, shape or form?

'Dad, I wish we'd known you were so stressed about money,' I venture tentatively.

'Oh, sweetheart.' Immediately his easy-going veneer snaps over his face. 'Don't worry about that.' He flashes me a confident Tony Talbot smile and I clutch my forehead.

'Dad. Stop. I'm not a child any more. *Tell* me. If you'd just told me the truth that time I found Krista photographing the bureau, instead of biting my head off . . .'

As I replay that scene, I see it so differently now. Dad was defensive. Embarrassed. He couldn't bear to admit the truth – that he had money problems – so he went on the attack.

Dad gazes back for a few silent seconds, then his expression changes and he rubs his cheek.

'You're right, Effie. I behaved badly that day. I apologize. And it's true, I forget that you're adults. Well, all right.' He takes a gulp of whisky, then gives me a frank look. 'Things became pretty scary. All my own fault. When Mimi and I broke up, it was obvious that our assets would be split and that we would have to sell Greenoaks.'

'I never even *thought* about . . .' I pause, embarrassed. 'Financial arrangements.'

280

'Well, why would you?' Dad gives me a sudden, penetrating look. 'Darling, please know that there wasn't any acrimony. Mimi received a fair settlement. We were both satisfied. But . . . it changed things. Of course it did. My financial planning hadn't included a divorce.'

There's a pause as he sips his drink again, and I find myself wondering who he's had to talk to about this.

'And the more I thought about selling Greenoaks . . . the harder I found the prospect.' He gives a long sigh as he glances around the room. 'This house feels like more than a house, somehow. Do you know what I mean?'

Silently, I nod.

'So I decided to see if I couldn't make one almighty push to keep Greenoaks. That was my huge, terrible error.' He gazes down into his glass. 'I took some big investment risks. Broke all my own rules. If I'd been my own client . . .' He shakes his head. 'But there was no one to stop me. And I had a degree of hubris,' he adds candidly. 'I thought I was better at this game than I was.'

'What happened?' I say fearfully.

'Oh, nemesis, of course. It was pretty catastrophic.' Dad speaks lightly, but his eyes are serious. 'There was a hellish couple of weeks when I feared we might end up not just without Greenoaks, but without any home at all. That's when I handed over the reins of family life to Krista. I couldn't think about anything except my desperate salvage operation.' He pauses, as though re-running events in his mind. 'The trouble is, I never took the reins back. It was easy to let Krista run things. I trusted her.'

'So . . . are things OK now?' I hardly dare ask the question.

'Oh, I'll survive.' He sees my face and leans forward to

touch my shoulder reassuringly. 'I'll be fine, Effie. Really. Maybe not in a grand place like this, but life moves on. I'll miss Greenoaks, but there we are.'

He pours himself some more whisky and offers me the decanter, but I shake my head.

'I understand, Dad,' I say. 'I understand why you tried to keep Greenoaks.'

'I was so proud when we moved in here, you know,' says Dad wistfully. 'A boy from Layton-on-Sea, in this house. I remember my old grandad coming to visit, once. Remember him?'

'Er . . . just about,' I say.

'Well, he came to visit us in Greenoaks and I still remember his face when he saw it. I remember him saying, "Well, you did all right, didn't you, Tony?" ' Dad's face brightens at the memory. Then he adds more ruefully, 'Of course, he was a scoundrel, my grandad. Did I tell you about when he and I decided to go into business together? We hatched all kinds of get-rich-quick schemes. None of them worked out, of course.'

'No.' I laugh. 'Why don't we go out to lunch sometime and you can tell me.'

'Thank you, my darling. I'd love that.'

I can see us in a cosy pub, maybe in front of a fire, Dad telling me funny stories about his past. Just the thought makes me feel warm and hopeful.

'But there was more to it than that,' continues Dad slowly, turning his glass round and round in his fingers. 'It wasn't just a status symbol. Greenoaks has been so dear to us. So central to our family life. I worried about what we would look like without it. Whether we would still . . . feel like a family.'

'We will,' I say with a conviction that takes me by surprise. 'We don't need Greenoaks, Dad. We'll still get together, we'll still be together, we'll still be a family. It'll just be . . . different.'

Where are these words coming from? I don't even know. But as I say them, I realize there's a new resolve inside me. I'm going to make them true.

'You're very wise, Effie,' says Dad, his eyes crinkling. 'I should have asked your advice all along.'

Yeah, right, I reply silently, but I won't ruin the moment.

'I need to talk to Bean,' he adds more gravely. 'I need to make things right with her.'

'Dad, you *can't* sell her furniture,' I say. 'It'll break her heart. Can't we take it out of the sale?'

'Oh, Effie.' He shakes his head. 'I'm sorry. The buyers have been tricksy enough, throwing in extra demands, here and there. I can't risk derailing the whole thing.'

'But—'

'Effie, we're not losing this sale.' He blows out, and I see a hinterland of worry behind that statement. 'I'll have to make it up to Bean in some other way.'

For a few moments we're both silent. There's no point pushing the issue any more just now, I think mutinously. But it's not right.

A shaft of sunshine appears from behind a cloud, then disappears again, and I glance up at Dad, who seems lost in memories. In this stillness, I feel as though I could say anything.

Feeling as though I'm walking on eggshells, I take a deep breath and say quietly, 'For a long time, I couldn't believe you and Mimi had split up. I just couldn't deal with it. I used to look back at photos of you both, all the time. Like this one, remember?'

On impulse, I take out my phone and summon up the photo

of me standing on the rocking horse. I hold my phone out and we both gaze at the picture. Dad. Mimi. Me, in my tutu, with my dishevelled bunches. All of us beaming radiantly.

'You look happy,' I say.

'We *were* happy.' Dad nods.

'That was real.' I suddenly realize I'm asking him a question. 'It wasn't . . . You weren't just . . . pretending?'

A tear spills from my eye and runs down my cheek, and Dad's face changes.

'Oh, Effie,' he says in dismay. 'Darling girl. Is that what you've been thinking?'

I stare at the screen, my nose prickling. I know I heard him tell everyone outside that it was a happy time. But what if that was a performance, too?

'The thing is . . . you seemed happy right until you told us you were getting divorced,' I say, still staring intently down. 'So now I look back, all the way back to when I was little, at all the lovely, happy memories, and I think . . . well, what was true?'

'Effie, look at me,' says Dad, and he waits until I reluctantly lift my eyes. 'Listen to me, please. Mimi and I were truly, genuinely happy, throughout your childhood. Until long after all of you left home. And even then, we weren't *un*happy. We just . . . weren't good for each other any more. But our happiness until then was real. You *must* believe that.' He leans forward, his gaze earnest. 'Nothing was contrived. The love that Mimi and I had throughout our marriage was real.' He pauses, as though thinking how to proceed. 'But the difficulties we went through were real, too. And the future, whatever it looks like, will be real in its own way. A relationship isn't a snapshot.' He nods down at the phone. 'It's a journey.'

'Do you think you might ever get back together?' I ask, because it's been the question burning in my head constantly since that bombshell day. But even as I say it, I know the answer. 'It's fine,' I say quickly. 'I know.'

'Oh, Effie.' Dad gazes at me, his own eyes a little sheeny. 'Come here.' A moment later we're hugging each other, my phone still clutched in my hand, his arms tight around me. I haven't hugged my dad in so long. I thought I might never hug him again.

'Um . . . excuse me?' We both look up to see Edwin Fullerton peeping round the door, looking taken aback. 'I don't mean to intrude on this . . . ah . . . moment,' he says, awkwardly staring at his shoes. 'But I did have a further question or two.'

'*Really?*' Dad mutters, but I'm already stepping away.

'Don't worry, Dad, it's fine. You have stuff to do. And so do I.'

NINETEEN

I walk out of the house into the warm summer's day, feeling a bit dazed by everything. It's good, I tell myself. It's all positive. Krista's leaving. I'm speaking to Dad. I'm back together with Joe. Things are resolved.

So why don't I feel resolved? I feel itchy, as if I need to *do* something, but I'm not sure what.

Find my Russian dolls, a little voice reminds me, and I exhale. I know that's what I came here to do; I know that was my goal. But it's not my doll family that's making my stomach all gnarly. It's my real family.

As I head round the house into the garden, I see broken plates still littering the terrace, and I survey them in dismay. Is this really going to be our last image of Greenoaks? Shouting and weeping and smashed crockery?

At that moment, my phone buzzes and I open it distractedly to find a message from Bean.

Where are you?? They've started serving cocktails here!
Shall I order you a Mojito?

I hesitate a moment, then type a reply:

Are you coming back to Greenoaks?

Almost instantly her answer appears:

Back?? Are you nuts?? I'm ordering you a Mojito.

I stare at her message uneasily, then type:

What about the bird bath? What about all the stuff you
wanted to keep? The souvenirs?

Again her reply is almost instantaneous:

Don't give a shit any more. Don't want any souvenirs.
Come and have a drink.

I send her a thumbs-up emoji, playing for time, but it's not
how I feel. This isn't the way it was supposed to be.

On impulse, I dial Temi's number, because if anyone can
give me wise advice, it's her.

'Effie!' Her cheerful voice greets me. 'At last! Got the dolls?'

'No,' I admit. 'I haven't really been looking for them.'

'You haven't been *looking*?'

'I started looking. But I kept being distracted. By family
stuff.'

'Huh,' says Temi. 'What family stuff?'

I sink down on to my heels, suddenly feeling a bit over-whelmed by everything.

'Temi, our whole family's splintered. Shattered.'

'Right,' she says, after a pause. 'I know, babe. You've been telling me that for a while.'

'No, it's different. It's worse. Bean stormed out of brunch, saying our family was broken and it would never be fixed.'

'*Bean* did?' Temi sounds incredulous.

'I know. It was awful. She started throwing plates around.'

'Throwing *plates*?' Temi erupts in laughter. 'Sorry. Sorry. I know you're stressed. But Bean? Throwing *plates*?'

'She injured Humph. He had to go to A&E.' I start gig-gling, in spite of myself. 'Although, on the plus side, Dad and Krista have split up.'

'You're kidding!' Temi gasps. 'It's all been going on, hasn't it? Next time you have a party, Effie, get me on the list, OK?'

'Oh God, Temi, you should *so* have been at the party,' I say regretfully. 'I'm sure half the people there had never been to Greenoaks in their lives. *You* should have been here to say goodbye. *That* should have been the party we had—'

And then I break off mid-stream, my brain suddenly gal-vanized. That's it. Of course. That's *it*. It was the wrong party, all along. It was stupid and fake and pretentious and it wasn't a proper goodbye to Greenoaks.

I stand up, suddenly full of energy, full of conviction, knowing exactly what I need to do.

'Temi, can you get on a train down here?' I ask abruptly.

'Do what?'

'I'm throwing a party. Farewell to Greenoaks. Tonight.'

'*Another* party?' She sounds astonished.

'Yes, but different. Not fancy. The party this *should* have been. Bonfire on the mound . . . drinks . . . a Talbot family party.'

'OK, I'm in.' I can hear the smile in her voice. 'I'm on the next train. You're not having a bonfire without me!'

As I ring off, I'm smiling too. I want to throw the party we should have had all along. With the right people at it. Not Humph. Not Lacey. Not a million strangers just there for the drinks.

Impulsively I open a new document and write out an invitation:

Please join me on the mound to enjoy our last view of
Greenoaks. 8pm. Drinks. Food. Bonfire. Love from Effie.
No need to RSVP. See you there.

I copy the text, think for a moment, then create a new WhatsApp group, consisting of me, Dad, Bean, Gus, Joe and Temi.

I title the group *Effie's Last Hurrah*. Then I paste in the invitation text. And then, before I can rethink anything, I send it.

TWENTY

The evening air is still warm as Gus lays another load of branches on the fire, in his tried and tested bonfire-stacking formation.

'Where do you want the rugs?' says Dad, panting as he reaches the top of the mound.

'There.' I point at the grass behind Gus. 'Where we always go.'

It's the spot with the best panoramic views. If you face one way, you look down at the house and the drive so you can see who's coming; if you turn the other way, you get an amazing vista across the fields. I never really appreciated the views from the mound till I was grown-up.

'Drinks!' Bean puffs as she reaches the top of the mound, too, clutching a brace of wine bottles. 'God, I'm unfit.'

'Well done, Bean,' says Dad, and she shoots him a wary little smile. We're all still a bit prickly. At least, Bean's still prickly. Gus is still drunk, though he's denying it. Joe's being the diplomat. And I'm in charge.

I like being in charge. I register this feeling, even as I'm telling Bean where to put the drinks. I must find something to do in life where I end up in charge.

'Got it!' Temi arrives at the top of the mound, clutching the bunting, which she's retrieved from the lawn. 'All parties need bunting.'

I glance down past her at the quiet, tidy lawn. Now that the bunting's gone, and we've cleared up all the broken china, you'd never think there had been a party there. Nor a family yelling fest. That party's over. *This* is the party.

Temi jams a bamboo cane in the ground and starts tying the bunting round it – then exclaims in frustration as it falls over.

'I'll help,' says Gus, coming over. 'What you need is a bit of muscle.'

'I've got muscle!' says Temi indignantly. 'I'll beat you at an arm wrestle any day, Gus.'

'Balloons!' Joe appears, looking like a children's entertainer with a bunch of helium balloons bobbing above him. 'Got them from the sitting room. What about the Versailles table settings?' he adds, deadpan. 'Shall I bring those up, too?'

'I think we can probably live without those,' I say, equally deadpan. As I'm speaking, Bean comes by and I touch her on the arm, because there's something I've been meaning to say. 'Listen, Bean,' I murmur in her ear. 'I think we should have another go at speaking to Dad about your furniture. Talk him round.'

'No,' she mutters back.

'But I'm sure we could persuade him—'

'Really, I'm over it.' She cuts me off a little savagely. 'I don't want it any more. I don't care.'

I watch her head back down the mound, feeling conflicted.

I think she does care. But I'm not going to push it right now. Things are fragile enough as it is.

'I think we could light the fire now,' I say to Gus, and watch as he approaches it in a businesslike way. Near by, Dad's opening the wine.

'Oh, Effie,' he says. 'I've just remembered, I *did* see your Russian dolls.'

'What?' I look up, alert.

'Yes, Krista had them.'

For a few seconds I can't speak. My face feels like stone. Krista had them?

'She'd been clearing out the window seat and she asked me what to do with them. I told her to keep them, of course,' he adds hastily, seeing my stricken expression. 'She told me she'd put them somewhere safe. So they're in the house. If we can't find them, I'll ask her.'

I almost want to laugh maniacally. Krista? Somewhere safe?

But this is the evening of building bridges. So somehow I swallow my dismay, and put on a smile.

'Thanks, Dad,' I say. 'I'm sure we'll track them down.'

After a few moments, Bean reappears with some cushions and I help her arrange them on the ground. We're all in our comfort zone now. We all know what to do.

Soon the fire's crackling, and we've all got glasses in our hands, and Joe has arrived at the top of the mound with a trayful of sausages. He's been a total star all afternoon, volunteering to go and shop for food, and then picking up Temi from a far-flung station when her train malfunctioned.

'I know lobster ravioli has its moments,' says Gus, looking at the tray hungrily. 'But *sausages*.'

As he speaks, the fire takes hold suddenly, and we all turn to watch it blaze and spark. How many times have we sat up here, just staring into the flickering flames? It feels natural, gathering around the bonfire. Unforced. A proper send-off.

Maybe our family has changed shape. Maybe things aren't exactly like they used to be. And maybe they'll be even more different in the future. But whatever happens, we'll still be us.

'Well, here's to you, Talbots,' says Temi, looking around. 'And thanks for having me.'

'You're welcome,' says Bean fondly. 'You practically grew up here.'

'Happy memories.' Temi looks around, taking in the house, the garden, the distant tree house. 'So many happy memories. But we'll all make new ones.'

'Yes,' says Bean resolutely. 'That's the plan.'

'It sure is.' I smile at her.

'You can't hold on to things just because of the memories,' continues Temi thoughtfully. 'Otherwise no one would *ever* move house. Or country.'

'Exactly.' Bean nods. 'Or chuck a crap boyfriend. Every crap boyfriend has at least *one* good memory attached to him. But you have to let them go. Otherwise you're all, "Oh, but there was that lovely time we walked in the autumn leaves."'

'Niall,' I say at once and Bean nods ruefully, because she stayed with her uni boyfriend Niall for far too long, and we've agreed on this many times.

'I still remember leaving our house in France,' says Temi reminiscently. 'That was a hard day. I was so happy there. It was sunny ... We were near the beach ... I could walk around in bare feet ...' She shakes her head disbelievingly. 'Then I find myself in London, can't speak the language, it rains all the time, everyone seems so unfriendly ... and I was like, "My life is *ruined*! It's *over*!"' She smiles at me. 'But, you know, it turned out pretty OK in the end.'

I feel a movement beside me and turn to see Joe joining me on the rug.

'Well done,' he says quietly. 'You've turned things around.'

'Well, I don't know,' I say cautiously.

'No, you have. This is great.' He spreads his arms around. 'It's perfect. Even if there isn't lobster and a DJ.'

'*What?*' I exclaim, in mock-horror. 'Are you dissing Krista's house-cooling party?'

'Some people marry the same woman over and over,' says Joe, looking thoughtfully over at Dad. 'You meet their second wife, and she's a duplicate of the first one, just with a different name.' He pauses. 'Your dad *really* didn't do that, did he?'

'No.' I can't help giggling. 'Not so much. Thanks for doing all the shopping, by the way,' I add. '*And* picking up Temi. I've hardly seen you this afternoon.'

'I know.' Joe nods. 'In fact, I've been meaning to ask you something. Did you get anywhere with your mission? And what was it, anyway? Will you tell me now?' he adds, his eyes twinkling. 'Will you trust me?'

'Well, *all right*,' I say, as though this is a huge concession. 'I came here for my Russian dolls. It's this set of painted wooden dolls that fit inside each other. I've had them for ever. My aim was to grab them and go. But then . . .' I gaze around the mound. 'I guess other things took over.'

'I remember your Russian dolls.' Joe stares at me. 'That's what you came back for?'

'They mean a lot to me and I was worried they'd get lost, which is exactly what seems to have happened.' I heave a gusty sigh. 'Dad says the last person who had them was Krista.

294

Apparently she put them "somewhere safe", which was probably the bin. But never say never. I'm not giving up.'

'You mean you haven't found them?' He looks at me with an odd expression.

'Not yet. I know this all probably seems really stupid to you—'

'It doesn't. It doesn't at all.' He gives a sudden, incredulous laugh. 'That's really what you've been searching for, all this time?'

'Yes!' I say, affronted at his amusement. 'Why?'

'Because I know where they are.'

'What?' I stare at him, stupefied.

'They're in the hall. Right by the front door, on the window sill.'

'In the *hall*?' I can't quite process this. 'The *hall*? They can't be.'

'Wait there.'

Before I can reply, he's getting up and hurrying down the mound, then breaking into a run across the grass. I watch him go, my head befuddled. How can *Joe* know where my Russian dolls are?

He can't. He's mistaken. He doesn't know what Russian dolls are. Or it *was* them, but now they're gone . . . I mustn't get my hopes up. As I wait, I'm breathless with tension, my hands knotted in each other, hardly daring to . . .

But then, just as my heart is almost juddering out of my chest, there he is. Returning over the lawn, back up the mound, a flash of red in his hand. My dolls. My *dolls*. I stare at them, my eyes filling.

'Here you are.' Joe hands them over, and I breathe out as my fingers close around the familiar, smooth, beloved contours.

'Thanks,' I gulp. It seems such an inadequate word. 'Thanks so much. I thought I'd never see them again.'

'I remember those,' he says, sinking down on to the rug again beside me. 'You've always had them.'

'Yes.'

'They're . . . nice,' he offers, clearly searching for something to say about them. 'I suppose they count as antiques, almost.'

'Maybe.' I nod.

I feel a bit wrung out. All that searching, and they were in the hall all the time. Krista really did put them somewhere safe. I can hardly believe it.

'But I was in the hall!' I say, suddenly raising my head. 'How did I not see them?'

'They were half hidden by the curtain,' says Joe. 'I wouldn't have noticed them myself, only I was hanging around outside the front door for a while. This one was staring at me the whole time.' He taps the biggest doll. 'She's a bit creepy. In my opinion,' he hastily adds, as I shoot a glare at him.

How did I miss them? I'm thinking incredulously. I guess I wasn't at my most observant when I entered the hall and dashed into the coat cupboard. But if I'd only paused and done a quick sweep of the area . . .

Joe has clearly been following the same thought process.

'If you'd just said in the rose bush, "I'm looking for my Russian dolls," I would have said, "What, those ones?" and I would have grabbed them for you.'

'I would have taken them,' I say slowly. 'And said, "Thanks." And then I would have left, straight away. *I would have got the next train back to London.*'

I feel slightly stunned at this realization. If I'd told Joe about my dolls, I wouldn't be here with him now. We wouldn't have had the conversation in the cellar. Or the tree house. Or any of it. I shiver as I contemplate the near miss I've had.

'That was a close one,' says Joe, raising his eyebrows at me. 'We might never have . . .'

'Yes. I know.' And suddenly, as I gaze up at the man I nearly lost, I'm desperate not to make another wrong turn, into another wrong universe. 'Joe, I know we've . . .' I swallow, my face hot. 'But are we . . . Do you want . . . ? Where are we?'

Oh God, I'm blathering. But I don't know what he thinks of us; of this. And I've suddenly realized I can't go a moment longer without knowing the worst. Or the best. What *was* that, this morning? Two old lovers having a last encounter, goodbye, thank you very much? Or was it . . . ?

There's a flash of surprise in Joe's face – then, as he surveys me, his eyes crinkle.

'Oh, Effie,' he says. 'My love. Do you have to ask?'

My throat thickens at the word *love*, but I persevere. I can't let his tender expression sway me.

'Yes, I do.' I stare back at him resolutely. 'If life has taught me anything, it's don't ever assume. Nail it down. Get things clear. Because otherwise . . .' I scrabble for the right words, and suddenly, madly, recall that stupid yoga sculpture. 'Otherwise you might think assembly *is* included. Whereas they say assembly *isn't* included. And that leads to . . . you know. Misery.'

'Misery.' Joe opens his eyes wider.

'Yes.' I lift my chin. 'Misery. So I do have to ask. And I'd like you to be, you know. Honest.' My voice gives a sudden treacherous wobble. 'Be honest.'

I force myself to keep my gaze steady. Joe looks at me, his face grave, then finally draws breath.

'Assembly is included,' he says. 'As far as I'm concerned. Assembly is included. If you'd be interested in that option?'

Something inside my body seems to let go. I think it's a muscle that's been miserably tensed for the past four years, finally relaxing.

'Great.' I rub my nose, trying to hide my feelings. 'Yes. I would like that option.'

'The option *I'd* really like,' he says matter-of-factly, 'is to build a life with you. A strong, put-together kind of life. I know you're pretty good at assembly yourself, probably better than I am, in fact. So maybe it could be . . . a joint project?'

'I'm handy with a wrench.' I try to laugh, but it doesn't quite work.

'I would go so far . . .' Joe hesitates, his eyes even more intense. 'I would go so far as to say I can't seem to build the life I want without you. Nothing fits.'

'Lives are tricky,' I say. 'Maybe you should have tried a set of shelves first.'

Joe gives a short bark of laughter, then pulls me into his arms, and as he kisses me, it's with a new, strong determination.

'We're us,' he murmurs in my ear. 'We're us again.'

I nod happily against his chest, one hand still clenched round my dolls, one arm clinging on to Joe. I'll never let either go again.

It feels like several hours later that we draw apart. As Joe watches, smiling, I separate my dolls into their individual familiar selves, checking them over, lining them up on the lawn from large to small. They beam back at me, their expressions fixed and happy, as if they were never lost. Never gone. Nothing was ever wrong.

As I reach the tiniest doll, I look up at Joe, turning the wooden figure round in my fingers.

'There's always been a Joe I could never get at,' I say. 'Hidden under all the layers. Right at the centre of you.'

'I know.' Joe exhales. 'I know. I clam up. I shut the world out. I don't help myself.'

I gaze for a few moments at my dear, familiar, tiniest doll, then up at Joe.

'Let me in, Joe,' I say quietly. 'Let me in. I want to be right in the heart of you.'

Joe nods, his eyes grave. 'I'll try. I want that, too. And I want to be in the heart of you.'

'You already are,' I whisper, my fingers unpicking the Blu-Tack at the base of the tiniest doll. As I release it, there's a flash from the hollowed-out place in the wood. A trickle of silver chain. The glint of the Smallest Diamond in the World.

'No.' Joe seems almost ashen with shock. '*No*.'

'It was burning all the time,' I say, holding the tiny candle. Joe surveys it silently, then takes it, and after a questioning look, fastens it around my neck. It feels warm, as though it's only been off me for five minutes.

'Effie . . .' Joe's eyes are suddenly anguished, but I forestall whatever he's about to say by shaking my head.

'Not backwards,' I say. 'Forwards. Only forwards.'

'Your dolls!' Bean flops down beside me and reaches to pick one up. 'You found them!'

'Joe did,' I explain. 'He knew where they were, all the time.'

'Of *course* he did.' Bean rolls her eyes humorously. 'Trust Joe. You should have just asked him straight away.'

'No!' I say with animation. 'It's exactly the opposite. I *shouldn't* have asked Joe straight away.' And I'm about to explain how, if I'd done that, none of us would be sitting here right now – when I notice Dad, over Joe's shoulder. He's quietly moved away from the main gathering to the side of the mound. Now he's just sitting there, alone, staring over the garden of Greenoaks. His body is motionless and his face is as sad as I've ever seen it.

I nudge Bean, who turns and claps her hand over her mouth anxiously. Then I glance at Gus, who breaks off his conversation with Temi, and the pair of them quietly come over.

'Dad?' I begin, without knowing what I'm going to say. He turns his head, and at his desolate expression, I feel a kind of inner plunging. 'We . . . we need some music!' I press on, sounding only a bit strained. 'Come on, let's sing, everyone!'

I hurry over to Dad and pull him encouragingly to his feet. Then I grasp one of his hands, crossing my own, and uncertainly start to sing, *'Should auld acquaintance be forgot . . .'*

For a few seconds, no one else moves. My voice wavers through the evening air alone and I feel a shaft of terror. Is no one going to join in? Was this a terrible idea?

But then, suddenly there's Dad's voice, resounding along with mine. He squeezes my fingers, and I squeeze back. Bean hurries over to take Dad's other hand, her faltering soprano singing along tunelessly.

'Good for you.' Joe's voice is suddenly in my ear, his hand in mine. 'Good for you, Effie.'

Now he's clasping hands with Temi, who's already singing lustily, and Gus is coming forward, bellowing as though he's at a rugby match. And within a few moments, we're linked together. We're hand in hand, all of us, arms rising and falling in clumsy rhythm. Our faces are lit up in the flickering firelight, and we're singing, tunelessly and raggedly, laughing awkwardly as we forget the words, shoving and jostling each other's hands, but still just about in time. Still just about together.

TWENTY-ONE

By midnight, all the wine is finished. And all the back-up wine. And the cider and sausages and the chocolate cake. Dad has left, claiming to be too old to spend the night out on the mound. The fire is out by now and I'm huddled with Bean, Gus, Joe and Temi, in sleeping bags, with cushions and all the blankets we could find.

'This is *really* uncomfortable,' Bean keeps complaining. 'How on earth did we sleep out here all the time?'

'We were drunk,' suggests Joe.

'We were young,' says Temi. 'I used to sleep all over the place at parties. On floors, rugs, in the bath once ...' She wriggles, and punches a pillow. 'Effie, don't you have an air mattress we could use?'

'Or a real mattress,' says Gus. 'We could bring one out.'

'Or a four-poster bed?' I retort. 'Honestly! You're all so feeble. This is our last night at Greenoaks. We *have* to sleep on the mound.'

I'm not going to admit that I'm totally uncomfortable, too.

That's not the point. The point is, we're all here, just like we used to be. Even if stones *are* sticking into our backs and there isn't any mirror for Temi to apply her five zillion vitally essential serums.

I drift off into fitful sleep at last, waking a few times to pull a blanket over me or huddle closer to Joe. At one point during the night I find myself gazing up at the stars, finding magical clusters in the darkness, listening to Bean murmur in her sleep. Then I drop off again. And so I go on, throughout the night, waking and sleeping and dozing – until suddenly it's seven o'clock in the morning and the sky is bright and everyone is still fast asleep except me, who feels wide awake. Typical.

I'm freezing, which might be because I've somehow worked my way out of my sleeping bag in my sleep. And my limbs are aching. I feel like a ninety-three-year-old, right now. But on the plus side, the day is brand-new and the air is clean and fresh, and there's nothing between my face and the sky. No walls, no windows, nothing. I take a deep breath, feeling a massive sense of satisfaction which overcomes the slightly bruised feeling in my shoulders. Here we all are. We did it.

I sit up on my elbows, contemplating the peaceful drive, wondering if I can summon the energy to go and make tea for everyone or whether I should wake Gus up accidentally on purpose and get him to do it. And then, as I'm watching, a car comes driving in. A Volvo I don't recognize. It draws to a halt and the engine is switched off and for a moment nothing happens. Then the driver's door opens and a woman gets out. She looks to be in her late thirties, and is dressed in jeans and loafers and a crisp, striped shirt. Her blonde hair is swingy and fresh and kind of adorable-looking.

I watch, gripped, as she takes a few steps towards the house, then just stares up at it. She peers around the drive, takes another step forward, then gives a sudden, childlike skip of glee. Then she glances up at the mound, spots me watching her and claps a hand over her mouth.

She has such an open, friendly face, I find myself getting to my feet and skittering down towards her.

'Hello,' she says charmingly as I approach. 'I'm so sorry to intrude this early. I'm Libby Van Beuren.'

'Van Beuren?' I stare at her, taken aback.

She doesn't look sinister. She doesn't look anything like how I pictured the Van Beurens to be. (Which I now realize was a family of frowning FBI agents in black suits.)

'The guy at the property agency said he thought you wouldn't mind if I popped round.' Libby Van Beuren's eyes sparkle. 'I know the house isn't ours till Wednesday, but I was passing, and I couldn't resist. Are you . . . one of the Talbots?'

'I'm Effie,' I say, and extend my hand. 'We were just . . .' I gesture up at the others, who are gradually surfacing now, rubbing their eyes and peering down at us. 'We were having a kind of house-cooling bonfire party. We slept outside.'

'You slept outside!' echoes Libby Van Beuren, her whole face lighting up. 'A bonfire party! How wonderful! This whole place is magical. *Magical*. The tree house. The turret. I have such plans . . .' She breaks off as a van comes wending its way slowly into the drive, with *Garsett Removals* printed on the side. 'Oh! This is your removers. Good luck!' She makes a comical face. 'Moving's the worst, isn't it? My husband is in denial. Anyway, I just had to come and have a look. I'm so excited. Were you happy here?'

'Yes.' I nod simply. 'We were happy here.'

'I just fell for the house as soon as I saw it. It's so *quirky*. The stained glass. And the brickwork.'

'Not everyone loves the brickwork,' I feel obliged to point out, and Libby Van Beuren tosses her head back.

'I don't care what everyone thinks. I love it. It's different! It's unique!'

'I always felt that way, too.' I smile at her, feeling an instant bond. 'It's a unique house. People don't forget it.'

'No, I can imagine.' I can tell that she's hanging on my every word. 'Are you a big family?' She peers up at the others on the mound. 'Did you grow up here? Was it a good place to raise a family?'

'Yes. My parents actually . . . they broke up. But it's fine. It's fine. We're all . . . you know. Adjusted.'

One of the removers has rung the doorbell, and Dad now appears on the doorstep, holding a cup of tea. He glances over at me and Libby Van Beuren in surprise and I wave back.

'Well, look, I won't disturb you any more,' says Libby Van Beuren. 'But it was wonderful to meet you—'

'Wait,' I say, seizing my chance. 'I have a quick question. I know you bought the Peter Rabbit furniture that's in one of the bedrooms. But my dad kind of sold that without . . . He didn't realize . . .' I pause, trying to get my words in order. 'It's my sister's. And she loves it. And she was really upset. So, could I buy it back?'

'Oh my goodness!' Libby Van Beuren's hand has gone to her mouth in dismay. 'Of course. Of course! And don't worry about buying it back. That's just my husband's way. Dan always has to strike a good deal. He was roaming around seeking out extras to throw in, just for the sake of it. You know? I mean, we do love the furniture, but if your sister's really attached to it . . .'

'Thank you. She is. Thank you.'

'I'll square it with Dan, don't worry.' She lowers her voice. 'Truth is, he won't even notice.'

Another van pulls into the drive behind us, and she makes a rueful face.

'I'm in your way. I'm sorry. I'll leave.'

'No!' I say at once. 'Please don't. Take your time.'

'Well, if you're sure . . .' She glances at the car. 'Would it be OK if I let the kids have a quick run around?'

'Kids?' I blink at her. 'Of course!'

'I need to drop them at day camp, but I'd love them just to get a taste . . .'

I watch as she heads towards the car, opens the back door and, after a bit of rummaging inside, helps out two little girls. They're dressed in jeans and sneakers, with shiny hair held back with clips. One is holding an old bunny, the other is sucking her thumb.

They take a few steps forward, hand in hand, staring up at the house with huge eyes.

'This is our new home!' Libby Van Beuren says encouragingly. 'This is where we're going to live, sweethearts!'

'It's scary,' says one of the little girls, turning away, almost looking as though she's going to cry. 'I like Grandma's house.'

'That's my mother's house,' explains Libby Van Beuren to me. 'We've been camping there a while. Hey, but we'll like this house too!' she says gently to her daughter. 'When we've got used to it. This is Effie!' She gestures at me. 'She used to live here when she was a little girl. Effie, this is Laura and Eleanor.'

I crouch down, so I'm on a level with the two girls, and look into their grave, suspicious faces.

'You're going to love it here,' I say seriously. 'There are attics you can climb in. And lots of grass to play on. And a tree house. And look, you can balance on these stepping stones,' I say, suddenly remembering a game I used to play with Bean.

I show the girls the old stepping stones set in the grass leading up to the mound, and after a moment they're playing follow-my-leader, jumping from stone to stone, just like we used to do.

'Thanks,' says Libby Van Beuren gratefully, as we both watch them. 'Moving's always hard. New house, new school . . . Did you go to the village school?'

'Yes.' I nod. 'And the same headmistress is still there. She's great.'

'Oh good.' Libby Van Beuren breathes out. 'I guess it's hard for you guys, too,' she adds, as though it's just occurring to her. 'Leaving this place, after so many years.'

'Oh, we're fine,' I say after a pause. 'We're fine.'

'Well, I hope we do it justice,' she says. 'It feels quite a responsibility, you know? Taking on a place like this.'

'I'm sure you will.' I meet her excited, anxious eyes and feel something inside me unwind. I know she'll love Greenoaks and I know she'll look after it. 'I hope you have fun. Stay as long as you like, by the way.' I gesture at the girls. 'Let them get used to the place. Nice to meet you. And good luck!'

'You too! Oh, and do return whenever you like,' she adds eagerly. 'Whenever. We'd love to see you for a visit.'

'Thanks,' I say, after a pause. 'Maybe.'

I climb back up to the top of the mound to find Gus still asleep, Bean sitting up in her sleeping bag, Temi peering at her phone and Joe waiting for me expectantly, his hair on end.

'Who was that?'

'New owner of Greenoaks.'

'Ah.' Joe gives me an appraising look. 'You OK?'

'I'm great,' I say briskly. 'Everything's good.'

'I need to get back to London,' says Temi, yawning. 'It's *Monday*.'

'So do I,' I say, remembering. 'I've got a catering job later.'

'I was thinking of catching the eight twenty.' Gus squints dazedly at his watch. 'Does that give us time for bacon and eggs?'

'Oh, look at those two,' says Temi, her face softening, and I follow her gaze to see the two little girls playing It, running round the rose bushes.

'I think they'll enjoy living here,' I say, watching them too. 'I hope they do.'

Everything inside me has shifted. I'm stronger. Not only am I able to let go, I'm happy to let go. I'm focused on the future. And I'm about to ask Bean if I can borrow her navy blazer to wear home, when I see a man walking towards the mound, who doesn't look like either a remover or a Van Beuren. He has a kind-looking face and thick curly hair and as he gets nearer my stomach lurches, because I suddenly recognize him. Oh God, oh God—

'My name is Adam,' he says, walking up the mound in his chunky boots, his voice wary but resolute, his eyes darting between us. 'Adam Solomon. I was looking for Bean?'

'I'm here,' says Bean, her voice tiny and apprehensive. 'Adam, I'm here. Hi.' She moves forward from where she was half hidden behind Gus, and I can see the tension growing on her face.

'Hi,' he says.

'Hi,' she says again.

Beside me, Joe is watching tautly. Temi's eyes are like saucers, and I can see Gus shifting position for a better view.

'I wanted to . . .' Adam swallows, the breeze gently blowing his hair. 'Would you like to . . . have breakfast?'

'OK,' says Bean warily.

'And . . . lunch?'

'OK,' says Bean again.

'And supper? And then breakfast again? And maybe . . .' He hesitates. 'Maybe every meal?'

As she suddenly understands his meaning, there's a kind of rippling on Bean's face. A kind of sunshine breaking out. And it's only now that I realize how long her night has lasted.

'Yes,' she says, her voice trembling, her mouth flickering into a joyful smile. 'Yes, I would like to.'

'Good.' Adam breathes out. 'That's . . . good.' He reaches out to her with an instinctive, loving movement – then, as though aware of his small but avid audience, limits himself to taking Bean's hands and holding them, tight.

I exhale, my eyes hot. From the way he's looking at her, steadfastly, protectively, I feel like he might just pass the test of Good Enough For My Sister.

'Let me . . . I'll get some coffee on and then you can meet everyone properly.' Bean breaks the mood at last, a little flustered, and it's like a signal for everyone to move.

'I need a shower,' Temi announces.

'We *must* have some bacon,' Gus is saying. 'Shall I make bacon rolls?'

'I'll help,' volunteers Joe, then he touches my shoulder gently. 'Coming?'

'I'll be a moment,' I say, and he nods.

I sit down on the grass and watch as Bean and Adam make their way down the mound, Adam still clutching her hand tight. Behind them, in a kind of procession, go Joe, Gus and Temi, trailing sleeping bags and blankets, with unruly hair and dishevelled clothes. Just like the old days.

They all trudge across the drive, then disappear through the front door into the house. And just for a moment there's total stillness. There are no removers in the drive. Libby Van Beuren has vanished from view and I can't see the two children. It's just me and Greenoaks.

On impulse, I reach for my Russian dolls and line them up on the grass, then take a photo of them with Greenoaks as the backdrop. Their five familiar faces stare back at me, fixedly smiling. Always connected, always a family, always part of each other, even if they're scattered.

I take a few more shots, playing around with filters, then put my phone away. I wrap my arms around my knees and breathe out, running my eyes for the last time over the turret, the stained glass, the outlandish brickwork. Dear Greenoaks. Dear, ugly old house.

I don't think I'll return, I find myself thinking. I won't come back. I don't need to.

EPILOGUE

One year later

I'm absolutely determined that Skye should be a bridesmaid for Joe and me. She's very advanced for her age and I'm *sure* she'll be able to walk soon enough.

'I read about a baby who walked at eight months,' I say casually to Bean. 'And another one walked at seven months. It was on YouTube. It does happen.'

'I'm not pushing her to walk early just so she can totter along at your wedding.' Bean shoots me a ferocious, mother-tiger glance. 'So don't get any ideas.'

We both survey Skye, who beams back in that sunny, adorable way she has. She's lying on her sheepskin rug in her Peter-Rabbit-themed nursery, apparently fascinated by her own hands. To be fair, I'm quite fascinated by them, too. In fact, I'm fascinated by all of her, and spend most of my spare time round here at Bean and Adam's place, helping as much as I can.

'What about crawling?' I suggest. 'Could she be a crawling bridesmaid?'

'A crawling bridesmaid?'

'She could have her own little white train.'

'She'd look like a caterpillar,' says Bean fondly. 'Or a little white slug, edging her way up the aisle.'

'No, she wouldn't!' I say. 'No, you wouldn't, would you, Skye?' I bury my face in Skye's tummy, just to hear her delicious gurgle. Late-summer sunshine is coming in through the muslin curtains and from downstairs I hear a pop, which means Aperol Spritzes are on the way. It feels like a celebration. Every family get-together has felt like a celebration, recently. There was Bean's engagement and wedding, and then the arrival of Skye, and then me and Joe . . . I twist my engagement ring round my finger, still unused to the feel of it.

'Nice rabbit,' I say, noticing a new blue crocheted bunny on the rocking chair, and Bean's face lights up.

'Mimi made it.'

'Of course she did.'

Mimi was *born* to be a granny. She's been round here most days, ever since Bean got out of hospital, putting on washing or taking Skye for a little walk round the block. As she's pointed out often enough, she never did give birth or look after a newborn, so it's a new adventure for her too. For all of us.

I feel different in the family, these days. More equal to my siblings. When Adam got caught up on a work trip and couldn't make one of Bean's scans, it was me who went and held her hand. And I keep sending her vitamins. It's become a running joke.

Bean still tries to do too much. She can't help herself. But Gus and I now try to get there before her. So at Christmas, I organized all the presents. I even hosted family festive drinks on Dad's birthday, and we decorated my tiny tree.

We all shifted generation, that day that Adam phoned up with the news about Skye. I became an aunt. Dad, a grandfather . . . we all instantly went up a level. Gus said it best, when I saw him at the hospital the next day. He gave me one of his wry, comical looks and said, 'We're really not the kids any more, are we, Effie? We'd better grow up or something.'

He's been dating a bit since Romilly, although he hasn't found anyone long-term. And Dad's been dating, too. It took a while for everything to shake down after the party, but a few months later, he announced at one of our new, regular lunches that he was buying a modest flat in Chichester.

It suits Dad, Chichester. He's started to sail a bit and he's neighbours with an old friend from university days. Recently he's been talking about a 'rather special lady friend' he's going to introduce us to, but he's keeping her low profile for now. No photos on Instagram, this time round. We've been to visit him lots, and the last time, as we walked along the coastal path, I actually found myself saying to Joe, 'Aren't you glad Dad moved here?'

Bean is blissfully happy in her cottage, with Adam, and little Skye gurgling in her nursery. I'm *loving* being engaged to Joe. (Apart from that hideously unflattering photo of me in the *Daily Mail*, caption: 'Childhood sweetheart of Doctor of Hearts flaunts new engagement ring on coffee-shop outing'. I was *just getting coffee*.)

I've had so many messages from old schoolfriends, saying things like 'We knew you would!' and 'What took you so long?!' Humph was particularly charming in his card, and promised us, as a wedding present, an alpaca-wool blanket from one of his seventy new alpacas. (He's given up on the Spinken method and now describes himself as a 'farmer'.)

And I have a job. At last. At *last*. I just kept applying. Every day. Never giving up. And at last I struck gold, with an events agency that I'd already applied to, but that had a new opening. It's early days, but so far, so good.

Gus is thriving, too. Ever since he got rid of Romilly, he's been a different person. Less lost in work, more engaged in the real world. Maybe because the real world is more appealing now.

Our family is like one of those games where you shake the plastic box and then try to get the silver balls into all the little hollows. Sometimes it seems impossible. But if you wait long enough, it'll happen; everyone will eventually find their place.

As we head downstairs from the nursery to the kitchen, I hear Dad chatting with Adam about bread dough, and I chew my lip, trying not to laugh. Something we've learned about Adam since he joined our family is he's borderline obsessive about making bread. He's twice pressed a jar of sourdough starter on Dad, and twice the sourdough starter has died because Dad didn't look after it properly. But it sounds as though he's trying for a third time.

'Yes, gluten content,' I can hear Dad saying as I walk into Bean's kitchen. 'Absolutely. I must bear that in mind.'

'Hear this sound? That's the sound you're waiting for—' Adam looks up from tapping his loaf as I walk in. 'All OK?'

'She's even more adorable than she was last week,' I say with a loving sigh.

'Especially at three in the morning,' says Bean, setting Skye in her bouncy chair, which is second-hand and re-covered in tasteful vintage fabric, because she's Bean and she doesn't do 'just any old bouncy chair'.

'Aperol Spritz?' Adam puts down his loaf on a wire rack.

'Yes, please!' I say.

'Always.' Bean smiles at him. 'I'll get out the hummus.'

We head out to Bean's terrace with drinks, bread, dips and Skye, who is deposited, still in her bouncy chair, in the shade, near the old stone bird bath from Greenoaks. It looks perfect in Bean's little garden. In fact, better than it ever did before, because you really notice it here.

'Hello, hello!' Joe's voice breaks into the conversation and he arrives in the garden via the side passage. 'Thought I'd find you out here.'

He comes over to kiss me, and as his hand squeezes my shoulder, I feel the disbelieving headrush I still occasionally get. *I'm with Joe.* For good. It all worked out. It so nearly might not have done. But it did.

When Joe has greeted everyone and poured himself a drink, he comes back to me and proffers his phone.

'So . . . I found a house.'

'What?' I look up, instantly alert, because we've been property-searching, but it's impossible. Houses might just as well be the Lesser Crested Dodo. Either they cost a gazillion pounds, or . . . No, that's it. That's the only issue. They cost a gazillion pounds. Unless you live out in the sticks, like Bean does, but Joe needs to get to St Thomas' Hospital and my job is in Soho, so we're trying to look in the general London-ish area. Even Temi has taken to biting her lip when I ask her if she's found us anything, and she pretty much considers herself a property consultant.

'A house,' he repeats. 'And we could afford it.'

'A house?' I crinkle my brow. 'No. You mean a flat.'

'A house.'

'A *house*?'

'It's . . . unusual. The estate agent said to me, "There *is* a house, but it's so ugly no one will go and see it."'

'Ugly?' I stiffen with interest, and Joe grins.

'That's what he said. "Quirky" was the other word he used. Thought you'd like to see it.'

He gives me his phone, and I look down at a photo of the weirdest house I've ever seen. It seems to be clad in about four different finishes, from brick to fake stone to pebbledash to a kind of clapboard. It has a lopsided gable and a falling-down porch and a ratty tree leaning up against it. But it's speaking to me. It has kindness in its lines. It's saying, *Give me a chance. I'll look after you.*

I scroll through photos of a terrible sitting room, a green bathroom, a brown decrepit kitchen, three bedrooms, then back to the exterior. Already my heart is swelling with love.

'Crikey,' says Dad, peering over my shoulder. 'That *is* ugly.'

'It's not ugly!' I say defensively. 'At least, it's ugly in a good way. Houses *should* be a bit ugly. Gives them character.'

'I've always thought so.' Joe meets my eyes and I know he gets it, totally.

'I mean, who wants some perfect palace?'

'Not me,' says Joe resolutely. 'Never.'

'Effie!' says Bean, peering over my other shoulder, sounding aghast. 'You can't be serious.'

'I love it,' I say stubbornly. 'It's *exactly* my kind of house.'

'But the pebbledash!'

'I love the pebbledash.'

'But the *windows*.' She sounds actually upset. 'And they'd cost a fortune to replace.'

'I love the windows,' I say defiantly. 'They're the best bit.'

'OK, chicken legs are up,' chimes in Adam, coming out of

the kitchen with a baking tray, and everyone turns towards the food.

As we all sit down at the wooden table, juggling plates and chicken legs and napkins and glasses, I'm half listening to the conversation about the herb marinade and I'm nodding and smiling. But at the same time, I keep glancing down at photos of the house and my mind is full of visions. Visions of the future. Me. Joe. A dear, ugly place to make our own.

And they're all good.

ACKNOWLEDGEMENTS

I would like to thank my wise editors – Frankie Gray, Kara Cesare, Whitney Frick and Clio Seraphim – together with everyone at Transworld.

Huge thanks also, as always, to Araminta Whitley, Marina de Pass, Nicki Kennedy and everyone at the Soho Agency and ILA.

The Shopaholic Series

Starring the unforgettable Becky Bloomwood,
shopper extraordinaire . . .

The Secret Dreamworld of a Shopaholic
(also published as *Confessions of a Shopaholic*)

Meet Becky – a journalist who spends all her time
telling people how to manage money, and all her leisure
time spending it. But the letters from her bank manager
are getting harder to ignore. Can she ever escape this
dreamworld, find true love . . . and regain the use of
her credit card?

Shopaholic Abroad
Becky's life is peachy. Her balance is in the black –
well, nearly – and now her boyfriend has asked her
to move to New York with him. Can Becky keep the
man *and* the clothes when there's so much temptation
around every corner?

Shopaholic Ties the Knot
Becky finally has the perfect job, the perfect man and, at
last, the perfect wedding. Or rather, *weddings* . . . How
has Becky ended up with not one, but two big days?

Shopaholic & Sister
Becky has received some incredible news. She has a
long-lost sister! But how will she cope when she realizes
her sister is not a shopper . . . but a skinflint?

Shopaholic & Baby
Becky is pregnant! But being Becky, she decides to shop around – for a new, more expensive obstetrician – and unwittingly ends up employing Luke's ex-girlfriend! How will Becky make it through the longest nine months of her life?

Mini Shopaholic
Times are hard, so Becky's Cutting Back. She has the perfect idea: throw a budget-busting birthday party. But her daughter Minnie can turn the simplest event into chaos. Whose turn will it be to sit on the naughty step?

Shopaholic to the Stars
Becky is in Hollywood and her heart is set on a new career – she's going to be a stylist to the stars! But in between choosing clutch bags and chasing celebrities, Becky gets caught up in the whirlwind of Tinseltown. Has Becky gone too far this time?

Shopaholic to the Rescue
Becky is on a major rescue mission! Hollywood was full of surprises, and now she's on a road trip to Las Vegas to find out why her dad has mysteriously disappeared, help her best friend Suze and *maybe* even bond with Alicia Bitch Long-legs. She comes up with her biggest, boldest, most brilliant plan yet – can she save the day?

Christmas Shopaholic
Becky is hosting Christmas for the first time. With her sister Jess demanding a vegan turkey, Luke insistent that he just wants aftershave again, and little Minnie insisting on a very specific picnic hamper, will chaos ensue or will Becky manage to bring comfort and joy at Christmas?

Other Books

Sophie Kinsella's hilarious, heart-warming stand-alone novels:

Can You Keep a Secret?
Emma blurts out her deepest, darkest secrets to the sexy stranger sitting next to her on the plane. After all, she'll never see him again . . . will she?

The Undomestic Goddess
Samantha runs away from her workaholic life and becomes a housekeeper in a country house. But what will happen when her past catches up with her?

Remember Me?
What if you woke up and your life was perfect? Lexi's life has fast-forwarded three years, and she has everything she's ever wanted – and no idea how she got there. Can she cope when she finds out the truth?

Twenties Girl
Lara has always had an overactive imagination. But when the ghost of her great-aunt Sadie shows up, asking for her help, Lara wonders if she's losing her mind . . .

I've Got Your Number
After losing her engagement ring and her mobile phone, Poppy takes a mobile she finds in a bin. Little knowing that she's picked up another man in the process . . .

Wedding Night
Lottie is determined to get married. And Ben seems perfect – they'll iron out their little differences later. But their families have different plans . . .

My *Not So* Perfect Life
When Katie's ex-boss from hell books a glamping holiday at her family's farm, Katie plans to get her revenge on the woman with the perfect life. But does Demeter really have it so good? And what's wrong with not-so-perfect anyway?

Surprise Me
Sylvie and Dan have a happy marriage and are totally in sync. But when they introduce surprises into their relationship to keep things fresh, they begin to wonder if they know each other after all . . .

I Owe You *One*
When a handsome stranger asks Fixie to watch his laptop for a moment, she ends up saving it from certain disaster. To thank her, he scribbles her an IOU. Soon, small favours become life-changing.

Love Your Life
Ava falls in love with a handsome stranger on an anonymous writing retreat. But when they return home it seems they just can't love each other's lives. Can they overcome their differences to find one life, together?

For Young Adults

FINDING AUDREY

Audrey can't leave the house. She can't even take off her dark glasses inside. But then Linus stumbles into her life. And with him on her side, Audrey can do things she'd thought were too scary. Suddenly, finding her way back to the real world seems achievable . . .

For Younger Readers

The Mummy Fairy and Me Series

Ella's family have a big secret . . . her mummy is a fairy! She can do amazing spells with her Computawand to make delicious cupcakes, create the perfect birthday party and cause chaos at the supermarket. But sometimes the spells go a bit wrong and that's when Ella comes to the rescue!

Prepare for magic and mayhem in this sweet and funny new series for young readers.

Sophie Kinsella is an internationally bestselling writer. She is the author of many number one bestsellers, including the hugely popular Shopaholic series. She has also written seven bestselling novels as Madeleine Wickham and several books for children. She lives in the UK with her husband and family.

Visit her website at www.sophiekinsella.co.uk and find her on Facebook at www.facebook.com/SophieKinsellaOfficial. You can also follow her on Twitter @KinsellaSophie and Instagram @sophiekinsellawriter.